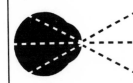

This Large Print Book carries the
Seal of Approval of N.A.V.H.

FOLLOW ME

FOLLOW ME

JOANNA SCOTT

THORNDIKE PRESS
A part of Gale, Cengage Learning

GALE
CENGAGE Learning

Detroit • New York • San Francisco • New Haven, Conn • Waterville, Maine • London

GALE
CENGAGE Learning

Acknowledgements: Special thanks to the Vermont Studio Workshop, the Santa Maddalena Foundation, the Center at High Falls in Rochester, New York, and Ruth Rosenberg-Naparsteck for her lively history of a river, *Runnin' Crazy.* For their invaluable input, I'm indebted to Maureen Howard, Lori Precious, Steve Erikson, Geri Thoma, Reagan Arthur, Jayne Yaffe Kemp, and to the three who fill our house with songs: Jim, Kathryn, and Alice.

Thorndike Press® Large Print Basic.
The text of this Large Print edition is unabridged.
Other aspects of the book may vary from the original edition.
Set in 16 pt. Plantin.
Printed on permanent paper.

LIBRARY OF CONGRESS CATALOGING-IN-PUBLICATION DATA

Scott, Joanna, 1960–
   Follow me / by Joanna Scott.
      p. cm. — (Thorndike Press large print basic)
   ISBN-13: 978-1-4104-1773-2 (alk. paper)
   ISBN-10: 1-4104-1773-5 (alk. paper)
   1. Grandmothers—Fiction. 2. Family secrets—Fiction. 3.
Pennsylvania—Fiction. 4. Large type books. I. Title.
PS3569.C636F65 2009b
813'.54—dc22
                                      2009013412

Published in 2009 by arrangement with Little, Brown and Company, a division of Hachette Book Group, Inc.

In memory of Walter Lee Scott,
1922–2007

Come with me, and we will go
Where the rocks of coral grow;
Follow, follow, follow me.

Anne Hunter,
from "A Mermaid's Song"

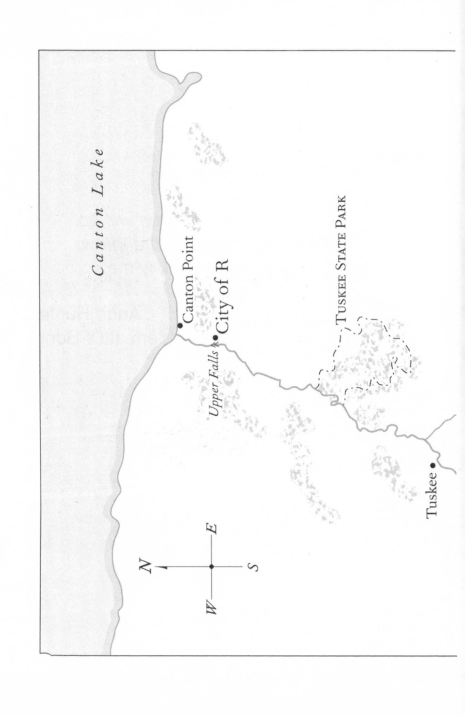

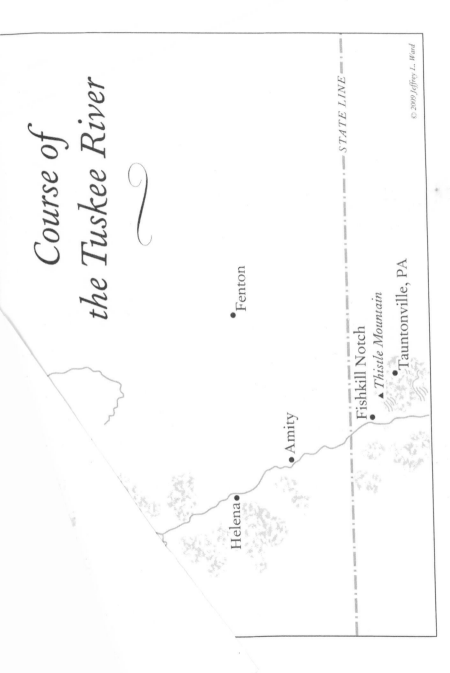

Course of the Tuskee River

Fenton

Amity

Helena

Fishkill Notch

▲ Thistle Mountain

Tauntonville, PA

STATE LINE

© 2009 Jeffrey L. Ward

November 6, 2006

One and two and three and —

That's about how long my father had to contemplate his life, to catch one last hungry glimpse of a sky that was likely the same steel gray as this morning's sky, to hear the river spilling down the cliff face of the Upper Falls, to see the spool of foam, tinged red from chemical waste, unraveling with the northward pull of the current, to note the strata of limestone and shale in the sheer walls below the ruins of Boxman's Mill, to feel his arms grappling helplessly, his legs buckling, his torso twisting away from the water while he anticipated his absence from the world and thought about my mother and abruptly and completely regretted his decision to jump.

My father was a mystery to me when I was growing up, though not because he threw himself from the pedestrian bridge six months before I was born. Here's the thing — he didn't die that day. He survived his plunge into the icy Tuskee, and as soon as he'd dried out and recovered his senses, he packed his bags and left town.

You might say he was lucky. But really, a man who'd concluded that the only release from his torment was to escape life altogether would have needed more than luck.

And so in November of 1974, on a day much like today, in the wake of a rainstorm, he climbed over the rail of the bridge and jumped, and as he fell he had enough time to acknowledge that if he'd had the wherewithal to consider other options he could have spared himself from the impending impact, which he must have felt in anticipation, with horrible, vivid clarity, before he experienced it as a distinct physical sensation, his body shattering the surface of the river right at the moment when he was probably condemning himself for being such a stupid fucking idiot, and wasn't it just so fucking typical for him to realize this too late!

Under ordinary conditions, the story would have ended with my father's death. But something extraordinary happened that morning, and Abe Boyle was saved from an outcome that should have been inevitable. As I imagine it, no sooner had he slipped

12

beneath the surface of the Tuskee than from the depths came a soft rumble, and the river, already swollen from the rain, abruptly smoothed out in response. The refuse stopped its spinning rush; the wind died down. A vacuum of silence sucked in all noise, and the gallons of water that a moment before had been plunging over the falls seemed to hover in the air, hesitating, uncertain. For an instant that was too short and too long to be measured by conventional time, all motion in the gorge ceased.

And out of that infinite stillness came my father's reprieve. Though I can't fully explain what happened next, I do know that heavy rainfall contributed to problems created by a rickety wooden cofferdam. A portion of the barrier had collapsed, and storm debris had been collecting over several days, clogging the spillway. The previous night an additional two inches of rain had fallen, causing the city's sewers to overflow, and a dense sludge pasted the debris into a full obstruction, blocking the surging river entirely. The water had nowhere to go except back into the gorge.

Ripples spread across the surface, gathering into a forceful swell. There was a great splashing noise of liquid washing against a confined space. Water began foaming and boiling, and that portion of the Tuskee reversed its direction. The current sloshed southward even as the river toppled over the falls with renewed force, and the gorge began to fill like a stopped-up sink.

I can only guess that my father, if he was still conscious, assumed he had already died and was descending through a vile, viscous fluid into hell. Or else he spent that brief moment stunned into a complete oblivion, thinking and feeling nothing.

Across from the brewery, in the lower parking lot of the Beebee Electric plant, a few employees heard an unusual roar echoing through the gorge. They approached the embankment and through the mist watched the river surging back into the stone channel. When it appeared that the water would keep rising, they prepared to flee. Some of them had even started to run when a wave crashed over the wall and spread across the parking lot. At the same moment, the debris blocking the opening must have been dislodged by the shifting pressure, for the river formed a liquid funnel in the gorge, gulping back the surge, and the water level fell.

But the people in the Beebee parking lot didn't notice the spillover trickling away through cracks and crevices in the wall. They didn't see that the Tuskee River was flowing steadily and reliably north again, toward Canton Point and the lake. Rather, their stares were fixed on the body of the sputtering, blue-faced, waterlogged man who had been deposited in a puddle on the pavement.

For reasons I'll go on to explain, I was thinking about this story earlier this morning. I was wondering if I should go ahead and write it down, tell the whole of it from start to finish. Would anyone believe me if I claimed to be telling the truth?

I felt too muddled to head directly to work, so I took a detour through the city. I parked my car in the lot beside the ruins of Boxman's Mill and walked partway across the pedestrian bridge. The air was damp, the sky overcast. Far below, the river looked as glassy and flat as a pond. I stood there for a long while, watching gulls circling between the walls of the gorge. When I heard the electric chimes of St. Stephen's ringing the hour, I decided to leave. But first I dug into my purse, found a penny, and tossed it over the rail. As it fell, I counted aloud: *one and two and three and* —

Between the bottle of vodka he'd polished off the night before he jumped from the bridge and the engulfing shock of the frigid water, my father would remember little of his actual ordeal. Most of my information comes from my grandmother. She was the one who first told me what happened that day. She described the unfolding scene in the gorge in impossible detail, as if she'd been there and had watched it herself.

After being spit out by the river onto the lower parking lot of the Beebee plant, my father, with no broken bones or obvious injuries, was helped to his feet. A blanket appeared out of nowhere and was draped over his shoulders. Clamping his shivering lips closed, shaking his aching head, he vowed silently to get on with his life and prove himself worthy.

He couldn't bring himself to contact my mother, and she never came close to guessing why he disappeared so abruptly. All she knew was that Abe Boyle went away without even saying good-bye, leaving her alone, brokenhearted, and pregnant with me.

My grandmother Sally Werner blamed herself for the turmoil that culminated that day in the gorge. Everything, she thought, was her fault. And yet she was convinced that none of it could have been prevented.

She entrusted me with her version of this story late in her life. In fact, it's a long story when all the pieces are added together, and it begins many years before my father jumped from the pedestrian bridge, when my grandmother was young and set out to follow the Tuskee River north. She confided in me because she wanted me to understand, as she put it, *how one thing led to another.* But I had to promise never to repeat what she told me to anyone.

She would be furious to hear that I'm about to break my promise. I'd like to hope, though, that by the end she would forgive me.

SALLY WERNER

Touch your fingertip to a bubble. Feel the pop of cold. Cold, clear water squeezed from subterranean stone. Water seeping into the spring, filling the basin, spilling over the mossy slate ledge, flowing with a persistence peculiar to rivers, tumbling across a wide plateau, over a hillock, and down, down, down, for two hundred and sixty curving miles to the lake.

Here at the source of the Tuskee. Look around. Balance on your knees upon the stone rim, cup the water in your hands, and drink.

Splish splash. Brrr. Drip, drip, drip. See the different paw prints pressed in rich mud. Fat muskrat scooting away, wood sparrow bathing in the shallows, carcasses of yesterday's mayflies spinning with the flow. Slugs and worms, snakes and frogs, hidden in the muck.

Gurgling source of life. Good, plain water

bubbling up out of the earth, widening into a lazy meadow stream, gathering depth and momentum along its descent. Clear current stirring silt into a dusky brown, stirring brown into a frothy yellow, eroding stone, cascading over precipices, carving ravines, powering turbines and generators, filling irrigation ditches, flowing past fields and houses, picking up sewage and chemical waste and runoff from the roads, ripening with a thick luminescence before spilling out into the lake.

Help me!

What was that?

Roar of the falls. Splashing shoals. Raindrops piercing the surface on a cold autumn day. A single spot of foam traveling along the water's surface, disappearing between ripples, sliding forward, splitting and converging in serpentines.

There it goes, there and there.

Have you ever heard the legend of the Tuskawali? They were little creatures said to have the faces and hair of humans and the spotted bodies of tadpoles. Hatched deep inside the earth, they squirmed from the molten center, through cracks in the sediment, up into the aquifer, and eventually they emerged with the fresh water into the spring and swam downriver in search of mates. The natives believed them to be the sacred incarnations of fate, begot in the underworld for the sole purpose of multiplying possibility in the world. Their goodwill could be cultivated simply by leaving them alone.

The early explorers at first dismissed the natives' accounts of the Tuskawali as superstition. Then they saw several of the minute creatures circling in the clear water of the spring, gliding just below the surface. They saw dappled clouds of Tuskawali swimming at the edge of the meadow, where the stream deepened before descending down the mountain. They even saw one stretched on a rock, soaking in the sun. The creatures were too swift to catch with bare hands, so the men used sieves and fine-woven nets, scooping up the Tuskawali by the dozens. They dumped the tiny captives into bottles filled with river water, packed them in crates, and carried them east, to be loaded onto ships and sent back to England.

Invariably, the Tuskawali died either during the journey to the coast or on board the ships. The men hoped to bring home the strange carcasses, if nothing else, as proof of their existence. But the bodies floating belly up inside the bottles disintegrated into a silt that within minutes became transparent. And then, of the twelve ships that transported the bottles, two went down in North Atlantic storms, four were sunk by Spanish frigates off the Azores, four others lost their cargo to a fire in Southampton Harbor, and one sailed off course, disappearing into the icy oblivion of the Arctic. Only a few bottles actually made it into the hands of scientists at the Royal Society, who tested the water with all the means available to them and found no impurities beyond a slightly elevated level of phosphorus.

The Tuskee River flows north across the state border, through the Southern Tier and up into Canton Lake. Its source is on the edge of a cornfield in the highlands of the Endless Mountains, the spring where the Tuskawali were said to have come out of the earth. After the natives were driven from the region and before tractors made the high slopes accessible to farmers, the forest undergrowth grew so dense and the outflow so thick with swamp grass that the exact location of the spring was forgotten — until the day in 1947 when a sixteen-year-old girl left her newborn infant on the kitchen table of her parents' home and ran away.

Splish splash, halluah, halluah. Where was

she? Oh, buddy, weren't they in trouble now.

If only she had a buddy.

Or a blanket to keep her warm.

Or soap. She'd give her little toe for a bar of perfumed soap. And for such a sacrifice she deserved a piece of milk chocolate as well, along with a guarantee that she'd never again go through what she'd just been through.

But with water, this good, fresh, pure springwater bubbling like happiness, she'd do all right. She didn't need nobody. Anybody, rather. She knew her grammar well enough to get by. *The cock's crow came with dawn.* Until she went to work for the Jensons, she'd had Miss Krumbaldorf for three-quarters of seventh grade. Miss Krumbaldorf with her narrow shoulders and string-blond hair and freckled nose: she was perfect and devoted herself to teaching students everything they needed to know so that when the time came, they could decide how best to make use of their God-given talents.

Was it because of Miss Krumbaldorf that Sally made the irreversible decision to leave her newborn son for her family to raise and run away from the world? If only the world weren't so darn big. Everywhere you go, there it is.

And just when you think you've had enough, you find a quiet place where the clear, cold water comes bubbling out of the earth. That's nice. And look at all the wild strawberries peeking out from behind their leafy curtains — enough to fill two buckets!

The afternoon sun offering a healing warmth. A wood thrush piping its three-note trill. If she weren't so all alone at this, the second beginning of her life, she'd have to consider herself blessed.

The first documented reference to Sally Werner is her birth certificate issued by the Peterkin county clerk in August of 1930. Her name appears once more on a list of children who in their twelfth year were welcomed as full members of the Good Shepherd Calvary Church, having been successfully *baptized in the Spirit.* But there are no surviving photographs of Sally as a child. She's absent from the family albums. Of her siblings, only her sister Trudy would ever look for her after she left home.

Her parents, German immigrants from the village of Utilspur in the Black Forest, settled near the father's brother on the outskirts of Tauntonville in the Peterkin Valley. Shortly after their arrival, they joined the local Baptist church, and their devotion to their newfound faith quickly became the center of their lives. The father, Dietrich Werner, was appointed an elder, while the mother, Gertrude, led the women's Bible study group. Sally was their first daughter and their second child of seven. Somehow they managed to grow corn and hay on their forty acres of stony land. They kept a small herd of dairy cows, and they sold Gertrude's homemade jam at a roadside stand.

An outbreak of polio in 1939 would take the life of their youngest daughter, Anna, and leave another daughter, Trudy, dependent upon a leg brace for the rest of her life. Dietrich and Gertrude Werner interpreted this loss as God's angry call for a show of stronger faith. And as anti-German sentiment spread with the escalation of the war abroad, they felt an increasing need to prove themselves patriotic Americans. They stopped speaking German even between themselves, and they spent less time running the farm and more time with their religious duties in town. They hardly noticed as their crop yield steadily decreased.

To help support the family, the oldest son, Loden, went to work for the local lumber company when he was fourteen. At the age of twelve, Sally was sent to the neighboring farm to help with housework and care for the young Jenson twins. For the next four years she was paid with room and board and a weekly allotment of sausages, which she brought home to her parents on Sunday mornings before church.

It was during a church picnic one mild October day when her older cousin Daniel offered her a ride on his new motorcycle. He was twenty-three. He'd come back from the war blind in one eye. Though he'd been a timid boy, slight and pale, who had always kept out of the way at family gatherings, as a wounded veteran he'd gained a special status among his relatives, and he was allowed to follow his own set of rules. He'd started smoking hand-rolled cigarettes and drinking from bottles tucked in paper sacks. He worked part-time as a clerk in a grocery store. No one knew how he came up with the money to buy a motorcycle. He was the type to keep his thoughts to himself, and Sally, who'd been watching him with interest from a distance, sizing him up and trying to get a better look at his damaged eye, was surprised when he offered her a ride.

She knew what her parents would have said if she'd asked them for permission to take a ride with Daniel. So she didn't ask them. She just snuck away from the picnic and met him on the dirt road behind the

Jensons' barn. She hiked up her skirt, swung her leg over the seat, mounting the bike as if she were mounting the Jensons' paint pony, and grabbed Daniel around the waist as he gunned the engine.

It was great fun riding back behind the reservoir and along the road that crossed a lower ridge of Thistle Mountain. Daniel made that bike go so fast that Sally's hat went flying, and when she screamed he just went faster.

Faster along the mountain's southern slope, faster along the zigzagging road, their bodies leaning together one way and then the other, down along the dirt road behind the junkyard, down through Stockhams Woods, careening into a field Sally had never seen before, bumping up and over a grassy mound at such high speed that the front wheel actually left the dirt road and they seemed to float suspended in the air, then dropped abruptly, slowed, and finally rattled to a halt in the middle of nowhere.

Crazy, one-eyed Daniel — when did you get so wild? You who would only ever eat your potatoes mashed, never fried or boiled. And always adding sugar to lemonade that was already sweet. You were changed by the war, along with the rest of the world. Because of the war, people now knew what could happen. But as Father Ludwig of the Good Shepherd Calvary Church liked to say: *knoving eez nawt veezdom.*

Daniel, lacking in *veezdom,* urged, "Come on, Sally."

"Where to?"

"Let's just have a walk around."

They walked for a while along the path that grew narrower toward the end of the meadow, the brambles scratching Sally's legs, closing in, until the path faded to nothing, there was no dirt left to see, the sun was low in the sky, and it was time to get back home. But Daniel wasn't ready to go home. Daniel had a confession to make: *all this time* —

"How long?"

"Forever."

For forever, he'd guessed that Sally had special feelings for him. The way she looked at him. Her smile. Gee, when she smiled at him, it was all he could do not to —

What was he trying to tell her?

Though she should have known better, she couldn't help but grin. That was her habit. Grinning Sally, who by then had a reputation for being able to charm all the youth of Tauntonville. As it turned out, she'd unintentionally charmed her cousin Daniel.

What a silly boy he was!

Such a darling girl — why, he absolutely had to kiss her!

He pressed so hard against her that she tripped and fell beneath him. She instinctively grabbed him as she went down, which he seemed to take as proof that she wanted him just as much as he wanted her. And while he tickled her and made her shriek with laughter, she did want him enough to tickle him back. His good eye sparkled; his bad eye stared at a skewed angle and was veiled with a pearly film. What a strange and fascinating fellow! No matter that he was her cousin — that was part of the fun of it. It felt right and natural to be misbehaving. That's all they were doing. Misbehaving in the way that can't be helped when you're young and full of life and out of your parents' sight. Until Daniel went too far, and by the time Sally realized what was happening, she couldn't stop him.

Doesn't it feel good, Sally? Doesn't it, doesn't it? He loved her and he couldn't help loving her.

It was over just like that — an action too quickly completed to be undone. And though she could see from the look in his good eye that her cousin was satisfied, all Sally could think to say in the cool bitterness that came with an understanding of having failed to protect herself was "Don't you ever do that to me again, Daniel Werner. Now take me home."

She worked for the Jensons six months more, until her swollen belly was showing too much to be hidden by sweaters. Daniel, eager to claim his cousin as his wife, made it known that he was the father, but Sally refused to have anything to do with him. She must marry him, her parents told her. She'd rather die, she said. Daniel wrote to Sally, describing the joyful life ahead for them together, in long, garbled letters, which she tore up without ever answering. At home, she worked as hard as she could, shucking, lifting, hauling, boiling berries into jam, and praying that exhaustion would put an early end to her trouble. She hissed at her mother's admonitions and invited her father's rage with her foul language, feeling with a secret satisfaction the sting of his powerful hand against her ear and then the ringing that she hoped signaled a deeper pain. They couldn't make her marry Daniel Werner against her will. Oh, yes they could. Oh, no they couldn't. Still her belly grew fatter as the snow turned to rain. And then the day came when there was nothing left to do but run away.

Running, running, running up the jagged slope behind the rows of new corn, over the stone wall, through the woods and meadows. Sting of nettles. Gray sky of dawn. Bark of a startled deer. *Don't be afraid, it's only me.* Running, running, running. Baby will have his bottle of warm milk by now and a clean soft diaper to replace the soiled one she'd left on him. *Good-bye, baby.* He'd been alive a whole forty-eight hours, and she hadn't bothered to give him a name yet. She would let her parents name him. They'd name him Moses. No, they wouldn't. They'd name him something shameful — Job or Ishmael or, worst of all, Sal — so he'd never forget his shameful mother.

Running, running, running, because that's what a girl does who has left her baby in a basket on top of the kitchen table, like a pile of fresh-baked biscuits. And all the while listening for the sound of voices filling the empty air, calling her to come back.

Sally!

O Lord our Governor, whose glory is in all the world.

Where's Sally?

Has anyone seen our wretched Sally?

Look what she forgot to take along with her!

And who's surprised?

Almighty and everlasting God, from whom cometh every good and perfect gift.

Laura, check the attic. Loden, check the cellar. Clem, ride over to the Jenson place, see what they know. Tru, watch Willy. And the baby.

Sally isn't here.

Sally's gone away.

Bad Sally. Doomed Sally. The flesh lusteth against the Spirit, and the Spirit against the flesh.

Give unto us an increase of faith, despite —

A mouth of cursing, deceit, and fraud. Tush, she said with vanity, I shall never be cast down. And look what happened.

Bad Sally will come to a bad end — that's what they'd been saying ever since her cousin taught her about love. While other Tauntonville girls her age were finishing their schooling and looking forward to marriage, she was —

Running, running, running —

Where's Sally?

Sally's gone away.

Is that her name carried on the wind? *Shhh,* says the breeze moving through the meadow. Don't speak. The world will watch in silence as she runs, the sky empty of consolation. No one is calling. They've

31

already given up on her.

But still she runs. Running, running, running. How many lives start over this way, by putting one foot in front of the other?

In this corner of the world, hidden from prying eyes, in the grainy light of dusk, on a June evening in her sixteenth year, Sally knelt at the mossy edge of the spring, cupped her hand to hold the fresh water, and drank her fill. The water was as cold as ice. Colder. She ate those sour strawberries by the handful, and then, in the darkness, she made a soft bed from dry pine needles and slept. She slept for one hundred years. And she woke to a whole different life.

How was it different?

It was raining.

Oh.

A soft, soaking rain fell all day. It was the kind of rain that washed away caked mud from fingers, blood smears from a sanitary pad, and dirt from the soul. She sat beneath a rocky ledge beside the spring and waited for the rain to stop. Late in the afternoon, she was as bad a girl as ever.

Bad Sally.

That's her.

In ancient times the oracle would have predicted a bad end. But there are no oracles in the modern world. There are only fears and hopes.

And hunger. Dear Jesus, she was so damn hungry she was ready to eat her shoe.

But still she sat beside the dripping shale, feeling cold through to her bones and furious at everyone she could think of — God, her family, Miss Krumbaldorf, the Jensons, the men who started the war, the German soldier who threw the grenade that sent shrapnel into Daniel's eye, and of course Daniel Werner himself, who couldn't see straight enough to know that he would never convince his cousin to marry him.

Dripping, bubbling water. It was early in the month, not yet summer, and with the rain the temperature was dropping steadily. She'd freeze to death if she didn't do something besides sit there watching raindrops melt into the spring, the bubbles pop, the foam swirl, and — why, look at that sneaky little worm slipping out from beneath a rock, sliding soundlessly into the water. Just a slimy gray newt with yellow spots. Yet in the tension of her loneliness, it was more than that.

She tried to catch sight of the creature as it swam away. At first she didn't see it moving in the water. Then she saw the tiny snout sticking out above the surface, the black beads of its eyes staring, as though challenging her to imagine the potential for conversation.

What else was there to do but say hello?

At the sound of her voice, the newt pulled itself underwater with a jerk, leaving only a single circle where its snout had been. As the faint ripple widened, Sally caught sight of thready brown hair trailing below the surface, hardly more than a shadowy blur in the water. And were those arms stretched out, along with the flickering motion of tiny hands paddling through the water? There and gone, leaving enough of an impression for Sally to wonder about what she'd just seen.

But wonder doesn't last long when a belly is rumbling its complaints. Sally had never heard the legend of the Tuskawali and didn't want to have to figure out how to make sense of what she'd seen. Why, a newt was just a newt! Forget about it. More important, the spring was a vessel of stone and mud spilling water in a constant stream. The water moved through the narrow channel and toward the meadow as if on a single-minded mission, going on its way with a certainty that Sally envied. Where, she wondered, was it heading? Where would it lead?

She couldn't begin to guess the answer. Her parents' farm was at the bottom of the south side of Thistle Mountain. Here on a distant northern plateau, the stream meandered through the meadow and then bent toward the slope. She'd never been on the north slope of the mountain before. She'd never been farther than the field behind the junkyard where one Sunday afternoon she'd lain with her cousin Daniel.

As soon as the drizzle had lightened to a warm mist and before the sun had sunk behind the far ridge of pines, Sally Werner set out walking, following the bank of the meadow stream, descending through the forest as the stream widened into a creek and fell over mossy stone shelves. The flowing water was the next best thing to an arrow mounted on a sign with her name on it.

This way, Sally Werner.

A girl in a plaid sheath dress and saddle shoes just walking along, stepping over roots stretched across the ground like knobby fingers, hoping that she was heading in the right direction, with a destination that would include a hot turkey dinner, walking to the rhythm of the ballad she was making up to tell the story of her life.

Mother, daughter, sister, lover.

Wretched Sally Werner.

And then what?

Then she disappears down the mountain-side.

Quick, come say good-bye to Sally.

Good-bye, Sally.

But she's already gone.

June 4, 1947, five o'clock on a Wednesday. And what in God's name did the two men see coming out of the bushes?

"D-d-don't shoot, Swill. It's a girl."

"I can see it's a girl."

Grizzled old Swill, with narrow eyes shadowed by the brim of his cap. Everybody on the north side of the mountain knew Swill. And the man who knew him best was his stuttering brother, Mason, standing there in Italian army boots his nephew had sent back for him from the war, woolen kneesocks knitted by his nephew's wife, a lumber shirt, and striped shorts belted above his waist.

"D-don't you d-d-do anything crazy, Swill."

"I wouldn't ever shoot a doe."

Together they watched her cross from one side of the creek to the other, stepping so lightly she might have thought those stones were eggshells.

"Hello, darling."

The shock of them — "What in hell!"

"Well, listen to that mouth. Won't you listen to that mouth!"

All she could think to do then was to stand there, stupid and helpless, the creek trickling merrily around the rock beneath her right foot.

Swill said he wouldn't have ever thought such an ugly sound could come out of such a pretty mouth.

Ticktock of a dead tree's branch knocking against the trunk of a tall elm. Gurgle of the stream. The rest of the world was silent as Swill took a step forward.

"Sw-Swill," his brother murmured.

"Shut up, Mason."

What should Sally do? After sixteen years in the Peterkin Valley, this situation was new to her. At least she'd known Daniel before he threw himself on her. She'd known him all her life. These men were strangers and seemed bent on causing harm. Should she turn and run and risk taking a load of shot in her back? Should she curse? Should she prepare to fight? Should she smile? She wasn't finished considering these options when she felt a slimy substance hit her left leg, a cold, wet wormy thing that latched on just below the crease of her knee, causing her to lose her balance and shift extra weight to her right foot, which slipped out from under her. She landed with a splash in the icy water, catching herself with her hands so she didn't fall too hard, though she got enough of a soaking to turn the butter-colored squares of her dress brown.

Now she was mad.

"You damn imbeciles," she said, surprising herself with a choice of words she'd never before uttered as a trio. She decided to elaborate: "You goddamn imbeciles!"

"The little spitfire," said Swill, laying his gun on the ground.

"P-p-poor girlie," said Mason.

They straddled the creek, curled their rough fingers around her elbows, and lifted her onto dry land. With a quick motion she felt the back of her leg to confirm that it was bare again, free of the worm or leech that had latched itself there.

She warned the men that they'd better not lay a hand on her — this after they had already released her.

"We w-won't," said Mason, taking a step back.

"And you," she snarled, turning to Swill. "Quit laughing."

"Who's laughing?"

"Tell him to quit laughing."

"Quit l-laughing, Swill."

"I'm not laughing. It's a cough. Feather on the back of my tongue. Ha, hach." He spit a gob into the creek, squared his shoulders, and announced, "That's better."

"Aw, Swill."

"Swill," Sally echoed. "It's a good name. Swill. Like what's in a pigsty."

"Hey now, I haven't done you any wrong."

"Not yet."

"Not ever, missy. Not if you get on home where you belong."

"I don't have a home."

"You sh-sure look like you have a home. That's a homemade dress like wha-what Georgie would sew," said Mason. He pointed at her, singling her out, accusing her of being who she was.

"You just appeared out of nowhere?" goaded Swill. "Like an angel, eh?"

"Like an angel, yep."

"You an angel?"

"What if I am?"

"Prove it."

"Angels don't have to prove anything. Either you believe or you don't. It's your choice."

"An angel wouldn't curse like you do."

"How do you know what an angel would say? Ever met one?"

"Swill, d-don't g-go pretending you know anything about angels. You of all p-p-people."

"Swill," sneered Sally, filling her mouth with the bad taste of the name.

"Let's go, Mason," Swill said, hooking the strap of his gun back over his shoulder. "It's suppertime." And to urge his brother along, he added in a hush that was more than loud enough for Sally to hear, "Can't you see she's got a screw loose?"

She slapped a mosquito into a red smear on her arm and watched the two men as they headed down the path away from her. At first she felt triumphant and certain that she had a right to be indignant. Then she started to feel a rising anguish as she thought about that good word *supper* and realized she would go another night without it.

Wait!

Did she say that aloud?

They went on without turning, climbing carefully down the steep path, holding those twelve-gauge shotguns snug under their arms.

Please.

All she could see by then was Mason's cap

bobbing above a jutting rock. "Hey there," she said in a whimper. "Hey, misters." Now that they were out of sight completely, she realized how foolish she'd been. Like what's in a pigsty, she'd said. Why had she said that? She sagged in a heap to the ground, taking up the space between a craggy boulder and the hard knuckle of a root, and hid her face in her arms. She held in her sobs in order to be able to hear their footsteps if they returned to help her. But they didn't return. That was her fault. She wouldn't last through the night. That, too, was her fault. She'd left her newborn son on the kitchen table. She'd made it impossible ever to return home. She had no home. She was born out of nothing and would become nothing. Like what's in a pigsty, sure. Out of her own pretty mouth. Shit and filth and blood and any goddamn chance she had left — all in the pigsty. It was her fault. Mistaking ignorance for freedom. All the facts that she would never know. A phrase from her seventh-grade studies came to mind: *failure of self-governance.* Meaning what? She hadn't understood then and she didn't understand now. And another dislocated phrase: *on the eve of.* And a word she didn't remember ever learning: *blimey.* Where did that come from? The unscrewed screw causing everything to lose its place. *Crosshatch* and *according to.* Bump, bump, bump. The world spinning like her mother's lazy Susan on the table, beans and potatoes turning round, along with baby.

For Christ's sake.

Amen.

Help yourself. Loden, pass the carrots.

Can't someone shut that baby up!

He misses his mum.

Tru, go warm the milk. And the rest of you — what are you waiting for? Eat.

Spinning on this, the second night of her new beginning. Cool breeze hardening into a frosty stillness. Low sun filtered by the trees. Creek burbling on its descent. Awareness growing of pain hardening in her right breast, and no one to help her. No one to comfort her. No one to save her from herself and the harsh night. She would drift away. Drifting, she would lose track. She would give up. She would forgive. She would forswear and forget, and life would fade into the dream of life, a woodland scene, Sally Werner huddled on the ground, birds chirping and whistling, indifferent to her plight, and a red cap bobbing up over the rock.

"P-poor g-g-girlie."

It was the stuttering man named Mason. Without his shotgun.

42

"Are you all right?"

"Sure."

"Can you s-s-stand?"

Though a small man, with white hair bristling from beneath the sides of his cap, he was wiry and sturdy enough to support her as she rose to her feet. He didn't appear strong enough to carry her, though he offered to try. She draped her arm over his shoulders and leaned against him.

"You d-don't look all right, g-g-girlie."

"I guess I don't feel all right," she said, and as if to prove it she collapsed in a faint.

The woman was murmuring, saying something that Sally didn't understand, and something else, and as clear as a bell, "She's sure been through it." And then the stuttering man was asking the woman w-w-what happened to the girl. But the woman said she needed hot water, and she directed the stuttering man to put a pot on the stove. The man continued to stand in the doorway, squeezing his cap in his hands, waiting for an explanation.

"What's your name, honey?" the woman asked gently.

Sally wanted to answer, but somehow her name came out all wrong, a string of complaining syllables that didn't make sense.

The woman took it upon herself to interpret. She told the stuttering man:

"She's calling for her mama. She doesn't know where she is. Honey, you're here with us, with friends. We'll take care of you. You don't need to worry yourself worse off than you already are."

"She need a d-d-doctor?"

"You go get the water boiling, Uncle, if you will. And could you bring Stevie in? He's out back with Daryl. Send Daryl home, and bring Stevie inside."

"How 'b-bout Swill's wife?"

"We'll start without her. I'll let you know if we need help. Honey, here's a sip of water. You like that? You've been through it, haven't you? Uncle, go on, please."

"I'm g-g-going."

"That Uncle Mason," the woman said, shaking her head. She explained to Sally that he only ever wanted to do good, and she didn't have to be afraid of him. "He says you're an angel. An angel visiting from heaven. He says your wings are broke, and he carried you all the way down the mountain. I can't hardly believe it, but Uncle Mason would never tell a lie." She lifted the glass to offer Sally another sip of water. And how about a bite to eat — a cheese sandwich and applesauce? Did she want to try? No, not yet? That was fine, they weren't in any hurry. She needed to rest a bit, and then she'd be hungry.

"There you are. Now let yourself get better. Don't fight it. I suspect you've been fighting something for a while. Just relax. You can tell me your story later. Don't worry about anything. You're not the first stray we've taken in, believe me. And don't you think we're going to blame you for something we don't even know about. I assure you, honey, I've had my own share, if you know what I mean. Who hasn't? Well, what matters now is making you comfortable."

She introduced herself as Georgina but went on to explain that she was called Georgie. The appropriate response from Sally would have been to offer her own name. Instead, she closed her eyes and basked in Georgie's words and Georgie's kindness. Everything was permeated with the grassy smell of witch hazel from the cloth draped across her forehead. As her thoughts moved idly through comprehension and comparison, she imagined that she was fully submerged in a bath of witch hazel, breathing through a straw. Somewhere in a corner of her mind she remembered to be wary, yet mostly she felt herself settling into a warm feeling of gratitude. She had a vague sense that this woman named Georgie was saving more than her life. She gave her the best smile she could muster to show her thanks.

"You sure look worn out," said Georgie. "Now don't mind me, we'll put you in dry clothes, slip your arm out of the sleeve like that. There, that's a good girl. And here we go, you've got a hot spot there. I bet it smarts."

The hot spot was a boil deep inside Sally's right breast, and Georgie was right, it smarted plenty.

"Hey, Uncle," Georgie called toward the kitchen, "fill a basin with the water off the stove, thanks, and leave it outside the door. Here you go, honey, slip this on. That's a good girl. Maybe we could use . . . you know, Uncle Mason, if you don't mind making a trip to Lawson's to pick up a couple of things we'll need, I'll give a call ahead. And you, Stevie," she said, motioning to a young boy standing in the doorway, "make yourself useful right now. Go find me some towels. Go on now, do as I say."

After she'd closed the door, Georgie draped a warm washcloth over Sally's infected breast. She fell silent for a few minutes. Sally watched her face through the witch hazel cloud of her fever and decided that she had no cause to feel wary. Here was a woman she could trust, at least for now. It was a luxurious conclusion, and it gave Sally a sweet, dreamy contentment, as if she'd just been told that she'd come into a great deal of money.

When the washcloth turned clammy, Georgie exchanged it with another one. She called her son to come into the room. A moment later a boy's voice right next to Sally's ear said, "Who's she?"

Sally blinked her eyes open.

"Hello. Uncle Mason says you're an angel."

"I'm Sally."

"Are you Sally Angel or Angel Sally? There's a difference."

"What's the difference?"

"Oh, don't bother with him," said Georgie. "Stevie, wring this cloth out in the sink and bring me another clean one."

"No, wait a second." Sally wanted to know the difference between Sally Angel and Angel Sally.

"If you don't know, I ain't gonna tell you."

Sally corrected him: "I'm not."

"You're not?"

"You shouldn't say, *I ain't.* You should say, *I'm not.*"

The woman named Georgie used this as evidence to prove to the boy she called Stevie that Sally was an angel. Angels knew everything, and soon she'd be teaching the boy all about the secrets of heaven. "But first we want to make her better."

If she was an angel, why was she sick? The boy addressed the question to his mother, but Sally answered. "Because I fell from heaven."

"Really?"

"Right out of the blue sky." As she said this, she gazed into the blue of the boy's wide, staring eyes, a thick, creamy blue that she imagined would help to soften the impact of her fall. She understood that these strangers were offering her a place of refuge. Not another home — it was better than home. Stevie, Georgie, Uncle Mason. They were ready to provide her with the aid she needed to start over again so she could continue on her way.

The little blue-eyed kid with a mop of thin, almost whitish hair, like an old man's. Like Uncle Mason's hair beneath his red cap. The kid and Uncle Mason led by Georgie, who looked too young to have such deep lines around her eyes — they were going to take care of her. She'd fallen from the sky, and they were going to make her better.

"Go on, Stevie," said his mother.

"Thank you," Sally said, and the boy nodded with a strange solemnity, as though until then he'd been testing her and now he was satisfied that she'd told him what he'd been waiting to hear.

By the next morning she was sitting up in bed and eating Georgie's canned applesauce, which through its sweetness tasted slightly bitter, reminiscent of the witch hazel that still saturated everything — her skin, her thoughts, the walls of her room. Everything in Georgie's house seemed to have been soaked in witch hazel, even Georgie, whose face had a wet gleam in the gray morning light.

"It looks like the rain is here for a while," she said as she watched Sally eat.

"Mmm."

"Do you like it?"

"The rain?"

"The fruit sauce."

"It's tasty."

"How are you feeling there?" She pointed to Sally's breast.

"Much better."

"That can happen in the first week, when

49

your milk comes in," she said gently. But Sally was more clearheaded now, and the comment made her feel suspicious, as though she'd just realized that she'd left a door unlocked — the door to her room full of secrets. While Sally had been disoriented from her ordeal, Georgie had gone inside without asking, and she knew all about what Sally was trying to hide.

"What do you mean?"

Georgie looked perplexed. She must have expected her guest to begin telling her story right then. But Sally, as grateful as she was, had already told the only story she wanted to tell: she'd fallen from the sky. She was Sally Angel, or Angel Sally, whichever the little boy named Stevie preferred.

"Well . . . ," said Georgie. Her voice was timid, and yet Sally sensed a stubbornness there, even a wily ingenuity.

"Well what?"

"The same thing happened to me shortly after my boy was born, and I tell you, it was like a knife cutting through me."

Sally didn't reply, just licked her spoon clean and replaced it in the empty bowl. She felt a disturbing impulse to be rude to this kind woman, to prove to her that she wasn't as pathetic as she appeared to be.

"Say, where are you from?" Georgie asked

abruptly.

"Rondo," Sally said with equal abruptness, surprised and proud to have thought of an unreal place so quickly.

"Where's Rondo?"

"Downriver."

"North of here?"

That confused her for a moment, and she wondered if Georgie had a hunch that she was misleading her. Maybe she should have said *upriver* instead.

"Sort of," she hedged.

"North along the Tuskee?"

Sally had only a vague sense of the Tuskee. It didn't widen into a significant river until the Southern Tier, and it didn't figure in importance for the farmers in the Peterkin Valley.

Sally shook her head no, then changed her mind and nodded yes.

Rondo, huh? Georgie had never heard of it. She looked Sally over as though she were searching her, head to foot, searching her face, her scratched arms and hands, and the contours of the bedsheet for some indication that there was more to disclose.

"Okay," Georgie said with a shrug, either with real fatigue or just worn out by the effort to separate truth from lies. She lifted the bowl away from Sally and quickly exited

51

the room, leaving behind the stark impression of her disappointment and with her absence giving her guest time to consider that by forfeiting this opportunity to confide, she was in danger of losing the best friend she might have made in Fishkill Notch.

A child's voice came to her then, traveling up from the porch below her window, rattling in play as the light rain dripped over the eaves, the mingling sounds reminding her of the gurgling creek she'd walked and slept beside, that clear, beautiful water and the music of its current. Chortling, gurgling, roar and giggle, words rattling, threats growled. Hurray, hurray! Don't you come near! Quick, hide! Jumping, crawling, hiding, warring, cheering in play, in dream, in fever. The boy was the creek turning into a river — Georgie's boy growing up in the close range of his mother's eyes and ears. She was always watching, listening, ready to hear and respond to a signal of danger. Unlike the mother of Sally's boy.

Sally's little boy.

She unbuttoned the collar of the nightie Georgie had dressed her in, squeezed the nipple of her left breast, and squirted a syrupy milk — the milk for her own boy, whose name she didn't even know.

A year ago she'd been a fifteen-year-old girl earning three pounds of sausages a week. Now she was a mother with swollen breasts who didn't know her own son's name. And that was as good a reason as any for telling a lie. She'd never let herself need anyone. If she was an angel, she was the fiercest kind, wielding a fiery sword in revenge, in destruction, in righteous fury.

Crash. Grrrr. You spy, you are my enemy. I will slay you with my magic sword. Slice, slice. Roar.

"Hey, kiddo," Georgie called in a plain voice, the voice of easy routine, from the kitchen. "Lunch is ready."

Sally let the pillow absorb her sobs. Raging, wretched Sally.

One thing Sally Werner would say about herself was that she didn't like to be idle. As a young girl she'd usually been the first one up in the house. She loved tiptoeing around in the winter darkness of the downstairs rooms, looking for treasure, pretending to be a princess aprowl in a castle. She learned to light the stove when she was just short of seven years old, and by the time she was ten she could cook a nice fried egg. When she went to work for the Jensons, she made herself valuable by doing more than she was asked. And back at home, she'd kept herself busy with chores that the rest of the family preferred to put off.

She woke later than her usual time after the second night at Georgie's house. Lying in bed, she took a long look around the room. The morning sunlight brightened the blinds and turned the unpainted walls golden. The three shelves of an old bookcase were empty. Next to the bed was a free-standing lamp without a shade. There was no bureau, but a single open drawer set on the floor held towels and sheets. She noticed that plaster chips had fallen into the drawer, and she looked up to see the big cracks in the ceiling and a hole around an empty light socket. It might have looked like work was being done on the room, but there was a thick dusty feel to it, and Sally figured that it was a room no one had bothered with for years.

She was wearing a baggy old cotton nightie sized for a fat woman. She wanted to change into clothes, but not into her own clothes. Putting on her own dingy dress would have been like going backward in time, and she didn't want to do that. Anyway, her dress wasn't even there in the room.

The rest of the house was so silent that

Sally wondered if she'd been left alone. She got up out of bed and went to investigate. Across the narrow hall was a closet with a toilet and sink. She stopped there first, used the toilet, washed her face as best she could, and retied her hair in a ponytail. Then she headed down the hall that led to the kitchen.

Georgie was at the stove, stirring something that didn't smell like anything Sally recognized. The man seated at the kitchen table was facing the entranceway where Sally stood, and he let out a low chuckle at the sight of her.

"There she is, the she-demon."

It was Swill. Swill of the pigsty. Ugly old Swill, capless now, the grizzle on his head and face thick and short and white, like a coating of paste. She was embarrassed to see him, or, rather, to be seen by him. But she also resented him for announcing her arrival as though she couldn't hear.

"You look like you're feeling better," said Georgie, turning, holding a spoon that dripped a thick, brown porridge onto the floor. "Are you feeling better?"

She was, yes, thanks, she said, and added that she didn't know what she would have done without, without . . . Unsure who to thank, she just let her voice trail off.

Georgie didn't notice the porridge on the

floor. Neither did Swill, who rose from the table, fit his cap back on, and said he'd best be going.

"You haven't had your breakfast yet," Georgie said.

With his eyes fixed on Sally, who stood there in her fat-lady's nightie, Swill announced that he'd lost his appetite.

Sally decided he was an enemy for life. She no longer regretted bringing up the pigsty comparison. She wished she'd thought of something worse.

"We'll be seeing you, then," said Georgie.

He said he had to stop by the A&P before he headed out to work at the Baker place. There was stuff he needed. Stuff — whatever that meant.

"Sure. See you later."

He was reaching for the back door when Georgie's boy squeezed past Sally through the entranceway and jumped toward Swill, who caught him in a swift hug, twirled him around, and set him standing on a chair.

"Hey, kiddo."

The boy raised his arm and pointed a finger. "Pow, pow."

"Aw, you got me good that time," Swill said, rubbing the boy's hair.

Sally looked on, feeling an unfamiliar envy for Swill's tender manner, along with a fair amount of anger at his deception. She guessed from the way he'd acted in the woods that he wasn't always a gentleman.

"I gotta go now, buster. See you later."

"Pow, pow," said the boy, shooting a couple of farewell rounds at the ceiling.

Sally walked into the small space of the kitchen and said, "Hey, buster."

"Steven," said his mother firmly, which Sally took as a signal that she should use his proper name, "say hello to our guest."

"Morning, Miss Angel."

He should call her Sally, she told him. He shrugged and hopped down from the chair, grabbed a bowl from the counter, and held it out to be filled. Georgie began bustling in an awkward fashion. After giving the boy his oatmeal, she set out the milk bottle and cups with a clatter, swished the percolator pot to check the level of the coffee, and urged the boy to eat. She had to get to work now and take him to Grandma's, so he'd better hurry up and finish his breakfast and run a comb through his hair.

Sally kept out of the way, accepting the cup of coffee and taking a seat with the boy at the table. From her position, she noticed that the floor was warped; the whole floor seemed tilted, the molding bulging with swollen joints, and the ceiling was so low that Sally was reminded of the Jensons' root cellar.

She watched the boy leap from his chair and whirl out of the kitchen. When he was gone, she asked if there was anything she could do to help. Georgie said what she could do was stay quiet for the day and make sure that infection didn't flare up again. She apologized for the condition of the house. One day soon she'd get around to fixing up that spare room where Sally was staying.

"But it's hard, you know," Georgie said.

"Sure, I know how it is."

"Raising my boy alone."

"Who's that man, that Mr. Swill?" Sally asked. And then, thoughtlessly: "What's he to your family?"

Georgie gave her that same cold, searching look she'd given her yesterday when Sally had lied about her home.

"Swill?"

"I mean —"

"Swill is Steven's grandfather."

"I see."

"You don't think much of him, do you?"

No, Sally protested, she'd never said that.

But Swill had already told Georgie what Sally said to him up there on the mountain. The words she'd used. As she started to apologize, Georgie held her hand up to silence her. "He doesn't always make a good first impression," she said. "You're not to blame. Well, listen, I'm going to work. You make yourself at home. I'll be back at six, and we'll have dinner. And then you can tell me your story."

"I'm a Werner," she blurted in a desperate effort to prove herself trustworthy. "I'm Sally Werner."

"Werner." Georgie thought for a moment. "I don't recognize the name. Oh, look, there's Mason's truck coming up the road. He'll keep you company. I'll be seeing you."

She headed off to the bathroom to help her boy wash up. Sally sipped the watery brew of her coffee. Watching Mason's pickup approach, she felt like a fugitive waiting for the sheriff to arrive. She had an urge to run, the way she'd run from the kitchen of her parents' house. And yet she also wanted to let things happen to her, come what may. Here in Georgie's kitchen, with its low ceiling and cockeyed floor, sixteen-year-old Sally Werner waited as time was marked by the sound of tires crunching gravel. She thought about the sound her name made when she'd spoken it aloud to Georgie, and she wondered if her parents were searching the yard, calling for her right then, calling through cupped hands. *Sally, you wicked girl! Sally Werner!* Did they miss her? Did they want her to come home? Of course not. They were glad she was gone. Good-bye and good riddance to the daughter who had brought the family nothing but shame and another hungry mouth to feed.

Sally watched through the screen of the back door as Uncle Mason stepped from the cab of his pickup truck. Maybe he'd tell her what would happen next.

"Hi, g-g-g-girlie." He twisted the soft band of his cap around his wrist as he nodded his greeting. He seemed embarrassed to see her. She pushed herself out of the chair and folded her arms. His embarrassment humiliated her. She resented him. If he couldn't find a way to help her, she wanted him to go away. And yet she also perceived him to be harmless. He must have been nearly seventy — a few years older than Swill. He was about her height, though with longer legs and a higher waist. His face lacked the gray grizzle of Swill's face and instead was a smooth, shiny marble with age spots that reminded Sally of the spots on the newt she'd seen that first day at the spring. She remembered the slimy sensation on the back of her leg just before she'd fallen into the creek. The memory caused her to reach around to touch the skin of her calf to make sure something awful wasn't still clinging there. As she twisted, she noticed a tear at hip level on her nightie, and when she looked back at Mason she saw he was staring right at the white of her panties showing through.

She glared at him and moved her forearm to cover it. He matched her glare with a smile. It was a melancholy smile, as though he were trying to cheer her up despite his own secret misery.

He asked her how she was feeling.

"Why, I'm feeling fine," she said with a shrug, unsure why she found it an odd question.

"Well then, where are you g-g-going next?" It was a straightforward question, but she didn't have a straightforward answer. In fact, she didn't have any answer at all.

He picked up the glass Stevie had left on the table and examined the inch of milk left in it. He said, "Let's not b-beat around the bush," and then paused. The pause made Sally wonder if he was expecting her to offer some suggestion. Or maybe he was telling her to go find some clothes and get dressed properly. She wanted to get dressed.

She didn't want to give the false impression that she was lazy. She was far from lazy — anyone who knew her would agree. If she was given work to do, she did it, and much more. She just needed permission to do things her own way.

She took a step toward the hall, but just then Mason dropped the glass he'd been holding. It bounced without shattering, dribbling milk, and he stepped quickly backward, as if to move away from something alive that had found its way into the house and was scuttling across the floor.

"I'll take care of it," Sally said, grabbing a dishrag and getting down on her knees to wipe the floor. The position made the sharp pain in her breast come back all at once. She sat up, sucking in her breath with a whistle.

"Y-you okay?"

"I'm fine."

He offered her his hand and tugged her to her feet. She was surprised at his strength and then remembered that somehow this little man, by his own account, had managed to pick her up from her faint in the woods and haul her down the mountain. She looked more closely at him, trying to figure out how all the pieces came together.

"You're looking at m-me," he said, "like

I'm a p-puzzle you want to solve." She blinked, startled by his accuracy. She would have asked him if he was a mind reader, but she sensed that the question would have sounded stupid.

Handing him the glass she'd picked up from the floor, she denied that she was looking at him in any special way, even as their eyes met.

"S-say," he said after a pause. "You have a p-plan for yourself?" It was a question that made her feel a little bit ashamed and a little bit suspicious, in equal measure. He was standing there judging her. Depending on whether he blamed her or forgave her, she would feel either more ashamed or more suspicious of him.

She wanted to say she didn't see how her plan was any of his business. But he clearly wanted to help. So what if she didn't want his help?

Funny that right then she heard a chickadee call outside the kitchen window. Its trill reminded her of her younger sister Tru, who used to translate birdsongs into words. Thanks to Tru, she heard, *Love me, me, me,* from the chickadee, a plea that roused in Sally the impossible but nearly overwhelming longing to believe that everything she'd experienced since she'd ridden away from the picnic on Daniel Werner's motorcycle had been a dream. All she had to do was go back to sleep and wake up again, and her mother would be standing over her bed:

Morning, Sally.

Where am I?

Why, you're at home. You've been sick. But you're better now. Get up, you lazybones.

And below her bedroom window, she'd hear the sound of the cows complaining, groaning from their fullness and with their low mooing urging her: Get up, Sally, get out of bed.

Moo.

Sally?

Where's Sally?

Who cares?

"You look l-l-lost in thought," said Uncle Mason.

"Who cares?" she asked, just to hear the words spoken aloud.

"I'm s-s-sorry."

"No, I mean . . . aw, forget it. Listen, I'll be honest. I'm in a fix. I don't have a dime in my pocket. I need to find work, but it doesn't look like there's much available around here. There's the cement factory where —"

"They're laying off r-r-right and left. G-Georgie will be lucky if she holds on to her job."

Sally wondered aloud about the sales work she'd seen advertised in mail-order catalogues. If she could stay with Georgie for a while and start earning commissions —

"You can't stay here," Mason said plainly, forcefully.

"Why not?"

"That room — there's no heat b-b-back there. It's closed off during the w-winter."

"Well, I could —"

Sally waited for Mason to fill in the blank. Instead he put his cap on his head, positioning it so the rim bent over his ear. "I'd b-best be going," he said. "I'll be seeing you."

"See you then, sure," Sally echoed.

And that was that. With Uncle Mason went Sally's sense that she had to plan anything. She didn't even get out of her nightie that day. She just sat around, paging through Georgie's old magazines, setting herself the task of memorizing details about the lives of movie stars to keep herself from getting too jittery with boredom. Georgie came home with Stevie at the end of the day and cooked scrambled eggs for dinner.

The next day when Georgie was at work and the boy was with Swill's wife, Sally sat around again, though at least she got dressed, wearing a denim skirt and yellow blouse that Georgie had lent her. The following day, she devised small chores to occupy her while she tried to figure out the direction of her life. The week turned into a month, and she was still trying to decide on her next move. Once in a while she'd get up and walk through the town. She thought about stopping at the beauty parlor to have her hair done, but she had no money.

On weekends when it was hot, Sally accompanied Georgie and her boy to wade in a swimming hole near the spot where Swill and Mason had found her the day after she'd run away from home. They watched the parade in town on the Fourth of July. And once Mason drove them to a country fair, where they watched barrel races and horse auctions. That was the best day of all. It happened to be Sally's seventeenth birthday, a fact she kept secret. But instead of feeling sorry for herself, she felt relieved to have put the last year behind her.

During the week, Georgie worked long days at the factory. She couldn't be blamed if she didn't have the energy to straighten up around the house. Sally, who felt ready to explode from boredom, spent the lonely hours setting things in order for Georgie, dusting her collection of ceramic animals on the shelves in the living room, washing the windows and the kitchen floor. When she saw how grateful Georgie was for her effort, Sally grew more ambitious. She washed the dirty laundry and hung it on the line. She found a screwdriver and tightened the loose knobs on the doors. After finding a can of white paint in the basement, she sanded and painted the flaking porch rail. She took apart a window sash and attached a weight to the cord. She filled a pail with raspberries from the bushes out back and boiled them down to jam.

Georgie never asked her to leave and never complained to her about staying there. Swill hardly came by at all. He'd wait to see the boy when Georgie dropped him off at his house for his wife to babysit. Weeks had passed, and Sally had only heard of the woman who was Swill's wife and Steven's grandmother — she never seemed to leave her own house. But Uncle Mason stopped by to visit Sally most mornings, and Sally found herself looking forward to the company. He wouldn't say much. He'd usually bring his pipe, and he'd spend a long time tamping the tobacco. Often, he wouldn't even bother to light it.

All summer long, Sally Werner stayed at

Georgie's house. At the beginning of September, little Stevie started school. Nights turned colder, and the chirping of the crickets grew weaker. Sally would have liked a second blanket, but she didn't bother to ask because she guessed that Georgie didn't have an extra to spare. And then one morning early in October she woke up from a restless sleep. Noticing a different quality of light in the room, she lifted the blind and saw snow on the ground — a light dusting shining like glitter inside the bottle of a winter scene.

"I've b-b-been thinking," Uncle Mason said later that day, chewing on his pipe.

Sally rocked fast in the chair on the porch. She had on an old wool jacket Georgie had lent her, though the snow had already melted, and the sun was saturating the earth with a velvety warmth.

"Now hear m-me out." Uncle Mason leaned back against the porch rail, drawing creaks from it as he shifted his weight. He stared off at something over Sally's right shoulder and stayed quiet for so long that Sally thought he'd forgotten what he'd been wanting to say. And then it came out all at once: He had a home that n-n-needed tending. Sally didn't have a home to g-g-go to.

She couldn't stay there with Georgie. Why, then, d-d-didn't she come stay with Mason for a while?

"You," she began in shock, trying to gather words in response to the offense. "You . . ."

"Me?"

If he thought she would, if he wanted . . .

"I d-d-don't understand."

"Are you asking me to marry you?"

At this, the old man nearly collapsed in a fit of laughter. "Oh!" he cried, holding his belly, reminding Sally of her father when he was measuring the effects of a good meal. "Oh!" he howled, overcome with amusement. "Oh, good Lord. Oh, girlie. Oh, oh, oh!" He moaned in glee. He had to take off his glasses and wipe tears from his eyes, he was laughing so hard. He had to sit down, he was laughing so hard. He was laughing so hard that Sally began to feel offended.

"Is it that funny?"

"Oh, g-g-girlie, no, yes, I d-d-don't know. I n-n-need a housekeeper." And then, through his chuckles, he murmured, "Unless you w-want to marry me?"

"Of course not!" she said. "I can't believe you'd come up with that crazy notion! Why, that's just cockeyed!"

What a cockeyed world she'd stepped into, she thought. A cockeyed family, a

69

cockeyed hamlet on a meager river, a cock-eyed old salamander of a man who dared to imagine that a seventeen-year-old girl would want to be his wife. The sky was too low and the ground was too high. No wonder everything kept slipping, glasses were dropped, and nothing made sense. And yet how odd it was to feel a growing commitment, as though just by choosing to remain there she would acquire a permanence, with roots growing from her feet into the porch.

"I'm going to take a bath," she said, using the same familiar kind of announcement she would have used at home with her own family. It was strange, she thought, how this old man was starting to seem familiar to her, how strangeness itself was becoming ordinary, how she was beginning to imagine that she could fit in here, she could belong.

"I'll b-b-be seeing you," he called after she'd gone inside. She was heading down the hall to her room when she heard him say, "Think about wh-what I'm offering. I p-p-pay a good wage."

She hesitated, then turned around. She intended to tell him okay, she'd think about his offer, and it sure was kind of him to be concerned about her situation. But he was already gone.

This was rural Pennsylvania in the fall of 1947 — a world of mud, sickly elms, stubbled hayfields, and backyard industries. The Tuskee was even dirtier then than now, or at least polluted in a different way, with a film of soot coating the surface and cement dust ending up as sludge along the banks. In the village where Georgie and her relatives lived, Fishkill Notch, the creek from the spring on Thistle Mountain met the Fishkill Creek. With the headwaters pouring in from the upper slopes, the water in Fishkill Notch spread into a deeper channel that on maps is marked as the start of the Tuskee River.

Hidden between its marshy banks, the river didn't draw attention to itself as it ran through the village. Anglers cast their lines there, but mostly the river flowed on without being noticed by the residents, and without noticing them.

Georgie's house was on a side road off of Main Street. Mason's house, though, was perched on a mound of land close to the wedge where the Fishkill bends into the Tuskee. In the spring and fall and after heavy rains, the sound of the river would make Sally Werner think that a storm was blowing in and wind was pouring through the trees. Years later, when she heard static on the radio or the TV, she'd think of Mason's house and the Tuskee rushing past.

She spent one more night at Georgie's. When Georgie came home from work, she brought a casserole that Swill's wife had made. She already knew about Uncle Mason's proposal and agreed that it was a good idea, promising Sally that they'd get together every weekend. She'd heard they were building a new movie theater over in the next town. She was planning to take Stevie to the Saturday matinees, and she hoped Sally would come along with them.

They ate supper, and Georgie put the boy to bed, ran a bath for herself, and called good night. Sally, who was ready to be forthright, asked if they could talk. Georgie came into the living room immediately, as though she'd been standing just around the corner waiting for the invitation.

The two young women stayed up most of the night, sharing Georgie's cigarettes, sitting on opposite ends of the couch, their knees drawn up under their nighties, their bare toes tucked between the creases of the cushions. Sally listened to Georgie talk about Steven Jackson, her fiancé, and the plans they had had. The wedding never happened, she explained, because Steve never made it home from the war and never got to meet his son, who came three weeks early and emerged like a king, bright blue from the squeeze of the cord around his neck. The doctor had taken it upon himself to pronounce the boy damaged for life. But he turned out to be just fine.

"He's better than just fine," Sally said.

"And your little one? Tell me about him."

So Sally told Georgie everything, beginning with the ride on Daniel Werner's motorcycle and the uncertain weeks that followed, her flat belly growing rounder, her prayers to God unheeded, the scorn of her relatives and neighbors, the birth of her son in the same bed where her mother had given birth to her, and ending with the day she ran away from home.

"It must have been something, leaving your baby behind like that," Georgie said finally. "I can't nearly imagine."

"It was" — Sally searched for a word — "unspeakable." It struck her as soon as she said it that she'd chosen the wrong word. But she couldn't think of another word that would do.

Georgie knew better than to say *you poor*

girl to Sally. But her sad eyes conveyed her pity, and this time Sally didn't mind.

"Won't they ever come looking for you?" Georgie asked.

I'm as good as dead, Sally wanted to say. I'm a squashed bug. I'm a fish floating belly up. I'm curdled milk. I'm a rotten apple. I'm — she searched for one more comparison — the girl in the moon, even as she said one word aloud. "No."

"And you don't ever want to see your baby again?"

"Of course I do. But he won't ever want to see me."

"That's not right."

"He's a Werner. I tell you, if you're a Werner you don't know how to forgive. Every mistake is given a number and carved in stone. That's the stone they put as your grave marker."

"I can't imagine. All the women I've talked to over the years, all the stories I've heard tell . . . I've never heard a story like yours, Sally Werner. You've sure been through it. I knew when I saw you you'd been through something. But now you just stick around here for a while, and you can figure out how to manage."

Sure, she'd stick around. Just to be in a place where she could say what she'd been through, to talk about it all . . . she'd felt comforted by the sound of her voice as she'd spoken of her unspeakable troubles. The conversation was like a light that went off gradually, fading from bright to a soft darkness over several hours.

It was long after midnight when she lay down on the bed in Georgie's spare room. For the first time in months, she began feeling hopeful. Georgie's sympathy had given her an idea, just a vague one, but enough to build on. She'd keep house for old Mason Jackson, who'd promised her a good wage, and somehow she would learn to manage. She'd do more than manage. With the money she earned, she'd have the freedom to choose how to live the rest of her life.

Daughter of satan! Babylon's whore! You foul embodiment of human filth! I tell you to kneel and pray for forgiveness. But there is no forgiveness. You are here, forever here, under my command. Now scrub the toilet! Sweep the porch! Milk the cows! Slaughter the pig! Pave the road! Brick the chimney! Raise the barn. Burn it down, and raise it again. Burn it down! Raise it again. Burn it down, down, down . . .

Burn what down? Her reeling thoughts were stuck on the cows that needed milking. Those cows with their full udders. Where were the cows? Uncle Mason didn't have cows. He didn't even have a barn. Or did he have a barn hidden somewhere in the house? Were the cows in the house?

Hurry, hurry, there was work to do. If she fell behind with one task, then she'd fall behind with everything. The cows? Where were the cows?

Running, running, running, to find the barn with the cows. But the hallway was endless, and every door was locked. Running, running, running, the sensation of slime latching onto the back of her leg, and —

Dear Lord in heaven —

It was only a dream.

Only. In reality, Uncle Mason would never have spoken to her like that.

Good morning to me.

Get up, lazybones. Get up and do something.

But there was nothing that needed doing.

Sunday morning, snow falling soundlessly into the shallow river, the house full of the good smell of frying bacon. Uncle Mason was rattling around the kitchen, making breakfast. Sally sat up in bed and pressed her hands against her face to feel the warmth left over from sleep.

Life waiting to be lived.

G-g-girlie. Was she up?

She'd be out in a minute. She had to get dressed.

Her breakfast was ready, a breakfast of eggs and bacon and buttered biscuits piled on a plate for Sally to find when she came into the kitchen. She'd dressed herself in the sweater and skirt Georgie had packed in a duffel for her. The sweater was the color of the deep red of a peach close to the pit and made of a wool almost as fine as cashmere, and the skirt was navy, a stiff corduroy hanging at knee length — a modern cut, if not exactly stylish.

Ten days had passed since she'd arrived at Uncle Mason's. In those ten days, it was all Sally could do to give the impression that she was useful. A house so sparsely furnished and pristine, with simple, functional chairs and tables and gleaming wood floors, hardly needed a housekeeper, and there were times when she kept herself busy by sweeping a room she'd already swept clean.

Uncle Mason had worked for thirty-five years at the cement factory. But his real love was wood, and he'd made all his own furniture — the chairs and tables, the lamp stands and chests and bedposts. He'd even built a model of a three-mast whaling ship, the *Charles P. Morgan,* which graced the mantel. He'd made most everything except an old Gabler player piano. Shoved against the back wall of the sitting room, it seemed to be trying to shrink into the shadows. Sally had never heard any music in the house, and she wondered why Mason Jackson bothered to keep a player piano that was never played.

A segment of the shallow river was visible through the back door, and while she ate her breakfast Sally watched the water between two yellow willow saplings, watched the snowflakes shimmer in a light that seemed to come from nowhere before they folded into the ripples of the surface.

"You l-l-like it here?" Uncle Mason asked as he stood at the sink and rinsed off the frying pan.

"I like it here fine." She hadn't meant the statement to come out as flat as it did. "I mean, I really do like it here," she said, making an effort to sound enthusiastic. "I don't know what I would have done . . ."

"M-m-maybe in the spring we can get you over to Amity for some typing classes."

"Why do I need to know how to type?"

"It's a g-good skill for a g-girl to know, that's all."

She thought she could sense what he was

implying: she needed a marketable skill for later, when Uncle Mason wasn't around.

"I guess," she said with a shrug.

She helped him dry the dishes and then watched as he got down to his work of whittling. He was whittling a cane for Swill's wife, who was having trouble with her hip, he'd said.

It was Sunday, and Sally had nothing to do. On other days of the week she cooked simple fare for their supper — chicken stew, Welsh rarebit, fried eggs. But on Sundays, Mason Jackson made it clear that she was supposed to fill the hours doing whatever she chose.

The problem was, she couldn't decide what to choose to occupy herself. She wanted to get out and have some fun. But from what she'd seen so far, there wasn't much fun to be had in Fishkill Notch. And it was snowing. What was there to do in the snow when she didn't even have proper boots?

She picked up an old movie magazine Georgie had given her. She'd already read everything in it, so she just paged through looking at the pictures. Uncle Mason's whittling knife made a sound that reminded her of her younger brothers when they slurped soup. He didn't say much while he worked.

He never said much.

Was that a bird? Sally asked after a long while, motioning to the feathery lines he'd carved along the head of the cane.

It was a swan.

Oh.

She noticed for the first time that he was left-handed. She found herself staring at the hand that held the knife and the dull gold band on his ring finger. She wondered what had happened to his wife, though she decided it would have been impolite to ask. But he guessed that she was hiding her curiosity, and he asked abruptly, "What are you staring at?" without looking up.

"Nothing."

"M-my ring?"

"No. Well, yes. You had a wife?"

"I did."

"She passed away?"

"She left."

"Oh."

He kept working, shaping the swan, peeling off curls of wood. Sally decided he preferred to be finished with the conversation, so she stood up and went to her room.

Shortly before noon he called to her, "I'll b-b-be seeing you." He was heading to his brother's house for the afternoon.

"Sure," she called back through her closed

door. "Bye-bye."

"Help yourself to wh-whatever you can find. I'll bring b-b-back some ham for s-supper."

"Thanks."

A few minutes later she heard his truck sputtering, stalling, revving again, and then clattering along the drive. She came out of her room in time to watch through the living room window as he turned onto the road and disappeared.

Leaving Sally behind to do whatever. Fixing a cheese sandwich, then eating it, kept her occupied for a short time. She smoked a cigarette and practiced blowing smoke rings. She smoked another cigarette. And then she searched among the piano scrolls for music she might want to hear.

While she was looking through the box she found the publisher's brochure, which included lyrics to the songs. It wasn't easy figuring out how to thread the first scroll onto the take-up spool, but she managed it finally. She pumped the pedals and played a song called "Blue Sky Blues," listened to it once, then played it again, singing along.

Sun don't care,
blue sky won't mind,
this aching heart you left behind.

Nothing left of rainy-day love
but a secret memory . . .

She played the song over and over, singing it with more confidence each time, with more of what Sally liked to think could be called *pizzazz*. She sang it for the boy she loved, whoever that was — any good-looking boy who treated her with respect and wasn't Daniel Werner. She sang it on the stage of a smoky nightclub. She growled it into a microphone in front of an audience of hundreds.

She paged through the brochure to another song — "Boomerang Girl" — and put the scroll in the piano. It was a song about a lover who keeps leaving and coming back —

She flies away and out of sight,
she's gone as far as I can see,
and then she's flying right back to me!

— and Sally sang it in a way she liked to think would sneak up on listeners, making them realize there was a reason they were paying attention.

High-flying girl coming right back,
boomerang right back,
right back to me!

82

She sang the few songs she knew without needing to read the lyrics: "You Brought a New Kind of Love to Me" and "My Darling Clementine" and "I've Been Working on the Railroad." She sang for hours in the empty house, pumping the pedals of that old player piano and singing as though she were trying to be heard across the mountain in Tauntonville. She imagined someone saying to her in appreciation: *Sweetheart, you sing like there's no tomorrow.*

But there was tomorrow, and by then the scrolls would be packed away in their box, the lid to the piano closed, Uncle Mason fixed in his chair whittling a stick's knob into a swan while Sally swept the floor around him, sweeping up wood shavings as they fell because that was virtually all that needed doing.

High-flying girl singing like a nightingale under a blue sky on a summer day. Oh, heartache. Oh, my darling Clementine. Humming life away. Strange life, trading one family for another. Uncle Mason better than any uncle she ever had, kinder, more generous, and he didn't have a son named Daniel. Georgie as good as a sister. Swill standing off to the side when he came to pick up his brother to go hunting, eyeing her suspiciously. His gun in the bed of his truck.

I wouldn't ever shoot a doe.

Swill an enemy for life. And if he was ever in danger of softening his attitude toward Sally, back at his house there was an invalid wife whispering in his ear, telling him about all the bad things a bad girl will do. Even though she'd never met Sally. So what? She didn't have to meet Sally to know what she was like. All bad girls were the same.

Hiss.

"Where's Sally?"

"She's out b-b-back in the garden."

No, she wasn't. She was in her room with the door open a crack, but Swill and Mason didn't know that.

"Mason, listen, I've been thinking."

"Mmm?"

Silence.

"Wh-what have you been thinking? Eh, Swill?"

"You still keep your savings in that box?"

"Mmm."

"You keep it hidden, don't you?"

"I k-keep it where I've always kept it, t-t-top of the shelf there."

"Right there in the open."

"It's no p-p-place anyone would look."

"You can see it if you stand on a chair,

84

can't you?"

"Who will be st-standing on a chair here?"

"Doesn't the girl ever clean up the cob-webs? Doesn't she dust up there?"

"Why, I suppose."

"And someday she'll see that box and wonder what's inside."

"Th-th-that's enough, Swill."

"I'm just trying to watch out for you. You got your whole life savings —"

"I d-d-d-don't w-w-w-want to hear it!"

The world, Sally considered, was divided into those who thought she'd amount to nothing and those who thought she'd amount to something. Between Swill and Mason. One who said she was a thief just waiting for an opportunity. One who trusted her alone in his house.

Here living this strange life inside an old man's house. La, la, la. Sharp lines of un-upholstered furniture. Vague, sweet smell of wood everywhere. Like cinnamon mixed with pine sap and dry leaves. Uncle Mason's trust in her as constant as the sound of the river. He was right — she'd never steal his money. Never, never! She wasn't a thief. He paid a good wage, like he'd promised — twenty-five dollars a week, plus room and board. He had never put a grimy paw on her, never touched her inappropriately and never would. He wanted only to enjoy the sense that he was helping her get by — and more. That spring he paid for typing lessons and drove her to Amity, to the secretarial school above the Fat Cat Diner, three times a week for a month.

The qick bown fox. The quick brown foz. The quick brown fox jumped over the lazy dog, at ten words per minute, then sixteen, then twenty-three, then thirty-two, then fifty-one words per minute, with no mistakes.

What a fortunate girl. When she no longer worked for Uncle Mason, she'd have a skill to offer and would be able to find a job. A girl who could type would never be without a job. And since she didn't plan to profit by thievery . . .

She was shocked just by the idea of it. There wasn't a thieving bone in her body. No, she wasn't a thief.

Say it again.

She wasn't a thief.

Since she wasn't a thief, she told herself that it wouldn't do any harm, would it, to climb on a chair on a Sunday afternoon when Mason was at Swill's? She had to dust those cobwebs in the corner, after all, up there above the shelf. It sure was dusty up there. She'd never thought to get up that high, not until she'd heard Mason and Swill talking about the box. And there it was, a nice, dark, shellacked oak box, there on top of the highest of the built-in shelves in the kitchen, above the shelf of canned vegetables.

It wouldn't do any harm, would it, to lift the box down and set it on the kitchen table and lift the tiny latch? It wasn't even locked, after all. The hinges creaked slightly. The wind preceding a spring storm rattled the windowpanes. Sally was hardly breathing as she lifted the lid. And then she forgot to breathe entirely, so baffled was she by the money — thick stacks of bills in denominations of ten and twenty, secured with rubber bands.

She'd expected to find money in the box. But not stacks of money — enough money to last a lifetime; money that smelled like fresh-cut grass, pipe smoke, and sanded wood, all at once; so much money that if she tucked a whole stack of bills in her pocket, it probably wouldn't be missed.

What a terrible thought. She almost apologized aloud. She wanted also, weirdly, to laugh, for she was conscious of the possibility that the whole thing was a trap set out for her, which she'd sprung, and she was being watched, the effect of the joke measured by spying eyes. Aha! Caught red-handed! Young ladies shouldn't pry into the affairs of old men. Who said that? Who said what?

Hurry up and close the box.

She closed the box.

Now put it back where you found it.

She put it back.

Now get off the chair.

She got off the chair.

Now breathe, Sally Werner.

She breathed.

She lived at Mason Jackson's house for a little more than two years, from the fall of 1947 to the spring of 1950, much as a niece might live with her elderly uncle for a time. She didn't manage to save much of her wages, as generous as Mason was. She spent the money thoughtlessly, buying straw hats she'd wear only once, going out to the Saturday matinees in Amity to see the same movies over again, getting fancy hairdos at Erna's Beauty Parlor on Main Street. Erna knew how to do a beehive before Sally had even seen a beehive in the magazines. She dyed Sally's red hair a silky blond. She could tame Sally's waves or curl them into corkscrews, and she and the other ladies there always had something interesting to say.

Though she was grateful to have shelter and secure work, Sally couldn't help but long for more out of life than she was getting. Her chores didn't come close to filling up the week. On Sunday afternoons, when everything in town was closed and people were home with their families, she stayed in, singing along with the player piano. But singing didn't keep her from growing restless.

Georgie had met a foreman at the cement factory in the spring of 1948 and within a year was engaged to be married, but she still invited Sally to go to the movies every Saturday afternoon. She made it a point to introduce Sally to other eligible young men from the factory and even succeeded in setting up some blind dates with friends of her fiancé. But nothing came of it. Sally didn't mind, though. She wasn't in any hurry to give up her freedom.

She found she was always welcome at Erna's Beauty Parlor. Sometimes she even helped with customers, setting up the hair dryers and answering the phone when the parlor got busy. She met Erna's sister, an older woman named Gladdy Toffit, who drove in once a week, nearly an hour each way, from Helena, a hamlet north of Amity. Gladdy was in her forties and, to Sally's fascination, had been divorced twice. She had one child, a grown daughter who had broken Gladdy's heart by eloping to California with a man she met at the tavern where she'd been working. Gladdy didn't work at all. She lived off what she called a *handsome trust* set up for her by the mother of her first ex-husband.

Gladdy Toffit told Sally just what a woman needed to know: First of all, said Gladdy, she needed to be prepared to be abandoned. Men liked two kinds of romance — the romance of first love, and the romance of new love, which meant that most every woman would have a chance to be discardable old love at some point in her life. Second, a woman needed to know how to hold her liquor. She couldn't turn silly from a few swallows of whiskey. Third, a woman needed to know how to shoot a rifle. Fourth, a woman needed to know how to choose a perfume that suited her.

Sally pondered all of these notions, especially the last. "How do I know what's the right perfume?" she wondered aloud.

Gladdy had no sure formula for finding an appropriate fragrance. But she could say with some certainty that women who smoked shouldn't wear lavender. Why not?

There was no single reason. It was just a fact. Also, a woman should never splash herself with rose water if she knew she'd be frying eggs later in the day.

Erna called her sister Gladdy a Fount of Knowledge. Gladdy would sit under the hair dryer, lifting up the helmet every few seconds when she thought of other important information to pass along. She was fond of Sally, she said, because she reminded her of her daughter. Sally could fill in as her daughter until the real daughter came home.

Sally learned something of the world during her visits to Erna's salon. More precisely, she was getting a sense of proportion, understanding the scope of her provincial ignorance. And as she became more aware of how narrow her life was, she felt increasingly dissatisfied with the confinements of Uncle Mason's house, the stark quiet of the rooms, and the repetition of the routine. Sweeping, cooking, dusting, washing, and singing for no one on Sundays. La, la, la. Mason Jackson was as nice a man as you'd ever meet — that's what she told Gladdy and Erna. But she didn't tell them how each day was like a song she'd grown tired of singing but sang anyway, returning to the same chorus over and over and always ending on the same note.

" 'Night, g-g-g-girlie. See you in the morning."

She wanted something unexpected to happen. But all the potential for surprise was closed up in that box on the high shelf in the kitchen, bundles held with rubber bands and hidden from view.

After she'd opened that box for the first time, Sally was determined never to open it again. Yet her determination weakened as the details of the memory were made more vivid by her imagination, the green of the bills greener, the stacks thicker. One day while she was sweeping around Uncle Mason, sweeping up those wood curls, she even pictured the box with its lid wide open. She wasn't sure whether she was imagining it just then or remembering an image from the previous night's bad dream.

She wasn't sure about much of anything. She'd watch Uncle Mason when he was whittling, hoping that with some gesture he'd give her a clue about himself. She'd forget that she was staring at him and would keep on staring, until he shook his head, shaking away her gaze like he'd shake away a fly. Then she'd stop staring and wait for another time, when she thought he was too deeply involved in his work to notice her. She'd wait tensely, half expecting him to leap from his chair and demand, *What is it you want from me?*

I want to know about the money in that box up there.

Months went by. Uncle Mason whittled, Sally cleaned and cooked, and on Sundays, when the whole Jackson family got together, she sang, *Nothing left of rainy-day love . . .*

She waited for Uncle Mason to tell her something remarkable. But he stayed away from subjects that would interest her. He liked to talk about the weather and the measurements in the rain gauge in the garden. When his brother stopped by, they sat in the kitchen murmuring, their voices barely audible. And when Sally entered the room and Swill fell silent, Mason would say something like, How 'b-b-bout that trolley line proposed for Amity?

Sally didn't want to hear about a trolley line!

Well, then. D-did she want a second serving of the p-p-pound cake Swill's wife made?

No thank you!

Sometimes, maybe just three or four times during the two and a half years she lived at Mason Jackson's house, he'd lift his eyes while she was staring at him and return her stare with a force that wasn't in any way cruel but involved a kind of penetrating vision, so she felt that he was reflecting the look she'd aimed at him. He'd give her a gentle nod, as though to reassure her that she'd done nothing wrong. But after he left the room she'd feel dirty from her own sorry struggle to see beyond what words could tell her. She'd feel like she'd been found out. And worse. She'd feel pitied by the look in his eyes when he'd returned her stare.

I'm not a thief.

Of course you're not.

She hadn't stolen any money. She'd never taken anything that Uncle Mason hadn't given her. But what was he planning to do with all that money? she wanted to ask him.

What money? he probably would have said, playing stupid.

The money up there.

Where?

In the box.

What box?

On a bright June morning, three months after she'd first opened the wooden box, she climbed up on a chair to check the shelf and make sure the box was still there. Finding it, she couldn't resist opening it. And after she opened it, she couldn't resist running her fingers across the soft paper of the bills. She was reminded of the stacks of bills she'd seen in the drawer of the cash register at Liggett's. She'd always wondered what all those bills in the cash register added up to. Five plus ten, ten plus twenty, twenty plus —

Quick, he's coming.

No, Uncle Mason wasn't coming right then. He'd gone off pheasant-hunting with his brother for the day. Funny about those hunting trips. Anything Uncle Mason ever brought back for Sally to dress and cook had been shot by his brother. If an animal was dead, Swill was the one who'd killed it. But he never shot a doe, no, not even if he happened to be standing in the yard, aligning the target in the kitchen in the back sight of his gun, aiming the barrel —

She cried out, startled by the shadow of a branch moving in the breeze outside the window. But no one was there. Of course no one was there. She quickly closed the box and returned it to the shelf. She was sorry afterward that she hadn't finished counting the money. But what did she care about how much money Mason Jackson kept in the box?

They were at Lawson's counter one day

after they'd gone to see an Abbott and Cos-
tello monster movie at the Amity theater,
waiting for their order, when Sally cleared
her throat too loudly and said, "Georgie,
I've been wondering."

Georgie was lost in a daydream, probably
thinking about that Mr. Harvey Fitzgerald,
the cement factory foreman who in eleven
months was going to be her husband.

But Sally wanted to know if . . .

"I'm going to suck your blood!" Stevie
bunched his shoulders into a high collar and
made fangs with his fingers. Sally gave him
a quick laugh and turned the seat of his
stool to spin him.

"What were you saying?" Georgie asked.

"I was wondering what happened to Mason's wife."

The waitress set the coffees and root beer
float on the counter and promised to bring
the pie straightaway. The boy occupied
himself poking his straw at the bobbing
mound of ice cream in his glass. Sally tried
to take a sip from her cup, but the rim was
too hot. With her eyes fixed on the clock
above the kitchen door, she asked if Mason
Jackson had ever been married.

Yes, he'd been married, Georgie said. He
was married to a woman named Shirley. For
how long? For all Georgie knew, they were

still married, least on paper.

"No children?"

Georgie explained that Mason and Shirley had had a child, a little girl, who drowned in the Tuskee when she was two. Fell through the ice. No one in the Jackson family liked to talk about it, though. The only one who ever told stories was Swill's wife, and only then when Swill wasn't around. Anyway, Shirley left Mason after the girl drowned. She just up and left town. Didn't even say good-bye.

"Where'd she go?"

"Disappeared. She was last seen at the station in Amity boarding a bus heading west."

"And Mason still wears his ring?"

"Remember, Stevie, when you asked him about that ring? Uncle Mason said the ring was stuck. He'd have to cut off his finger, he said, if he wanted to take off the ring."

What a fine thought! "Chop, chop," the boy said, slicing the air with a butter knife.

"You, stop that. Anyway, it was the only time I ever heard Uncle Mason mention that ring. If I were you I wouldn't ask him about the past. He doesn't like to talk about it."

"No, I guess not."

The waitress swooped in, setting the pieces of pie in front of them. "Hey, handsome," she said, leaning on her elbows toward Stevie. "Do I make a mean float or what?"

He looked uncertain about how to reply, and then he growled, "I'm going to suck your blood!"

"Oh, you'll be a heartbreaker," said the waitress.

And that was the end of the conversation with Georgie about Uncle Mason. Stevie wanted to leave as soon as he'd finished his float. Georgie wanted to go look in the window of the bridal shop to see what they had on the mannequin this week. She was planning to sew her own dress and two for Harvey Fitzgerald's little sisters, who would be the bridesmaids.

Sally thought a lot about what Georgie had told her, how trouble had once struck in Uncle Mason's quiet life. He'd lost a daughter to the river, and his marriage had gone sour. He had no interest in spending the money he'd earned over the course of his life. All he could think to do with it was put it in a box, stacks of bills tucked safely away for him to ignore.

The day after talking with Georgie, and then the next day and the next, Sally stared at Uncle Mason, wondering if while he whittled and puffed on his pipe he was remembering his troubles. And when her wonder was too expansive and abstract a feeling to tolerate, she'd wait for him to leave the house, and then she'd get the box and open it.

Opening the box, she'd think about what she would have done with all that cash, if it had been hers. Stacks and stacks of bills. She'd stare at the money until she'd think she heard the sound of someone coming. No one was ever coming, but she was scared of being caught. And after she put the box away she'd regret that she didn't take the time to count the money. How much money he'd accumulated, she couldn't begin to estimate. She'd count it someday, just to see what Mason Jackson of Fishkill Notch was worth.

On a brisk, clear November Sunday in 1949, she discovered that Mason Jackson was worth four thousand three hundred and forty dollars. Who would have expected it? He never bought anything extra, just what he considered necessary or, for Sally, what he felt she deserved. But a fortune of four thousand three hundred and forty dollars — that was bigger than any nest egg Sally had ever seen. In truth, she'd never seen the money of any other nest egg, only heard stories about what her mother or her aunt or uncle kept under mattresses or in coffee cans in the back of a closet. This nest egg, all four thousand three hundred and forty dollars, seemed a whole lot of money to a nineteen-year-old girl from Tauntonville.

The truth was, humble Mason Jackson was a rich man. All those tens and twenties were worth . . . how much? It occurred to her that in the rush of secrecy, maybe she'd counted wrong.

On a Tuesday in December, she took down the box and counted the money again. This time she counted four thousand three hundred and seventy dollars. She recounted the bills, just to make sure, and came up with the same sum she'd counted the first time — thirty dollars less than what she'd just counted. Did she count correctly the first time, or this time?

She pondered the mystery for so long that she still had the box open on the table when she heard the truck coming up the drive.

She hurriedly returned the box to the shelf and was in her room by the time Uncle Mason and his brother came into the house. Through the closed door she tried to hear what they were saying, but they kept their voices low. Later, after Swill had gone, she emerged from her room and headed to the kitchen, passing Uncle Mason in the hall, meeting his gaze for a moment, returning his nod and wondering about the expression in his eyes, as black as lake water and too deep to see to the bottom.

A few weeks later, when she was alone in the house, she opened the box and counted the money. Twenty dollars had been added since the last time she'd looked. But the following week, she counted the money and came up with a different sum, thirty dollars less. From one week to the next, over the course of several months, she never came up with the same amount twice. She didn't believe that the amount was changing. Rather, she was aware of a strange influence in the air that made her mix up her numbers when she was trying to count.

How had her life gotten so complicated? In the early days working as Mason Jackson's housekeeper in Fishkill Notch, she'd been given the opportunity to start afresh, free of judgment, if not exactly blameless. She had worn clothes as unadorned as the furniture in Uncle Mason's house. She'd cooked and cleaned. She'd swept wood curls from the floor. On Sundays she'd pumped the pedals of the player piano and taught herself to sing. She'd learned to type. And she had even started imagining that she would make things right: one day she would return home and get her baby boy and show him that she wasn't as bad as she'd been made out to be.

Then she'd found Mason Jackson's box. And it wasn't long after that she started to think up new ways to count money.

Brooms and kitchen pots, music, friends, beehive hairdos and picture shows. It would all have been manageable without that box on the shelf. If only she hadn't found that box. The effect of it was like a strong wind that had blown through the window and turned the pages of the book she was reading, if she'd ever bothered to read a book. She'd lost her place and didn't know what was going on or who was who — Georgie, little Stevie, Swill, Gladdy Toffit, Erna, and the mysterious Mason Jackson. And what about all the earlier chapters? Why didn't they matter anymore?

She tried to look in the mirror on the medicine cabinet to see herself, to make sure she was still there — the same Sally Werner she remembered — but the glass was all steamed up from her bath. She used her hand to wipe away the steam, and just when she thought she'd see what she expected to see, the door to the cabinet popped open, and her reflection set out walking away.

Did that make sense?

No.

Where was she?

Floors to sweep, songs to sing, and there she was making twenty-five dollars a week for doing hardly nothing. Anything! How could she make a slip like that?

It was easy to slip in Fishkill Notch. The very ground was tilted beneath the tilted floors. She'd slipped all the way down Thistle Mountain — slipped and spread and flowed on her way elsewhere, until the current hit the dam that was Uncle Mason's house.

It all should have been so simple. She was a housekeeper for a nice old man with good manners. He'd never reprimanded her, not once. And he'd never been inappropriate. He was a good man with a sad story that he didn't like to tell.

And she was nineteen-year-old Sally Werner from Tauntonville. She'd made mistakes, sure. She didn't pretend to be completely innocent. But she wasn't a thief.

"No," she said aloud, to no one. "I am not a thief."

■ ■ ■ ■

May 20, 1950, the day of Georgie's wedding to Harvey Fitzgerald, started out rainy, with thunder rumbling to the south. But by ten o'clock the rain had stopped, and a wind picked up, whipping the clouds away. By noon, the sky was a fresh blue, and the lawn behind the Cadmus Party House was almost dry.

Sally woke early to the sound of a cardinal singing its *tawitt witt witt* in the rain. She wrapped herself in a robe, plugged in the percolator, and cooked a pot of oatmeal. After she put on the temporary outfit of a cotton skirt and a high-necked sleeveless shirt, she waited for time to pass. Uncle Mason came out of his room later than usual, at about eight thirty, looking so pale and worn that Sally asked him if he was feeling ill. He assured her that he was fine and gave his chest a few pats to show that his lungs were clear. But he ended up coughing anyway, bringing up mucus from the back of his throat. All he needed to set things right, he said, was a glass of fresh water.

"Here you are, Uncle."

"Ah. Hhh-cha-mm — that's b-b-better."

But still he looked weaker than usual, deflated, like a balloon that had lost air overnight.

"You sure nothing's wrong, Uncle? You're happy for Georgie, aren't you?"

Sure, he was happy for her. Who wouldn't be happy for her? But look at the time! They'd be late to the wedding if they didn't hurry!

The wedding wouldn't start until noon. Forty of Georgie's and Harvey's relatives and friends had been invited. Georgie expected about eighty people to show up. *That's just the way it is here,* she said, which Sally took to mean that everybody was welcome.

Though Georgie had never officially married Steven Jackson, the Jacksons treated her as one of their own. They were the only family she had. They didn't mind that she was going to marry another man. They were pleased she'd found someone to love. Harvey Fitzgerald wasn't taking Steve's place. *Those are shoes no one can fill* was the line Georgie used most often to assure the Jackson family that Steve wouldn't be forgotten. But Harvey Fitzgerald was a dependable man, by all accounts, and he'd be a good father to her boy.

Even if she wouldn't admit it, not even to

105

herself, Sally felt envious of Georgie. Yet she also felt tender toward her, like she would have felt if her little sister Tru were getting married. And she was looking forward to dancing at the wedding, spinning fast enough to turn her new yellow dress into a blur of gold.

Really, though, the dress wasn't exactly *new.* Gladdy Toffit's daughter had worn it once, to her senior prom, and Gladdy had given the dress to Sally — *for keeps,* she said. It was a rich yellow color with sparkling sequins around the neckline and a creamy chiffon waistband.

At nine o'clock she folded the dress carefully and put it in a shopping bag, along with the dress shoes she'd borrowed from Erna. Then she called good-bye to Uncle Mason and walked over to Erna's Beauty Parlor. Georgie was already there when she arrived, her hair pinned in preparation for an updo. Sally volunteered to help with the Fitzgerald girls, fourteen-year-old twins who were having their hair curled.

The rest of the morning passed quickly. Swill stopped by the parlor to pick up Georgie. He waited in his truck while Erna put on the finishing touches, winding glittery ribbons through Georgie's hair. There was a moment of panic when Georgie stood up from the chair too suddenly, her high-heeled shoe slipped from under her, and she turned her ankle. At first it seemed as though she had a real sprain, but the ache passed quickly, Georgie declared herself miraculously mended, and she headed out the door at a run.

There was another sign of trouble when one of the Fitzgerald girls started crying because she didn't like her curls. But Erna managed to comfort her, whispering something in her ear, which aroused the suspicion of the other Fitzgerald girl, so Sally took it upon herself to assure this sister in a whisper that she'd catch the boys' eyes that day. Both girls left contented. And while they waited for Gladdy Toffit to join them, Erna fixed Sally's hair in a French braid secured at the end with a ribbon that matched her waistband. They kept waiting as long as they could without being late for the wedding, but Gladdy never showed up.

The ceremony was held in the gazebo at the edge of the lawn, along the bank of the narrow Tuskee. There'd been plenty of rain that season, and the current was stronger than usual, the water running so loudly over the loose stones that it was hard to hear the minister who was presiding, or the bride and groom as they were led through their vows. At that point there were about fifty guests either sitting on wooden chairs or standing about the lawn. But as soon as the vows were completed and the bride and groom had kissed, other guests started to arrive, some appearing at the back door of the Party House, as though they'd been given the signal to emerge, and others coming from their cars in the parking lot.

Uncle Mason was dressed in an old-fashioned white tie and tails that looked, to Sally's eyes, more than a little ridiculous, especially since the waiter pouring the champagne was wearing a similar outfit. Swill wore a plain black suit, as though in mourning, Sally thought — a contrast to the contented smile on his face. He made dozens of toasts, and when the fiddler played a fast jig, Swill was out there on the platform bouncing higher than any younger man, catching the girls by the elbows and swinging them around. At one point he even grabbed hold of Sally, skipped along with her, and called to her over the music, "You're looking lovely," as though the weight of his disapproval had lifted in an instant.

His wife watched serenely from her chair, Uncle Mason by her side. During nearly three years in Fishkill Notch, Sally had never met Swill's wife face to face. She didn't even know her proper name. She was only ever *Swill's wife*. People called her that as though she didn't have another name and wasn't even real enough to fill up the passenger seat of a car. Sally had come to think of her as a woman who existed only in a shadow form.

But there she sat in a polka-dot dress and red hat, a plump woman with freckled arms and cheeks already brown from the spring sun and a heavy bosom that she propped up with her folded arms. Sally was surprised to see Swill's flesh-and-blood wife — and even more surprised to see her tapping the foot of her good leg to the music, tipping her head back and forth in time, and grinning a grin that matched her husband's.

Life felt good and simple again at Georgie's wedding. Sally was reminded of a day when she was eight or nine and had gone to watch her father and uncle help the Jensons raise a new barn. The way the boards came together into a frame was like the way everyone here came together to make a celebration. Georgie looked lovely in her sky blue satin dress trimmed with rose point lace. Swill and Mason Jackson, unused to their suits, managed to look more like themselves as the day went on, Swill more ruffled and messy, Mason more modest. Little Stevie strutted around with an air of being someone very important and held out his hand to greet every stranger in his path. Harvey Fitzgerald was a bearish man, burly, with a heavy beard, but his face expressed shy sweetness, and he let Stevie ride on his back while he was dancing with Georgie. And what a fine dancer he was, stepping nimbly across the crowded floor.

"Well, won't you look at that," Sally said to Erna over by the banquet table. "Georgie has found herself a real fox-trotter for a husband." She'd meant it as a true compliment, but Erna looked at her suspiciously and said, "He's a decent fellow," and Sally had to explain in defense that she'd meant to say just that.

It was a trite exchange, without consequence. Erna and Sally went on to taste and compare the hors d'oeuvres together. But later, when Sally thought back to the wedding, she'd wonder if that's when she started to become aware of feeling slightly removed from everything, as though she'd come in late and didn't quite understand what was going on.

Surely it didn't help her effort to blend in when the bandleader announced that he had a special song to play, and a special girl to sing it for him. With everybody watching and waiting, he called, "Sally Werner, will you come up here and join us?"

Erna shoved her with an elbow. "He said your name," she whispered. But Sally was too stunned to move and just stood there pretending that she'd disappeared, which would have been better than continuing with her life right then, for even a twitch of a nose would give away her secret to all those staring eyes, and they'd realize that she was still standing there dumbly — in reality a living, breathing girl who was terrified of singing in public.

"Is Sally Werner here?"

No, she wanted to call back. I'm not here.

"Here she is!" cried Erna.

"Hush!" Sally caught Erna's arm and pulled it down.

"Sally Werner," said the bandleader into the mike, "come sing us a song!"

How did anyone know that singing was her secret pleasure? By keeping it secret, she'd meant to avoid scrutiny and judgment. She felt like she was becoming aware of some sort of deep betrayal. And here she was being called upon to defend herself.

But wait a second — she didn't even know if she could sing.

"Sally Werner!" someone in the audience shouted.

"Sally Werner!"

"Sally Werner, Sally Werner," others began chanting.

She cast a searching look at the faces, mostly strangers, and then her eyes met Uncle Mason's; their gazes locked for a moment that was long enough for him to offer her that understanding nod of his, conveying his confidence in her and revealing that he was the one who had come to know more about her than she'd ever intended to let him know. When she was singing along with the scrolls on the player piano, when she was belting out those songs on Sunday afternoons — why, either the furniture in the house had ears, or Mason Jackson wasn't always quite as far away as she'd thought. And that meant . . . she couldn't think clearly about what it meant.

She kept her gaze on him as she would have gripped a rope rail along a wobbly bridge, holding him in view as she moved toward the band.

"Sally Werner, Sally Werner!"

All those people watching, calling, waiting for her to prove to them that she was worth something.

"Sally Werner! Sally Werner! Sally

Werner!"

The bandleader, a neatly groomed, ruddy man nearly a foot taller than Sally, leaned toward her and murmured a song title in her ear. She looked at him in confusion, not because she didn't know that song — she did know it, backward and forward — but she couldn't imagine how he knew she knew it.

"Sshh, hush," people said impatiently. "Let her sing."

Sally looked over the faces, seeing in them what she interpreted as a particular kind of anticipation; she recognized it as the same kind of interest that she herself felt when she was at the county fair watching a man dressed up as a clown come into the ring riding a bull. It was the anticipation of people waiting for a fool to perform.

The band was already playing, moving so quickly through the opening chords that Sally couldn't enter the song on time. The bandleader made a discreet signal with his finger, and the musicians repeated the opening chords. Sally stepped forward toward the microphone. She'd never sung into a microphone before.

It's easy to smile . . . , she sang, and then she stopped, startled by the strange volume of her voice and scared of the audience's concentrated attention. But the band kept on playing, and the audience remained silent with expectation. She didn't know what to do. She thought she saw a woman in the crowd mouthing *I-told-you-so,* and Sally worried that she was getting ready to call out a loud boo. They were all going to boo at her. They were going to boo her out of Fishkill Notch.

She searched for Uncle Mason, but the place beside Swill's wife was empty. Swill's wife was looking like she'd rather be sitting there than anywhere else in the world, stationed in the audience at Georgie's wedding waiting for Sally Werner to sing. Sally focused on her, mesmerized by her cheerful face. Swill's wife grinned widely, communicating her pleasure. It didn't matter what Sally did — Swill's wife was going to enjoy the show no matter what.

"It's easy to sigh . . . ," the bandleader whispered to her.

"It's easy to sigh," she sang . . .

It's easy to know
That you and I
Were meant to fall in love.

It was strange to hear her voice amplified and coming back to her as a new sound.

114

She felt stupid and vulnerable. But she also felt an unfamiliar strength filling her, making her bend her fingers into fists. She sang louder:

It's simple to wish,
And simple to dream . . .

It was helpful to watch Swill's plump wife nodding and grinning, grinning and nodding.

It's simple to guess . . .
That you and I . . .
Were meant to fall in love.

A hoot of praise rose from somewhere in the audience. Someone else yelled, urging her on. Sally kept her eyes fixed on Swill's wife as she sang,

Oh, you and I,
Yes, you and I,
Were meant to fall in love.

There, she'd done it, sung like there was no tomorrow. And in the empty space following the end of the song came applause, loud and merry applause, whistles and calls for an encore.

"Ladies and gentlemen," said the bandleader, "that was your own Sally Werner."

"Sally Werner," called the audience. "Sally Werner, Sally Werner, Sally Werner!"

"How about another song, Sally Werner?" the bandleader asked her through the microphone and then murmured to her, "You know 'Walk with Me'?"

Sure she knew "Walk with Me."

Walk with me, walk with me,
Darlin', won't you walk with me . . .

She sang with full confidence right from the start. She sang because she liked singing. She liked it more than ever now that other people wanted to hear her. For the first time in her life, she was worthy of admiration. It didn't matter that she was singing with a bunch of farmhand-musicians in front of an easy-to-please crowd. She might as well have been singing in a concert hall before an audience of thousands.

After singing the two songs from start to finish, she stepped off the stage to the clamor of applause that wouldn't fade. They wanted more, more, more! Sing another song, Sally Werner! Keep singing until the cows come home!

But she felt wise beyond her experience right then and knew that she should stop while she was ahead. She waved to the audience to signal that her part of the show was over. She returned to the mike to say, "Thank you, thank you very much," and then offered a quick curtsy.

The applause faded slowly, reluctantly. Sally held on to the sound until the last person had stopped clapping and the fiddler had begun a new song.

"That was fine singing, Sally Werner!" someone said to her as she brushed past.

"Oh, young lady, you have talent!"

"Sally," said Georgie, giving her a hug, enveloping her in the satin folds of her dress. "My friend Sally!"

"That took some guts," said Erna, handing her a glass of champagne.

Everyone was praising her, even surly old Swill, who raised his glass to her and said, "You brought down the house!" He might as well have said, *You're part of the family now, and you can't go on hating me forever.* That motley Jackson family — they were ready to take in any stray that made it over the top of Thistle Mountain. But where was Uncle Mason? Sally wanted to hear directly from him that she'd done fine. Better than fine. Everyone looked happy because Sally Werner had sung for them. She hadn't known she could sing like that. Or if she'd

117

known, she hadn't known what an audience would think of her. But they all thought she was special, all of them except Mason Jackson. Why hadn't he sought her out to congratulate her? What was taking him so long?

With the champagne and the dancing and the music, she soon forgot about Uncle Mason. She was swept into a blur of motion and felt herself snug in the arms of men she didn't even know, men who called her "doll" and turned her in circles. She felt as though she were getting married, too, and had finally earned the right to fall in love.

Finally, after hours of dancing, she had to stop and rest. She retreated to a back corner of the dance floor, where tables were set up and guests were still gnawing on cold corn and chicken. She didn't want to be noticed right then — she didn't want to be asked to dance until she'd gotten her breath back — so she stepped behind a stack of plates. She touched her hand to her face to feel the warmth of her cheek. She realized she was hungry and scooped up a handful of sugared almonds. Chewing absentmindedly, she let her thoughts wander. And that's when she heard someone nearby say her name.

"Sally Werner."

She turned toward the voice. But the

woman wasn't talking to her. The woman was sitting at a small table in front of the banquet table, with her back to Sally as she leaned toward the fat woman — Swill's wife — who was seated next to her.

The woman, whom Sally didn't recognize, spat out the next word as if she'd just discovered the rotten taste of it in her last bite of chicken. The word was "slut," or at least that's what Sally thought she heard.

"Dear little Sally" — it was Swill's wife speaking now. "She's a good girl."

"Then you don't know?"

"What's there to know?"

"The girl . . . with her own cousin!"

The voice faded behind the rise in the music and then came out forcefully. Her own cousin. Sally pressed closer to the table to hear better.

"And birthed a monster."

Did she really say *monster?* But Sally's baby wasn't a monster. Sally had seen enough of him to know that he was an ordinary baby with ten fingers and ten toes. He had come out pink and mewling and then promptly fallen asleep when she'd laid him in the basket. Those words, though — *slut* and *cousin* and *monster* — a stranger was using those words to tell her story. The story of Sally Werner. Wretched Sally Werner.

"My husband works with her brother," the woman said, her voice suddenly as clear as a bell. "Her own family won't have anything to do with her. Go up to Tauntonville yourself. You'll hear what they say about her there. Frankly, they all think she's dead. There's a rumor that maybe she drowned herself in the river. But they'll be hearing otherwise soon as I get home. And won't they be disappointed."

Sally Werner wasn't dead. She was only desperate. Desperate to get out of there.

Run, Sally!

She backed away, knocking against a chair and freezing. Everyone was staring at her. No, no one was staring at her. She wasn't there. She didn't exist.

She moved the chair to the side and kept backing up for a dozen or so steps, then turned and fled from the tent and across the lawn and around to the front of the Cadmus Party House.

Fuzzy, motionless trees around her. Champagne bubbles bursting in her head. Sandal heels sinking into mud.

Dragging, stumbling, running.

How dare you raise your voice in song after leaving your baby to rot on the kitchen table! Daughter of Sodom! Run as fast as you can, but you won't run faster than the devil. Feel the heat of his breath on your neck. He's there with you, wherever you go. You slut.

All she could think to do was to follow her running legs up Marsh Lane to Main Street to Brindle Street to the dirt road that led to Mason Jackson's house, the only home she knew.

Running, running, running.

The quiet of aloneness was a hard pressure, the weight of air squeezing against her ears. Deep fathoms of an empty room. Nothing in the process of change, no one to observe that Sally had entered the room, no one to hear her breathing, the silence beyond her only partially relieved by the distant gurgling headwaters of the Tuskee.

Sally felt a sharp cramp in her gut as she stood there in Mason Jackson's living room, staring at that wood, gulping the scene as though it could cool her parched throat. But there was no comfort in the hard surfaces around her. The furniture looked only temporarily motionless rather than inanimate, hanging fire, suspicious rather than blank. Strange how the emptiness was divided by the hard lines of the straight-backed chairs pushed up against the wooden table, the stiff-cushioned sofa, the rocking chair, the floorboards that gleamed with every possible tint of brown. Here in the domain of a whittler, wood offered itself as the reason for everything, conveying the truth that the natural world was made to be cut up, shaped, and turned into a place of refuge.

Not Sally Werner's refuge.

She'd done what she'd done, no getting around it. She was like the beat-up old player piano, an oddity, a mistake that couldn't be corrected, the one item in the room that didn't fit in. And oh the lies it told. Pump the pedals, and it fools you into thinking that you're a star.

Sally Werner Sally Werner Sally Werner.

Nineteen-year-old Sally Werner, who had grown up to nourish the seed sown by her cousin and gone on to birth a monster.

Don't matter what side of the mountain you hail from. You're going to hear about Sally Werner sooner or later. That slut. Satan's paramour revealed in all her infamy.

Everywhere she went, she was who she was. Even standing there in a quiet house: she was the girl the others preferred dead. Too bad for them, she was alive enough to sing at a wedding.

You sure brought down the house, Sally Werner. And now you're standing in the rubble of Mason Jackson's modest life, having made a wreck of things. See how everything you touch falls apart.

The ceiling caves in.
The floor collapses.
And the walls come
tumbling,
tumbling,
tumbling
down.

She slipped out of her borrowed sandals and left them in the middle of the floor before moving toward the kitchen, each step tentative in her effort to be nonexistent. Though the truck wasn't in the driveway and there was no one else in the house, she couldn't bear the thought of being heard. Tiptoe, tiptoe, one bare foot after the other. Mason Jackson's housekeeper. What did he need with a live-in housekeeper anyway? People in Fishkill Notch might have thought it odd or at least questionable if they weren't convinced that Mason Jackson did only what was proper. He was too innately honest ever to invite doubt. People liked knowing that he was there, in his house built on the gravelly wedge where the creeks converged and became a river. Mason Jackson gave the world something to admire: an old man who could take any piece of wood in the world and make it functional, permanent, and appealing all at the same time. Working, scraping away peels of wood in his clean, quiet house. The piano sitting in the shadows, pretending to be useless, finished with its life of music.

The soft, shushing sound of running water.

Uncle Mason's housekeeper moving as soundlessly as a fish.

And then, shit, bumping a toe against the hard leg of a kitchen chair. Damn that chair.

Won't you listen to that foul mouth.

Shush, said the water.

Soundless exhalation of thick air.

Soundless ascent, as Mason Jackson's housekeeper climbed onto that damn chair and reached for the box on top of the high shelf. Soundless effort, as she lifted it down carefully, holding the box against her chest as she would have held something far more fragile.

She set the box on the table and gently opened the lid, breathing in that good smell of money and wood and pipe smoke all mixed together. How much money? Ten plus twenty, thirty plus ten, sixty plus twenty plus ten plus — no, wait, she'd counted wrong. She had to start over. Twenty plus ten. Ten plus twenty.

As time passed, the sum increased. And as the sum increased, so did her anxiousness. She wouldn't be alone forever. Mason Jackson would be coming home at any minute, and he'd wonder what his housekeeper was doing with the box that held his savings, the fruit of a long life of hard work. Ten plus twenty plus thirty.

Quick, Sally Werner! Someone was coming!

No one was coming. No one was ever coming. Each time she'd opened the box, she'd thought she'd heard the sound of Uncle Mason coming home. And each time, she'd been wrong.

Still, she knew that a theft should happen fast, without delay. She told herself to take what she needed and get out of there. But how much did she truly need? Enough to pay for a bus ticket to a destination so far away that disgrace couldn't follow her. Enough so she wouldn't go hungry. And wouldn't it be something if with a portion of the money in Mason Jackson's box, she could make amends and bring the child she'd left behind back into her life? If she started all over again, she would like to start with him, the boy she hadn't bothered to name. How much would it cost to give him a name? To buy his affection? All she could do to figure out what a new life with her son would cost was to count the money slowly, as though caution would clarify the future: ten plus twenty plus thirty —

"T-t-take it all."

She froze, condemned to remain for all eternity in that same position, standing at the table, bent over the open box, forever and ever. End of story. Time would go on without offering her the cleansing experience of change. She would remain the fine-hewn statue carved by the knife of Mason Jackson's sharp-edged voice as he stood behind her in the entranceway to the kitchen. Today would become tomorrow. A thousand years dating from that moment in May 1950, a wanderer would enter the empty house and find her there . . .

"I mean it. T-t-t-t-take it all."

What could she do? Being who she was and what he'd made her — both at once, in wooden form. She was helpless. The crime was permanent.

"N-n-no," she whispered, her voice a mirror.

"I w-w-w-want you to have it."

Wooden creature, caught red-handed,

stealing an honest old man's life savings. Her fingernails had been painted a smoky red by Erna earlier in the week. Red-tipped hands of a girl in a yellow silk dress. Her hair, auburn again, plaited and bound with a ribbon. Nineteen years old, and no one had ever told her she was beautiful.

For a moment she closed her eyes and with a great effort of imagination pictured what Uncle Mason saw: the image of her guilt a fixture that would always be there. She felt his disappointment in her. She felt that he would maintain a strength of love for her, despite her crime. This was so puzzling, so unexpected and disorienting, that she opened her eyes and turned her head to look at him. With that effort she came to life, twisting back into motion, into time. She met his gaze, saw in him a gentle little man who had an ability to forgive her — an ability that right then seemed no less than magical.

And in the next instant that magical apparition of Mason Jackson was gone, having slipped away abruptly, vanishing, leaving her standing there wondering what to do, with her red-tipped hands still in the box that held his life savings.

She could call out to him. And then what? She could close the box and go to her room. And then what?

He wanted her to take the money. He'd said as much. He'd given her permission and made it clear that he wouldn't hold her responsible for stealing. Why he wanted her to take it didn't make any sense. Or she convinced herself that it didn't make sense because it helped her avoid the truth. Really, it made too much sense. But in the panic that returned to her as she grabbed the bundles of bills, she wouldn't let herself think clearly enough to understand that she was capable right then of understanding more than she would have thought possible.

She didn't allow herself to think of what Mason Jackson had been through over the course of his long, hard life. She didn't consider the gold band on his finger. She didn't let the ring call to mind what Georgie had told her about the wife who'd left Mason after their little girl had fallen through the ice of the Tuskee. She didn't think about the little girl. She didn't think about the frigid water flowing below the ice. She didn't stop to remember how one day three years earlier Swill and Mason had lifted her by her elbows out of the cold creek. All these thoughts could have come to her vividly right then, yet she didn't let them. She was too busy stuffing the money

128

into an empty paper bag, frantic to get out of there.

She'd have to use two bags if she was going to take all the money. But she wasn't going to take all the money. She wasn't so cruel that she'd leave him with nothing. She'd leave at least half of it behind — her parting gift and her only way of apologizing to the man who had been so kind to her.

And then, watch how she runs out of the house in her bare feet, running away from this chapter of her life, running along the path that fishermen had made in the swamp grass.

She followed the river a couple of miles until she reached the Route 36 bridge. She climbed up the sloping bank, slipping once on the wet grass, muddying her nice yellow dress. She started walking along the road, keeping just inside the gravel edge to avoid the sharp little stones.

A few cars sped right past her. She kept walking, minding her own business. But when she turned at the loud approach of a station wagon, the driver slowed and the children sitting in the back waved and called something to her. The car stopped a few yards ahead along the road.

She jogged up to the passenger door,

which swung open before she reached it. A sullen, pimply boy sat in the passenger seat, and a man with a broad, sunburnt face and buzz-cut hair was at the wheel. The man leaned over the boy and said to Sally, "Need a lift?"

"Sure, thanks."

"Go on," the man said to the sullen boy, who dragged himself out the door without acknowledging Sally. She climbed into the seat while the boy squeezed himself into the back beside the other children.

The man started driving.

"Where you heading?"

"Rondo," she said.

"Where's that?"

"Downriver."

The man had never heard of it. But of course there were lots of places he'd never heard of. He asked Sally if she'd heard of Sarabelle, where he was from. He knew a doctor there, if she wanted to see one.

"Why would I want that!" Her eyes blazed, and her voice was harsh.

"No, sorry, it's just . . . if you had trouble, you know. . . ."

She assured him that she was fine, she'd just been walking to the bus, and wouldn't you know, the heel on her shoe broke so she threw both shoes away. That's all.

"You want to get the bus in Amity? I'll take you to the station there."

"That would be helpful."

He drove along slowly, as if he meant to delay their arrival in Amity so he could hear something of her story and satisfy his curiosity. With each bump and dip in the road, the children in the back yelled joyously.

"Say," the man asked after a while, "what's your name?"

"Sally."

"Just Sally?"

"Sally Angel," she replied in a cold voice. She turned to watch a tractor plowing a field in the distance and didn't speak again until the end of the drive, when, as she was stepping out of the car, she thanked the man for giving her a lift.

March 15, 2007

Scrappy changeling, there and not there, transforming herself with a snap of her fingers. Good-bye, hello. Dear Sally, I'm your namesake. Wait for me. You should listen to what I have to say. I have the advantage, after all, of living in your future. I know what's in store for you. Of course, that makes it more difficult to be accurate in my description of the past and keep the facts compatible.

Ever since discovering that my grandmother's grasp of this story was incomplete, I've made an effort to fill in the gaps. I've retraced her journey upriver and beyond, all the way back to Tauntonville. I've talked to members of our extended family, along with some of my grandmother's old acquaintances, and I can say with confidence that my version, even if it's not infallibly correct, is closer to the truth than hers. I admit, though, that I can't always keep straight who told me what.

Girl, my grandmother would say to me when I was caught causing trouble: you sure are a Werner through and through. I used to think I heard in her voice a note of conspiracy, as if she were concluding, in light of my bad behavior, that I was obliged to repeat the mistakes she'd made. Over time I came to believe that she was only pretending to disapprove of me, and in reality she was secretly pleased with my antics.

In one picture from the late seventies, we're standing facing each other on the terrace behind her house on Anchor Heights. I'm about five in the photo, and my grandmother Sally is still young enough to look spry. I'm holding up a bouquet, though not a bouquet of cultivated flowers from a garden. They're weeds, unglamorous, aggravating stalks of dandelion and yellow rocket from the looks of them. Just weeds I must have plucked from the side of the road.

I only ever collected weeds — out of ignorance when I was little, and then as part of a game. Over the years, my grandmother and I engaged in a fierce competition involving weeds, each of us trying to outdo the other, gathering as many weeds as we could find in an hour. We'd rate our hauls at the end by counting the different stalks in each bundle. I usually won the contest. My grandmother managed to find the colorful weeds, but I'd collect more of them.

She kept a *Golden Guide* to weeds in her kitchen, and we took to drying and pressing examples of individual species, though we didn't make much effort to keep track of our collection. Even to this day, I'll pull an old book off my shelf and find in its pages an ancient sprig of pigweed or goosefoot.

In this photo of the two of us, I'm proud to be showing off my winning weeds, and my grandmother is proud to acknowledge her defeat. There's something wily in her expression. It took me years to realize that I won our games because she wanted me to win.

Weeds might be infesting, unattractive plants, out of place everywhere they spread, but the way they adapt to the most adverse conditions — *well, it's something,* my grandmother liked to say whenever I told her about a patch of weeds I'd found growing in an unlikely place around the city, in a sidewalk crack, between bricks on an outside wall at the mall, in the middle of the Wegmans parking lot.

More than something, she'd add.

My mother was standing at the kitchen

counter flipping through a magazine when her water broke. My grandmother, slouched in her chair, had surrendered to the lulling glow of the TV and was singing in a whispery voice to Lawrence Welk's orchestra.

Ay-yah. Hmmm, most any afternoon at five . . .

Mama, it's time.

We'll be so glad . . .

It's time!

It's a familiar scenario: a suitcase already packed, a doctor on call, a pregnant woman saying, *It's time.* What's missing is the jittery husband standing ready to transport his wife to the hospital. In this story my grandmother is the one who's ready. She'd been the one who packed the suitcase. And she'd been sleeping with the car keys on her bedside stand, along with a flashlight and a battery-powered clock radio in the unlikely event that a storm blew down the electrical lines and she had to orient herself in the dark.

There was no storm that night. There was a rising moon casting a silver light, turning the contrails of a cumulus mass into streams of melted iron. There was a warm breeze rattling the cones that had fallen from the pines onto the driveway. And there was my grandmother, standing with the suitcase in her hand, urging her daughter, my mother, to hurry, hurry, hurry.

My grandmother and mother would often laugh about what followed: the rush to the car, the wild drive to the hospital with my grandmother blasting the horn as she ran through every red light. My grandmother parked the Chevette half on the sidewalk in front of the emergency entrance and swept my mother through the open doors, shouting for a doctor, the violence of her voice causing a temporary stir among the medical staff, though what the nurses found as they gathered around was my pregnant mother resting her folded arms on the ridge of her swollen belly, calmly surveying a fire-hazard notice on the wall while she let out a leisurely burp.

As punishment for causing unnecessary havoc, my grandmother was directed to a bench and given a dozen forms to fill out before any help would be offered.

Name, date, address, policy number, patient history, reason for visit. Name, date, address, policy number, emergency contact. Name, date, policy number, home phone, work phone. Name, date . . .

Like as not, folks won't be noticed until they generate a folder stuffed with unnecessary forms, my grandmother would grumble. You'd think life begins and ends on paper.

Only after she'd finished signing her name on the last sheet was my grandmother taken to the waiting room and my mother officially admitted to the hospital. Irked at being left alone, my grandmother ignored the No Smoking sign and lit a cigarette. In the story she tells about that night, no one came to tell her to put her cigarette out. She didn't wait long after finishing the first one to light another.

Meanwhile, I wasn't making my entrance easy for my mother. I'd accomplished a full somersault during my last week of gestation and was presenting breech, as if to demonstrate my reluctance. And though my mother's contractions intensified, by the time of her first exam in the maternity ward her cervix had hardly dilated.

She was given a shot of morphine to relax her. The drug relaxed me as well, causing me to loosen my grip, and I began slipping into this world, though my resistance continued to slow the process, so what should have progressed quickly from that point took ten hours, along with ten Lucky Strikes and the remaining fluid in my grandmother's lighter.

Ass-first I descended through the squeeze

of the canal. Ass-first in what my grandmother Sally would cite as my first great act of disrespect.

Craziness mirroring craziness. You and me, Grandma. I knew there was something I wouldn't want to face, so I turned my back and tried to hang on to the center, gripped my mother the way I'd grip the branch of a tree high above the ground. And then, helpless to gravity, feeling my hands weaken, the weakness spreading numbness up my wrists. Centimeter by centimeter, letting go. One Lucky Strike after another.

The sky above the courtyard was a velvety blue when a mockingbird outside the window suddenly changed its irritating sounds from hungry clicks to a lovely warbling reminiscent of a wood thrush's song in spring. That's when my grandmother knew that I'd been born.

She took advantage of an open door, slipping into the restricted area as a doctor let himself out. She made her way to the nurses' station and demanded to see her daughter and grandchild without delay. The nurse at the desk sympathized, and without asking for the supervisor's permission she led my grandmother into the birthing room, where my mother was resting and a pediatric nurse was putting silver drops in my eyes.

Assured that my mother had made it through in good condition, my grandmother held her breath as she approached me, even as she directed her mind to the task of willing away all the nightmarish fantasies that had been haunting her through her daughter's pregnancy. She was admittedly impressionable, and her imagination was still populated with hoofed demons from the illustrated Bible of her youth. Oh, they would have their fun with me, my grandmother feared, branding me as the product of my parents' unnatural love, stealing essential organs and adding extra body parts — an eleventh toe, a third arm, or even a pink tail curled like a pig's.

I was more than a mistake. To my grandmother, I was the consequence of a long series of bad decisions traceable back years before my mother and father fell in love, back to the time before my mother had been born, when my grandmother was a young woman fumbling along, following the river north.

I was lying under a warming lamp, not yet swaddled, when my grandmother first saw me. She counted my fingers and toes, eyed my proportions, studied my bunched, angry face. Was I adequately symmetrical, or was I cursed with deformities? Had I been marked by my parents' sin? It demanded such intense and lengthy concentration for her to be reassured of my normalcy that she didn't notice how lightheaded she'd become. She staggered, clutching at the air. She would have fallen to the floor, but a nurse took quick action, sliding a chair behind her, catching her as she collapsed.

My mother, who'd been watching the scene from her bed, was only partially right in thinking that my grandmother was overcome with joy at the birth of her grandchild. It's more accurate to say that she was overcome with relief because I wouldn't have to go through life advertising the fact that I never should have been conceived.

My grandmother Sally, with her peach-white thistle hair, her speckled green eyes, and dimples multiplying into fine-lined wrinkles. I didn't realize how much we were alike until after she was gone. It's not just that I'm reminded of our obvious resemblance when I look at photographs of her as a young woman. I'm convinced that I recognize the potential for disarray, as though I could tug the end of a frayed thread sticking out from her cuff, and the tidy package she'd squeezed herself into would unravel.

Of course, if she comes apart, I'll do the same. And then we'll both have the opportunity to start over again. If she's not the woman she was led to think she was, then neither am I the result of her mistakes.

There's still much I have to consider in order to come up with a convincing new version to replace the old one. Like all stories that are pieced together from different accounts, this one involves a fair amount of guesswork, and sometimes I look at an unfinished sentence and feel stumped. It's then that my thoughts will drift and I'll start imagining what I would have done in my grandmother's place.

SALLY ANGEL

The only bus leaving Amity that evening was heading north, so Sally headed north with it, taking the seat directly behind the driver, hoping that no one had noticed she was barefoot. There were just three other passengers: two old women wearing dusty black capes over black dresses, looking as if they'd been riding the same bus in the same clothes for days, and a blank-faced boy of about fourteen who'd been waiting alone at the stop on the outskirts of Amity and yawned the whole way up the aisle when he'd boarded.

The motion of the bus was jerky, and the interior rattled over every pothole. Smoke hung in the air from the last set of passengers, stirring in Sally a longing for a cigarette. She blinked drowsily, but sleep wouldn't come to her. She sat up a little straighter. Bumping along toward her new life, she studied the back of the driver's head, a tangle of gray, brown, and white hair that reminded her of batter for a marble cake.

Wouldn't she rather have been stirring a cake batter's chocolate into swirls, dipping in her finger for a taste? Sure. Pouring, measuring, creaming sugar with sweet butter. And the good smell of the cake baking in the oven. Mmm-mmm. The spongy holes from the prongs of the fork, and it was done, la-di-da, see what Sally made all on her own, sure, you can have some, there's enough to go around, but wait your turn.

Loden and Willy would be right there holding out empty plates to be filled. And Tru and Laura and Clem. And a little boy, his face smeared with chocolate frosting.

He likes the cake so much, he's not coming up for air till he's cleaned the plate.

Look how happy he is.

Happy to be eating cake.

And the rest of them — what had they been up to these past years?

Doing and doing and doing. You know, the same old thing. They always liked best doing as close to nothing as they could get away with. Leaning against the trunk of a sycamore at noon, looking up through the cool shade at the highest branches and the sunlit green of the leaves between patches of blue sky. Not that they'd ever put it that way. But there were some things they would never take for granted, like the coo of a dove. Who doesn't love that sound? And the sweet racket of a cricket's chirp. And at night a full moon, a soft breeze, and the pulsing glow from a firefly trapped in cupped hands. What a life.

Well, we'd best be going. Come along now, finish your cake and say thanks.

Thanks.

Wait, don't leave!

It was you who left.

Then and now separated by the wall of Sally's foolishness, an unbreachable wall built stone by stone, reaching high and wide enough to block the view. Sally on one side, her little boy on the other. Why was she heading in the opposite direction, away from him? Because she was only riding on the bus, not steering it.

Good-bye, Sally.

Who's Sally?

I'm your mother, damn it, and one day I'm coming to get you.

Trouble was, she'd paid for her fare all the way to the last stop on the bus route, the end of the line — not Rondo, not her unreal city, but close enough. Before too long, she'd go back home and find her little

144

boy. But for now she wanted to get as far away as possible, as quickly as possible, from Fishkill Notch. Upriver, downriver, it didn't matter where she was going, as long as she was going away from Mason Jackson's house and that box on the shelf.

Bumpety-bumping through the darkening land. The rattling shell of the bus made talk impossible, so Sally would never know whether the two old mourners across the aisle were on their way to a funeral or coming home from one, or why the boy was traveling alone, or what the driver with his marble-cake hair was thinking about while he piloted the bus along the uneven road, from Amity through the hamlets of Garlinport and Canadice and — look at the sign illuminated by the bus's headlights, look there, why, it was Helena. What was so important about Helena? Sally knew the name, yet at first she couldn't remember why she knew it.

That her recognition was imprecise initially made her all the more interested in the place. Helena. She recalled that Helena was . . . what? She associated the place with all things sophisticated, gleaming, sharp, and witty. Why? She wasn't sure. But here she was, in the town . . . yes, she remembered now, where the worldly Gladdy Toffit lived.

She leaned forward. "Do you stop here?" she asked the driver.

"What's that?"

"Do you stop here?"

"You want to get off?"

"I was just wondering . . ."

"Yes or no, miss?"

"Well . . ."

The next thing she knew, the bus was slowing to a halt, and the hinges were creaking as the doors folded open. The driver dropped his arm with obvious impatience. The other passengers were silent. All attention was focused on Sally, who sat there staring ahead, trying to pretend that she wasn't solely responsible for this interruption. It was a long, awkward moment, and it became more awkward with every second that passed. She might as well have spoken a different language from the rest of them. She couldn't make her desires known because she wasn't sure exactly what she wanted, and no one was going to make a move to help her. She was condemned to fulfill the expectations of these strangers, which meant that she had no choice but to tighten her grip on the rolled edge of the paper bag full of Mason Jackson's money and get off the bus.

She was left standing barefooted on the sidewalk. A row of streetlamps lit up the block where she'd inadvertently landed — the center of the town where Gladdy Toffit lived. There were several empty stores across the street, and on one of the boards that had been nailed over the window, someone had painted a skull with gaping black eyes. On Sally's side of the street was the local credit union, a small grocery store, and, down at the end of the block, a neon sign for a tavern, the Barge. The *B* of the sign blinked weakly, off and on again, and then surprised Sally by suddenly going out altogether.

Clutching the paper bag, she headed toward the tavern. Since she didn't hear music or the noise of a crowd when she stood outside the door, she expected to find the interior quiet. Instead, when she pushed open the heavy oak door and stepped inside, she was met by a blast of music from the jukebox and the clamor of voices trying to be heard. People were packed against the bar, others were standing idly, and there was a group of men, all bearded, all in baseball caps and sleeveless shirts, hovering by the entrance.

To move farther into the tavern, Sally had

to pass between the gauntlet of these men. She pressed forward. But the space between them narrowed, and she heard their murmurs as they became aware of her. She considered the ridiculous impression she was making: a young woman in a mud-splattered yellow silk dress, with no shoes. She'd have expected strangers would prefer to keep their distance from a girl like her. But the men seemed eager to claim her as their own, pressing in, raising their voices to announce, "Why, won't you lookie here, we got a vee-zit-or!" and "Hello, baby doll!" and "Hey, how come I don't know you?"

"Excuse me," she said, trying to push through the crowd. When the men wouldn't budge, she seethed, "Get on out of my way, you dumbbells!" thinking this was closer to the language they spoke.

In response, an arm came up and wrapped around her waist. A man put his face close to hers, flashing a grin that revealed bloody barbecue sauce filling the cracks between his teeth. She felt another hand slide more stealthily down her buttocks, smoothing her dress. She tried to free herself, but the group of them were surrounding her, bearing down, the lot of them becoming one brutish force.

She should have been offended. But all

Sally could think about right then was protecting the bag full of Mason Jackson's money. Whose money? She'd stolen it — or he'd given it to her. Which? Both. Either. It was hers now. No, it was still his. How disorienting it was to consider this while she was trying to push her way through the men. With their groping and fondling, they were coming too close to Mason Jackson's money.

Stay away, you perverts!

Did she say that aloud? She wasn't sure. But it wouldn't matter what she said because they weren't listening to her words.

Then listen to my elbow, you bastard, right in your fat gut!

"Uh!"

And how about a kick in the kneecap?

"Uh!"

That'll show you, baby-dolling a girl you don't even know . . .

She watched their mouths move, but their voices seemed to come from elsewhere, to belong to others hidden behind the curtain of bodies. They asked her, "What are you doing here?" and "Why are you alone?" and "Where are your shoes?"

"I'm looking for a friend."

"He's not here."

"She."

"Who's she?"

"Gladdy Toffit."

"You're looking for Gladdy? Why didn't you say so? Hey, she's looking for Gladdy."

"We should have guessed."

"She's Gladdy's friend."

"Gladdy! Where's Gladdy?"

"There she is!"

A hand cupped gently under her elbow, steering her through the crowd.

"Move aside, boys, let us through. I'll take you to Gladdy. Come on now, out of the way, make room, here we are." Men stepped back, opening up a path straight from the entrance to the bar. The song on the jukebox finished, the record clicked back into its slot, and as the voices in the bar softened to a hush, the man who was guiding Sally tapped the shoulder of a woman drooping on her barstool.

She straightened, tipped back the wide brim of her straw hat, and blinked against the ceiling lights. The foundation greased on her face made her skin shine. The penciled line of her plucked eyebrows seemed to move independently of the muscles of her face, bunching when she smiled.

"My darling Lily!"

Gladdy grabbed Sally's arm and pulled her into an embrace. Her breath had a sickly

150

smell of licorice, with a hint of vinegar.

"You've come home," she said. "Why didn't you tell me you were coming? Why didn't you write?"

"That's Lily?" a man in the background asked.

"That's not Lily," someone else declared.

The man who had accompanied Sally through the crowd asked her directly: "Are you Lily?"

"Who's Lily?"

"Why, we all thought you were out in California."

"I'm not Lily. I'm Sally."

"Sally who?" Gladdy asked, wobbling slightly on the stool, squinting against the blur.

"Don't you know me, Gladdy?"

"That's Lily's dress," Gladdy announced, suspicion in her voice.

"You gave it to me," Sally reminded her, but just then the jukebox started up again.

"What?"

"You gave it to me," Sally shouted, "to wear at Georgie's wedding!"

That was enough of a clue for Gladdy to guess the answer to the riddle. "Sally! Why, Sally!" The heave of her hiccup would have sent her flying from her stool if she hadn't still been holding on to Sally. And now Sally was holding on to her.

"Hello, Gladdy."

"I thought you were my Lily," Gladdy said loudly, in an effort to be heard above the noise. "Just appearing out of the blue in Lily's dress and all. And with that light shining in my eyes."

Sally could guess that it wasn't the light confusing Gladdy. It was drink after drink after drink. And now she wanted Sally to sit by her, sit here on the stool that her friend Mick would give up, what a gentleman, and they could talk, Sally and Gladdy, over drinks, and laugh about old times — as if their brief history of gabbing at Erna's parlor was already that far back in the past.

"What'll you have?"

The question was put to her as if it were a test, and Sally realized even as she answered, "Lemonade, I guess," that she'd failed.

"Lemonade? Lemonade!" Gladdy hooted. "Give her your famous Wallop, Bill," Gladdy directed the bartender. "And the same for me. You're in my town," she said to Sally. "Let the fun begin!"

The fun began with a bitter concoction of Wild Turkey and soda water, which Gladdy goaded Sally into drinking in gulps. A full glass replaced the empty one, and Sally kept on drinking, though more slowly. Between sips, she asked Gladdy why she'd missed Georgie's wedding.

"I hate weddings," Gladdy replied, and with that flat declaration she made Sally aware of how little she knew her or knew about her. The woman who lived on what she'd called a *handsome trust* and who had always seemed to have more advice to share than there was time to share it — it was hard to match that woman with this one. Sally hadn't known, for instance, that Gladdy spent her nights drinking at this dingy bar. She hadn't known that Gladdy liked to get so drunk she couldn't think straight. She hadn't known that Gladdy hated weddings. Why did she hate weddings? Sally wanted to ask. But Gladdy preempted her, demanding with sudden clarity, "Why are you here?"

"I . . ." Sally didn't know what to say. The pronoun hung there, without meaning. Just a dumb, reckless, forgettable *I,* unaccountable and attached to only one thing: the paper bag stuffed with Mason Jackson's money. She gripped the rolled edge more tightly, making a small tear in the paper.

"Taking a vacation, are you? Or did you up and quit?"

"Yeah, I quit."

"Just like that?"

"Just like that."

"Cheers. Welcome to Helena."

They clinked, and with that toast Sally entered Gladdy's world — a world that was turning out to be far less predictable than she would have thought, a world that didn't conform to any of the advice Gladdy had ever offered during those hours at Erna's Beauty Parlor. She sat there wishing she'd had the nerve to turn around and walk out of the Barge, leaving Gladdy Toffit behind. But she felt trapped by the older woman's friendship, protected by her, dependent upon her, buffeted by her whims, helpless, ignorant, and eager to be whatever Gladdy wanted her to be, in particular, to stand in as a substitute for her daughter, who had once worn to a dance the yellow dress that Sally had managed to splatter with mud.

"You came to the right place," Gladdy drawled, patting Sally's thigh. "First thing tomorrow, we'll find you some shoes."

Helena, fifteen miles north of Amity, was even less of a town than Fishkill Notch, with more than half the commercial buildings boarded shut. The land to the east behind Main Street sloped down to the Tuskee. The water was shallow and clear, and the pull of the current turned the water weeds and moss into green streaks below the surface. Willows lined both banks, forming a canopy before opening to gravel. Downriver, an old railway trestle had partially collapsed. The current poured around the broken wood and steel, rushed on and over the crumpled stone lip of a dam, and widened into a basin beside an abandoned gristmill.

All in all, Sally thought Helena a dingy place. Gladdy had moved there years ago with her second husband, a land speculator who had bought up property and, failing to sell it, had fled, leaving his wife with a slew of foreclosures. Why, Sally wondered, had Gladdy stayed in Helena? Why didn't she go back to Amity, where she'd been born and raised, or go forward to the nearest lively city? Why didn't everybody keep going and going until they found a better home?

Even at the beginning, Sally sensed that Gladdy wasn't exactly the worldly woman she'd pretended to be back at her sister's beauty parlor. She'd given the impression that she had more money than she knew what to do with. But she wasn't close to rich. She lived in a small, asphalt-shingled cottage along Route 36, with just two bedrooms and a porch closed in with dusty, torn screens. It was true she didn't want for basics. She had enough money to cover her bills and buy food and plenty of liquor. But she didn't live the splendorous life that Sally had been envying for months.

On the other hand, Sally wasn't the same young woman she'd been back in Fishkill Notch. Gladdy seemed to have forgotten Sally's surname, or else she'd never known it, so she didn't ask her why she'd changed it. Nor did she ask about the paper bag that Sally had brought with her — her only possession besides the yellow dress. She'd probably been too drunk even to notice the bag that first night. For a short time she didn't seem inclined to care much about what Sally was hiding. But as the days passed, she began to look at her guest with a sharper eye, and Sally sensed distrust in the air, as if Gladdy Toffit were just waiting for her to fess up to her guilt.

Finally, later in the week, Gladdy came right out and asked her why she had left Fishkill Notch in such a hurry. Sally didn't have a good answer for her. She didn't have any answer at all, in fact, other than a shrug. And when Gladdy offered to drive Sally back to Mason Jackson's house so she could pick up the clothes she might have left behind, Sally had to say that she never wanted to go back there, though she didn't want to talk about *why.* She added that the outfits Gladdy had slated for the rummage sale, along with the sandals she'd bought off the rack outside the convenience store in Helena, would do just fine for the summer.

Gladdy said she understood that there were some things too painful to revisit. But it was clear that she didn't like being so mystified. Later that same day, she announced she was driving to Erna's to have her hair done — not unusual in itself, since she had her hair done once a week. But Sally guessed that it was Gladdy's way of getting at the truth. Inevitably she'd ask lots of questions at the parlor and try to find out what Sally was hiding.

Go ahead, Sally didn't say, do all the prying you want. She wasn't worried about being caught red-handed with Mason Jackson's money. She knew she'd never have to answer for the theft or ever have to return the money. Anyway, *theft* was the wrong word. She didn't believe that she'd stolen Mason Jackson's money because she knew he didn't believe it. And he wasn't going around Fishkill Notch accusing Sally of doing anything wrong.

What worried her most was that her good friend Georgie was back there thinking poorly of her for running off without a word. Someday, she told herself, she'd write her a letter and explain everything. But she wasn't ready for that. The best she could do was extract a promise from Gladdy that she'd keep Sally's whereabouts a secret. And this was one promise guaranteed to be kept. Gladdy loved being in charge of secrets, and she was ready to guard this one. When she set off for Fishkill Notch that day, she looked smug and purposeful, proud of being privy to part of the mystery and keen on finding out the rest of it.

But since Mason Jackson wasn't wasting his time spreading slander, there wouldn't be much to learn. Indeed, when Gladdy came back from Erna's that day, she was in a huffy mood. She even hinted that Sally couldn't stay around for long, there wasn't enough space in the house, and anyway, she said, she was thinking about boarding up the house for the winter and moving to Florida.

And then, toward evening — that same evening after she came back from Fishkill Notch and then every other evening Sally spent with her — Gladdy poured herself a hefty bourbon, poured one for Sally, and they sat out on the porch looking through the torn wire mesh at the cars speeding by on the street, one passing every minute or so. Most nights, Gladdy drank three glasses to Sally's half. And then they'd get up and go have their supper of barbecued ribs and drinks at the Barge. When she'd drunk enough to forget that she'd ever cared about the opinions of others, Gladdy would make it a point to stir up some fun, dropping change in the jukebox and sashaying from one man to another.

You gave me
a cotton tree,
a bristle belt,
a piece of felt,
but not what I want most.

What I want most,
I'll tell you,
ain't no bristle belt,
no piece of felt,
no cotton tree.

What I want most,
oh, honey bear,
what I want most,
is a skyful of love,
that's what I want most.

Starry love,
skyful of love,

that's what I want most.

Gladdy spun out of the arms of the man she'd been dancing with and back to the bar. She pounded twice with her fist, signaling to the bartender where she wanted him to set her drink, which she proceeded to empty in a gulp. She slung her arm over Sally's shoulder, rocked her to the rhythm of the song's last chords, and then, once the music was over, said, "Now, don't be shy, Sally. These boys, they're starving for company. You can have your pick of the crop. But I don't blame you for sitting it out today. Lordy, the heat. There's no escaping it. Gee, those fellas on the road crew, they're something. Sure, hit me again, Bill. Bottoms up. Skyful of love. Mmm-hmm. Cheers, honey bear. Sally here, won't you look at her. She's our little lost wallflower. Oh, starry love, skyful of love. Uh-huh. Doesn't she remind you of my Lil? I used to tell my Lil, I used to say, whatever you do, beware of a gentleman's promises. That's the mistake I kept making. Never again, ha, now that it's too late. Life flies so fast, by the time you remember to notice it, it's out of reach. That's fine, just as long as you have money for jam and don't get mixed up with those mud kickers in Amity.

Oh, yeah. A cotton tree, a piece of felt. I'll tell you, honey bear, what I want most, mmm, yeah, what I want most. Soft breeze blowing. Song in my heart. Why won't you get up and dance, Sally? Mmm-hmmm. Here we go again, Bill, bottoms up. Cheers, mountain girl. Another day, another year. If you pay attention, you might learn something, I'll show you how to get a good thing going. Mick, sweetheart, Mick, why don't you ask Sally to dance? Sally? Where's Sally? Has anyone seen Sally? She was here a moment ago . . ."

Gone out for a breath of air, that was all. Sweet, fresh night air after the suffocating closeness of the Barge, touch of the coming autumn's cold raising bumps on her uncovered arms as she followed the path behind the building, drawn there by the mumbling of the river, yearning to escape the din of the tavern and find a little peace and quiet where she could sit and think.

She ended up following the sound of the flowing water to the riverbank. She wandered along the well-worn path that led past the willows, beneath the intact part of the trestle, and to the old mill. There was enough moonlight to give the river a surface sheen but not enough to illuminate the path clearly. Sally stepped carefully in her sandals, avoiding the dark bulges of roots and stones, using a long stick she'd found to stake out her steps. She sat for a while on a flat-topped rock, bobbing the stick like a fishing pole, touching the end of it against the water as she thought about what she might do with herself next. She'd had enough of Gladdy Toffit. She had to make a plan and start living a life that would rush like this river toward happiness, rushing away from the dingy world of Helena, where there was nothing to do but get drunk and dance to stupid songs about love.

"Nothing to do," she warbled, making up a tune. *"Nothing to do . . ."* The tip of her stick dented the water. The cool air was even cooler here by the river, and she folded her legs up under her skirt. Feeling some sort of debris catch on the stick, she raised it from the river, pulling from the water soggy brown weeds that clung to the stick, their weight bending it, drawing the tip back toward the surface. The stick made a creaking sound. Pushing it away from her, she tried to lift it again and succeeded in drawing the weeds a few inches farther out of the water, revealing, just for a second or two, their slender forms, separate shapes sleeker than she would have expected, look-

ing more like frogs than weeds, yes, like little frogs dangling from the stick, startled by the air, wriggling to free themselves. Frog weeds, Sally decided, whatever that meant, just as the stick went . . .

Snap, half of it disappearing into the rushing water and the other half springing back, loosening from Sally's grip and flipping free, disappearing into the darkness of the brush behind her.

Moonlight rippling. River flowing. Thready, sodden weeds rooted in the mud. Fish gliding, invisible in the dark water. Crickets chirping. Frog head poking from the glassy surface of a little inlet behind the rock where Sally sat, frog eyes watching her, but Sally didn't notice because she was too busy feeling sorry for herself. A young girl in good health, not unattractive or unmannered . . . how was it possible that she would end up in such a dismal place, in a dull mill town beside a dull river, having fled Gladdy Toffit's foolishness, only to while away the time fishing weeds from the Tuskee? She felt as lonely as she'd ever felt. If someone would just give her permission to act on the only desire she had left, which was to go back to Tauntonville. But then she remembered that they didn't want her back in Tauntonville.

Slut, they called her. *Mother of a bastard.*
Shut up!
What did you say, Sally?

"Take me to my home away from home . . . ," she sang softly. It would have been the beginning of a fine song. But she'd promised herself at Georgie's wedding that she'd never sing aloud again. "Walk with Me" had been her last song.

Darlin', won't you walk with me,
Left and right, day and night,
No stoppin' once we start.

She would learn to hate singing; her own voice would make her shudder.

Step by step went Sally, pushing away the brambles that had grown across the path just as she'd pushed away the men that first night at the Barge, not quite as balanced as she would have been if she hadn't drunk a couple of cocktails. Damn that Gladdy Tof-fit, leading Sally so far astray that she had to stumble through the dark to get back to where she'd begun, or at least to reach the nearest light, which at that moment hap-pened to be beyond the trestle, shining through the lower windows of the ruined mill and reflecting off the river. She headed toward the mill for no other reason than that she needed more light to see accurately: to see for sure that weeds were weeds, to see the difference between water and land, to see the path in front of her.

The path eventually became easier to navigate, widening into dirt for a stretch and then flattening into a brick-paved drive that led to a rear entrance. Sally approached the building, but instead of heading toward this door, which was tightly sealed with planks and crisscrossed boards, she climbed the crumbling stone steps up the slope.

With each step she took, another set of crickets in the brush on either side stopped chirping, their hushes meeting her in intervals. She stood on the top step for a few minutes and with her stillness encouraged the crickets to chirp again. While she waited, she became aware of a distant crackling music — it was coming through the open window, along with the light. She approached the window slowly, moving to the side of the frame so she could look in from an angle.

The light came from a propane lantern set on a stool near a pile of shingles. The music was issuing from a transistor radio beside the lantern. The roof of the mill had long since collapsed, and the floor of this main room was dirt and weeds; the ceiling was the open night sky. Blankets were spread out on the ground, and a few couples lay off in the shadows, absorbed in their embraces, while the rest of the group enjoyed their cigarettes and a game of cards. Sally couldn't tell what they were playing, but she felt a bitter sense that she would be forever on the outside, looking in at the fun. She felt too worn out to have fun; as Georgie liked to say, she'd been through it. Yet she wasn't too old to feel regret for what she'd missed. She'd never had a proper youth of her own, never had a chance to hang around on a summer night with kids her own age, acting up in ways that didn't matter and playing games that had no consequence.

She kept watching as a girl in the center of the half circle laid out cards one by one, faceup, Sally guessed, for no one reached to turn them over. The girl continued distributing the cards. And then she laid a card in front of one of the boys and stopped, leaning back with a motion that indicated her job was finished. The group made a noise in unison that reminded Sally of the murmur of the Tuskee. It was an expression that combined calm with wariness and expectation.

The card must have been significant. The group waited for the boy to do something.

He was supposed to stand up and dance a stupid jig — was that it? Or he had to kiss a girl he didn't like. As his penalty for receiving whatever card had been dealt him, he was supposed to do something ridiculous or dangerous. He had to make a fool of himself. He had to pull down his pants or eat dirt or leave the game altogether and go home for the night.

Sally considered all these notions while she stared at the boy. He sat close to the light, facing the window, but he was too absorbed in his predicament to notice Sally there. She could see that he was pale, slighter than the other boys, though tall, with dark welts of acne on his cheeks and blond bangs that he should have had trimmed weeks before. Sally thought he might have been older than the others, maybe sixteen or seventeen, and yet he seemed weaker, more vulnerable, maybe because of the card he'd just been dealt or maybe because that's just the way he was.

"Go on," one of the girls urged.

"We're waiting," a boy said.

"We don't have all night."

"Chicken."

"Bawk, bawk."

The couples had stopped their smooching and were sitting up, watching the game along with the rest of the group, waiting for the boy to do whatever he was supposed to do. The song playing on the radio had a sorrowful melody, Sally thought, though she couldn't make out the words. She felt sure that whatever the boy did would have an awful finality to it. Though she wanted to look away, she went on staring. As he reached to retrieve something on the ground, she wanted to shout out a warning, yet she kept quiet. And when she saw the pistol in his hand, she wasn't more surprised than she would have been if she'd been dreaming the whole scene.

It was similar to a dream, inevitable and natural and illogical. A slanting light shone from the lantern; the radio crackled its song; the river splashed; the crickets chirped; the tension made breathing impossible; the air was so thick that the boy could hardly lift his arm, raising the gun to his head in an attenuated motion, the effort exhausting him, drenching him in sweat, the heat of fear turning his pale skin into melting wax.

Far away, a dog barked, the sound urging duty, like snapping fingers — *do it, do it!* Slowly, slowly. As gradual as the light of the rising sun stretching across the ground toward the halfway point where fate was waiting.

Strength of life. Set me upon a rock of stone. Mark what is done amiss. The awful stupidity of man. A girl dealing cards. A boy pressing his finger against a trigger. *Do it, do it!* Click. Silence.

Um, what just happened?

Nothing. Nothing ever happened in this dingy backwater. The chamber of the gun was always empty. Life was always unremarkable. One day after the next, nothing worth remembering, not even this stupid game played by boys and girls so bored that they didn't care whether they woke up the next morning. Yawn.

Sally couldn't contain her outrage. "If that's not the dumbest thing I've ever seen!" she cried out. "You are all a bunch of lunatics." She liked that word: *lunatics.* "Crazy lunatics! You all should be locked up. Every last one of you. Get out of here, go on home," she ordered, shaking her fist as she leaned across the sill.

The kids stared at her with frozen expressions that mixed shock and dismay and humiliation. The boy with the pistol was the first to move, raising his arms as though in surrender. And the girl who had dealt the cards jumped to her feet and grabbed the gun, pointing it at Sally.

"Put that down," Sally ordered.

"Aw, Belle, sure, it's all in fun," said another one of the girls enigmatically. "But still —"

Ding. That was the sound the bullet made as it glanced off a beam near the window before it crackled into a brick in the wall opposite. Sally was too startled to duck. She stood there numbly, wondering if she was understanding correctly: Did the girl named Belle nearly kill her?

"Oh my God," Belle exclaimed, shaking the pistol before she dropped it, as though it had burned her hand. "Oh, my God. Oh, no. I didn't . . . I thought . . . I thought . . . I thought it wasn't loaded!"

Sure, was the unsaid response from the group. *Yeah, right. Like we believe you.*

"Mole!" cried another girl.

Mole was the idiot who'd pointed the pistol at his head and pulled the trigger. Mole was the poor sucker who'd been dealt the fateful card; Mole, pale, sweat-drenched Mole, had folded forward from the position he'd been sitting in and was sprawled over his bent legs, lying facedown on the grassy floor of the mill, looking as if he'd been dead for a week.

Watching the whole scene through the window, Sally put two and two together: a pistol had been fired, ding, and a boy had been shot. He was dead, of course. What else was she supposed to think? She climbed over the sill and rushed toward him, though not out of any sense that she could insert herself into this part of the disaster and come to his rescue. Rather, she went to him because she thought that either by accident or on purpose he'd put himself in the path of the bullet, preventing it from striking her.

Yet by the time she reached him, he was propped up by the arms of one of the girls, panting, then breathing deeply, then shaking his head, shaking away the fright of it all. Well, then he hadn't been shot, it appeared. He had merely collapsed in a dead faint. The idea of a fainting boy made Sally laugh aloud. But seeing the shine of embarrassment in his eyes, she changed her response to a forced solemnity.

"Are you all right, Mole?" the girl named Belle asked.

"Are you all right?" Sally echoed.

"I didn't mean . . . gee, Mole . . . ," Belle faltered.

"You could have killed him," Sally scolded, feeling a need to clarify Belle's responsibility in the affair.

"We checked first, didn't we, Mole? Didn't we? We all did, isn't that right?" Belle pleaded for support, turning to the rest of the group. "The gun wasn't supposed to be loaded," she said. The others nodded and murmured agreeably.

Sally decided that she deserved as much sympathy as Mole, the fainting boy. "You could have killed me," she said.

"Who are you, anyway?" Belle asked.

Before she could answer, Mole said, "You could have killed her." His tone was surprisingly reasonable, as if he were offering a simple observation. Sally was impressed. "You could have killed both of us," he said. "Both of us with one bullet." Sally was even more impressed. The fainting boy was turning out to be unexpectedly keen, with a calm, convincing authority. Sally liked the feeling of having come through a dangerous experience together. They both could have died with terrible abruptness, killed by the bullet that wasn't supposed to be in the gun. Then they never would have eaten another meal or seen the sun rise again or even, if this were a possibility, gotten to know each other. Instead, here they were alive, looking into each other's eyes, both of them searching for a clue that would tell them something about their prospects.

When the fainting boy felt strong enough to

stand, the party ended. They all went home, Belle up front holding the pistol like a dead rat by its tail, Mole leading Sally by the hand through the darkness along the rocky path to the street. "Careful," he kept saying. His hand was clammy, the fingers spidery and strong. When he looked at her, his eyes seemed to widen more than was physically possible, with the pale skin at the corners folding into ruffles. Sally judged him to be no older than fifteen or sixteen and because of that she felt superior to him, the same way she felt superior to her younger brothers. And yet she liked being led by him along the path. It stirred in her a feeling of trust that was as unfamiliar as it was immediate.

"Of course," he'd said with a laugh after she'd told him her name. Of course she was Sally Angel. A name must suit its subject, and Sally Angel suited her. Dropping from the sky like that — she would be forever associated in his mind with the miracle of his survival.

And why was he called Mole? "Such a funny name," she said. No, she corrected, she didn't mean funny, "not like funny-funny. Just funny," she explained limply. Mole laughed at her and then with her when she joined in. He told her that his full name was Martin Oliver Langerton, and Mole was what his family had called him from the start.

Sally asked him about the game back at the mill. He said that it was meant to be a harmless game. "Still," he mused, if the gun had fired . . . if his hand had slipped and the gun had fired . . . ? He didn't want to think about it. He didn't want to imagine himself dead. He wasn't dead. He was alive, truly alive, and to prove it, look.

He whooped as they broke through a screen of brambles and stepped onto the road. Then he lifted her in his arms, spun her around, and set her back down. The fainting boy was turning out to be bursting with giddy spirit. "You're swell to come along like that," he said in gratitude. "You're a real nice gal," he added. And, more solemnly, with a touch of awe, he murmured, "You're . . . ," and then he paused for a long interval, searching the night sky for the right word. "A peach," he declared.

Sally flinched, as if she'd caught a splinter in her toe. She was, by his estimate, a peach. Wasn't that kind of noncommittal? Well, she told herself, it was a start. She'd found at least the possibility of something more.

They headed toward the block of buildings on Main Street, and Sally motioned with her free hand to indicate that the Barge was her destination. But as she approached the tavern, she began dragging her feet, making each step more sluggish than the last, slowing nearly to a standstill in an effort to give the boy named Mole ample opportunity to say what she wanted to hear. And when they'd reached the door and he still hadn't asked if he could see her again, she asked him.

The next evening, as Sally stood at the mirror in Gladdy's front hall fixing her hatpins, she said coldly, "I won't be at the Barge tonight. I'm going out." She was surprised that Gladdy didn't ask, *Out where?* for she'd been prepared to reply, *Out for a walk.* Gladdy didn't ask her if she was going out alone. Sally didn't say, *Yes,* though the truth was *no.* Gladdy, already four ounces into her bourbon, didn't seem to notice or care that Sally had trimmed her hat with blue freesias and baby's breath from her weedy garden. Stirring her drink with her finger, she'd spent the last hour reminiscing about long-ago summers when she used to chase the iceman's cart down Volner Street in Amity. Those carefree, hazy days, before the war, before both her marriages went sour, before she'd seen the truth about men . . .

She'd trailed off with "If I'd known then what I know now," and by the time Sally was at the mirror, she'd fallen into a reflective silence. When Sally said good-bye and headed out the door, Gladdy didn't try to stop her. Other than lifting a pinkie to wave as Sally left the house, she remained absorbed in her own thoughts and her bourbon, leaving her guest to drift away without bothering to ask when she planned to return.

Sally had been excited about meeting Mole that evening, but Gladdy's indifference threatened to put her in an ugly mood. She could have disappeared for good, and Gladdy Toffit wouldn't have cared. No one would have cared. Ever since she'd left home to work for the Jensons at the age of twelve, it had been far too easy to run away and leave behind all that was familiar, or walk, like this, thump thump thump, down the porch steps and along the brick path, closing the gate behind her, making sure the latch clicked before she ambled through the cool summer twilight.

But of course she wasn't going away for good. She wasn't even going away. She was just going to meet a local boy who'd shown an interest in her. This was how she probably would have spent many of her evenings back in Tauntonville, if she'd been allowed to grow up gradually, day by day, in an ordinary fashion — stepping out like this to meet up with an ordinary boy, a boy named Mole, who, thankfully, knew nothing about her past.

And there he was at the end of the street, leaning against the hood of a car, resting on his elbows and blowing smoke rings. He waved at her with the hand holding the cigarette, scattering sparks as the ash dropped off. She waved back, pleased to find him waiting right where he'd promised to be.

When she reached him, he grabbed her hand and shook it vigorously, as though he were sealing a business deal. She laughed loudly and abruptly but stopped when she saw the blush splotching his cheeks. He was easily mortified. She squeezed his hand to convey her pleasure at seeing him, and he cheered up, offering her a cigarette and waving his lighter with a flourish before extinguishing it with a loud click.

"Mr. Mole," she said in a husky voice, after exhaling smoke in a long, slow stream.

"Sally Angel." He pronounced her name slowly, as if he were reading it from a list.

"Where shall we walk to, Mole?" she asked.

"Walk?"

"Aren't we going on a walk? It's a real nice evening."

"I thought —"

"You don't want to walk?"

He looked uncertain. "If you want to walk, we can walk. But, well, okay, let's walk."

"Is something wrong?" By then she'd slipped her arm around his and locked elbows. They were walking along the side of the street, stepping around puddles left behind by a thunderstorm that had blown through that afternoon. Now, with the sun below the horizon, the sky was brilliantly clear, a dark, shining topaz.

"How could anything be wrong when you're around?" he said, a question that he delivered flatly, as if he'd been rehearsing it all morning. But when he smiled, it felt good and honest, with his inward smile matching the outward one, as far as Sally could tell. She already was convinced that this boy, this Mole, was the sweetest fellow she'd ever met.

She bumped her hip against his, knocking him slightly to the side. He bumped back. She bumped, he bumped, and they staggered along the road, laughing together, bumping together, and suddenly rearing backward to get out of the way when a car came speeding around the turn.

Sally and Mole clung to each other, still chuckling, as they watched the car, a stub-finned green Cadillac, go by.

"There goes the cream-cheese prince," said Mole when the car was out of sight.

"Who?"

"Heir to the throne."

"What are you talking about?"

"You don't know Benny Patterson?"

"I haven't been here long."

"The Pattersons own a dairy farm east of Fenton. They got rich selling cream cheese. Benny, what a gorilla. He bought that car with cash. Aw, will you listen to that." There was a bird shrieking in the darkness, a jay calling and then answering itself. "Crazy bird," murmured Mole. But Sally was still thinking about the prince of cream cheese speeding by in his Cadillac.

"Wouldn't it be nice to be able to drive around? I mean, if we could just get in a car and follow the road," she said dreamily. Mole didn't say anything, and Sally interpreted his silence as agreement. "If only I knew how to drive," she continued. "Gee, I wish . . . if I had a car . . ."

"You say you want to learn to drive?" There was an unfamiliar sharpness in Mole's voice, and Sally guessed that he was envious of Benny Patterson's fancy car and all the privileges that money bought. She decided to talk about something else, and the best she could come up with was to comment on the good smell of honeysuckle. She added, in an attempt to reassure him, "It's nice to walk along." But he didn't let go either of her arm or the subject.

"So you want to learn to drive?" he repeated.

"Who wouldn't?"

"Some girls are flat-out scared."

"Bah, that's just what boys think. They're afraid their girls will learn to drive and then drive away and leave them in the dust."

"Where would you go, if you could drive?"

"To Amity. To shop."

"And what would you buy?"

She sensed that he was teasing her now, so she teased him back: "I'd buy you your own deck of cards."

"What do I need with cards?"

"You'd get to call the game."

She laughed to show that she was joking, and he laughed along with her and then pulled her toward him, tipping his head down as she tipped hers up, their lips meeting in a brief, tender kiss that thrilled Sally not just because it was happening but because she sensed in it a bid to make something serious, respectful, and lasting out of their mutual affection. Sweet Mole with his menthol breath and tousled hair. He cared about her too much to take advantage of her. And she felt for him a different kind of attraction than she'd ever felt before, something that right here in its early stages was enriched with the possibility of permanence. She wasn't certain yet — she hardly knew him, after all — but it could be that this kiss signified a release from all her troubles.

"Mole."

"Sally Angel."

How could she let him think of her under that guise, a false name, a veil for her sins? *My real name is . . . ,* she tried to say. *I'm not . . . ,* she tried to say. "I . . . ," she began. But before she could utter another word he'd leaned forward and they were kissing again, their mouths open this time, their tongues moving greedily, their eyes squeezed shut. Oh, he was a nice boy, an innocent who assumed there was an empty place in Sally's life that only he could fill. And he wasn't far from the truth, was he? Maybe she hadn't been looking for a boy like Mole, but now she was glad she'd found him.

They finally came up for air, blinking, each waiting for the other to speak, the silence stretching into an awkward pause that Sally could think to break only by telling Mole that she needed to go home. Wasn't that what a good girl was supposed to say? But she didn't want to say it. She didn't want to go home. She had no home of her own and was fighting a swell of desperation when Mole asked in a whisper, "You want to learn to drive?"

"Yes," she said softly. She would have said yes to any question he'd asked.

"Well then, I'll teach you," he announced, taking her hand and leading her around the curve of the road that had returned them — magically, it seemed to Sally, as though they'd crossed a fold of time and space in a single stride — to the street corner from where they'd set out on their walk. And at the corner was the car that had been parked there earlier, a tired old Pontiac with a webbed crack in the corner of the windshield and dents along one side, front to back, that were outlined in rusty scratches.

The scratches were black in the dusk. The corner of the rear bumper was anchored with twine. Mole patted the hood as though to calm a nervous horse, and then he opened the passenger door for Sally.

"Meet Phoebe."

"This is your car? Why didn't you tell me

earlier?"

"You said you wanted to walk."

"But . . . this is your car? Really, Mole? You have your own car?"

He didn't answer. He'd already closed her door and was walking around the front of the car. She watched him settle in beside her and fit the key into the ignition, and she was reminded of the ride she'd taken four years earlier on the back of her cousin's motorcycle. But this ride would be nothing like that one. She already was sure that this ride would be like the kisses she'd just enjoyed, marking the beginning of a story that would go on and on.

She didn't mind that the seam of her vinyl seat had split and she could feel the coil of the metal spring. She didn't mind the dents and cracks. She felt the pleasure of Mole's pride as he described the car to her, a '46 Pontiac sedan complete with a radio and a heater that actually worked! To prove it, Mole turned the heater on, turned it off, turned it on and off again as he drove down the street.

He had an odd way of driving, with his hands gripping the steering wheel as though to hold it on the stem and his foot pressing and then releasing the accelerator, creating a jerking motion that kept throwing Sally back against her seat. She wondered if he'd only recently learned to drive or even if he was old enough to drive. What did he know about the world? What did he assume about her? Surely it wouldn't occur to him that she'd *been through it.* Or maybe he was wise enough to guess that Sally had secrets he didn't want to hear.

She had an impulse to divert him from this thought, even though he'd given no sign that he was thinking it. "Say," she said, sliding her hand behind his neck, "where are you taking me?"

"To the moon!" he cried. "Hold on, baby!" With that he pressed the accelerator, turning the car with a screech down a dark lane that led to a school and speeding around the front loop and into an empty parking lot, where he stopped so abruptly that Sally had to throw her hands forward to keep from colliding with the dashboard.

"Your turn," he said in a tone that reminded her of the way her brothers would dare her, when she was just a little girl, to jump off a high rock shelf into the pool at the bottom of the gravel pit.

But what Sally experienced that evening in Mole's beat-up '46 Pontiac sedan was not the sensation of falling. Nor was it much like the dangerous thrill she'd felt on the back of her cousin's motorcycle. Rather, after she'd taken her place in the driver's seat and Mole had showed her how to put the car in drive, she felt as though she were riding on a raft, carried by a steady current. Why, it turned out to be surprisingly easy to drive, almost effortless! She had only to rest the ball of her foot against the pedal and hold the steering wheel at an angle that kept the car moving in a circle, around and around in the parking lot, following the beams of the headlights.

"I'm driving!"

"Go ahead," he urged. "Go a little faster."

She obliged, following the road that girdled the earth, speeding along from hemisphere to hemisphere. Mole turned on the radio and turned up the volume of the sportscaster who was reporting on last night's headliner at the Elks Club, in which Abe Walden had been —

"Dumped by Bruce Brewster!" Mole cried.

"Who?"

"Welterweight from Hornell, the best, good God, dumped on the seat of his drawers!" He hung on to the vinyl handle above the passenger door and swayed with the motion of the car. "Go for it!" he shouted as Sally changed direction and steered the car in a tight figure eight.

Fast, faster, fastest. The darkening twilight gave the playground a strange depth, as if the flat field went on and on. The Pontiac sped round the parking lot in dizzying loops.

So this is happiness, Sally thought. This was the power that would save her from her own mistakes. The ability to go anywhere, to just get in a car and go with the current, leaving everything behind.

But now Mole was yelling that she had to do something, find something, figure it out for herself because *whoops,* he'd forgotten to show her the brake.

"The what?"

"The pedal there, to stop." He tried to kick his foot into the space, but Sally beat him to it.

"I know what a brake is." Sally pressed lightly, expertly slowing the car, bringing it to a halt with its nose pointing toward the fence. "How was that?"

"I told you," he said. "You're a natural." He reached for the gear handle, shoving it into park.

They sat in silence for a moment, staring at the metal links glinting in the headlights. "I guess . . . ," Mole said vaguely, giving a timid smile. She braced her shoulders as she turned toward him, offering him her lips. He hesitated, so she wrapped her arms around his neck to pull him closer, and they kissed another gulping kiss.

A newscaster was droning on about yesterday's swirling dogfight over Korea, though Sally and Mole weren't listening. Nor did they notice the dark form of a moth fluttering in the headlight beams or the white-tailed doe that bounded across the edge of the playground behind the fence. They kept kissing for so long, with such absorbing passion, that by the end of it, Sally was certain that she knew Mole thoroughly and knew that she could count on him to be a good and honest sport no matter what. So desperate was she to put the tumult of the last three years behind her forever that by the time they'd stopped kissing, she'd concluded that they should marry and spend the rest of their lives together.

"It's a good thing that pistol didn't fire when you pulled the trigger," she whispered, fingering his collarbone, pressing tenderly to explore the line of his neck.

She expected him to say something charming in return. But he surprised her by admitting in a murmur that he had something to tell her — a *something* in a tone that promised to be an unwelcome confession. Her fingers curled in tense anticipation. He was going to tell her that he didn't want to be involved with her or couldn't be involved because of what she'd done, he'd heard about her, he knew about what she'd left behind in Tauntonville and what she'd taken from Fishkill Notch. He was going to call her a slut. He was going to say he wouldn't have anything more to do with her. He was going to say —

"It's about Phoebe. Well . . ."

"What?" Her confusion was smothering. All she would let herself understand was that he was telling her something he thought she didn't want to hear.

"The car, it's Phil's. Phil's my brother, see —"

"What?"

"I should have come right out and told you earlier. You see, Phil lets me use his car when he doesn't need it, except he needs it to drive to Fenton. He's a manager on the graveyard shift at the diner there, and he needs the car to get to work. If I'm not back by ten —"

"That's all you're telling me, about the car?"

"I mean, I hope you're not mad."

"You darling," Sally said with relief. His ignorance of her guilt was almost as good as forgiveness. "Of course I'm not mad."

■ ■ ■ ■

They met the next time Phil lent Mole the Pontiac, three nights later. They met again on the following Sunday and stayed out well past midnight, since it was Phil's night off. They met again on Tuesday night, and then the next Thursday, dividing their time between driving instruction and kissing, incrementally driving less, since Sally was quick to master the necessary skills, and kissing more, expanding their kissing to caresses, their caresses to more excited groping. They took to parking along the gravel drive leading to the mill. They'd move to the ample rear seat, and Mole would open Sally's blouse button by button with a slow, intoxicating persistence. Sometimes he'd have to struggle with the hooks of her bra, bunching the clasp, pulling with two hands before he discovered that a simple pinch with a slight rubbing would do it. His fingers were always cold, even on a steamy summer's night, but they'd warm up from the heat of Sally's skin. And she'd make sure to move her body into positions that gave him room to explore, shifting her hips to stretch her torso into a long curve, lifting her chin, raising a knee, until finally, after

several weeks of caresses gentler than anything she could have dreamed of, she separated her thighs for him.

She'd been afraid that with this new
intimacy he'd ask about her history. But
though he must have understood that she
wasn't a virgin, he was too absorbed in his
pleasure to care. And she felt her need to
confess to him evaporate. He'd fallen for
her in her incarnation as Sally Angel; there
wasn't any need for him to find out about
Sally Werner.

She did ask him one night about his own
past romances. He insisted that she was his
first real love, though he'd had what he
called "a dress rehearsal" with a girl named
Annette, the older sister of Belle, the girl
who'd fired the gun in the mill. But Annette
had gone away to a junior college, where
she'd met someone else, a sergeant in the
military, who at the time was on leave from
Korea. When she came back to Helena the
next summer, she was already engaged.

"But I don't want to talk about all that,"
Mole said.

Mostly, they talked about the future. He'd
dropped out of school the previous year,
but he was planning to enroll in an electrician's course at the Career Training Center
in Fenton. Once he was certified, he hoped

to get a job with a county contractor for a while, and then he'd make a go of it on his own, work full-time out of his own truck, after he bought a truck. He had his eye on one of those shiny, red, almost new Dodge pickups that were lined up in the lot at the Gleason dealership.

Sally said she had already begun to look for a job. She didn't want to live at Gladdy Toffit's for much longer, but first she needed to find something that paid enough to cover her expenses. She'd probably go to a city, she said, maybe to New York or Chicago. There were plenty of jobs in the big cities, especially secretary jobs, more jobs than there were girls to fill them. She could type fifty words a minute, and she'd get faster with practice.

Mole said he'd consider a town but never a city. He couldn't live in a city, with all that filth and noise and the rivers thick with stinking sludge from the sewers. Sally, hearing this, was quick to modify her ambition. She'd like to live *near* a city, not right in one, or in a town big enough to have offices in need of secretaries. Also, she wouldn't mind living within a bus ride of a dancing hall. Now, that would be fun, the two of them dancing all night and walking home arm in arm as the sun was coming up.

Imagine, Mole. The two of us . . .

She didn't bother to say this aloud. The more time they spent together, the less they needed to speak, since most of their communication was exchanged in silence, through touches and glances. Away from him, during the day, she'd savor the nugget of heat he'd left inside her. Lost in thoughts that combined memories and anticipated pleasures, she'd feel far away as she wandered through Gladdy's house. She'd stumble, stub her toe, hit her elbow against a counter, knock over the cereal box, but she'd always recover and clean up the mess before Gladdy noticed.

Gladdy failed to notice many things. She didn't emerge until early afternoon, her throat full of sand and her black curls unraveled. Some mornings Sally would catch a glimpse of one of Gladdy's male friends from the Barge as he snuck from the bedroom out the back door, but Gladdy herself never made mention of them. She'd eat a late breakfast of scrambled eggs and toast, and then she'd spend an hour or two talking on the phone to friends she called "dearie" and "honey" but who never appeared in Helena. Sometimes she'd drive to Fishkill Notch. Other days she'd dress in one of the three rayon skirt-suits she owned, gather bills from the rolltop desk in the living room, and get in the car and drive to the bank in Amity to confer with the person she called her *financial adviser*. Late in the afternoon she'd come back home to pour her bourbon, urging Sally to join her because, as she claimed, she didn't like to drink alone. But soon enough she'd drift off into one of those dull reveries, and that's when Sally would slip away to meet Mole. When she returned later in the evening, Gladdy would be off having the time of her life at the Barge.

Sally didn't much like staying there, dependent upon Gladdy. She kept scanning the classifieds in the county paper for rooms. But she couldn't complain because, after all, Gladdy had assumed she was penniless and never mentioned money, never asked her to contribute to the cost of food, never asked her to pay something for board. True, Sally overheard her whispering in her phone conversations, evidently reporting on different ways that "the girl" was taking advantage of her kindness. But Gladdy must have liked the idea of having a freeloader in residence, or else she would have come right out and told her to leave.

That Sally had thousands of dollars stuffed in a brown paper bag in the closet of the guest room would never have occurred to Gladdy Toffit. And Sally felt justified in keeping it a secret. She thought of the money as something to protect in its original form, to keep contained in the vault of its paper bag. She would check on it nightly, counting as she separated the bills into equal stacks. But to use the money, she was convinced, would invite damnation; she would let herself starve before she spent a single dollar on herself. She clung to the conviction that Mason Jackson's money had come with an obligation: he wouldn't have let her run off with half his life savings if he hadn't expected her to use it wisely. And the wisest use she could imagine involved making reparation for her negligence. While she hadn't yet formulated a plan, she believed that the money in the closet was meant to help her son. He deserved better than what her parents would ever offer.

For several months, she was able to live off Gladdy's grudging charity. As the time passed, she believed that she was moving closer to a secure future, when she and Mole would marry, buy a house and a shiny Dodge pickup, and from the earnings of their good jobs accumulate enough to put away in a Savings Club for the children they'd go on to have together, for Mole

194

wanted at least three children, while Sally, hiding her reluctance, insisted that two, a boy and a girl, would be nice.

A hot, humid summer cooled to brisk, wet September days. Mole began his electrician's course. Gladdy whiled away her sober hours waiting to get drunk. Sally watched the minute hand on the kitchen clock, waiting for the time when she was to meet Mole at the corner; and he was always there, puffing on a cigarette and leaning against the Pontiac, ready to grab her and kiss her and bury his face in her hair, inhaling the smell of her shampoo. She couldn't believe how much he cared for her. And while they both spoke of the future as though they were practically engaged, Sally was relieved that he never invited her home to introduce her to his parents and brothers or even brought her to parties with his local chums. She liked the feeling that they were living in a world of their own making, where they were spared from the judgment of others.

She had a few days of worry when she didn't start bleeding on schedule; in the dark hours of the night, when she was alone in Gladdy's guest room, she told herself that she was destined for ruin and would bring only misery to all who associated with her. But before the week was over, her period arrived with a bloody burst, seeping through her bedsheet and staining the mattress. She spent the next day alternately crying secretly, for no reason she could fathom, and grinning stupidly, grateful to be spared.

In October of 1951, Sally found part-time work typing the correspondence of Mrs. J. T. Mellow, the widow of a banker, a stooped, elderly woman, frail but purposeful. Mrs. Mellow didn't say much ordinarily; she'd leave a pile of letters on the desk, handwritten in an awkward, childish print, and after greeting Sally at the door, she'd close herself up in the parlor for most of the morning, emerging just before noon, collecting the typed letters, wrapping herself in a shawl, and heading to the post office, leaving Sally to let herself out.

At first Sally was disappointed that Mrs. Mellow never commented on how well the letters were typed, but she grew used to the old woman's solemn manner and the quiet rooms. She had the feeling that the hours marked by the chimes of the mantel clock passed more slowly here than elsewhere, each minute stretched longer than its usual span, and that someday soon, time inside this house would stop passing altogether — at which point, Sally thought, Mrs. Mellow would have nothing left to put in her letters.

For now, though, the old woman wrote occasionally to her husband's former clients, inquiring about business he'd been overseeing before his death. But most of her letters were to a niece in Albany and a nephew in Boston, and they were full of marvelous information about disparate things — a new species of bird discovered in India, the position of the twin stars, Castor and Pollux, in the autumn sky, or sneak thieves who stole $395 in cash from a Fenton motel room while the occupants slept. How did she know so much? Sally wondered. She knew the date of Claudette Colbert's birthday. She knew where to find a mahogany Ironrite cabinet on sale. She knew that fir green would be next spring's stylish color.

But Mrs. Mellow's house wasn't at all stylish. Sally guessed from the stale fragrance in the air that long ago she had hidden potpourris around the house and then forgotten them. The ancient stenciled-paper shades over the front windows were blotched with stains; the leather seats of the dining room chairs were marred by hairline cracks; old crazy quilts were slung across the banister and the sofa; on a tarnished silver-plated card receiver in the front hall was a stack of yellowed calling cards that must have been decades old; there was a dish full of dusty seashells on the mantel; mismatched ceramics were stacked in a glass cabinet; sentimental prints had been hung on all the walls, including a lithograph above the desk of a bearded man reading Scripture to his wife.

It would all have been too stuffy and boring to endure if it weren't for the lively letters that Mrs. Mellow wrote. From these letters Sally learned a little about a lot. She learned about Champillon and the Rosetta stone; she learned about Florence Nightingale's common sense; she learned how to make scalloped eggs and deviled chicken; she even learned that brainpower would be enhanced for those who left the cake alone and ate the pickles.

And then Sally gleaned that the niece was due to have a baby early in the new year.

Dear Marguerite, wrote Mrs. Mellow, *do not be afraid to ask for pain relief when you are in labor. There is no reason in our modern era for a woman to suffer.*

Another letter began, *Dear Marguerite, It occurs to me to remind you to be sure that the milk you drink is pasteurized.*

Or *Dear Marguerite, I want you to know that the trust fund will be administered through the*

Romulus Savings Bank. Your task will be to design the education for your child in such a way that our family's privileges will be put to good use.

Privileges was a word Sally kept mistyping — as *privleges* and *pivileges* and *ptivileges.* The paper wore thin beneath the wheel of her eraser. Twice she had to start over and retype the letter. And as she kept typing, the word echoed in her thoughts: *privileges, privileges, privileges.*

There were children born with privileges and children born without them. There were children who would want for nothing, and children who would grow up knowing only want. There were children, like the child to be born to Marguerite of Albany, whose education would be carefully supervised. And there were children, like Sally's son, who were born only to be abandoned.

Sally had gone without privileges all through her life, and so would her child. He was a monster, according to the woman at Georgie's wedding. What kind of monster? Was he monstrous because he was stupid or wicked or just plain ugly? Or was he monstrous because he was poor?

Privileges, privileges.

. . . *in need,* Sally typed, and then she continued impulsively, *like it or leave it,* and

199

added, *Sally* and *was here* and *passing by.*

Of course she crumpled the paper and threw the letter away. Then she typed it straight through without a single mistake, singing a song under her breath, singing over and over the only two lines she could remember:

Passing by, mmm-hmmm,
On a slow train to Paradise.

But singing, she reminded herself when she was done typing, was to be resisted. She'd forsworn it, hadn't she? Sally Werner liked to sing, not Sally Angel. Singing was not what she would do while she was rocking her son to sleep, if she ever had the chance to rock him to sleep. Why, first of all, she would have to introduce herself to him. And then, then, then, imagine — that little honey child, probably freckles all over his face like her brothers, snub nose, maybe even a redhead, tattered shirt, bare feet, too young to recognize that other children had what he lacked and too old for his mother to return and pretend that she'd never gone away.

Did he like to wade in the flooded meadow after the spring rains, like Sally used to do? Did he ever wake from a bad dream? Did he suck his thumb, and did Dietrich Werner beat him for it? Maybe. Probably. Of course he'd beat the child. He'd smack him to wake him up to the reality of his life. He'd smack him to remind him that he was the bastard son of the devil's whore. He'd smack him to prove that he was too stupid to amount to anything, and he'd keep smacking him until someone made him stop.

"Are you finished, Miss Angel?"

If gravity hadn't held her in place, she would have been so startled by the voice coming from the doorway of the study that she would have flown out of her chair and hit her head on the ceiling.

"Yes. No. I mean, here's what I've done so far."

"That's fine for today. You can go."

Sally was too baffled to move. Mrs. Mellow usually left the house before her; now, as she walked across the room, planting her cane ahead of her halting steps, she was smiling a tight smile, as if to assure her that everything would be all right, despite what Sally had been thinking. What had she been thinking? She was confused less by the old woman's authority than by her implicit knack for reading minds.

Sally noticed for the first time the dull blue shine of cataracts in her eyes. And that musty, rose-petal fragrance — it was easy to imagine that it had its source in her, that she was stuffed with dried flowers, her thin skin like wrinkled cloth, her hair the fringe of the cushion. She was so very old, older than anyone Sally had ever known, old enough to see beyond appearances and understand what needed to be said, which, in this case, involved the simplest of directions. She didn't tell her to stay or wait or even take her time. She told her that she could *go,* offering what Sally heard as permission to return to the place where she'd stop her father from hitting her son.

On the Wednesday before Thanksgiving, a gray November day, they borrowed the Pontiac from Mole's brother. When Mole asked her where they were going, she said, "Nowhere." He said something about how there was always *somewhere* up ahead and left it at that.

The road was still damp from the previous night's rain. Sally was at the wheel and drove south along Route 36 in the direction of Amity. She knew from the map to make a sharp turn just north of Amity, where they'd turn onto Route 253, and on the outskirts of Fishkill Notch she would take the right-hand fork onto County Road 27.

The few straggling leaves on the maples

along the road were a charred dark red. Brown bristle filled the cornfields. Most of the pastures were empty, and the barns were shut up tight against the damp cold. There weren't many cars out, and the only other signs of activity Sally noticed were the muddy tractor lines crisscrossing the road in front of the farms, along with white smoke rising from some of the chimneys.

Although she'd passed along this same route once before, in a bus and mostly in the dark, she had the vague feeling that she knew this scenery from earlier in her life, as though she'd seen it as a child or maybe dreamed about it repeatedly and in her dreams had gotten hopelessly lost here.

But she wasn't lost. She'd studied the map back at Gladdy's and memorized the directions. It was less than fifty miles from Helena to Tauntonville, a distance that should have been impossibly long given all she'd been through since she'd run away. But how easy it was to return, miraculously easy, really — a left turn, a right fork, a few stoplights, and on toward nowhere.

"That's the Patterson estate, Benny Patterson's place," Mole announced. They were passing fields lusher than the others, carpeted in velvet green, mounded with hillocks and divided into rough squares by pine brakes. The fields close to the road were empty, but cows could be seen grazing farther away, on the slope above the barn. Down a long drive lined by sycamores was the homestead, a fancy, pink-bricked Georgian mansion. The scene suggested prosperity and ease, and yet there was something desolate about it all, with the land like wind-whipped water surrounding the island of the house, a building that looked out on the world with a squint of contempt. Sally was glad to drive past and leave it behind. Once the estate was out of sight, she thought to herself about how she didn't need much in the way of material goods. She didn't need a big house or a fancy car, she didn't need jewels or minks, she didn't even need the money that was in the paper bag she'd stuffed into the old purse she'd found in Gladdy's rummage box. That she could so readily give the money away to her son, as she was intending to do, seemed the simplest of the choices available to her. But someone — her sister Tru, probably — would have to counsel the boy on how to spend the money responsibly, to offer the guidance that Sally wouldn't have the time to give him. It would be hello and good-bye when she saw him; she planned to stay just long enough to be reassured that he was getting proper care, but then she would disappear before her parents could catch her and make her answer for the scandal she'd caused.

Wretched Sally Werner.

Run, Sally.

Where's Sally? Has anyone seen Sally?

There were patches of brown loosestrife along the roadside. The smell of burning leaves hung in the air, though they didn't see any smoke. The shadow of a hawk crossed a field and disappeared into the shade of a cloud.

Passing by, mmm-hmmm.

"Hey," Mole said.

"What?"

He ran his hand along her right thigh, gliding over the ribs of her corduroy skirt, smoothing it against her skin. "You look lost in thought."

"I'm thinking about how I wish we could just drive and drive," she said. "I wish we could keep on driving till we reached the gates of heaven."

"And what if those gates were closed?"

"Why, I'd do this!" She blared the horn as she sped along the road, filling the gray expanse of sky with the noise. "Open the gates!" she called. "Come on! Open the gates or I'll crash down the doors!" She pressed the pedal to the floor, sending the car into such a fast surge forward that the tires squealed, and an acrid smell filled the interior. But there was no real danger. Sally easily slowed the car and drove calmly along the next stretch of road, the horn quiet again, the radio crackling, in search of a signal, and Mole measuring her with a wondering stare, as though he had just realized that the girl at the wheel was a stranger.

Which of them was it who asked, "Do you love me?"

Which of them replied, "You're crazy"?

Or countered, "You're crazy, too," providing all the proof they'd ever need that they were made for each other.

He slid closer toward her and stretched his arm across her shoulders. She stayed focused on the road, both hands gripping the wheel, while he ran a crooked finger against the back of her neck, collecting loose strands of hair and pressing them up against the underside of her ponytail. His touch blended warmth with a shivery lightness, and Sally felt soothed and grateful. When a car passed in the northbound lane, she was certain that the driver had seen enough of them at a glance to feel envious. Who wouldn't feel envious of two young lovers who looked so sure that they'd never need more than each other?

They reached the turnoff onto Bluff Road shortly after four o'clock. Mole had been dozing on and off for the last twenty minutes and didn't open his eyes to see where they were. When they drove beneath the bare-branched canopy of red oaks and onto the dirt drive leading to the Werner farm, he fell into a deeper sleep, lulled by the boat-like motion of the car. And when Sally stopped and turned off the engine at the point where the mud was furrowed with the deep ruts from her father's tractor, Mole murmured from the depths of his dream, shifting his torso, tucking his hand behind his own waist, hugging himself in sleep.

Wasn't it right and inevitable that her lover boy would sleep through the impending encounter? If only she were sleeping, too, and this visit was happening in some remote place in her mind, where memory could play its dirty tricks and turn the past into the present. It was the same house, unchanged by time, as decrepit as it had been, though no more, since she'd seen it last. It had the same shingle roof patched with tar, the same stained, peeling clapboard, the same sagging porch. And from the chimney came the same gray wisps, as if the old furnace had been burning and never stopped burning for the four years that she'd been gone.

With stringy briars blocking the view from the lower yard, it was possible that the car couldn't be seen from the downstairs windows of the house or from the barn. But someone upstairs in the house might be able to spot it and alert the rest of the family to the arrival of uninvited visitors. Soon the activity would pick up inside the house, one voice would call to another, and someone, Loden or Clem probably, would come marching down the drive to see what the intruder wanted.

Sally waited, taking breaths that were too shallow to sustain her, until she had to inhale sharply, drawing the whole rotting spirit of the place into her lungs. She watched the windows for signs of life. The brambles brushing the car were overgrown raspberry bushes, and they reminded her of gathering berries when she was a young child. She loved pressing open the thicket to uncover the best berries, lifting each berry with a slight twist of its stem, picking with such painstaking slowness that her mother used to send her older brother, Loden, out to scold her. But her mother knew that at the end, Sally's harvest would be perfect, the bucket filled to the brim with berries that weren't too green and weren't too ripe, their tender skin unbroken. That's why she was always the one chosen to do the picking.

A big, bottlenose fly living beyond its season and worn out by the cold bumped against the windshield looking for a way into the car. At the same time, a crow landed nearby and bounced along the mud ridge of the drive. It hopped sideways, cast a glance at Sally as if to make sure that she was following, and then hopped toward the house, wings folded tightly against its sides.

The quiet here was the quiet of emptiness, of abandonment. It was the quiet of the dream that Mole was dreaming in the passenger seat. It was the quiet of her own indecision as she sat there waiting to decide what to do, watching the house, wondering if she'd been wise to return, regretting that she hadn't sent a letter ahead to prepare her family. Despite the easy drive, they seemed so far away from where she sat, separated by the thick, oppressive silence. And yet how abruptly the silence was shattered when she opened the car door and swung it shut behind her.

She followed the crow for a few yards. As

she gained on it, the bird hopped faster and finally began trotting across the grass to get out of her way. She felt angry at the crow, as though she knew it had something to do with the ordeal awaiting her inside the house. She tried not to look beyond the house at the barn. She wanted only to go back to the car and drive away. But the rhythm of her approach was too strong to resist, her legs were carrying her up the steps and onto the porch, her hand was knocking on the door, her face was suddenly crimson hot, and with her sight momentarily blurred by a watery haze she wouldn't have recognized her sister Trudy if she didn't hear her voice, a sandy sort of growl that came from trying to contain her shriek in a whisper.

"Dear Lord, is it really? Oh, Sally! Where were you all this time, where have you been, why didn't you write, why did you go away, just go away like that, without saying good-bye?"

"I don't know" was all Sally could manage to reply, though that wasn't accurate. She did know why she ran away from home. Everybody knew why.

"Come inside, but don't . . . oh, shhh. We can't let the others know you're here, not yet, not until we have a chance to talk."

They had to squeeze through the narrow doorway of the foyer, across the hall, and into the small living room. Tru had gotten so much taller and rosier that the room seemed too small to contain her, too cluttered, with a fat box of a radio, Sally was surprised to notice, and a worn-out sofa that hadn't been there before. But there were no toys scattered about, no hobbyhorse or puzzle pieces indicating that there was a young child living in the house.

Tru said her name again, called her "my Sally," and threw her arms around her big sister, careening with her across the room. Sally wanted to ask about her child, but she couldn't get a word in as long as Tru was going on and on, repeating that she couldn't believe it, she couldn't believe it, here was her own Sally, she couldn't believe that just yesterday she'd put on a sweater that Sally had left behind, and now today here Sally was, under the same roof, her dear Sally, life hadn't been the same without her, everything was so serious, and she hadn't had a good laugh in who knew how long. But now here was Sally, and Tru couldn't believe it!

It was all said in the same growling whisper, for as much as she loved her very own big sister, she couldn't bring herself to tell the rest of the family that Sally had come home. She didn't have to tell them, for while they were spinning around in that dance of greeting, their brother Loden appeared in the doorway and stood watching them.

He cleared his throat loudly. The sisters stopped their hugging, separated, and stared back at him. It took a moment for Sally to realize that he was her older brother and not a younger, thinner version of her father, his hair a sandy red instead of gray, with long sideburns framing his face. She was about to reach for him, to touch him on the arm just as a gentle way of making sure that he was real. But when he pursed his lips, she cringed, for she was sure he was going to spit at her.

Instead of spitting, he said, "Hello there."

She said hello back.

He said, "You been gone awhile."

She nodded.

He asked Tru, "Did you ask her to come?"

Tru said, "No."

Loden said to Sally, "Well, why are you here?"

Tru said, "Shut up, Loden."

Loden repeated, "Why are you here?"

"Can't you guess?" It occurred to her that they might not want to let the boy meet his real mother. But she hadn't come all this way just to be disappointed, and she announced in a way that made it clear she wouldn't be defied, "I want to see my baby."

Loden shot Tru a fierce, silencing glance. Tru looked down at the floor. Loden asked flatly, "What baby?" — a question so unexpected that Sally was dumbstruck.

"What baby?" Loden asked again.

"My baby. I don't have to explain. I have something for him."

"What are you talking about? What's she talking about, Tru?"

Were they trying to fool her? Were they feigning ignorance, or could it be that the baby she'd left behind had disappeared before her brother and sister ever knew of his existence?

"Then let me talk to Mother."

"She's gone with Father to Aunt Lena's. There'll be a funeral soon. Aunt Lena's failing, though I doubt you much care."

"Of course I care. But I've come all this way to see my baby, and I'm not leaving until you tell me where he is."

"What baby?" Loden asked once more, with such implacable bafflement that Sally had to face the fact that he wasn't going to tell her where they'd hidden her baby. The Werner family was determined to pretend that Sally's child had never been born in the first place. And if he'd never existed, then neither had his mother. She who had made a career out of running away — she'd left behind all evidence that she'd ever lived, her past like the footprints she'd made in the snow when she was racing her little sisters. If she'd even had little sisters.

On your mark, get set —

Wait for me, Sally!

Running through the storm, had they done it once or twice or hundreds of times? Running against the slanting snow, running ahead and away, stopping at the fence to let Tru and Laura catch up. Stamp, stamp, stamping her feet to get the blood moving, and while she was waiting, thinking about what she wanted for Christmas.

Penny candy, a felt pony with glass eyes, and a doll's pie cupboard made of wood and tin. Hinky-dinky parlez-vous. This is the way we build a house, build a house, build a house. Funny to think that someday we'll be all grown up. I'll tell you about the man I'm going to marry. He'll have straight brown hair, gray eyes, he won't be too short or too tall, he'll play the banjo, and he'll always be stronger than the Sea Hag and her goons. Take that, umph, and that!

And then her cousin Daniel gunned the engine of his motorcycle, and she hung on for dear life.

Run, Sally!

Wretched Sally Werner.

And here she was back where she'd started, at the top of the slope of her life, her feet sliding out from under her.

"You poor girl." Tru caught her in her arms and held her upright. Sally wanted to call out for her mother. Instead, she said, "I'm fine," and left it at that, too stunned to say anything more, even to press the issue and demand to know what they'd done with her child. Tru's concern was too much for her. Loden's judgment was too harsh. The weight of the thick air made her weak. But she was still strong enough to separate herself from her sister and walk out of the room and out the front door. She wondered if they were waiting for her to change her mind and come back or at least call to them and say good-bye. But they must have known that Sally never said good-bye. She just squeezed her arm against her fat purse and left without telling her family where she was planning to go. And they didn't try to stop her as she walked out the door. They didn't come after her and weren't going to explain why there was a tricycle resting on the lawn below the porch, with the back end hidden by the corner of the house so only the front wheel was visible. Sally hadn't noticed it when she'd entered the house, but she noticed it as she left, and she knew what it meant: a tricycle meant that there was a young child nearby, a child the Werners were hiding from Sally.

"Where were you?" Mole asked. He'd moved to the driver's seat and had started the car as he'd seen Sally returning.

He wanted answers to his questions: Who lived here? And why had they driven all this way if they weren't going to stay for dinner? But Sally had nothing to tell him, other than to insist that they had to get out of there now.

Mole put the car in reverse, backed toward the fence, then shifted to drive, rolling the wheels over the muddy ruts. As he headed out to the road, Sally looked over her shoulder to take one last look and saw a crow perched on the gatepost, maybe the same crow that had been hopping ahead of her earlier. Its black eyes stared at nothing and it sat there so still that years later, whenever Sally thought about her last visit home, she'd forget that the crow had been alive and would picture it as a painted figurine fixed there, nailed in place. It had been there, she'd believe, for as long as she could remember.

■ ■ ■ ■

Coming from this direction, Sally wasn't sure whether to go left or right when they reached the second main intersection, but she pretended to be certain when she told Mole to turn left. Left was wrong, they began to suspect after they'd traveled along the road for a good twenty minutes without seeing any landmarks she recognized. When they passed a long stretch of meadow crowned on its rise with a boarded-up, decrepit old mansion, Sally knew they'd gone the wrong way. But Mole didn't complain; he just swooped the car around in a U-turn and headed back along the route toward Amity.

Sally closed her eyes for a while, trying to feel what Mole had felt when he'd let the bumping of the car lull him to sleep. But she couldn't sleep because Loden and Tru and the rest of her family, along with a little boy whose name she didn't know, were crowding her head, waiting for the opportunity to give her nightmares. Because of them, she'd never sleep again.

Mole was quiet, waiting for her to explain. She wanted to tell him something worthy, though she couldn't bring herself to tell him the truth. Instead, she hatched a story. She said that though she'd once told him before that her parents were living, in fact they'd passed away, her mother in '41, her father in '46. She was sorry she hadn't told him the truth, but the truth, she said, had been too hard to face. She'd wanted to pay a visit to the farm for old times' sake. Well, the new owners hadn't been welcoming — not very welcoming at all!

She was surprised by how easy it was to make up this new lie, so she kept right on lying, spinning one deception out of the web of another. She said that the new owners — the Haggertys, she named them on a whim — had been church friends with her parents, but they'd moved away. They came back to Tauntonville on holidays, and when they visited they always brought Sally a box of ribbon candy, yet now that they owned the farm, they pretended not to know her. They must have coveted the property all through the years her parents were alive, she said. Her father was still warm in his grave when the Haggertys bought the farm for next to nothing, with the help of a no-good lawyer. Sally had been too young to fight them in court. She'd grown up since then. She'd thought about finding a lawyer of her own and trying to win the farm back. Really, though, she didn't want to live on a dreary old farm in the middle of nowhere. That wasn't what she'd been born for.

The story roused Mole; he kept shaking his head and interrupting to tell Sally that she sure had been dealt a bad hand, and it was hard to tell a crook from a friend these days, and she shouldn't sit back and let others take advantage of her. No, she should claim what was rightfully hers.

Having taken a sharp turn into a gas station lot, he sealed his last statement with an emphatic cluck of his tongue and shut off the engine. While he was out chatting with the attendant, waiting for the tank to fill, Sally came up with a good reason to explain why the farm was worthless.

"The thing is, they started using some newfangled fertilizer, something Mr. Haggerty bought on discount, and it turns out they've gone and poisoned all their land," she said as Mole drove from the gas station. "The Haggertys won't have a harvest next year or ever again. Serves them right, huh?"

"I guess."

She'd thought he shared her indignation and was surprised by his noncommittal response. She wanted to ask him to say more. But he was too busy watching the road, searching the land as though there were something he expected to find.

"Looking for something?" she asked after a moment.

"Mmm" was all he said.

To their left, a wall of tall pines was black in the twilight; to their right, the empty fields were a gray blur. The occasional farmhouse seemed insubstantial, like a cardboard cutout. Front yards were cluttered with tires and hubcaps and the shells of burned-out cars — the kind of junk that would survive the people who lived there.

"Aha!" Mole said when he finally spotted the sign he'd been looking for. He was already turning into the lot as he announced, "Let's have dinner."

"Dinner," Sally echoed lamely. She didn't say, *I'm feeling miserable, and all you can think about is dinner?* She did exclaim with unnecessary anger when, stepping from the car, she stubbed the toe of her shoe against broken pavement. "Damn you!" she seethed, as if she blamed Mole for her stumble, though he was already ahead and holding open the door to the tavern.

Sitting across from him in a booth and watching him lick beer foam from his top lip with the tip of his tongue, she felt convinced that he was to blame for everything. It was his fault that she'd had to lie about her visit home. It was his fault that he didn't know the truth about her. If he'd been the kind of person who could read between the lines, he would have realized that Sally wasn't upset because she'd lost her parents and the farm. She was upset because all this time she'd been mistakenly thinking that she would see her child again.

It was Mole's fault for getting so worked up over the thought of barbecue ribs the attendant back at the gas station had called the best in the free world.

"I forgot to have lunch," he explained to the waitress, a girl who looked at least a couple of years younger than Sally, plump and rosy, with a great mound of bleached hair pulled back in a braid.

"I'll have the kitchen speed it up, honey."

"She called you honey," Sally said after the girl had disappeared through the swinging doors. Mole smiled, as though to indicate that he considered himself deserving. But he wasn't deserving. He was just ignorant.

It was his fault for not sensing that Sally was about to burst into tears. It was his fault that they were sitting in this dive with creaking benches and lime green walls and a revolving dessert case holding only one-third of a cream pie. It was his fault that when Sally tried to lift her glass, the bottom of it stuck to the Formica, the glass tipped, and some beer splattered.

Damn you.

She was using her napkin to wipe away the spill when the waitress came over and swirled her rag over the table, a handy action that Sally should have known was logical but in her unsettled state took on a vexing meaning, as if the girl were demonstrating for Mole's benefit how competent she was.

It was Mole's fault that Sally was left out and her suffering went undetected. It was his fault that if she didn't start sobbing soon, she'd start screaming. And it was his fault that he managed to remain oblivious to it all and could think of nothing else to do besides picking up a painted plywood game board from the table beside him. Sliding the board between them, he said, "Checkers?"

Oh, she was ready to transform her fury into action. She was ready to grab Mole by the collar and shake him until the fog cleared and he saw her for who she really was. But now that he knew his empty belly would soon be filled, he looked so pleased with himself that she couldn't help but envy him. He leaned back against the cushion of the bench, less in a swaggering way than in a manner that suggested guidance, offering his own example to Sally, proving that she, too, could be happy — at least as happy as Mole.

She moved a red piece. He moved a black piece. They continued playing, barely glancing up when the waitress delivered their food and then both hurriedly pulling their racks apart so they could each hold a rib in one hand while moving a checker piece with the other.

Mole was concentrating intently. Sally sensed that he was building up an offense along the right side of the board. She moved stealthily in from the left and after a couple of turns made a multiple jump, capturing two black pieces before he knew what had hit him.

"Just you wait," he said in warning.

He jumped her. She jumped him. They played and they drank, they ate and they played. The longer she concentrated on the game of checkers, the less Sally thought about her visit home. The less she remembered, the more she could savor the delicious immersion in the here and now, playing as if the sheer, teasing fun of the game were all that mattered.

She signaled to the waitress and ordered a

second pitcher of beer. They continued to play slowly, intently. There was nothing else going on in the world, no cause to worry about affairs they couldn't control. The game absorbed them, and beyond the board was a blur of lights and sounds and memories. It didn't matter who won or lost, only that they kept playing. And so they took their time, moving a piece only after a long pause spent pondering the options.

Eventually she'd gained three kings to his one. She was expecting to win at the end and wanted to delay the inevitable, so she made a simple move to stall. In response, Mole brought his own king back toward her offense, clacking the stack along a zigzag, claiming two of Sally's kings and a single piece with a triple jump!

She sputtered in disbelief. He offered to take back the move, but she insisted that it was fair and square. She didn't mind losing, she said. She didn't say that she wished the game would go on forever, though she wondered if he could guess what she was thinking as he stared at her over the rim of his glass.

His affection for her was like the beer — there was too much of it, and the more there was, the more she wanted, but the quantity made her head spin. She decided that she'd better set the story straight and match things to their names before it was too late. Mole might be wondering about the Haggertys, for instance. She should explain. But first she had to determine their connection to the disappearance of her baby. They'd taken him away, hadn't they, giving Sally justification to despise them? But they were in a made-up story. What, then, had they done with her baby? What baby? She felt as though years had passed since she'd last spoken with her brother and sister in the living room of her parents' house, and she couldn't remember all the details of the exchange. Had they even been speaking the same language? The conclusion she'd reached at the time seemed stupid and inexact to her now. She wished she'd stayed long enough to give herself something clear to understand in the aftermath.

Confusion made her thirsty. She took another sip of beer. Mole drank from his glass, his motion matching hers like a mirror reflection. She drank again just to see him do the same and then refilled her glass and his.

The beer was tasting better with every sip. It was also weakening her resolve and loosening her tongue. It had been so easy to tell him a lie about herself. Why wouldn't it be just as easy to tell him the truth?

"You want to know something?" she asked.

"That can't be right," he said.

She didn't understand his response and wondered if she should apologize peremptorily. But then she followed his gaze, turning to look over his shoulder at the wall clock, which had on its face the picture of a Jeep splashing through mud. The motto read "traction through action," and the second *h* was covered by the point of the hour hand.

"Aw geez," he said with a moan. "I told Phil I'd be back by six. He's gonna kill me. He's gonna squash me like I'm a worm." He thumped his fist on the table to demonstrate. "A goddamn worm. Hey, miss, can I have the check? Excuse me, hey, miss!"

The waitress was sitting on a stool behind the cash register dipping a french fry into ketchup. She nodded to the bartender, a fat, bald, lugubrious man, who plodded over with the check and after setting the slip on the table turned his back and belched into his fist. The waitress kept eating her french fries, lost in her daydream. It was a strange place, Sally thought. Everything seemed out of sync and yet deliberate. She looked hard at Mole to try to gauge what he was thinking, but he was busy fishing in his wallet for money. He left a five-dollar bill to cover the three-dollar cost, explaining to Sally that he didn't want to wait for change.

At the tavern door they discovered it was raining in torrents. They held hands and ran across the gravel lot, but they were already soaked by the time they reached the car. Slipping in on either side, slamming the doors behind them, they forgot their haste and dove, as though on cue, into each other's arms. They began pecking at each other, their kisses broken up by bursts of absurd giggles, their cheeks slick from the rain, their hands fumbling to find a way in through their wet coats.

With lips and tongues, they traded hot spice from the ribs along with the sweet aftertaste of beer. Mole's hand slid inside the elastic waist of Sally's pants and moved toward her crotch. The damp inside her body warmed the cold damp of the surface of her skin. They couldn't get out of their coats fast enough. They rubbed and dipped, bumping against the steering wheel, kissing and caressing, forgetting the public setting in pursuit of their private pleasure until the raking headlights of a pickup truck turning into the tavern lot reminded Mole that they were late, he had responsibilities, and they were far from Helena, where a fuming Phil was waiting to flatten his little brother.

Sally tilted her head. Mole fit his mouth against her neck, just below her chin, for one last greedy kiss before pulling away. With the sluggishness of a couple awakened in the middle of the night, they smoothed and tucked themselves back into order.

Mole drove north, slowly at first, then faster and faster through the downpour. Sally loved the sensation of flying effortlessly, chasing the headlight beams while the wipers flicked away the streaming rain. Though she was dizzy from too much beer, she felt safe, anchored by her trust in Mole. She was impressed with his agility as he maneuvered the car around sharp curves and over the peaks of hills. He seemed entirely capable, confident, even fearless — not at all the awkward boy who had nearly put a bullet in his head by accident back at the Helena mill. Why, he knew the difference between above and beyond, between a will and a way. Lordy, there they go, galumph, galumph, around the sharp turn at a breakneck pace. It sure felt swell to be going so fast. The past would never catch up to Sally at this rate. She could at least try out the belief that her family had released her from the consequences of her actions, and she was free to follow her own design, never having to answer for something that others insisted didn't even happen, never having to wake from the dream of their denial, never going back, the circle never coming around, the remnants of what couldn't be helped washed away by the pouring rain, worry soothed by the swish, swish of the wipers, headlights gleaming, and the whole future waiting for her to catch up.

Wasn't she a lucky girl to have found a boy as fine as Mole? According to those who knew better, she didn't even have the right to insist on the reality of her experience. But thanks to Mole, she could relish the thrilling, becalming gift of love. Thanks to Mole, experience was as precise as a checkerboard, the game never ending. Like her father used to say: behold the glory. What once had splendor has no splendor at all because of the splendor that surpasses it — something like that. Nonsense making perfect sense in the absence of the truth. That's how it should be, life announcing itself with a juicy *burrrp*. Laughter and adventure and the sheer fun of being propelled through space and time, away from all her troubles, fast and faster and too fast to see —

That devil of a car, that fancy green stub-finned Cadillac soaring over the bump of the hill's summit as if it owned the world, crossing the line into the northbound lane and forcing Mole to jerk the wheel to the right to avoid a collision, sending the Pontiac off the road, the front right wheel dipping into a narrow gulch and the forward momentum causing the left wheels to lift into the air, the car turning over, crashing onto its top with a great bump that wrenched open the passenger door and catapulted Sally out onto the slope as the car continued to roll down, thumping toward the river, coming to rest, wheels jammed in the mud of the riverbank, the engine's whir sputtering out, the swollen Tuskee rushing north while up on the road Benny Patterson realigned his Cadillac to the southbound lane and sped on through the rain.

Something was supposed to happen next. What? Following from therefore and whence. How easily we forget. In other words. Just think, think, think. If, then. Oh, of course, why not?
Hello, Sally.
Tell Sally it's time to get up.
She couldn't hear anything, not even the clatter of rain and the shushing of the paper

reeds and the bubbling of the swollen river. Deep within her, though, she felt the imminence of the next thing. There would always be a next thing, until it was over. It wasn't until it was, and never everywhere. Here, there was mud that smelled of mint and the taste in her mouth of that awful milk from cows after they'd grazed in a pasture infested with oniongrass.

Sally, finish up and clear the table.

Wash the dishes.

Sweep the floor.

Swish, swish.

Hurry up, Sally!

She can't hear you.

Dreamin' a dream of no return.

Good-bye, Sally.

Aw, let's give her another chance.

Repent!

Rejoice!

"Oh."

Shhh.

What's going on?

She's waking up!

Drenching rain convincing her that she would only ever be cold, as cold as she was now, for the rest of eternity. Eye to eye with the rotting tuber of a duckweed wrapped in the knotted string of horsehair worms. Gross. Where was she? In the reeds. Why?

Because.

Hello, Sally.

Oh, her aching head.

Seen from below, plumes of cane brushed the heavy clouds, painting them gray. There was no sky beyond, no space, only layer after layer. It hurt to keep her eyes open. She preferred the dark behind closed lids, where here was there. But listen . . . someone was at the door.

Knock, knock.

Who's there?

Think, Sally.

It hurt too much to think. It hurt too much to cry, to gulp, to breathe, to wonder about anything.

It helped to hear, though, beyond the rain, or between it, the sound of the river. Why, she recognized that sound! She knew it from another time. She couldn't remember when, exactly, but she would never forget it. At first she was reminded of the rustling that a piece of cellophane made when it blew loose from the top of a bowl. But that wasn't right. She told herself that she must be patient. She must let the mist of recognition clear of its own volition, wisp by wisp, like notes of a melody — debris swirling, then the water rushing between soft banks, dislodged stones overturning, ravines eroding, moss thickening, time passing with the current of the Tuskee.

The Tuskee!

Of course it was the Tuskee. As long as she heard the river, then she wasn't lost. Comforted by this awareness, she closed her eyes again and let herself drift away from the feeling of cold and the dull aching of her body all over and the rain that would never let up. It was easier to think of nothing.

Sally?

Sally Werner!

She's gone.

She'll be back.

When she awoke again, it was close to dawn and the bottom of the black cloudbed was streaked with a metallic gray. The storm had passed, though drops still flew through the air, blown with the gusts off the soaked cane. Hundreds of crows roosting in the woods across the river made a racket, silencing any other wintering birds that might have wanted to greet the dawn.

Sally sat up and held her head in her hands, shivering, trying to will the ache away. She sat there like that for a long while, long enough for the crows to fly off and the sky to brighten enough so that a rich, promising blue could be seen between cracks in the clouds. She had no idea where she was. So much didn't make sense to her right then that she didn't even try to gather her scattered bits of memory into a single understanding. She preferred to put off the effort for as long as she could.

Slowly, the aching began to relent a little. She clenched her fists to fight the numbness in her fingertips. She rubbed her bruised legs. She opened her eyes and at first perceived the dense cane around her as the locked gate of a trap — somehow she'd been able to find her way into the center, but she'd never be able to find her way out. That thought was enough to motivate her to stand on wobbly legs and get moving.

She had no broken bones, though she felt sore everywhere. Her head hurt worst of all, and she suspected that the mat of her hair above one ear was wet with blood, though none came away on her hands. She had a vague sense that she was lucky to be alive. Yet with her thoughts still bunched up in a knot, she didn't connect her current predicament with its cause and didn't remember the accident.

She pushed her way through the thick reeds, heading down the slope in the direction of the river. She was surprised when she stepped forward and her foot sank ankle-deep in mud. Pulling free, she stepped around the muck and reached a rock outcrop above the river. She saw that the moss was thick along the sloping sides of the rock. She planted her feet carefully in the uneven grooves, balanced, and looked out over the broad expanse of the Tuskee.

The water flowed directly beneath her, through a channel cut out of the rock. The breeze carried the Tuskee's familiar smell of sour mud. The sky seemed to grow brighter as she stood there, and with the light her thoughts started to untangle, giving her a vague feeling of premonition, though she also had enough awareness to know that the important thing about to happen had already happened, and that's why she was standing there bruised, cold, and alone.

She stared idly at the river, waiting for nothing, watching twigs and leaves swirl over the surface, beneath a veil of steam fog. She watched the debris piling up against the branches of a toppled elm and then spinning around it, dragged by the force of the current. Sally was impressed by the power of the river, which proved far stronger than the barrier formed by the elm. For a moment she seemed to sense the surge of the river in the wind, and she felt as though being above the surface was no different from being below. She took a deep breath to remind herself that she wasn't drowning. And then she remembered Mole.

She set out in search of him, thrashing through the reeds along the riverbank, calling out to him, following her voice as it disappeared into the silence. The air was raw and empty, and she had the feeling that multitudes of birds hidden in the trees were watching her, waiting for her to leave. But she wouldn't leave until she found Mole. Really, though, it was his responsibility to find her, not the other way around. She would have concluded that he'd intentionally abandoned her if she wasn't so certain that he loved her. It comforted her to think about this. Mole would be worried about her right now and at the same time racked with guilt. He hadn't meant to leave her behind. He'd spend the rest of his life trying to make it up to her, while she'd spend the rest of her life assuring him that he wasn't to blame.

When she spotted the car sitting at a tilt just a few feet above the river, she was more puzzled than anything else, for she couldn't understand why the same car that had been traveling at such a high speed not long ago was now so perfectly still and quiet. Or why Mole, slouched in the driver's seat, didn't get up and get out of there, why, since he sat with his back to Sally as she approached, he didn't turn, why he didn't hear her through the shattered window, why his neck was bent and his head hung back at an odd angle, why, though his eyes were open, all that remained of their green were thin rims around expansive blackness, why, when she reached in to touch him, his skin was so waxy and cold, why he didn't answer when she called, why any of this was offering itself to her perception as a real experience, in real time. Well, it wasn't anything she'd been prepared for, not in a thousand years. And her sense of having been caught by surprise made her so frantic that she could only perceive the next action to follow the last out of sheer necessity.

She climbed into the car through the open passenger door and searched until she found her purse lying on the floor beneath the seat, covered with splintered glass. Then, because she believed she had no choice, she left Mole behind and went for help, even though she knew he was beyond help.

Somehow she managed to scramble up the steep slope, tearing through brush that reeked of gasoline. Somehow she managed to find the road and flag down a mail truck. When the driver, a gaunt, gray-bearded postman, signaled to her to convey that he was deaf, she began to wail. And though she wailed for the whole ten miles to the nearest town, the old man didn't seem to mind.

Martin Oliver Langerton was buried in the Hopewell Cemetery in Helena; Sally saw his family for the first and only time at the funeral service, and then they wouldn't acknowledge her. She understood why they blamed her for Mole's death. They had a right to blame her. She'd been a bad influence in all sorts of ways. She'd kept him out past midnight when he had to go to Fenton the next day. She'd been drinking with him on the day of the accident. That Mole hadn't ever introduced her to his family was proof that he'd known she was a bad sort and his family wouldn't approve of her.

Everyone disapproved of her in Helena. The other mourners wouldn't speak to her after the funeral service. Mole's friends, the ones she'd seen playing that dangerous game at the mill, wouldn't come near her. A few days later, when she went to purchase shampoo at the five-and-dime, the clerk pretended that she couldn't make change for a five-dollar bill, and she advised Sally to buy her shampoo someplace else. When she accompanied Gladdy to the Barge one night, the bartender ignored her. Mrs. Mellow met her at the door when Sally arrived for work. She told her that she wouldn't be needing a typist for the foreseeable future and handed her an envelope with a month's pay. And Gladdy, who at first made an unconvincing show of trying to comfort Sally "in her tearful sorrow," as Gladdy put it, made it clearer than ever that she didn't want her around. She kept saying that she would be packing up and moving to Florida any day now and told Sally to start looking for other accommodations.

Sally had every intention of leaving Helena, though for a long while, she couldn't bring herself to go. Helena had been Mole's home, and she preferred to stay as near to his memory as possible. But she knew she had to leave. She was just so afraid of being alone, and even Gladdy Toffit, in all her drunken indifference, seemed better company than no one at all.

On a gray Saturday morning at the end of January, she woke up, dressed, boiled water to make herself a cup of Nescafé. After she discovered that there was no milk in the refrigerator, she decided to walk the half mile to the market at the gas station.

When she returned, she found Gladdy's door locked. She wondered if she'd locked the door behind her. She knocked loudly, first on the door, then on Gladdy's bedroom window, until she noticed that the car was gone from the driveway. She waited on the porch for an hour or more and finally went to the Barge. The tavern was closed, but she met the bartender, who had come down from his apartment on the second floor and was sitting on the steps smoking a cigarette. She asked him if he'd seen Gladdy, and he said she'd moved to Florida.

"Where in Florida?"

"Florida is all I know," he said, tossing away his cigarette. He might as well have told her that it was her turn to get out of there.

Back at Gladdy's house, Sally smashed a pane in the back vestibule door with a stick and was able to reach in and turn the lock. Inside the house, she became aware of the heavy feeling of abandonment and an oppressive cold. She turned up the thermostat but didn't hear the surge of the furnace starting up, so she went to check it in the basement and discovered that it wasn't firing. She tried to light it manually but couldn't get a flame going and gave up.

Instead of packing her few belongings and leaving on the next bus out of town, Sally moved her things into Gladdy's bedroom and made herself at home. With the furnace out of oil, the house grew brutally cold over the course of the day, but Sally turned on the electric oven, opened the door to spread the heat, and wrapped herself in some extra clothes Gladdy had left behind — a thick flannel robe, flannel pajamas, wool socks.

It was her right to stay there, she told herself. She couldn't be expected to leave without having somewhere else to go. Besides, Gladdy was lucky to have her remain, for without the extra warmth from the oven, the pipes would have frozen and cracked, flooding the house. There would have been a terrible mess.

A brief, unseasonable thaw the following day made the house more tolerable. Sally put on an old denim dress she found in Gladdy's closet, something that probably had once belonged to the daughter, and she hauled in wood from a dingy woodpile behind the garage. She kept the fire going all evening and then relit it the next morning, comforted by the crackling as much as by the warmth. She cooked herself meals on the stovetop, and after the electricity was shut off she made sandwiches, ate vegetables cold from their cans, and at night read by a lantern fueled with kerosene she bought at the store.

She lived like that, alone in Gladdy's house, for far longer than she would have thought possible. She cried often, though only when there was no one around to hear her. In town, she put on a show of calm. People started to treat her with casual acceptance. Somehow weeks added up to months. By the spring she began showing up at the Barge regularly in the evenings, and she took to drinking with a newfound thirst. The booze made her chatty, and the men gathered around her as they used to gather around Gladdy, trading jokes and competing for her laughter. She would focus on one and then another, happy for the conversation, and sometimes she'd spend part of the evening dancing. Closing her eyes as she swayed in their embraces, she'd imagine them each as a different version of Mole — Freddy Mole and JJ Mole and Billy Mole.

Though she liked each of them because, in different ways, they helped distract her, she never brought a man home, not for a long while. Not until she met the fellow in the plaid suit who introduced himself to her at the Barge, with a clink of his glass, as

Bennett, but who turned out to be Benny Patterson, the famous cream-cheese prince. He was the only one she invited back to Gladdy's.

He'd breezed into town on a Saturday night looking for fun and had decided, after meeting Sally, to stick around for a while. He was wide in girth and voice, the boom of his greeting filling the room, his belly filling his shirt and stretching apart the cloth between the lower buttons. Pools of liquid gray filled the slits of his grinning eyes, and his blond curls made a floppy halo. He was big and loud and impossible to ignore. And he used his merry mood as a charm, winning Sally over with his teasing ways, convincing her to trust him enough to buy her a drink and then to buy her another.

"Angel!" he bellowed in echo after she'd told him her name. And while she watched him over the lip of her glass, he called into the crowd at the Barge, "You boys, you have an angel in your midst! A real live angel! How come this ain't national news?" And then he said in a quieter, silkier voice, "Miss Sally Angel. Why, you're something else."

She was something else. Did she believe it? Not quite. But she had the sense, mistakenly or not, she couldn't tell at first, that

243

there was a worshipful quality to his affection, and in this single way he seemed more like Mole than anyone else she'd met in Helena.

But the real lure of him for Sally was in the gamble. Though he didn't reveal much information about himself, he had an insistent manner and implied that she had to make her choice about him quickly. He wasn't a man who would let himself be strung along. It was now or never. Either she followed through or she gave up the possibility of ever getting to know him any better. Without putting any of this explicitly, he offered her an ultimatum, making the opportunity seem tantalizing and the timing urgent.

In the six months since Mole's death, Sally had come to think of loneliness as an aspect of herself, inescapable and defining; she really wasn't so different from a woman who'd been widowed after fifty years of marriage. Having lost the boy she loved, she expected to be mourning him for the rest of her life.

But here was Benny Patterson to prove that she didn't have to stay lonely forever. Sally could almost persuade herself that he'd been sent by Mole to deliver her from her loneliness, or at least she could hope that Mole wouldn't mind if she tried out an alternative ending to the story that had begun for her in Helena.

Back at Gladdy's, in Gladdy's own bed, Benny Patterson covered Sally so completely that she couldn't see past him and couldn't raise her head to see their reflection in the mirror above the bureau. The weight of his body was in itself a comfort, and the fragrance of his skin — cigarettes and sweat and a faint scent of glycerin combined — made him seem worldly and important. He moved decisively, obviously confident in his knowledge of physical pleasure.

They slept through the next morning until noon. Like Sally, Benny Patterson had no place he had to be, no responsibilities or schedules to follow; if he was telling the truth, there were foremen to oversee the workers on his family's farm, and he didn't even have to show up for meals.

Sally wasn't convinced that he was telling the truth. In fact, as she observed him over the next few days, she perceived something furtive in his sweetness. And then over breakfast their fourth morning together, after she'd poured his coffee and spilled some drops on his lap, he thrashed his arm in sudden rage, smacking the back of his hand hard against her chin. He was immediately full of remorse. He was sorry, so sorry, he hadn't meant to hit her. Would she ever forgive him? Sure, she said. How could she blame him for something he hadn't meant to do?

She watched him more carefully after that and noticed that he had a habit of suddenly shaking his head, as though trying to empty it of an unwanted thought. Or maybe he was just prone to sudden bouts of irritableness, without motive or depth. She wasn't really sure what to think about him. But she didn't need to trust him. In fact, she preferred not to trust him and to enjoy his bulky body without worrying about his intentions. Just by filling so much space, he distracted her from her grief.

He stayed with Sally at Gladdy's house for five nights altogether. The lack of electricity in the house amused him. Everything amused him. Sally didn't lie to herself about the potential of this romance: whatever they had going on between them didn't add up to much. It would be a brief chapter in both their lives. And yet it was this, the very brevity of the affair, that made her desire something permanent to take away with her and gave an intensity to her recklessness. She'd already lost so much in her life. But she wasn't yet twenty-two. She felt her youthfulness more strongly than ever when she lay with Benny Patterson. And because she was still young, she deserved a second chance.

On the sixth afternoon Benny offered to take her driving in his green Cadillac wherever she wanted to go. She carried the purse containing all of Mason Jackson's money, along with the few dollars she had left of the pay from Mrs. Mellow. She asked Benny to drive to the town of Fenton, which had its own department store. It made him proud to dole out money for a beautiful girl, and he didn't hold back. He bought her a bottle of French perfume and a necklace of freshwater pearls, and as he was paying the clerk he winked at Sally, communicating to her his anticipation at the thanks he expected when they returned to Gladdy's.

They headed over to the Woolworth's next and ordered milk shakes at the coffee counter. While they were waiting to be served, Sally excused herself to go to the ladies' room. She lingered at the back of the store, watching Benny as he took out his fancy gold-plated lighter to light his cigarette. The flame failed to rise, and he jammed his thumb on the lever repeatedly, his upper lip curling in a sneer, his teeth gritting, his whole face bunching and turning a hot, furious red.

Sally would never know that it was Benny Patterson in his Cadillac who had forced Mole off the road. She didn't need to know. The image of the cream-cheese prince sitting there trying to force the flame from his lighter was enough for her to admit to herself the truth she'd been avoiding: it was plain that he hadn't smacked her by accident, and he would do it again. She'd be better off without him. And even if he didn't feel the same about her, he would feel it sooner or later. They'd be miserable if they stayed together. And so it was a welcome coincidence when, in the ladies' room, she looked out the window and spotted a Northway bus drawing up to the stop beyond the store's awning.

She made it outside just as the driver was closing the doors. She ran along the sidewalk, calling for him to wait. He opened the doors for her, and she fumbled in her purse for money to buy a ticket to, to, to . . . She couldn't think straight and couldn't come up with the name of any place she wanted to go. The best she could do, finally, was to spit out "Rondo," the name of a place that didn't exist.

"What's that?" the driver asked. "Rondo," she repeated stupidly, desperate to escape before Benny Patterson realized that she wasn't coming back.

"Rondo it is," said the driver, to her amazement — or that's what she thought she heard him say. "Three dollars seventy-five cents, please and thank you," he added. Sally counted the money into the box. When the driver pulled the lever to shut the doors, she felt weak enough to faint right there in the aisle, but somehow she managed to make her way to a seat.

She gazed out the window at a lanky young man pedaling on a bike, racing the bus. She wondered where the bus was taking her, where Rondo was — the real Rondo and not the place she'd made up. She thought about Gladdy Toffit's cold, dreary, abandoned house in Helena. She thought about Benny Patterson waiting for her at the coffee counter. She was relieved that she'd never see him again.

The bus went straight through the town's last intersection while the man on the bicycle made a wide, arcing turn to the right. Sally stared as he lifted his feet from the pedals and glided down the street, enjoying, she assumed, a sensation that was close to flying.

As the bus picked up speed, she decided that after all she'd been through, she deserved a new name. She settled on a name that she believed would last for the rest of her life. She kept repeating it to herself so she'd get it straight the first time she had to say it aloud: *Sally Mole, Sally Mole, Sally Mole.*

May 3, 2007

For years I've used this cheap slab of plywood as my desk. It's wide enough to absorb the clutter. Along with the screen and keyboard, there's a pen, a crumpled tissue, a yarn coaster knitted by my boyfriend's mother, a glass paperweight in the shape of a heart, a bottle of clear nail polish, a pad of yellow Post-its, an envelope with a bill to be paid, and all 2,664 pages of *Webster's Third New International Dictionary.*

Outside, the mail carrier slides the door to his truck closed and crosses the street, reaching into his duffel to take out a package as he approaches the house next door. On the house's brick side facing our apartment, there's a shadow play going on — mottled, shifting shapes from the silver maple's wavering branches. A passing car is reflected in the glass of the neighbor's kitchen window, slipping in and out of view. Their azaleas are in bloom, the rhododendrons swollen, ready to pop, and their lawn, groomed by landscapers, is a bright, pure green.

It seems strange that the dire escalations on the other side of the world aren't registered here; there's no smoke in the air, no blood spray speckling the sidewalk. We take this calm for granted. Spaces are wide in this region, buildings are low, most families carry more debt than they'll ever be able to pay off in their lifetimes. There's little here that would be worth the risk of an attack, though at the same time I'd wager that there's nothing not worth the risk of a story.

The ladybug bumping against my windowpane, trying to get in.

A woman in sweats pushing a stroller along the sidewalk.

The wail of a siren in the distance.

The words hoarded in this box of a machine, along with all the dubious information available at the touch of a key.

It was in one of the neglected, asphalt-shingled houses by the train tracks on the other side of the city where I assume I was conceived, over in the Maplewood neighborhood or maybe in Edgerton or Dutchtown — in a rented room, in the dark secrecy of an August night, a freight train laboring

252

along behind the house, silt swelling the cracks between the floorboards, cigarette burns scarring the rugs.

In the one photograph I have of my parents together, a fading Polaroid from 1974, they're sitting facing each other, surrounded by their friends, at a picnic table cluttered with empty beer bottles. But when I imagine them alone together, I picture a satin sky outside the window, the curtains wafting, the chugging of a freight train filling the room along with the rattling and knocking of the headboard. And in the cave of sheets, pure happiness, a man and a woman rediscovering the potentials of their bodies and confirming that what they'd already experienced with each other the previous month and the month before could be found and repeated and still enjoyed as if for the first time.

I know from my mother that my father wasn't her first sexual partner, but he was the one she considered her first real love. He was the one who wanted to be sure that she was satisfied every step of the way, with whispers that must have been as tantalizing as his stroking fingers.

How does it feel? Do you like it?
Mmm, that's all right . . .
Baby Doll and *Buster Boy,* they took to call-

253

ing each other behind the closed door, probably in jest at first, or maybe in an attempt
to slow the momentum of their emotions
with some foolishness because they would
already have started to sense without saying
it that such a heady rush toward love, into
love, was perilous.

But doesn't it feel good when I —
And I —

They hadn't bothered to consider legiti-
mizing their connection with a formal
engagement. They believed that the freedom
to experience love without commitment,
without obligation, was essential if they were
going to enjoy a future together. But even
more powerful than the indulgence of
freedom was the sense that in each other
they'd found their reward, which they'd
earned simply through the hard work of
spending their entire childhoods apart,
unaware of each other's presence. How was
it possible that they both had been in the
world for so long, and neither one had
known of the other's existence? In the midst
of their infatuation, they became convinced
that they were meant for each other, it
couldn't be any other way. If they'd suffered
loneliness through their earlier years, it was
part of the necessary preface to their happiness. They had to suffer in order to recog-

nize the value of what they'd found in each other, with each other.

Surely they didn't mind that dingy setting — the sheets' scratchy cotton, the stifling air in the room, the thin mattress, the noise of the trains. And even if they hadn't bothered to eat dinner beforehand, they wouldn't have been distracted by hunger. They'd eat each other, nibble and drink to the point of satiation and beyond, awakening after a sleepy pause to their desire, which would have seemed as fresh as ever. Baby Doll and Buster Boy, as oblivious to their surroundings as fairy-tale children lost in the woods.

They weren't children in legal terms. They were both registered voters, old enough to drink and get drunk, old enough to hold jobs and report their income to the IRS. He was a graduate of the state university in Buffalo, while she was a student at a small college downstate. Given the troubles both experienced in childhood, they liked to say to each other that they'd been around the block. And yet I can see in the photograph that there's an innocent carelessness visible on the smooth skin of their faces, along with a vague expression of hope, as though they know they're deserving and are patiently waiting for their reward.

They were each other's reward, these

255

sloppy, ragged spirits, long hair — his tinged strawberry, hers more auburn — cut in a straight line across the middle of their backs, he with the wisps of a red beard, she with rhinestone baubles dangling from her ears, he with the pocket of a dimple on his right cheek, she with a dimple on her left. And how about this: according to my mother, they discovered that they'd both gone back to see *Five Easy Pieces* a second time the week it was released because of that one great scene, when Jack Nicholson jumps up on that flatbed truck in a traffic jam and plays the piano. They also found out that they both liked to watch *The Dating Game,* along with Minnie Pearl in *Hee Haw.* And they both knew all the words to "Psychedelic Shack" by the Temptations.

Psychedelic Shack, that's where it's at, oh yeah.

As they got to know each other better, they discovered other similarities. They both loved to laugh at bad jokes, to gargle with whiskey, to smoke a bong, to play shortstop, to ride the Jack Rabbit at Seabreeze and scream until they were hoarse, to fall asleep listening to music on headphones, and to dive into a cold lake on a hot day. Thanks to luck and destiny, they'd found each other in the crowd, and here they were, in one of the dingy rooms he rented by the month. She rested her head on his chest, listened to the thumping of his heart while he held her hand with his, bringing her fingertips to his mouth to taste her salty skin again. The sound of the passing train as it slowed down on its approach to a crossroad reminded them that they were captives of time, rousing in both of them a premonition of the weeks they'd be apart while he was driving his company's van in its zigzag route across the country and she was at school.

To have to wait so long to move in together struck them as one of the many unfair consequences of being poor. They had no say over the responsibilities assigned to them and so they were left to drift toward the melancholy close of this scene, drawing together once more before she had to go back to the house where she still lived during school breaks with her mother, my grandmother Sally, who at that late hour would have been lying awake in her own bed, waiting for the creak of the door to signal that her daughter was safely at home.

And I was waiting, too — waiting in the deep darkness of insentient potential for the strands to touch and stick and braid together in an inextricable knot.

SALLY MOLE

Step into the boat delicate barefoot tipping this way and that don't lose your balance you can stand or sit there that's better sit and feel the river swells tip with the river swells sit and float and wave good-bye gently bobbing in a boat without oars no oars in a boat you can't stop from gliding or the river from flowing you're not God after all you're just a young woman without oars in a boat turning around and around on a warm day sun on your face on the river your river like home if you had a home it would be this the banks farther away than you could throw a stone but close enough to see all the different greens of pine and melon and grass and waxy sumac on a sunlit afternoon you just a woman a young woman in a boat thinking what will be will be it's not your fault no more than being born just a young woman in a boat without oars gliding turning drifting as the river widens and the current slows and still the boat moves across the flat water somehow the forest shrinking to a solid line until it's too far away to see only the hot sun beating down and a slight wind dying and the slow gliding motion taking you farther from shore gentle tipping turning cool water at your toes wiggling toes water seeping through the shell that should be made of wood but now that it's too late you see is made of straw a boat made of straw whoever heard of a boat made of straw adrift in the middle of a lake in the middle of the day the water rising seeping turning to a steady trickle that will eventually submerge you a young woman in a boat a straw boat a sinking straw boat without oars.

Cold water rising.

Soggy straw unraveling.

Land nowhere in sight.

Look at the fix you've gotten yourself into this time, Sally.

Well, she was sure glad she knew how to swim.

"Oh!" She gasped, sputtered, coughed up a lungful of sour lake water. Blinked. Sputtered some more. "Oh."

"You been dreaming?" The question came from a girl in the seat next to her. As the girl grinned, she pressed the tip of her tongue through the gap between her front teeth.

"Mmm," Sally murmured, shaking her head to clear the fog of sleep.

"Was it a bad dream?" the girl asked. She was too old, at least sixteen, Sally judged, to be so forward with a stranger. Her question invited an insulting answer. Really, though, she didn't look like the kind who was easily insulted. With her crooked smile, a band of blotchy freckles crossing the bridge of her pug nose, her hair a mess of brown curls, a comic book open on her lap, she looked as though she expected the whole world to be nice to her.

When she'd given Sally long enough to reply, the girl offered, "I had a dream once." Her front teeth came down on her lower lip, and she chewed thoughtfully while Sally stared.

"You've only ever had one dream?" Sally asked.

"Yep."

"In your whole life?"

"Yep."

"What did you dream?"

"I dreamt I was throwing my Nestor a flake of hay, and he opened up his mouth and talked to me."

"Who's Nestor?"

"My Appaloos'."

The bus creaked as it slowed for a traffic light. Turning to look over the back of the seat, Sally saw two new passengers in addition to the girl. She must have slept right through at least one stop. She had no idea how long she'd been traveling, though the cramps in her neck and legs probably meant that she'd been on the bus for at least a couple of hours.

"Don't you want to know what he said?" the girl asked.

"Who?"

"Nestor, my Appaloos'."

"Your horse?"

"Where you from? My guess is Canada."

"Pennsylvania."

"Well, I was close."

"Not that close." Sally said this harsher than she'd meant it. The girl looked down and seemed to be considering the remark. Then she rolled up her comic book and tucked it in her pocket. She shook two cigarettes from a box. Sticking them both in her mouth, she struck a match, lit them, and handed one to Sally. After smoking thoughtfully for a few minutes, the girl said, "Nestor, he started tearing at his hay and then he stopped and looked at me. He gave a little snort. And he said one word."

"Really?" Sally asked. "Your horse can talk?" She felt a little bit of interest and a lot of impatience.

"Sure, my horse can talk. And there's a blue elephant driving the bus. What do you take me for? My oh my, lady. It was a dream!"

The girl stared past Sally, watching the activity in the street while the bus approached its next stop. "Where you headed?" she asked after a few minutes.

"Rondo."

The girl considered this. "We're in Tuskee," she said quietly.

"Where's Tuskee?"

The girl's expression flashed from incredulity to acceptance, as though in an instant she'd judged Sally to be a harmless idiot and that was that. She gestured out the window, indicating, *There, that's where Tuskee is.* Then she crushed her cigarette beneath her shoe and stood, reaching to lift a beat-up vinyl suitcase from the overhead rack.

"I'll be seeing you," she said abruptly.

"Hey," Sally called as the girl moved awkwardly down the aisle, holding her suitcase in front of her. "You didn't finish your story. What did your horse say? What was the word?"

"Tomorrow."

At first Sally thought the girl was promising to tell her later, tomorrow. But then, as she watched other passengers line up, she realized *tomorrow* was the word the horse had spoken, in a dream. She pondered that as the driver opened the doors.

The girl was the first to exit. Out on the sidewalk, she turned to look at the bus, raising her free hand to wave, and bumped into an oncoming woman who'd been walking hunched over. The fringe of a green shawl hung down below the woman's waist, reminding Sally of a similar shawl that her sister Tru used to wear to church. She'd twisted her brown hair in a bun, the way Tru wore hers. She limped away from the freckled girl, and as she did, she raised her head just enough for Sally to see the features and recognize her sister.

Trudy Werner! It was her own Tru, come to wherever they were all the way from home. And wouldn't you know, as Sally pulled up in a Northway bus, Tru just happened to be walking by. Oh, the good grace behind coincidence! Dear Tru. There was so much Sally wanted to ask her, so much she hadn't gotten a chance to say the last time they'd seen each other. Without Loden or the rest of the family to censor her, Tru would tell Sally what had happened to her son. Even if someone else was raising him, Sally bet that her sister was keeping an eye on the boy, making sure that he got proper care and affection. She must have been dying to tell her all about him that day Sally had appeared at the farm. Maybe Tru had left home in search of her and that's why she was out on the street. Maybe she was looking for her sister right at that moment.

Sally grabbed her purse and rushed into the aisle. The same doors that had almost closed her out and kept her from entering the bus almost kept her from leaving.

"Please! I'm getting off here," she said to the driver.

"Here," he echoed flatly.

"Yes."

He opened the doors. She leaped from the bottom step and ran past the freckled girl to her very own Tru, put a hand on her shoulder, whirled her around with a great exclamation of joy — and saw that the face belonged, in fact, to a stranger, a middle-aged woman who up close didn't look like Tru at all.

"Excuse me," Sally said, backing away. "I'm sorry. I thought you were my . . . someone . . . a friend. I'm sorry."

"Don't worry about it," the woman offered cheerily. "I hope you find her . . . your friend."

While Sally watched the woman continue down the sidewalk, the freckled girl from the bus approached. She murmured something Sally couldn't decipher. Sally murmured back, "What?"

The girl said softly, "This isn't Rondo."

"No?"

They stood in silence for a long moment. The girl set her suitcase on the sidewalk and scratched an itch behind her ear. She yawned, stretching out her arms. She rolled her shoulders to loosen the stiff muscles. And then she held up her hand, beckoning Sally to take in the scene around her — the line of storefronts, two newsstands on opposite corners of the intersection, cars coming and going, the bus disappearing down the street, belching exhaust, another bus approaching from the opposite direction.

"Welcome to Tuskee," she said, and Sally heard in her voice something not unlike the squeak of a rusty old iron gate swinging open.

The small city of Tuskee was more than big enough for Sally Mole. It had three drawbridges and a seven-story office building, along with a library, a small hospital, more bakeries than she could count, and several tailors, haberdasheries, laundries, and apothecaries. On North River Avenue there was even a shop specializing in watch repair. Sally was impressed. A city that had enough broken wristwatches in it to support a repair shop was of a different order from the other towns she'd passed through since leaving Tauntonville.

When the freckled girl introduced herself as Penny, Sally heard, *Benny. Benny? Who? What?* Ha, that was a funny gaffe! *Penny, not Benny,* had come to Tuskee to look for a job. She was from Bellona, a village notable for being the place where Henry Ford was once issued a speeding ticket. She was just a month shy of eighteen. She told Sally that she was in a hurry to get going with life. After selling her Appaloos' to her little sister for a dollar, she was ready for any adventure. She cared less about the money she would earn than the stories she would hear. She wanted to hear as much as she could before she got married.

She'd planned to stay with her uncle and his family, who lived just a few blocks from the bus station. When she found out that Sally was alone in Tuskee, without a place to stay, she declared that her aunt and uncle would have an extra bed for her. At first

Sally resisted. She was ready to use what was left of the money from Mrs. Mellow on a hotel room while she decided what to do with herself. But Penny just looped her arm around Sally's elbow and pulled her along, promising her she'd have a hot bath and a good meal before the day was over.

The Campbells' house was an overfilled red saltbox at the end of a lane. With seven children, three dogs, and innumerable cats, the family was too big for the house, or, as Mrs. Campbell would complain, the house was too small for the family. But it was ample enough for anyone who needed a place to stay. Mrs. Campbell met them at the front door and gave Sally a hug just as crushing as the one she gave her own niece, welcoming her as if she were another relative and had been missing for years. Yes, here Sally was, saved from whatever terrible fate she would have suffered if she'd stayed on that Northway bus. She'd been on her way to Rondo, Penny explained. Rondo? Mrs. Campbell had never heard of Rondo. No one had heard of Rondo. No matter. Sally was in Tuskee now, where anyone in need would never be denied a helping hand.

"I hope you're planning on staying for a long while," Penny said as they followed Mrs. Campbell into the house.

Why not? She had nowhere better to go. And about that bath — she wouldn't mind one, if indeed there was hot water to spare.

Almost before she knew what was happening to her, Sally found herself being treated like another member of a family in a household so crowded and wild that no one could keep track of how many people truly lived there. There wasn't a quiet corner to be found. Children shouted and banged on the upright piano, dogs barked, cats ran skittering across the kitchen table, and the telephone rang. The telephone was always ringing at the Campbell house. Mr. Campbell was Tuskee's favorite plumber, and he had more work than he could handle. Basements were flooded and sinks were clogged all over the city; every problem was more dire than any other problem. But as soon as the people got to chatting with Mr. Campbell on the phone, they'd forget their urgency, and by the end of the call they'd be saying that they hoped Mr. Campbell would come by whenever he had the time to spare.

It seemed to Sally that Mr. Campbell was home an awful lot for a plumber who had customers waiting. He wandered quietly from room to room, stopping to survey each scene, his face lit up with happy puzzlement. The children would race past him and sometimes bump against him, bouncing off and then rushing on their way. Sally wondered if he was as confused as she was about the family. She found it hard to be sure who was a Campbell and who was a guest. The fact that they all were clothed and fed amazed her. Somehow Mrs. Campbell managed to put food on the table every evening, big platters of pork or chicken and boiled vegetables for the family and any guests around to grab in passing. The first evening she was there, Sally followed Penny's cue, helping herself to the food, eating with her fingers while she was standing, nibbling on a chicken leg while across from her a small boy hunched over a corncob, the dogs jumped and barked, two girls fought over the last drop of milk in the bottle, and the telephone rang and fell silent and rang again.

And always in the middle of the pandemonium was Mrs. Campbell, who remained as impossibly serene as her husband, though evidently less baffled by the liveliness of her big family. While Mr. Campbell was a wispy man, drifting aimlessly through the crowded rooms, Mrs. Campbell was a large and solid woman. Just by hovering in one place for more than a few seconds, she provided a steady center around which all activity swirled.

There were more children than beds available in the house, but that didn't stop the Campbells from having guests. The pair of black-haired twin boys slept in the backyard in a tent. And since the Campbell girls were in the habit of adding to their numbers with friends, they couldn't fit in the small bedroom and instead had a slumber party in the living room. There were too many girls for Sally to keep track of their names. That first night there were ten of them, including Sally and Penny, and they sprawled across blankets piled on the floor, lay head to head in a star-shaped pattern. For a while they traded gossip, then jokes that got bawdier as the hour grew late, and then they started to sing. It turned out that Penny could play any tune by ear on the piano, and she played the Campbells' upright in accompaniment while the girls kept singing late into the night.

Though she didn't sing along, Sally enjoyed listening. She thought it odd and wonderful that the parents didn't march downstairs and tell them to be quiet. It seemed a house where expectations weren't bolstered with any rules. As she drifted off to sleep, she remembered the story Penny had told her about the horse named Nestor and the word he'd said in a dream: *tomorrow.* It was a good word, she decided, a hopeful and useful word. Now it was Sally's turn to look forward to *tomorrow,* something she hadn't allowed herself to do for months.

After just one day of searching, Penny found a job as a salesgirl at a shoe store — not the most lucrative kind of work, she acknowledged, but it was a good way to begin meeting people. Watching her get dressed early the next morning and set off for the store, Sally was surprised to feel a shade of envy. And while she wasn't quite prepared to make a decision about her future, she did head out to the corner newsstand, where she bought the local paper so she could check the classifieds.

She kept herself busy that day by getting her bearings, tracing the grid of streets downtown, noting the different stores and municipal buildings, and then heading farther out along the river, past the industrial section into the suburban neighborhoods, where tidy brick houses were shaded by flowering magnolias and fat, lazy dogs lounged on the front walks. As she passed an elementary school, a bell rang, summoning the children on the playground; a girl high on a swing leaped off, landed in a nimble crouch, and ran to join the line forming at the door. Sally was amused to feel herself resist a sudden urge to take the girl's place on the swing. A few blocks farther on, she stopped in a bakery and bought a molasses cookie, which was still deliciously warm from the oven. She ate it as she walked along.

Everything she experienced that day reinforced her conviction that this river city was ideal. While she hadn't traveled that far in terms of miles from the Woolworth's in Fenton, where she'd left Benny Patterson at the counter, she'd come far enough.

She bought the *Tuskee Chronicle* three days in a row but found no suitable listings. By the end of the week, she made it known to the Campbells that she was willing to take most anything that came along. And when what came along was a full-time clerking job at Potter's Hardware on Mead Street, located around the corner from the bus station and just a couple of blocks from Penny's shoe store, Sally didn't hesitate. At seventy-five cents an hour, it was a start.

The owner of the hardware store, Mr. Potter, was a good friend of the Campbells. He hired Sally to take the place of his former helper, Arnie Bly, who had worked for him twenty-three years before being felled by a tumor in his gut. Arnie Bly had died back in the winter, but only now was Mr. Potter getting around to replacing him. He made Sally swear that she was too healthy ever to fall ill before he agreed to hire her. He didn't ask about her experience and didn't seem to mind that she knew next to nothing about hardware supplies. He was happy to teach her.

Mr. Potter had a face that changed as the daylight changed, from a ruddy morning glow to a placid shine to a dusky fatigue by five o'clock. He spoke slowly and precisely, almost as if he thought Sally wasn't completely fluent in English. He kept on talking even after he'd told her everything he thought she needed to know about the store. She hadn't been working there long before he began trusting her with the details of his life. She learned that his wife was busy helping their daughter take care of her young children; his son was a schoolteacher; he had two brothers in Tuskee; and he proudly claimed among his ancestors a Seneca queen, a Portuguese fisherman, and a Scottish thief who'd been exiled for his crimes back in the 1700s.

Mr. Potter was unfazed by Sally's inexperience. Like everyone else she'd met since she'd stepped from the bus, he didn't worry about falling behind. There were more than enough hours in the day for the people who lived here. Even when they were in a hurry, they had a carefree way of showing it. Though they made sure that in the end, nothing was neglected, they carried on their affairs as if there were no world beyond the borders of Tuskee and therefore no pressing need to produce more than the residents themselves could generate. They didn't worry that they'd disappoint strangers with higher standards than their own, and they didn't worry that strangers would disappoint them. They just pitied all those who passed through on the bus without stopping.

Surrounded by such contentment, Sally didn't take long to begin settling into her new life. Her routines found their shapes, their simple contours. She had finally landed in a place where she truly was welcome. Though she couldn't yet know for sure, so far it seemed that there was nothing these people wouldn't forgive. No one blamed her for the rash actions of her youth; no one whispered about her behind her back. And with every day that passed, she felt less afraid of her own potential for making a wreck of things. It wasn't that she was unaware of the long-term consequences of her earlier indulgences. She understood that some consequences couldn't be left behind by boarding a bus. But this time around, her future wouldn't be something she just stumbled upon by mistake.

The first mistake she meant to avoid was overstaying her visit at the Campbells'. As much as she liked it there and as kind as they were to her, she didn't want them thinking she was taking advantage of their hospitality. If she really intended to remain in Tuskee, she couldn't begin by living off handouts from a couple who had a huge family to support. So when she learned that the apartment above Mr. Potter's hardware store was empty, she asked if she could rent it. Mr. Potter insisted that she live there for free.

The rooms had been vacant since Arnie Bly had died, and the furnishings were meager — a tattered sitting chair, a pine-wood table stained with coffee rings, a foldout cot for a bed. Mr. Potter was apologetic about the conditions, but Sally was grateful to him. And she wasn't given a chance to feel lonely. Penny came over the first night with a bag of groceries and made a spiced meat loaf, waking up the sleepy, dank rooms with the spitting noise of onions frying in oil.

She waited until she had supper on the table and they'd taken the first taste before beginning to tell Sally about the people she'd met that day.

There was the old woman who'd come into the store that morning carrying her little white poodle in her purse. While she browsed for shoes, she fed the poodle tiny peppermints.

And there was the bank executive who insisted on buying size-ten galoshes to cover his size-twelve shoes.

And the little boy who had names for each of his toes — Fiji and Samson and Mr. Doodlepuss and . . .

"I couldn't believe it. Right when I was fitting that boy with loafers, some feller came riding down North River on a donkey. He stopped in to buy boot laces."

"Really?"

"It's true!"

It was also true, Penny said, that the mayor's wife had webbed feet. And six pairs of women's pumps, size nine, on sale, were bought by Father Macklehose, the priest at St. Bernadette's.

"He likes a three-inch heel."

Oh, how Sally laughed at Penny's stories. She would keep begging her friend to stop so she could take another bite of her delicious meat loaf before it got cold. And while she was savoring the food, Penny would begin another story.

Life was promising to be comfortable for Sally Mole, who had learned not to take comfort for granted. Late the first night, lying awake in the darkness above Mr. Potter's hardware store, she thought about the people she missed most: Mole, her sister Trudy, her son, Uncle Mason and Georgie, and even Gladdy Toffit. As she drifted off to sleep, they all got mixed up in her mind, the dead with the living, and she wondered if she would ever see any of them again.

By the end of her third week in Tuskee, Sally had opened her first savings account at the local bank. She'd stocked the cupboards of her kitchen with canned soups and rice, crackers and cookies. She'd purchased a new pair of saddle shoes from the clearance rack at Penny's store. She'd been to the Immaculate Word Church on Hewitt Avenue twice for their Sunday service. She'd made biscuits and brought them to the Campbells in thanks for their kindness. She'd learned her way around the downtown streets. She'd come to understand the difference between a ripsaw and a crosscut saw, between tongs and pincers and pliers. She could answer most any question that a customer put to her.

She wasn't working because she was expected to work. For the first time in her life, she was working steadily, if slowly, toward a goal. She'd calculated that every dollar she tucked into the cash register would come back to her in the amount of a nickel. And a nickel plus a nickel plus a nickel would eventually add up to a substantial amount.

When she looked at herself in the mirror of the medicine cabinet in her bathroom, she looked at a new Sally. She wasn't the same used-up girl who couldn't keep out of trouble. Not that trouble wouldn't come after her. No, she wasn't such a fool that she thought nothing would go wrong ever again. Sure, things would go wrong. There would be challenges. She even had a hunch about the kind of challenge she'd have to deal with next. But in her reflection she saw someone who was unrecognizable simply because she'd learned to be hopeful.

Hopefulness wasn't just a mood for her; it was the logical conclusion she'd reached based on the evidence around her in Tuskee. The way people nodded and smiled at her along the street — why, they treated her as though they'd been saving a place for her at their dinner tables. And the sights she saw just walking around the block: spikes of velvety red snapdragons in the gardens, willows dripping green, and a drawbridge yawning open above the river. It was all so simply beautiful, as close to paradise as she expected to come.

It would have been pure paradise if she hadn't been bothered by that distracting little hunch she had. That one particular notion. By the middle of July, with her period two weeks overdue, her suspicion was getting stronger, the details coming into sharper focus every day. And as the substance of her hunch solidified, she felt herself preparing to despair. She had tempted fate in order to give herself a second chance and make up for her earlier negligence. But something so inevitable could never be used as recompense for something she'd already done. It didn't occur to her that she might give herself the moral freedom to change her mind and start looking for a way out of her predicament. All she could do was start preparing to spend the rest of her life dealing with the consequences of her recklessness.

But at least she'd made it to Tuskee. Everyone who settled in Tuskee prospered, and she could do the same. She didn't have to give up hope just because she'd have more responsibility than she'd planned for. Yes, she could be happy here. If she kept saying it to herself, she'd believe it. Yes, yes, yes, she could be happy here.

She celebrated her twenty-second birthday by writing a letter to her family, addressed to her parents. She volunteered little information about herself, though she did include her return address. She wrote that she hoped everyone in the family was in good health. She promised to visit soon and enclosed a twenty-dollar bill, which she specified was to be saved for her son.

Though she would never receive a reply from her parents, she would keep sending money through the years. Eventually it would add up to thousands and would equal exactly the money she deposited in the bank at regular intervals. From that first installment, she aimed to divide her earnings fair and square, with half of it going to her lost son and the other half saved for her second child, the one growing inside her — a last, unexpected gift from Benny Patterson.

The swath of park that ran along the east bank of the river was mostly a wide, unkempt lawn where boys played football and people brought picnics. Dandelion cotton carpeted the grass. Gnats gathered in thick, suffocating clouds. From the distance could be heard the steady clanging of the trip-hammers inside the Dyson Tool Company across the river. The grate of the Ferry Street Bridge creaked beneath the wheels of passing cars and buses. And the river, clearer here, without the film of cement dust or sewage, bubbled and splashed against the shore on its way north.

At one end of the park was a small railed platform, just wide enough for a plank bench that had been gouged over the years with hearts and initials. During her lunch break, Sally would sit there and watch Dyson workers loading crates on a barge, and she'd listen through the city's noise for the music of the river. Sometimes she'd hum quietly, so quietly that her voice would be inaudible even to her own ears. But she could feel the melody inside her. And when a smoky column of minnows gathered below the platform, she imagined that they were waiting for her to sing.

Left and right, day and night . . . no stoppin' once we start.

It was soothing to sit there, humming to herself and rehearsing words of songs she'd sung long ago, in her other life. She would

have liked to sing so loudly that the minnows would be able to hear her above the
rushing water. Sure, they'd be grateful to
her for giving them something to listen to
besides the river. She'd make them forget
about fishing nets and pike jaws and winter
ice. That's what music can do — make you
forget the dangers. This song or that,
crooned for an audience of fish. Dozens of
little fish, maybe even hundreds.

It's simple to wish,
And simple to dream.
Mmm-hmmm.
Is Sally here?
Who?
Sally Werner.
Who?
Sally Angel.
Who?
Sally Mole, Mole, Mole!
Hush.
Let her sing.
Sing for us, Sally.
Mmm-hmmm.

She had her eyes closed when a little boy
climbed the platform, thrust his head and
torso beneath the lower rail, and tried to
reach far enough so he could skim his hand
along the river. She didn't see him swish his
arm in an attempt to catch some minnows.

And with the clamor of the city mixing with the rushing water, she didn't hear the boy growling an invitation to the fish to come get caught, come on, you dummies.

But she didn't need to hear the boy or see what he was doing to sense what was about to happen, or would have happened. Even without seeing the boy wriggle forward on the platform, even without quite knowing that he was there beside the bench, she became aware of the sensation of impending disaster. It was something between a dream and an idea, involving more presumption than apprehension. And though she continued to sit with her head tipped back, her eyes closed, her thoughts adrift, the prospect of danger caused her to shift her position and thrust her left leg to the side so the boy bumped against her ankle instead of falling from the platform.

Her eyes opened wide. She saw the dusky sky. Her first impression was of the universe's infinite depth, and at the same time, sensing the boy's weight against her leg, she understood in a flash that if she moved her leg, he would slip forward and plunge into the river. He would drown. No, he wouldn't drown because Sally had already hooked her fingers through his belt loop and pulled him back to safety, away from the edge of the platform.

Oh, but wasn't he a rascal, his mother said with the kind of saintly calm shared with the rest of Tuskee's citizens, who could not be shaken from their general optimistic belief that everything happened according to a reasonable plan. As she gripped him by the elbow, pulling him gently to his feet, she explained to Sally that her son sure knew how to get into trouble. If she let him get out of her sight for a second, just one second —

"Fishy!" the boy was insisting, stomping his feet. Either he'd be allowed to catch one of those little fishies in the river, or he'd throw a tantrum.

Sally judged the boy to be about three, a couple of years younger than her own son.

"Once when he was a baby," his mother was saying, "I couldn't find him anywhere. He'd gone and crawled into the laundry basket and fallen asleep."

"Fishy fishy fishy!"

"We had the whole neighborhood out looking for him," the mother went on, brushing back the boy's wet bangs. "You rascal," she said, planting a kiss on his forehead. "We gotta get on now. Sweetie pie, say thanks to the lady. She saved you from a soaking. Say thanks."

"Fishy."

"Fishy to you," said Sally.

"Have a nice day," the mother offered in a plain, friendly manner.

"See you, then," Sally replied. After they were gone, she sat for a while watching the river as its surface turned waxier beneath the darkening sky. The school of minnows had disappeared, though not for good, Sally was sure. The next time she came back, the minnows would be there, waiting for her. And she knew that though the current seemed to have slowed almost to a standstill and the water beneath the platform looked like a big block of ice, solid, with nothing inside, really the river was full of mysterious life.

Sally had arrived in the city of Tuskee in the late spring of 1952. She worked steadily at Potter's Hardware through the summer, into the crisp fall days, and then through a winter that was colder than she was used to and yet more beautiful, with the streetlamps candy-striped with red ribbons, the pond behind the library crowded with skaters, a thick snow cover on the ground that lasted through to the beginning of March, and blustery winds that kept the clouds moving and cleared the sky to a crystal blue almost every morning.

With so few expenses of her own, she was able to save over five hundred dollars — this was on top of Mason Jackson's money, which she'd come to think of as a fortune she was holding in trust. Having failed once to give it away, she couldn't help but wonder whether, instead, she was meant to keep it. She never intended to spend it on herself. But in a strange way, all that cash, the whole lump sum of it hidden in a hatbox in the back of her closet, was of more use to her if it remained intact. It was a hedge against uncertainty. It was the foundation for the settled life she was going to lead.

As the months passed and the pregnancy began to show, she found herself enjoying her solitude more, though not because she was ashamed of her condition; if shame ever occurred to her, it was only as an idea to consider briefly and dismiss, something to send away from Tuskee while she stayed on. She was grateful to have purposeful work that put her in contact with people each day. And it helped to know that she had a good friend in Penny and could count on being invited to join the Campbell family for holiday meals. But she was happy just to sit by herself at the window of her apartment watching snowflakes collecting on the sill while she thought about the child growing inside her.

She felt certain she was pregnant with a girl, and when she thought about what to name the child, she didn't even consider names for boys. At first she decided she liked the name Judy, in honor of Judy Garland. But the next day she changed her mind and settled on Francesca. She went on to consider that Winifred was a fine name. And how about the names of her sisters, Trudy or Laura, or even her own name? How about Millicent? Now that was a name with stature! And really, there was nothing to compare with the friendly, inviting name of Brenda. Or maybe Phyllis or Carol, Daisy, or just plain Sue? All the names available were like candies on display. She'd choose one and give it to her child, her little girl, who with her fluttering presence was the reason Sally didn't mind the evening solitude, why, with the dark sky spilling snow, the shop below her apartment closed for the night, the intersection of Mead and State below her window empty of all activity, she didn't feel in the least bit lonely.

Close to term, she settled on the name Rebecca, but she managed to forget this in the hospital during the rush of her quick, searing labor, and in the first minutes after the birth of her child — the daughter she'd been expecting — Sally knew that she had to be called Penelope, after her friend who had first welcomed her when she'd stepped off the bus.

Penelope Mole, born at 6:31 a.m., March 17, 1953, in Tuskee General Hospital.

But good Lord, wasn't she the funniest-looking child anyone had ever seen! So ugly with her big, swollen eyes bunched shut and her fat lips and her wet cap of hair that the nurse declared her the next Miss America out of pity, failing to foresee that the infant's lopsided proportions would gradually shift and settle neatly into place, and the girl would develop into such a startling beauty that strangers, men and women alike, would stop in their tracks and stare as she passed.

And that's just what Sally did. She stared as the infant settled in her arms, not quite believing that the funny, wonderful creature was hers, marveling until marvel became an inevitable aspect of their interaction, implicit and constant. Even if she didn't speak of it, she'd often feel it, marveling at the child's sheer presence in the world. And now and then she'd wonder if she would have felt the same for her son, her firstborn, if she'd just given him a chance.

■ ■ ■ ■

She had every intention of writing to her family in Tauntonville and telling them that she had a new daughter. But in the letter she sent them on March 28, 1953, she didn't mention Penelope. She expressed the hope that her parents and brothers and sisters were all in good health. Spelling *raspberry* without the *p,* she announced to her mother that she missed her jam so much that she was going to try to make a batch herself come summer. She went on to ask her little brother Clem if he was behaving himself. She directed her little sister Laura to pay attention to her teacher, and she wondered if she had a sweetheart yet. She said that the fairy in the new movie *Peter Pan* reminded her of Tru. Sally asked Tru if she remembered the night long ago, before she became sick, when Tru had a dream that she could fly. For many days afterward, she tried to fly. She jumped off the bed and she jumped off the fence and she jumped from the loft. Did Tru remember? She flapped and flapped her arms so hard there were times Sally thought her sister just might fly, but then splat, down she'd come, every time.

Sally went on to write that she found it

hard to believe Tru was all grown up. She wondered if Tru was thinking of marriage. Sally assured her that she would find a nice and suitable young husband.

She hoped there were no worries about the rain this year and pointed out that the almanac predicted it would be a good year for corn. She told her parents that she went to church regularly and worked hard at her job at a store in town, though she didn't say which store. She assured all the members of her family that they were in her prayers every day, and she wished them good health and happiness. She noted that she was enclosing a gift of money for her son. She signed the letter, *Your loving daughter Sally.*

After sealing the envelope, she picked up her baby, who was blinking contentedly at the ceiling light, lying on her back on an alphabet quilt Mrs. Campbell had given her. Sally whispered nonsense to her, putting together any meaningless syllables that came to mind: *Nutterbutter* or *humf-fafa* or *lubadubdubdub.*

In a letter dated April 17, 1953, she wrote again to her family, hoping that they were in good health and wishing a happy Easter to each and every one. She said she hadn't forgotten that Loden's birthday was on the twenty-first and Laura's birthday was two weeks later, if she was counting correctly. She enclosed small presents for them, a locket for Laura and a wooden tie clip for Loden, both of which were small enough to fit in the envelope. She guessed that Loden had moved out of the house and started his own family by then, though she didn't put that in the letter.

She wrote that she'd read about the development of a polio vaccine, and she wondered if that might mean they would soon have a medicine to strengthen Tru's legs, and she wouldn't need her brace anymore. She named all the members of the family in order of age — *Father, Mother, Loden, Tru, Laura, Clem, Willy* — and assured them that they were in her prayers. She noted that she was enclosing a gift of money for them to save for her son and thanked them for looking after him.

After she'd sealed the envelope she picked up her baby and recited an old rhyme that came suddenly to mind, a simple rhyme for counting: *Goody goody two shoes. Three shoes, four. Five shoes, six shoes, seven, and more.*

She wrote to her family to wish them a happy Fourth of July. She hoped that they were enjoying good weather and good health. She predicted that the corn would be knee-high by the end of the week, and the raspberries would be ripening. She spelled *raspberries* without the *p* again. She wondered if her mother remembered, as she did, the time they thought there was a dog in the bushes, and her mother went out to chase it away, but when it came out into the open they saw that it was a bear. Her mother ran up on the porch as the bear waddled back into the woods all full and fat from the berries it had gorged on. They were sure mad to lose those berries, but they laughed. Did they all remember how they laughed?

It was so long ago, she wrote, *so much has happened since.* She enclosed a gift of money for her son and signed the letter, *Your loving daughter Sally.*

She pressed the moist stamp onto the envelope and then picked up Penelope, bouncing her on her lap, reciting, *Monday is a Monday, Tuesday is a brick, Wednesday is milk shake nice and thick, Thursday is a fairy tale, Friday is a lark, Saturday's a'passing, Sunday in the park.*

She wrote a letter to her family in August, and then again in October, November, and

December. She sent presents for their birthdays and Christmas, and she enclosed a portion of her earnings to give to her son. Without going into specifics, she assured her family that everything was all right. *Better than all right,* she wrote, *not counting what you read in the newspaper these days.*

She always included a return address, though she didn't really expect her parents to contact her. She convinced herself that she didn't care whether or not they replied. She wasn't going to waste the rest of her life waiting to hear back from them.

But, oh, if those Werners only knew the truth; if they could have seen chunky, funny-looking Penelope, who grew chunkier and funnier-looking before she began to grow beautiful. Surely the sight of her would have softened their hearts.

Her fat cheeks fattened into two stuffed pouches, and her eyes had the startled, sparkling glare of a raccoon caught in a lantern's glow. She sucked her thumb with great energy; upon discovering her feet, she took to chewing on her big toe. She was smiling before she was a month old, and her proudest smiles accompanied her juiciest farts.

She went to work with Sally and lay

contentedly in a cradle that Mr. Potter had set up for her, charming the customers who bent down to have a look, gurgling and cooing sweetly. So what if her proportions were odd? Odd was cute when it came packaged in a splendid little girl. It didn't matter to the people of Tuskee that her mother didn't have a marriage license to make the child legitimate. *Legitimate* wasn't a word in the local vocabulary. Neither, as far as Sally could tell, was *sinner* or *shame* or *bastard.*

Come to think of it, there were a whole lot of missing words. While Sally swept the aisles at the end of the day, she'd make a mental list of familiar words she never expected to hear in Tuskee: *catastrophe, gloom, horror, damnation, humiliate, massacre, vile* — and *whore,* of course, she'd never hear that around here, or *slut,* not because such words were forbidden, but because they simply weren't available for common conversation.

If Sally was judging correctly, the language spoken in Tuskee didn't provide an opportunity for slander. How lucky she was to have found her way to this haven, where she was free to carry on her life protected from the world's dangers, to work and raise her child here, to talk with friends, to point a customer in the direction of a ladder or a garden hose, to be useful, to nurse her baby and quiet her when she cried.

Coaxing her, *Shhh, don't you cry.*

Persuading her to *Go to sleep, my little baby.*

Promising to give her all sorts of treasures when she woke — *pretty horses, mockingbirds, golden rings, shortening bread.*

And wouldn't you know, one humid day late in the summer, when the sticky heat was making Penelope uncomfortable and her whimpers were building up to wails, Sally Mole heard herself singing. She'd probably been singing aloud to her baby for weeks, and she just hadn't thought to listen to her own voice. But now she heard herself singing to soothe Penelope when she was irritable.

She sang, *It's simple to wish.* She sang, *Darlin', won't you walk with me.* She sang to cajole her daughter out of a fuss. She sang to make her giggle. And once, months later, without thinking, she sang to Penelope in the hardware store. It was a song Sally had read as a verse in a children's book, an homage to the Cheshire cat, his saucy manner and lingering smile, and Penelope liked the melody Sally had made up so much that she clapped her hands together to beg for more. So Sally sang it again, *Grinning his grin and fading away, grinning and fading away, away, away,* and again, *away, away, away,* and again, noticing only after she'd whirled around, twirling the baby, that two men were standing at the end of an aisle watching her, listening to her sing. And the sight of them brought to Sally's mind words that were supposed to be absent from Tuskee, reminding her that she'd had a good reason for swearing off singing forever.

"That's a dandy song," said one of the men, a young man in a droopy tweed cap.

The other man, older than the first, perhaps his father, took the frayed, unlit stub of his cigar from his mouth, and said, "Don't mind us. You go ahead and sing."

"No, that's enough," said Sally, more angrily than she'd intended, drawing from the baby on her hip a grunt to express her dissatisfaction and then another grunt to indicate that she would burst out crying if her mother didn't resume her song.

"Quiet now," Sally said to her, truly an outrageous direction from the point of view of the baby, who might not have understood the exact meaning of the words but must have sensed that her mother was signaling that she would no longer comply with her daughter's simple desire. Penelope's frown bunched her whole face into an expression of despair, and she erupted in a sobbing frenzy. All Sally could think to do was to whisper a promise that she'd sing to her later.

For a moment Penelope fell silent and peered at her mother suspiciously.

"She wants you to sing is all," observed the younger man.

"Go ahead and sing for her." The older man offered this more as an expectation than a suggestion; he inserted his cigar stub back between his lips and folded his arms across his chest, waiting for Sally to continue. But Sally wasn't going to continue, and Penelope, sensing this, burst out crying again.

"Can I help you find something?" Sally asked, raising her voice above her baby's wails.

"We're looking for . . ."

She thought she heard him say *gadget.* He corrected her: he was looking for *a gasket, a graphite gasket.*

"A gasket, you say? Okay then, let me think, graphite gasket. Graphite, you said. Right, yes, okay, down there, next to the boiler tape . . ."

As the men disappeared down the aisle, Sally bounced and swayed her screaming baby. When the motion didn't comfort her, she whispered the words of the song into Penelope's ear. When that didn't work either, she opened the door and stood on the threshold, soaking in the brisk, bright cold of a January day, hugging her daughter close to keep her warm.

She had to raise her voice to be heard above the slur of tires on slushy macadam, the rattle of a bus's engine, the chimes outside the gift shop across the street. She sang to her baby, *fading away, away, away,* loudly, nearly bellowing the words *away, away, away.* And as she sang, a woman passing by, bundled in a wool coat and braided scarves, picked up the melody and hummed it as she continued down the street.

Penelope's smile suggested that her pleasure came more from manipulating her mother than from listening to her sing, but her mischievous delight was contagious, and Sally felt it, too, and she liked the way the tune was returning to her as an echo, hummed by a stranger.

All she had to do was sing. Of course she'd sing. She decided right then and there that it had been ridiculous to forswear singing for her entire future when she couldn't have guessed that the future would evolve into a present time in which she was a clerk at a hardware store holding a daughter in her arms who loved to cajole her into singing.

Grinning and fading away, away, away.

Sally Werner had stopped singing. Sally Angel had never allowed herself to sing. But now that Sally Mole had finally begun singing loudly enough for others to hear, she didn't want to stop:

Walk with me, walk with me . . .

Left and right, day and night . . .

"Thank you, miss!" the younger man called from behind her in the store's foyer. She looked at him in confusion. "The gaskets," he prompted.

Of course, the gaskets. Sally Mole had a job with responsibilities, she had customers who needed her attention, and Mr. Potter was off helping Wally Campbell install a dishwasher in a fancy house on Montague Street.

Another customer appeared and followed Sally and Penelope back into the store. He needed her to mix a gallon of paint — and while he was there he'd get some lightbulbs, he added, a comment that was overheard by the older of the other two men, reminding him that he needed batteries for his flashlight.

As all three of them went off in search of bulbs and batteries, the bell over the door jangled, and Penny Campbell entered the store. She was on her coffee break, stopping in to say a quick hello to Sally and to give her namesake a big fat kiss. She called the baby her scrumptious little goose, her funny creature, her darling, and took her in her arms, lifting her high. Penelope snorted at her; Penny snorted back. Back and forth they went, snort snort, leaving Sally free to ring up the purchases for the first pair of men and then fill a can with paint.

All three men knew one another and Penny as well, and soon they were in conversation, talking about the forecast for six inches of fresh snow overnight. With the prediction of a thaw later in the week, they wondered if there was a danger of flooding.

Sally pivoted the can to secure it in the mixer while the men and Penny traded more thoughts about the weather, debating the patterns of this winter versus the last and last winter versus the decade of winters before.

Oblivious to them, Sally sang as she worked the mixer, raising her voice above the motor's noise. She wouldn't have thought she remembered that particular song after all this time, but she did remember it, every word and every note.

If the sandman brought me dreams of you

I'd want to sleep my whole life through . . .

She failed to notice that the conversation across the counter had stopped. Not until she'd finished pressing the lid on the can did she look up and realize that she had an audience.

Funny how a single note surrounds itself with the company of other notes, words collect in lyrics, and a singer creates the need for an accompanist. Sally wouldn't have expected it to be so easy. One day she was singing lullabies to her baby; the next day after work she was at the Campbells' sitting on the piano bench next to Penny. They began with a song they both already knew, "Shoo-Fly Pie and Apple Pan Dowdy," Penny leading, then nodding for Sally to catch up, urging her to jump right in, to sing the chorus straight through, sing louder, sing the whole thing again on her own.

When they were done, Mrs. Campbell stepped in from the doorway, where she'd been listening. Why, Sally Mole sang like a lark, she said, and Penny agreed. With a little training, Sally would give Dinah a run for her money.

"Who's Dinah?"

Had Sally been living in a root cellar for

the past twenty years? Was it possible that she'd never heard Dinah Shore sing "Dear Hearts and Gentle People"? What about "Blues in the Night"? Penny preferred Peggy Lee's version to Dinah's. Mrs. Campbell wasn't so sure. Her favorite Peggy Lee song was "I Got It Bad and That Ain't Good." She hummed the opening, which Sally recognized. Yeah, she knew that song. Okay, it was a start. And how about Ethel Waters? Even if Sally hadn't heard a recording, maybe she'd seen her in *Pinky*? Well . . . no, in fact. But she had loved Judy Garland's vaudeville act in *Easter Parade.* Sure, everyone loved Judy. But how about Kay Starr or Ella Mae Morse?

Sally had plenty to learn, and Penny, who admitted to being cursed with a creaky hinge of a voice, had plenty to teach. She began with "Yes, My Darling Daughter" — *I gotta be good or Mama will scold me, yes, yes, yes.* She taught her "Buttons and Bows" and a simple ballad she'd made up herself about Nestor the talking Appaloos'. They quit at midnight, satisfied that they had something amounting to a repertoire.

The next day on their lunch hour they tried out their songs in the back room of the hardware store, with Penny gently coaxing Sally on the different ways to hold a note. The following day was Sunday, and Sally spent most of it at the Campbells' piano, Penny blending notes into songs that Sally would pick up in snatches while the children raced around the living room.

Sally enjoyed singing, but she wasn't engaged in any kind of effort she thought was worth developing, despite the Campbells' praise. Singing was what she did to pass the time, and if there were appreciative listeners, well, that was just good luck.

The Campbells shared her sense of luck. News of the impromptu performances traveled quickly around Tuskee, and by the end of that first Sunday there were a dozen extra guests who had stopped by to listen. The next Sunday afternoon the Campbells' little house was packed again with visitors. Some who came by brought a dish to share or beer or fresh fruit. There was more than they could eat, and Sally ended up taking home enough leftovers to last a week.

In that same period, Buddy Potter raised her wage, and by the beginning of the year Sally could afford to split the rent with Penny for a two-bedroom garage apartment on the same quiet lane where the Campbells lived. The Campbells lent them linens, and Mr. Potter's wife gave them an old Emerson portable TV. As a housewarming gift to themselves, they bought a record player and set it up on the kitchen counter. Sally paid just seven dollars a week for her share of the rent, and with her raise she succeeded in saving almost as much as she had when she'd been staying in the apartment above the hardware store. Now, though, her daughter would have a yard to play in, there was usually an older child among the troop of Campbells willing to babysit, and no one complained if they left the windows open in the evening and turned up the volume of the music.

Sally learned to sing every song on Penny's records. She recognized that her singing was naïve, but she wasn't about to add music to her list of responsibilities. Her lack of training would keep her from having to improve.

She caught on quickly, though, and at the Campbells' piano they produced something approximating music without much work. It was lively music, "real catchy," according to their listeners, memorable mostly for the setting where it was performed, Sally assumed: the Campbells' welcoming house in the pleasant city of Tuskee, where you could go and hear a tune for free on any Sunday afternoon.

This was the period of which Sally would later speak as the good old days, those years in Tuskee when she was sentimental about life and couldn't help but idealize the minutiae of experience. She loved the feeling of happiness and convinced herself that its inspiration was everywhere, not just in the predictable moments involving her baby and her friends, but also where she would have least expected it. Once, for instance, when she was carrying out the garbage and walking barefoot across the soggy grass, the soft earth molding to her feet made her instantly happy. And once, pushing Penelope in the stroller, she heard Bing Crosby singing over a transistor radio propped on the shelf of a newsstand, and she started singing along with him:

No, it isn't a dream . . .

Bing Crosby made her happy. So did Dinah Shore every Tuesday and Thursday evening. So did the antics of Lucy Ricardo. She was happy watching clothes tumble behind the glass of the dryer at the Laundromat. She was happy selling handsaws and screwdrivers. She discovered that she loved bologna sandwiches with French's mustard, strawberry Jell-O, and Cracker Jacks. She was happy when she filled in blocks of a crossword puzzle, even if she didn't finish it. Her first whiff of her first bottle of Breck shampoo — that was nice!

So was Play-Doh, Scotch tape, and an old plastic tablecloth that had been soaked by rain and left to dry in the sun.

She understood Tuskee to be the place where the truth of life's potential was vividly apparent. Sweet, dazzling happiness — she couldn't resist it and would seize upon whatever happened to fall in her path, whatever by luck or chance made itself available.

There were times when she resolved to put on a show of cool indifference, in response, say, to a compliment she thought excessive, and once when she was watching a silly romantic movie in which the hero everyone thought was dead suddenly appeared at the birthday party of his fiancée. More often, she wondered if there was an element of self-deception to her enthrallment. Yet whenever she vowed to become more neutral in her responses, her daughter would snort her snorting laugh or clap her hands with pleasure, or she'd call out *Mama* for the first time or take her first steps, and Sally would feel plainly, simply happy all over again.

If from time to time she caught a glimpse of distant trouble coming from elsewhere in the world, it didn't change her mood. She happened to be at the Campbells' watching a television broadcast when a clip came on showing some lawyer interviewing Senator Joe McCarthy. She could guess what dangers important men believed they were holding at bay. And she even saw that Tuskee was as vulnerable as anyplace else during the summer of 1955, when the river flooded the lumberyard, dragging a season's worth of timber downriver. That kind of trouble didn't last, though. It was like the iron grapefruit of a meteorite that fell through a lady's ceiling in Alabama and crashed into her console radio. Everybody talked about that meteorite for a while, and there were people willing to pay a fortune for it, but by the time that rock was put up for sale the next year its fame had waned and a buyer couldn't be found.

During the five years she spent in the city of Tuskee, from 1952 to 1957, Sally Mole gained an intimate knowledge of happiness. That the word had a breezy, carefree sound was appropriate, since the feeling had a palpable lightness to it, giving her a buoyancy, actually diminishing the pressure of gravity. And even if she wasn't convinced that she'd earned her happiness, it always seemed logical, following from previous experiences the way one year followed from the next.

There continued to be moments when she was provoked to think of the past. It wasn't as though her memory had been emptied the day she stepped off the bus in Tuskee. She continued to wonder about her son. And there were nights when she missed Mole so badly that she'd invite him to visit her dreams; he'd almost always make an appearance, filling the aching emptiness with his old jokes, making love to her in his slow, tender fashion. Sometimes in the aftermath of those dreams, the awareness of the absolute fact of his absence would leave her bereft. But in the time it took her blinking eyes to grow used to the light of morning, the world would find a way to remind her that *happiness is everywhere.* And though she could predict that such a claim might strike a more sophisticated person as mawkish, she knew that she could always add a little tune, and then it would sound reasonable enough.

By the summer of 1955, Sally was a single mother of a two-year-old daughter. She was content with her life in Tuskee and had no plans to alter her routine or move on. As it happened, the year brought three developments, relatively minor at first glance, though each would eventually have unexpected consequences.

The first one was a long-haired calico cat, a stray male that during a thunderstorm decided to make his home in the storage room of the hardware store. The tufts of his ears were too matted to comb out, there were oozing sores from fleabites on his belly, and one eye dripped a creamy mucus. Sally found the cat, or the cat found Sally, when she went to fetch a can of satin gloss in the back and was fumbling in the dark for the light switch. The cat curled against her leg, begging for food, but Sally, thinking she'd surprised a rat, screamed and kicked out her leg, sending the cat sailing through the air. He landed on the head of a broom, levering the shaft forward to bump Sally lightly in the face. She screamed again. The room abruptly filled with light. Buddy Potter had rushed back and turned on the switch, revealing Sally holding her cheek and the pitiful stray shivering on the broom bristles, starved and filthy, squinting, its mouth yawning in a growling complaint.

Sally filled a pan of water and fed the cat pieces of bologna from her sandwich; following the initial plan agreed upon with Buddy Potter, she would nurse the cat back to health and then find him a home. But within a few days, as the animal grew stronger and more stubborn, it became clear that he intended to make the hardware store his home for good.

Named Leonardo by Penny Campbell, he turned out to be a handsome cat with his glossy, mottled hair, his tufted ears, and his emerald eyes gleaming yellow in the dark. Even when he reached the plump weight of twenty pounds, he was regal rather than absurd, and as he marched down the middle of the aisle in front of customers he made it clear that he would answer to no one.

Or to almost no one. The cat allowed Penelope to use him as she pleased. He would let her yank his tail or grab at his tufts, and his temper never flared. And as she grew fonder of the cat, her acts of torture turned to rough demonstrations of affection. Instead of pulling his tail, she'd lift the heavy sack of him and spin him around; instead of grabbing his ears, she'd use him as a cushion and sit on him. Through it all, he seemed entirely resigned to and sometimes genuinely cheered by the abuse.

With customers, though, and sometimes with Sally, the cat could be stony, grand in his shiny fat stature, aloof and judgmental, all at once. He was generally a quiet cat, though his silence seemed deliberate, a calculated reticence rather than an innate quality. At first Sally had thought the poor creature was timid by nature, but it turned out that Leo was a vain and lazy animal, and if his needs weren't met with satisfying alacrity, he'd sit on the counter and glare at Sally, swishing his tail angrily and occasionally washing a paw in a way that suggested his dangerous potential, as though he were polishing a gun. He was the sovereign of the store and would not be disregarded.

This immense, imperious cat, then, was the year's first unexpected addition in Sally's life. The second came with the annual Tuskee Jubilee in August, when a singer named Dara Bliss performed on the last night of the festival. A magic show going on at the same time across the park attracted the bigger crowd, so Penny and Sally were able to claim front-row seats for Dara Bliss's act and could hear every crackle and sigh, every spill of breath as she sang.

She was middle-aged, maybe forty-five or fifty, with a mass of black curls, thick lips painted a gleaming purple, a huge bosom, and bands of gold bracelets spiraling from her wrists to her elbows. But it was her voice that fascinated Sally. It was a throaty voice, coarse at its core, yet with a delicacy around the edges, as though it were encased in a sheet of glass so thin it would have cracked with the wrong sound. There were no wrong sounds. Every note that came from Dara Bliss's mouth was right, whether she sang deep into an alto rumble or way up the scale, and Sally listened transfixed, wondering how a voice could be so seductive and confident, so clear, so singular, and yet seemingly boundless.

Dara Bliss was the first singer Sally had ever heard in live performance outside of church and school. Her husband, a fat, bald man with a thick beard carpeting his chin, played the electric keyboard, and between sets he hawked Dara's latest album at the stand beside the Airstream they traveled in. This LP, he announced, was the first of ten that were under contract to be professionally recorded in a studio in Savannah, Georgia. Sally bought the album after the show, and when her husband called her, Dara Bliss came back out from the Airstream and autographed the cover, drawing a flat line from a wild *D* and another line from the *B* right across her photograph on the front. The crackling of the fireworks display drowned out Sally's thank-you.

Sally listened to the record when she got home that night. She kept the music playing while she was cleaning the kitchen, taking dishes from the dish rack and stacking them in cabinets. She played the record again the next morning, while she was making biscuits with Penelope. And she played it again that evening after work, over and over.

Before she went to sleep that night, she'd memorized all the songs on Dara Bliss's album, from the bluesy "Turn Around, Lou" to a gospel hymn called "Alleluia Grace." She'd go on to sing them more often than any other songs she knew, sometimes with Penny accompanying, but mostly when she was alone. She roughed her voice in an attempt to mimic Dara Bliss and catch that raspy transition between notes, easing down to a low growl, breathing out the melody until she had to gasp. When she failed to do an adequate imitation, she sang in her own voice, as expressively as she could, to honor her.

The next week, while Penelope was napping and Penny Campbell was at the grocery store, Sally paged through the newspaper and stumbled upon a picture of Dara Bliss above the notice of her death. From the obituary, Sally learned that Dara Bliss had fallen asleep smoking a cigarette, and the lit cigarette had dropped onto the mattress and set the parked Airstream on fire. Her husband, who'd gone to the store, came back to find smoke seeping from the trailer, but by then it was too late. Dara Bliss was already dead.

She was fifty-two years old at the time of her death, according to the newspaper. She'd been born Dorothea Burton in Omaha, and she'd run away when she was sixteen to join a traveling vaudeville show. She had performed live on local radio stations hundreds of times, but she'd recorded only one album. She had crisscrossed the country several times in her touring, but her favorite venue was Icy's Lounge on the Boardwalk in Atlantic City. She'd performed there every summer for the past thirty years.

Rereading the obituary, Sally didn't miss the similarities between herself and Dara Bliss. Hadn't she run away when she was sixteen? And hadn't she nearly died when Mole's car went off the road? But she'd been spared, unlike Dara Bliss. And so she had to ask herself, listening to Dara Bliss sing, *I got you good, don't make a sound, turn around, Lou, oh turn around,* shouldn't she do more than just go on living? Alone in the apartment, with only the music for company, Sally studied the picture of the singer on the album cover, the lines of her flat signature crossing the face, dividing it along the bridge of her nose. In the photograph her hair had been teased into two puffy mounds on either side of her ears, and the way she glared through fake lashes, with her lips pursed almost angrily and two round dollops of rouge on her cheeks, she looked as though she were offended by her own ridiculousness, like a queen dressed up in a clown suit.

On stage at the Jubilee, she had seemed larger than life — big in body, big in voice. In Sally's memory, she seemed as invulnerable to the physical hazards of the world as she was to the opinions of her audience, the kind of woman who should have lived forever.

Yet she was dead. According to her obituary, she was survived by her husband, her mother, two sisters, three nephews, and one niece. Donations in her memory, the newspaper noted, could be sent to the Dara Bliss Scholarship Fund at St. Mary's School for Girls in Omaha.

Dara Bliss. Sally pictured the singer dead in her coffin, her face bronzed from the thick makeup, her hands folded across her puffy pink blouse, resting on the mound of her bosom. Of the ten albums her husband had said were under contract, only one had been produced. What would happen to the other nine? Why, the other nine would never exist, along with everything else that was lost when this death or any other cheated the world of something beautiful that hadn't yet been made.

Sally thought of her seventh-grade teacher, Miss Krumbaldorf, who had tried to teach her students how to make use of their God-given talents. Wasn't Sally's singing voice a talent God had given her? And didn't she, therefore, have an obligation to make use of it?

Her initial response to the death of Dara Bliss was a new determination. Though she didn't have a clear plan in mind, she recognized that there were steps she could take to develop her voice. She practiced more often on her own, sang with new concentration. She discovered that Penny had been right when she said it would help to drop her lower jaw, raise her arms, and sway to the rhythm. She tried to sing each note just the way Dara Bliss had sung it. But even as she worked to improve, she decided that she didn't need to make a decision about her ultimate capabilities. Her limits would reveal themselves over time. As long as she didn't identify precisely what she couldn't do, she wouldn't worry about being disappointed.

By the end of November 1955, Sally was happily experiencing a potent combination of satisfaction and anticipation. She was proud of managing on her own. She had a steady job, good friends, and a daughter whose features were starting to align themselves in an attractive symmetry. She could indulge in secret dreams of success. And she was the owner, by default, of a very fat cat.

The only real inconvenience in her life was the lack of a car. Tuskee's transit schedule was erratic, and she'd lost track of the number of times she'd walked home in the snow because the bus never came. After reviewing her finances and visiting all the dealerships in town, she decided to purchase a used Mercury sedan, her third and final addition of the year, as a Christmas present to herself. It was a fine blue car with a beige cloth interior, and even with seventy thousand miles on it, it didn't show much rust. Sally bought it on loan, at a rate discounted to a manageable two percent by the friendly dealer, who threw in the snow tires for free.

On New Year's Eve 1955, Sally left Penelope with the Campbells, and she sang before a crowd at the Rotary Club, with Penny accompanying on an out-of-tune upright piano at the back of the stage, playing in such a muted fashion that Sally heard her own voice overlie the music more confidently than ever. She had never sounded so accomplished to herself, so effortlessly fine. Yet still she was surprised when, after their finale of "Turn Around, Lou," a man in the audience called for Sally to sing the same song again.

Sing for us, Sally!

The spotlight held her in place; the mike was tipped on its pole; music rose magically from the shadows where Penny sat on a stool, an irresistible melody that Sally matched with words.

I got you good, don't make a sound . . .

She felt the sweet perfection of sound on her tongue and gave up her resistance to vanity, let herself indulge without humility in the certainty that she was breaking through to a new dimension flooded with dazzling light. Why, she was dazzling.

Sally Mole, Sally Mole, Sally Mole!

. . . a source of light dazzling the members of the Rotary Club, who as soon as she had finished her encore rose to their feet and applauded. She could have kept on singing for the rest of the night. But before she could begin a new song, the man serving as the MC stepped forward toward the mike. He thanked the lovely girls for their performance and then waved them away, launching right into a list of names, the results, as he explained, of the club's annual elections.

During the five years Sally lived in Tuskee, a new elementary school was built, the main library was renovated, the Dockery Bar and Grill opened for business, the abandoned Pinecrest Hotel on the outskirts of the city burned to the ground, the fencing team at the high school won the state championship, a new mayor was elected, Adlai Stevenson gave a stump speech on the porch of city hall, the river rose and shrank with the seasons, ice thickened and thawed, sycamores shed bark, road crews filled potholes, gardeners pulled weeds, dogs barked, cats fought, hammers hammered, engines sputtered, money was made, saved, spent, and borrowed, and Sally managed to pay off the loan for her Mercury sedan.

In that time, Penelope Mole grew from a funny-looking baby into such a lovely little girl, blue-eyed, with creamy skin sprayed lightly with freckles and her thick auburn hair bundled in a ponytail, that Buddy Potter featured her on his flyers advertising sales. And as the "Potter Girl," she came to be associated with the jubilant mix of charm and trade that drew customers to the store.

What Penelope would remember of her early years in Tuskee, though, was a more raucous experience — hours and hours filled with the clamor of everyday life. She remembered that the noise used to bother her, for she was always longing to hear her mother singing, and as much as Sally loved to sing, she couldn't do it often enough to satisfy her daughter. And so Penelope learned how to hear what she wanted to hear, though not in the ordinary sense of choosing ignorance. Rather, she devoted such effort to listening that she could discern music even in some of the dullest chatter around her, hearing in odd shreds of noise the hint of a tune. She was sure that there was music hidden in almost everything she heard.

If, for instance, an empty jar fell from a shelf and bounced on the wooden floor of the hardware store without shattering, Penelope heard it as a *thud thud thudding,* reminding her of an elephant knocking on the door with its trunk. Thud, thud, thud, she stomped on the floor in echo, in delight.

She listened to the ceiling fan whirring and heard a song about rabbits. She listened to the phone ringing and heard a song about bees. When she heard the radiator pipes knocking at night, she heard a drummer setting the beat. And sometimes she listened so carefully to the endless chatter of grown-ups that she heard the steady hum of time rushing by.

Tuskee, New York. October 23, 1957.

It was because Mr. Campbell asked Buddy Potter to help him with a rush job installing a new water heater at the Dockery, making it necessary for Buddy to ask Sally to stay late at the store to lock up, that Penny Campbell offered to take Penelope, who was growing cranky with late-afternoon hunger pangs, back to the apartment to prepare supper for her. It was because the gumbo was attracting crowds from around the county that the Dockery's owner had bought a new water heater to support the second industrial dishwasher that had been installed. It was because the Dockery's cook, Walter Stackhouse, had been born and raised in New Orleans that the food was so good. It was because employment was scarce in New Orleans for a black man who had lost a leg to melanoma that Walter Stackhouse moved north to Tuskee, where his wife's cousin lived. It was because this cousin had studied horticulture with a botanist from Tuskee that he'd landed a job with the city park service way back in 1932.

And it was because the residents recognized the value of their open spaces that the park service had a sufficient budget and the cousin of Walter Stackhouse's wife never had to worry about the prospect of being laid off.

Even if Sally wasn't fully aware of this trajectory, she would conclude, in retrospect, that she had the residents of Tuskee to thank for giving Penny Campbell a reason to bring Penelope back to the apartment, leaving Sally free to attend to last-minute duties at the store.

So it goes, she would hum to herself when she thought of this day, for it was the song she was singing quietly as she tabulated supplies in Buddy Potter's ledger.

So it goes, so it goes,

So I found you,

So I lost you . . . It was one of Dara Bliss's songs — not one of Sally's favorites off the album, but with its easy tune and lyrics she could keep singing it while she was concentrating on something else, at that particular moment on the surprising fact that they'd sold one hundred and seventeen brass transom window hooks so far that month. Why was everybody in Tuskee buying brass transom window hooks, she was wondering, even while she murmured the song, the sound of her voice barely audible even to her own ears — *So it goes, so it goes* — when who should be standing there, casting a shadow over the page of the ledger . . .

But she wasn't wondering about *who.* In Sally's experience of that moment, she wasn't asking any questions in her mind. She knew immediately, between one blink and the next, before she could even ask the question — *who are you?* — that the man standing across the counter was Benny Patterson. He had a rounder girth and thicker neck, without the bristle on his chin but with bushier sideburns, an odd scab on his right temple, the crust of it almost black, as though it had been there for months, and his hair hidden by a cap advertising motor oil. But still, without a doubt, it was Benny Patterson.

The cream-cheese prince of the Amity environs.

How ridiculous — Sally didn't even know the word *environs.* But even after five years, she would have been able to pick Benny Patterson out of a lineup.

"Can I help you?"

Can, she said. Not *may.* So what. Her ability to utter the offer aloud at that moment would continue to amaze her for the rest of her life, for it implied that she was engaging in complex calculations in her mind, judging his manner, estimating his potential for recognizing her as easily as she recognized him, looking for any sign that he knew what he'd found, either on purpose or by accident, it didn't matter which. The key was whether after five years he recognized her.

She'd cut her hair, and now that she no longer dyed it blond, the reddish streaks in it were visible again through the brunette cast. Her skin tone had changed, darkening slightly through the course of her pregnancy. She was at least ten pounds heavier than she'd been when she'd met Benny Patterson at the Barge in Helena. She wore overalls and heavy boots, and she was suddenly conscious that her fingernails were rimmed with grease from a repair she'd done that morning for an elderly woman who'd brought in a broken Hoosier hinge.

All this was somehow conceived and processed in an instant, stirring in her the judgment, if hesitant, that those milky blue eyes belonging to Benny Patterson weren't manifesting any visible sign of recognition, making it possible for her at least to try to follow the most natural routine, to offer help in a congenial tone, clerk to customer.

There was a short delay in his response, a barely measurable pause, perhaps insignificant or, more worrisome, Sally considered, maybe an indication of his suspicion. She blinked and looked at the floorboards beside the edge of the counter, noticing for what felt like the first time that the grain was outlined with embedded grime. But the smell of the dirty wood, damp from shoes trekking in the light rain that had been falling for the last hour, was pleasant in its familiarity. It was a fragrance peculiar to a hardware store with a wooden floor, and it would comfort her later, when she entered other hardware stores in other towns.

"Sure you can help me," he said with an easy jocularity. She wanted to feel relieved. He seemed oblivious, too absorbed by his self-importance to remember that he'd ever known her.

But was his tone appropriate for the circumstances, or was there something unnatural about it, a hint of the kind of tension that usually accompanies subterfuge? Had he come here seeking her out? Did he know her? Did he guess that she knew him?

While in her mind she pleaded with him to go away and leave her alone, with her manner she presented a bland docility combined with a hint of impatience, which she indicated by tilting her head slightly while she waited for him to tell her what he was looking for. She cast an obvious glance at the clock on the wall — five minutes to six, and while she was pleased to be of service, she hoped her customer understood that, though she wouldn't have been so impolite to put it this bluntly, *closing time was closing time.*

"You can help me," Benny Patterson said, stringing out each word in a drawl, "sharpen a butcher's knife I got here."

She guessed that he was drunk, that he'd started drinking at lunchtime and had gone through a six-pack since then. But this didn't match the scrubbed, polished quality to his skin. He wasn't unkempt enough to be drunk, and he smelled of mouthwash and aftershave rather than of stale beer.

"Oh, I'm terribly sorry." She emphasized the apology by shaking her head for a moment, then stopped, thinking that he'd judge the gesture histrionic. "We only offer that service on weekends. If you want to come back . . ."

"I can't come back."

His words were too deliberate for their simple meaning. What else was he trying to say? He stood there expecting her to respond, but she was at a loss, unable to formulate a sentence that would seem nothing less than perfectly appropriate. He'd said he couldn't come back. Should she ask why not? Should she commiserate? *That's a shame . . . ?* No, she mustn't say the word *shame,* not to Benny Patterson and not in Tuskee. Beautiful Tuskee. She felt oddly nostalgic all of a sudden, as though her fondness for the city were born of loss, though not because she was remembering a place where she'd been happy, where her daughter had been born and she'd made good friends; it was more like the tingly longing that followed a pleasant dream.

"I'm on my way to Chicago."

"Chicago?" She repeated the word as though it were unfamiliar to her and immediately regretted this demonstration of confusion. What was there to be confused about? The customer could not return on the weekend because he was on his way to Chicago.

"Oh."

"My sister is getting married."

Why did he tell her this? Why was he telling her more than she needed or wanted to know? He was testing her, wasn't he? Playing with her, nudging, needling, trying to unnerve her.

"That's nice."

"Not really. The guy's a dope."

"A dope?"

"Her fiancé. But you girls, you don't know heads from tails." Now that was funny, so funny he erupted with a series of grunts, forced laughter, a put-on, Sally suspected, though she couldn't be sure because she couldn't recall the sound of Benny's true laughter; she couldn't recall ever hearing him laugh.

When she heard the bell over the door jingle, she was relieved. She could attend to another customer and turn her back on Benny Patterson. But when the bulky stranger elbowed Benny in the back, Sally's relief evaporated.

"What the hell," Benny said, his tone more wry than surprised.

"Let's go."

"Slow down."

"Store's closed, it says on the sign. Aren't you supposed to be closed?" the man asked Sally. His seersucker suit was so wrong for the season that Sally wondered if even this outfit was planned as part of an intricate deception contrived to trap her.

"We're about to close."

"Let's go. You gotta excuse him, ma'am. He goes gaga in the presence of a pretty girl. Come on, Benny."

"I was just saying that girls, they don't know heads from tails."

"Shut up, Benny. My friend here," he said to Sally, "they named the Dumpster after him. A bin full of garbage, that's Benny. Benny Dumpster." The smirk on the stranger's face signaled complicity with Sally, didn't it? He was trying to convey to her that he shared her revulsion of this fool. Or else he was secretly amused by Sally's foolishness. Did he think she didn't recognize Benny Patterson?

"I was hoping to get my knife sharpened." Benny moved his hand to slice the air with his knife. But he didn't have a knife; he'd only been pretending — a ruse to draw Sally into conversation.

"We'll get your knife sharpened, oh yeah, sure, you can count on it. We'll get your knife sharpened, Benny. Now say good-bye to the pretty lady."

"Good-bye, pretty lady."

For an instant, Benny's face was a mirror. He was squinting with the hatred that she felt for him, reflecting back to her the evidence of her revulsion. She wasn't sure why, exactly, she hated him, but she did, and he knew it right then. And he hated her because she hated him.

The two men shoved each other as they turned to leave, their laughter swallowing the jingle of the bell as the door eased shut behind them, one of them — she couldn't tell who — interrupting his laughter to call out distinctly, if inexplicably, "Fly in the ointment!" and then joining the other in laughter again.

Sally recognized the car, Benny's own fancy green stub-finned Cadillac, a dingy old car after all these years. She stood to the side of the window and watched the men get into the car, the stranger into the driver's seat, and Benny into the passenger side. He was probably too drunk to drive, Sally thought — if he was drunk at all. She couldn't be sure if anything she'd just witnessed had been authentic, or if Benny and his friend had planned and rehearsed the whole scene just to humiliate her. Well, if that was their intention, they'd failed mightily. Those two idiots had no idea how impervious she was, how strong and confident she'd grown in her years in Tuskee.

Fuckers, she mouthed, watching the Cadillac pull out into the street. She wished she could have been brave enough to say it aloud, but she couldn't, even in the privacy of the empty store.

She hated Benny Patterson with the certainty that he deserved to be hated, though she couldn't really point to anything particular he'd done to her. But she was sure she had a right to hate him, if only because of his obvious potential for wrongdoing.

"Dear God." She let herself say this aloud as she watched the car roll along through the drizzle. Once they'd turned at the intersection and were out of sight, she realized how scared she was, her fingers numb as though from cold, her knees aching. "Turn around," she sang almost as an instruction to herself as she went back behind the counter to retrieve the key. "Turn around, Lou, turn around." She double-locked the bolt on the front door. Leaving the last column on the inventory list incomplete, she grabbed her hat and raincoat and headed back through the rear door, an exit she rarely used but chose now because she wanted to avoid the more public State Street, in case the men in the Cadillac circled back around the block.

The narrow alley behind the store led from State Street and ran between high slat fences to the small parking lot where Sally had left her car. In her befuddlement following Benny's visit, she'd forgotten that she'd given the car keys to Penny, and that she'd been planning to take the bus. Right then her thoughts were racing through the sequence of things she needed to do: make sure all the lights were out in the store and that there was food in the cat's dish; lock both the knob and the bolt of the back door, one click signaling that the first lock was secure, the next click signaling that the bolt was in its slot and she could leave, and would, but couldn't because he — who? — who else? — was dragging her backward through the air, spinning, arm in a vise around her neck, flesh at the wrist, her own hair in her face, and words she hadn't heard in the longest time, words like *slut* and *bitch* and *wasn't she a goddamn cunt who thought . . . she thought . . . she thought she could just* —

It was happening too quickly, in jagged flashes, her awareness was blurred by the speed with which the assault took place, the sequence of blows delivered faster than light.

Fist in the face, bouncing off the hard ridge of her cheekbone. Head propelled down with a yank of her hair. Her whole body twisting in a way she hadn't known was possible.

Realization seemed to take forever, but it must have come quickly, for she'd been struck only once before she understood what was happening to her and began stiffening in defense, her strength coming to her in little surges. She slapped away his arm when he tried to hit her again. Whose arm? His arm, of course — his name escaped her right then, or else the fact of it was so clearly useless that she didn't bother to waste her time identifying him. She knew him without knowing him, this man who was hurting her, his violence fueled by accusatory rage, destruction the only possible way he could conceive to end the action he'd begun.

He had never forgiven her and never would, the slut, the little whore who'd had the nerve to up and leave him sitting there at the lunch counter in the Fenton Woolworth's, treating him like shit, taking off without a word when she belonged to him, she was his girl, she was supposed to do what he told her to do, and he hadn't told her to go, but she'd gone anyway, she'd left him sitting there looking like a complete fool. And then she'd tried to hide from him. She really thought she could hide?

With the word came another punch, splitting her lip. *Hide* — what did it mean? It meant pain and the sour, metallic taste of blood and a wrenching force too powerful for her to block. It meant he hated her and wanted to kill her. It meant she hated him and wanted to kill him. It meant she had to get back to her daughter and take her away

— *to hide* her from him, her daughter's father who was not her daughter's father, at least not according to the lineage that Sally would have wished for her, for he was not Mole, and since Mole should have been her daughter's father it meant that he *was* her father, Mole was, not this man, not the one attacking her, beating her, who, she'd known from the start, had always been capable of this, what he was doing to her now, and why she'd tried to . . .

Hide: It meant she had to cover her face, so the next time he hit her his knuckles struck the back of her hand, bouncing her head away from him but not actually hurting her, which only enraged him more, and with a swift movement he yanked her arm away, and though she wanted to scream she didn't have time, his fist caught her in the mouth, driving into her gullet, shattering bone, filling her vision with a blank darkness that matched the sky.

There, he'd done it, she thought as she fell to her knees. He'd killed her. But she couldn't be dead if she could think that she was dead — proof, wasn't it, that she was still alive enough to be thinking, also to notice the shine of a puddle, though she couldn't identify the source of the light it was reflecting?

Where was the light?

Who cared?

Not Sally Mole — all she cared about was that she was still alive, and since she was alive then, watch out, she was furious! She had a right to be furious, didn't she?

And she had a right to fuel her fury with the indignant certainty that God was on her side. And if He was on her side, then she could appeal to Him, in silence. . . . Dear God, she was red-hot mad, so please give her strength! She wanted to surprise the man doing this to her with her own power, and she would have succeeded if he weren't so much stronger, she would have returned the blows and magnified them tenfold if the nature of physical force didn't rely on such fixed laws.

Bam, bam, bam! That was the sound of violence in cartoons. But Sally was discovering that in real life the sound of flesh against flesh was far more muted, more of a thumping and shuffling, with the occasional crackling that seemed to come from far away, not from a measurable distance but from another dimension.

She was on her knees, half on the wet pavement, half on the muddy ridge that ran between the alley and the side of the fence. Her hands were flat on the ground, with the first two fingers of her right hand touching the edge of a rough, rounded object, just a rock, a simple rock the size of a baseball, and in an instant she'd seized it in her hand and with a desperate contortion flung it toward him, heard his grunt that meant the rock had hit its target, though with the sting of drizzle and the blood in her eyes she couldn't see where the rock hit him or even what he was doing, could feel only that the pinching force on the back of her neck slackened.

She scrambled to her feet, swinging blindly, knocking his cap off but missing his face. He grabbed her elbow, but she shook free. She would escape him, she would leave him sitting at the counter in Fenton once and for all, that's what she wanted to do, not to hurt him, only to desert him, and she would have succeeded if he hadn't caught her from behind and pushed her up against the fence, binding her wrists together against her side with one of his bulky hands and with the other yanking at the collar of her raincoat, even as he promised her in a whisper, his mouth close to her ear, that she'd never get away from him again.

That old song.

You can run but you can't hide.

Had he said *run?* Why, she knew that word.

Run. That was one of the words she'd never forget. Sometimes it was followed by the clattering of shoes on pavement. Sometimes it revealed its meaning with the shush of grass being pushed away from an overgrown path. And sometimes — listen! — it provoked frightful caterwauling.

Cats, Sally knew, never said *meow,* nor did any two cats sound exactly alike, no more than two human voices ever matched exactly. The sound that Leo the cat made when he landed on Benny Patterson's head could not really be conveyed with a decipherable arrangement of letters.

But Sally could guess what the sound signified and looked up in time to catch a glimpse of Leo leaping from the peaked roof above the door. But she didn't know he had landed on Benny Patterson until she felt her attacker veer backward. He would have pulled her with him if she hadn't ripped herself free of his grasp. He stumbled, tripped over the corner of the step, and as the cat leaped forward, Leo's weight exacerbated Benny's fall; he plunged backward, his feet came out from under him, and his head snapped hard against the brick wall of Potter's Hardware.

All this thanks to a cat that unbelievably had come to Sally's rescue. Some crazy things happened in this world, things that sure would seem impossible in any account of them.

As she watched Benny Patterson roll in agony onto his knees, she understood the danger he presented to her daughter, and her certainty came to her in a full sentence that she almost uttered aloud: *he must never know of her existence.* Right then it seemed that everything depended upon keeping the child a secret from her father. She must *hide* her daughter, and in order to do that, she had to . . . what?

What does a woman do when the man who has beaten her has himself been injured and is moaning on his knees, cradling his aching head in his hands? Does she offer to help him? Or does she club him with a stick and deliver a fatal blow?

Of course not. Not at that particular moment, at least. Not when another man was approaching from the parking lot, walking hesitantly at first, picking up his pace when he saw Benny on the ground.

Then what else should she do?

Remember that word, *run?*

Run, Sally Mole!

Where to?

Follow the cat!

The huge, loping cat, with his big belly jiggling, would have preferred to take his time, but he seemed to understand the urgency. And he knew the way, at least from one end of the alley to the other, to State Street, where Sally could take over the lead while fat Leo ran panting along behind her.

Run.

Turn right on Beverly Place, Hamlin Street to Lincoln to the labyrinthine streets between downtown and her apartment, left, no, right, stop, go back, go forward.

Her lungs burned, and she was trying to blot the blood dribbling from her chin with her raincoat sleeve, but still she ran. She knew how to run. And if she kept running, she'd eventually reach where she wanted to go.

It felt magical, this ability to fly through the air, her feet barely touching the ground. Forget the absurd fact that a huge cat had come to her rescue and felled the man who'd been pummeling her. That could be attributed to a combination of divine intervention and good luck. But this flight . . . why, the motion of her legs seemed to have an inexplicable separateness from the rest of her body. If there was anything in her life that could be called a miracle, it would have to begin here, with the simple, miraculous action of running.

Run, Sally Mole.
She's running.
Look at her go.
Good-bye, Sally.
She'll be back.

Gurgling sound coming from the downspout of the Tuskee Presbyterian Church. She would remember that sound. She would remember the place on Everett Street where the macadam crust had broken, revealing the checkerboard of old cobblestones underneath. She would remember the haze around the streetlamps on a misty night. She would remember the story Penny told about Father Macklehose and his six pairs of women's pumps, size nine. She would remember thinking when Penny played the piano that she must have had eyes on her fingertips. She would remember Penny's meat loaf, her freckles, her talking Appaloos'. She would remember the little boy who would have fallen into the river if she hadn't saved him.

She would remember the way a summer breeze would waft through her apartment when she left the front and back doors open, drying her daughter's damp bangs after a bath. And for some reason, she would remember a magazine article she read about campers who survived a grizzly bear attack.

And a line in a library book about singing: *Pretend your mouth is a rubber band.*

She would remember the set of phrases the book's author instructed her to repeat: *Selfish shellfish, fresh flat fish, sharp shrews sweet shop,* and *letter.*

Over and over: *Letter letter letter letter letter.*

Ma, me, mi, mo, mu.

How much did you say? My damn hearing aid . . .

Month after month . . .

Or just gilding the lily . . .

But still, you know, she won't believe you.

You don't mind?

See, it's dreams that it's about.

Peekaboo.

Now bow your head, like this.

For I the Lord thy God am a jealous God.

Herein is love.

Amen.

The smell of applesauce in a bowl left overnight in the sink. Graham crackers soggy from spilled milk. Lifting fistfuls of cold spaghetti from the colander that night after she and Penny had the whole Campbell family over for dinner.

And the day she followed the sound of buzzing and discovered a swarm of ground bees in the ivy.

What about that hairy centipede the size of a small frog. Eek!

Dreaming about a squirrel perched on the kitchen counter, gnawing on an apple core. Dreaming about missing the bus. Dreaming about Mole, tasting the salt on his skin. Only afterward would she consider how his hands had changed, the nails far too clean and oiled, as if he'd been for a manicure.

"The test of our capacity for self-government," intoned Adlai Stevenson from the steps of city hall, "is in our ability to deal with the unknown."

Now it's time to push, Sally. Push!

Push, pushing, pushing a baby girl, six pounds twelve ounces, into the world. Little Miss America.

She would remember the variegated edges of a new hybrid lilac in the park, lavender rimmed with white. Her breasts leaking milk while she was ringing up a sale at the cash register. The sound of waves crashing on television. The list she made with her daughter of the places they would visit: Beverly Hills, Coney Island, the Empire State Building, the Grand Canyon, London

Bridge, Miami Beach, the North Pole, the Sahara Desert, and Timbuktu.

I'm yearning for you. I'm yearning for you.

How she wanted to give the impression that she felt whatever she was singing about. Though no one had to tell her to be careful not to overdo it. Sometimes she wished Penny had been more critical in her coaching. But Penny wouldn't ever complain. She loved spontaneity too much and was too amused by mistakes to offer advice to avert them.

The mayor's wife with her webbed feet. Buddy Potter with his coal black hair. The man who rode into town on a donkey.

The creaking and rattling as the Ferry Street drawbridge was raised.

Sliding with Penelope on a flattened cardboard box down a snowy slope after a freak snowstorm in October.

Again!

Soup simmering atop the stove. Dandelions yellow one day, gray puffs the next. A child's growth measured by penciled lines on the wall.

Listen . . .

She listened.

Running through Tuskee, New York, on the evening of October 23, 1957, with Leo the cat at her heels. She was conscious of the solidity of her body and yet how light she felt, almost weightless. She was running, running, running away, and nothing could hold her back.

She used the knocker on the front door rather than letting herself into the apartment, and when Penny Campbell appeared she grabbed her, pulling her outside. Penny, roused abruptly into a wild state of disbelief by the sight of her bloodied friend, pushed her away in order to study her and understand what she was seeing. But the only way she could understand the image in front of her was to mistake it for a theatrical deception, as though Sally had put on a ghoul's costume a week ahead of Halloween.

"Good God, Sally Mole, what did you do to yourself?"

Just as Penny was mistaken about Sally, Sally was mistaken about Penny, and the hint of accusation in her friend's voice threw her into a state of such stunning isolation that she could only stand there blinking, baffled, without any means available to communicate what she was feeling.

Communication, then, was Penny's job; from the awful sight in front of her, she surmised that Sally Mole wasn't pretending to be hurt. "You really are hurt," she said with simple desperation, drawing Sally into her arms. She tried using the fleshy side of her fist to wipe the blood from her friend's face and then thought better of it and pulled a tissue from the pocket of her shirt. "Poor Sally," she said, "dear Sally."

Her sympathy helped orient Sally, reminding her that she was not alone and enabling her to think clearly enough to decide what she needed to say, first of all to insist that she stay out of sight, for she didn't want to frighten Penelope, they must be quiet while Sally cleaned herself up. "Shh," she kept saying, a command that Penny echoed back, "Shh," in an attempt to reassure her, as though it were in her power to declare that the trouble was over and Sally would be all right. She just needed to let Penny take care of her.

But the trouble wasn't over, and there wasn't time for care, only for a quick wash and a change of clothes, she needed clothes for Penelope, as well, she had to pack a suitcase, but she didn't have a suitcase of her own, she recalled. Could she borrow Penny's suitcase?

Sure, she could borrow whatever she needed — not even borrow. She could have it for keeps, along with anything else, *everything* else, Penny pledged, only vaguely comprehending that she was saying good-bye to her friend even as she was trying to assist her.

They had to make their way to the one bathroom at the far end of the apartment. Penelope was watching television, and her own laughter accompanying the loud canned laughter on the show helped to cover up the sound of their shuffling steps as Penny and Sally snuck past the open doorway down the hall.

The bathroom light switched on by Penny was brutal, too bright and revealing for Sally to endure. She grabbed a towel from the rack and held it over her face, blotting the oozing cuts on her lip and brow. Perhaps sensing her embarrassment, Penny kept her gaze averted and instead of immediately set-ting out to help Sally wash, she fumbled around in the cabinet for supplies, mutter-ing the list of things she was searching for, "Cotton balls and bandages and tape . . . the tape . . . and the peroxide, there should be some in the medicine cabinet, and don't we have any Mercurochrome, my ma swears by Mercurochrome, I thought about pick-ing up a bottle of it just the other day, and then wouldn't you know, I forgot, I just forgot, and now all I can find is a box of Band-Aids. That's a start, but still . . . did I ever tell you about the time I stitched up a cut on Nestor's neck —"

"Penny!"

"A big gouge from a broken board —"

"Penny!"

"What?"

"Soap and water will be fine."

"You should see a doctor, Sally."

"Don't worry. Let me just wash up and change."

"Isn't there anything I can do?"

"A cup of tea would be nice," Sally said, lowering the towel to steal a glance at herself in the mirror.

"I'll get the water boiling," Penny said, but she didn't move.

Sally said she sure was looking forward to a hot cup of tea, and Penny's voice returned in a weak echo, "Cup of tea."

Sally tried to find a way to tell Penny how grateful she was for her help, for the whole of it, for everything since they stepped off the bus in Tuskee, but all she could think to say was "Thanks."

Penny mumbled something, *It's nothing,* or, *No problem,* as she retreated from the bathroom, leaving Sally alone.

Alone, face-to-face with the woman she'd become, inadvertently vulnerable despite her strength, coarse in manner despite her best efforts, bruised, bloodied, but nonetheless grateful to be who she was. It was because of her innate agility, wasn't it, that she was safe in this bathroom rather than lying in a puddle in a dark alley? The cat couldn't have held off her assailant indefinitely — and the other man, Benny's friend, more likely his accomplice, hadn't he wanted to get his hands on Sally? But Sally had escaped from both of them, spoiling their plans for her, flying off into the night, leaving the two brutes to wonder where she'd gone.

She filled the sink with cold water, splashed with the bar of soap to make suds, and plunged her face in up to her ears, soaking away the dirt and blood, holding her breath in order to savor the sensation, just for a moment, of being elsewhere, floating beyond her body, separating from her condition. There, *phew,* she exhaled, blew bubbles through the water, and lifted up, settling back into reality.

After drying herself, she draped the towel over her shoulders and took a good look at her reflection to assess the damage. The cut above her right eyebrow was surprisingly small for the amount of blood it had produced. The same was true for the cut on her lip. It was hardly visible, really just a hairline split, though the whole lip was swollen. The main injuries were to her throbbing nose, which already was discolored with a petal-shaped bruise, and to two of her bottom teeth, one of which was loose and the other broken in half. This disappointed her. A bruise was one thing, just a temporary effect, and a cut would heal eventually. But a broken tooth was broken forever, creating a permanent gap that would remind her of what Benny Patterson did to her every time she looked in the mirror.

You can run but you can't hide.

That was as much a lie as its inversion would have been: *you can hide but you can't run.* See, she could do both. The woman in the mirror would never be found, not by the man who would be looking for her. The world was too vast, the streets of cities too crowded, and night erased the day with its concealing darkness. She would disappear into the night, Sally with Penelope beside her, the two of them too fleet and sneaky for any hunter. They would go . . . where would they go? To Coney Island, to the North Pole, to Timbuktu. They would go wherever Sally could find a steady job.

The thought of money occurred to her.

She would need lots of it when she set out, she would need money for gas, for hotels, for the down payment on an apartment, adding up to much more than the ten dollars plus change she had in the purse.

Her purse! She'd lost her purse, probably dropped it in the alley when Benny Patterson grabbed her — her cheap vinyl purse containing sunglasses she hardly ever wore, lipstick, a nail file, a pack with one stick left of Wrigley's gum, a pack, half-smoked, of cigarettes, a wallet with money, a photograph of Penelope, and her license with her name and address.

By now, Benny Patterson might be rifling through her purse, or maybe he was already on her trail, following a map from State Street to her apartment. Soon he'd be pounding on the door, thud thud thud of an elephant's trunk. All that was left to do was scream, she'd scream for help, and all of Tuskee would come running to save her and Penelope.

Penelope.

The girl was standing in the doorway, holding Leo as if he were a stuffed animal, her arms encircling his fat middle. His heavy hindquarters sagged so low that his back paws brushed against the floor, and with his eyes half-closed and his tufted ears flattened to the sides, he had an expression of complete, placid compliance.

Sally's gaze met her daughter's in an exchange that took place entirely on the surface of the mirror. The girl was staring, dumbfounded by the monstrous, discolored thing that had replaced her mother. And Sally couldn't help but stare back, experiencing through her daughter's vision the mesmerizing encounter with an image too strange even to warrant an explanation. Her broken tooth and bruised nose, the skin of her right brow split and swollen into a lump over her eye, her straggly hair, her raincoat torn and spattered with blood — she saw herself just as her daughter saw her, the mother transformed into a stranger, the daughter spellbound, and the cat resigned to its fate.

It was a scene that both of them would consider pivotal through the rest of their lives, with every detail easily recollected in sharp definition, along with the sensation of being held in place by a mystery that would never be solved.

Who are you? Penelope would have asked if she could have thought of the words.

I don't know would have been the only answer possible.

In another time and place, Sally might

have been ashamed. But part of the sensation of being mesmerized was accepting the impenetrable aspect of the scene. Out of that acceptance they would each realize in their own fashion, if only vaguely, without self-consciousness or regret, that there would always be something inexplicable about the other. It couldn't be helped.

The girl would break the spell with the defining word *Mama.* Sally would respond by naming her daughter, as though for the first time: *Baby.* Back in the realm of graspable meaning, Sally would catch Penelope in her arms, the cat would drop with a complaining squeak, and they'd hold each other to regain the feeling of familiarity.

And then Sally would recall the urgency of her predicament — danger pressing, dire need for flight, she had to change her clothes and grab only what she could fit in the suitcase, she'd send for the rest later, and she'd have to wire the bank, which reminded her of the money in the hatbox, Mason Jackson's money, she'd need that, at least to get started.

Frantically digging through the clutter in her closet, with Penelope trailing her and Penny trailing Penelope, Sally searched for the hatbox that contained her freedom, her future, her ability to choose how to live her life.

"What are you doing, Mama?"

"We're going on a trip, baby."

Penny Campbell asked mournfully why she couldn't wait at least until the morning.

Sally promised to write to her and explain. But there wasn't time now. She had to find the hatbox, the blue hatbox with the paper bag full of money. "Here it is. Okay. Come on," she said to her daughter. "Where's your sweater? You can put the sweater on over your pajamas."

"I don't want to go."

"You don't even know where we're going."

"Where are we going?"

"The North Pole."

"Will there be reindeer?"

"Sure."

"And Santa?"

"Put these socks on."

"No!"

"Yes!"

"Sally," Penny interrupted, "why are you leaving?"

Sally couldn't think of a succinct answer to her friend's question, so she didn't bother to reply at all.

"I want to help." Penny said this in a

whisper that came out strangely amplified.

Now the child was really upset. She'd thought Big Penny, as she called her, was coming on the trip, too. But Big Penny was staying in Tuskee, where Little Penny was determined to stay, and to prove it she took the scarf Sally had thrown at her, wrapped one end around her wrist and the other end around the spoke of a chair. "I'm not going."

Sally tried pleading with her sweetheart, her baby, please, she needed her, she couldn't leave her there. When pleading didn't work, she unwound the scarf from the chair, lifted the girl over her shoulder, and carried her out to the car while Penny followed with the suitcase.

By the time Penelope had been deposited on the passenger side, she'd given up trying to resist. As she already knew, such was the nature of the world of adults that their irrational tyranny, whatever it was called, would always triumph. There was nothing to do but stick her thumb in her mouth and pout.

Sally and Penny clung to each other in such a long embrace that Penelope knocked impatiently with her knuckles on the window. If they were taking a trip, then they should get going!

As she opened the driver's door, Sally asked Penny to tell Buddy Potter she was sorry, to tell everyone she was sorry for leaving Tuskee without saying good-bye.

Was it possible? She wasn't coming back? Big Penny asked. Never?

"Never?" Little Penny echoed inside the car, her tone more sullen than outraged.

Sally promised to write to Penny and explain. She said good-bye. And then she remembered something she'd been meaning to say. "Arthur Steerforth who works at the Dockery, he has a crush on you."

"How do you know?"

"It's obvious. Good-bye, Penny," she called over the engine.

"Good-bye, Sally."

She put the car into reverse, backed up, heard the sound of gravel crackling under the tires, turned the car to head toward the street. She drove slowly, at a crawling pace the first few yards, watching in the rearview mirror for headlights, in case she was being followed.

"Stop!" Penelope shrieked.

Sally slammed on the brakes, jerking them both forward. Penelope lightly bumped her nose against the dashboard, but she wasn't hurt and didn't complain. And she didn't answer her mother, who called to her, demanding to be told what she was doing as Penelope opened the car door and dashed out into the night.

At first Sally thought her daughter was escaping back to the apartment, the only home she'd known. But she didn't head home. She ran in front of the stationary car toward a dark lump ahead in the road — a dead animal, Sally presumed, just ordinary filthy roadkill, and she was telling her daughter not to touch it when the animal demonstrated that it was far from dead by standing and lazily stretching out its front legs.

The girl caught it in her arms, and only then did Sally recognize fat Leo, the hero of the night. Penelope half carried, half dragged the cat back to the car, and she held him on her lap while Sally leaned across her and slammed the door shut.

Sally drove on, unable to think of anything to say to her daughter, who sat with a sour, unforgiving look, focused on the road ahead. With each mile the silence seemed to grow heavier, more unbearable, until finally Sally decided to sing. She began by humming and then she added the words:

Walk with me, walk with me
Darlin', won't you walk with me . . .

At the intersection with Route 15, she

headed north, following the river. She sang "Buttons and Bows" and the few lines she could remember from a new song she'd heard recently called "Blue Monday." She sang "Alleluia Grace." By the time she got to "Turn Around, Lou," both Leo the cat and Penelope were asleep.

June 14, 2007

Yesterday morning I drove to the Bonville pier, where the Tuskee River empties into Canton Lake. There was a crane on a barge below the Lake Avenue drawbridge, which was closed for repair, and the crane's operator sat idly in his cab, perhaps waiting for some signal from the workmen on the bridge. Farther up, between the bridge and the pier, a dredger on a second barge moved in slow motion, its steel jaws widening in a bored yawn above the surface of the water.

The river is a sludgy red at Canton Point, shallow and sluggish, too polluted from the chemical plants, I would have thought, to be attractive to fishermen. They're here, though, dozens of them sitting on foldout stools along the pier. While I was walking out to the end, one of the fishermen suddenly braced and lifted his rod as it started to bend. I stopped to see what he would pull from the water, watched as he slowly wound the taut line, the reel signaling its progress in intervals of stuttering clicks, and by the time the top wire of the hook appeared at the surface, the fisherman's neck and shoulders were glistening with sweat. The struggle continued as he tried to lift his prey into the air, with the line dipping and rising, dipping and rising. Finally, just when I thought the line would snap, the rod sprang backward and the empty hook flew into the air.

The fisherman's face was shadowed by the lip of his cap, but his patient manner as he reeled in the line and steadied the hook and restrung it with bait suggested that this was the usual experience for him. It was all he ever expected, with the contest itself the reason for his effort and the source of satisfaction.

I walked on to the end of the pier. The wind mixed the sour smell of the dredged mud with smoke from fresh pitch on the drawbridge. From where I stood, it looked as though the river widened its mouth and took in the huge lake in a gulp. But I've seen from above, when I'm in a plane approaching the airport from the north, that the river's current spreads in murky tendrils and eventually disperses, not so much absorbed by the lake as it is washed away.

Not far from the pier, hidden by the buildings of the marina, is a pavilion with a carousel, still closed that early in the morning, or otherwise I would have gone to ride on it. My grandmother used to bring me to the carousel when I was little. I always chose the same white horse, hand-carved, with real horsehair for its mane and tail, while my grandmother preferred to sit in the teacup and spin around and around. After the ride she'd stumble from the carousel laughing her growling laugh, thrilled by the dizziness.

It was almost inevitable that my trip to the pier and this memory of my grandmother would merge in an elaborate dream I had last night involving fish heads and carousel horses, most of which I've forgotten, except for the image of my grandmother spinning down the Tuskee in a teacup, gripping the handrails, her hair blowing wild.

My grandmother must have loved the way dizziness washed thoughts and memories into a blur. As a young woman she spun through her life the way she spun around in the teacup on the Bonville carousel. At pivotal moments she tended to act rashly, abandoning her plans without bothering to consider alternatives, moving so quickly from the location of trouble that she would lose track of how one thing was connected to another. Absorbed in the effort of escape, she'd forget that the same problems she'd left behind had a tendency to reappear when she came to a stop.

According to my mother, the first few times my grandmother met her boyfriend Abe Boyle was in passing, when she was on her way out the door, and she sized him up quickly, without much interest. My grandmother had other concerns and didn't give much thought to her daughter's evolving romantic life. It doesn't matter, though, what my grandmother thought of Abe when she first met him. It was what she *didn't* think of him that would end up having consequence.

Abe and Penelope met at a bar on a June night in 1974. They converged because one of Abe's friends was the new boyfriend of one of Penelope's friends. Abe was the oldest among the group and the only one from out of town. The others were former high school friends on summer break from college or working in the area. They had planned to hang out at the bar for the evening, but they ended up taking the girls back to the room where Abe lived and making an impromptu party, the numbers swelling as word got around, so by nine o'clock the group of six had grown to sixteen.

Some of the friends sat on the bed; others sat in a circle on the floor, passing around a bong and exchanging meaningful glances in lieu of talk since the volume of the stereo was turned up too loud for anyone to hear beyond the music.

I assume it was without words that Penelope and Abe first became acquainted, communicating with their eyes, shyly at first, then in a more relaxed way through the haze of smoke, and then seductively, my mother batting those famously long lashes of hers, twirling a strand of her hair around her finger while she waited for her next drag on the bong, my father conveying with his grin that he was sure the two of them belonged together.

Only when the last song had finished playing did my mother and father speak.

Nice party.
Mmm.
Sweet hash.
Mmm.
Hey.
Hey back.
You busy tomorrow?
Naw.
Wanna go somewhere?

Like where?
Oh, like anywhere.
Sure, why not.
Cool.

And all the while, even as they floated on the surface of a hazy, potted high and feigned a happy stupidity, their senses were more keenly alert than ever, greedily absorbing everything they could about the other in an attempt to consign the whole portrait to memory so that they'd have something substantial to savor, a vision detailed enough to satisfy the intense yearning they expected to feel after they'd separated for the night.

When my mother reminisces about my father, she tends to grow irritable quickly. *Oh, he had that sweet smile,* she'll say. *And he had that long hair, long auburn hair. He knew he was irresistible,* she continues with rising anger, *he thought he could do no wrong.* Even after thirty years, two marriages and two divorces, she still blames Abe for seducing her and then abandoning her when she was pregnant. And she blames my grandmother for not giving her better advice about men.

The truth is, though my mother doesn't realize this, my grandmother blamed herself for missing the warning signs. She would go on blaming herself for the rest of her life. With what she saw as the distinctive color of his hair, the green of his eyes, and the dimple in his cheek, he should have struck her as familiar. But when she saw him for the first time, she didn't bother to look carefully enough to recognize him. It took her months, she told me, *to put two and two together,* and by then it was too late: the damage had been done, and I was on my way into the world.

SALLY BLISS

Blur of deep night beyond the drops streaking the glass. Weight of the cat on her lap. *No stoppin' once we start.* Penelope wanted to stay awake and listen to her mother sing. Her bad mother, bumped and bruised, who made her get into the car and go away to nowhere. If only she could trade her for another mother, one who wasn't bumped and bruised and who would sit and watch television all night at home where she belonged. But what if she couldn't find a mother who knew all the words to all the songs ever written? Keep singing, Mama. She didn't have to say it. Singing came from her mother like light filled a room when the chain was pulled. Not always, though. Not after bedtime, and not that once when the bulb popped with a spark and went out. That was a funny surprise, and after being afraid for a little while in the darkness, she was laughing. She was laughing because her mother said, "Where are you, peanut?" and all the while she was right there behind her, all pajama'd and washed and ready for bed.

She missed her bed so much all of a sudden, she wanted to cry. But she was too tired to cry. She was too tired not to be tired, so she gave up trying to resist and fell asleep.

Sleep passed faster than she could count, and she was awake again. Awake was good but not so easy right away with the taste in her mouth like the time she ate paste in Mrs. Murray's nursery school class. Naughty girl! She was slapped on the face for eating paste, the only time she'd ever been slapped, and it made her so mad she decided right then and there to hate Mrs. Murray forever. She hated her now just thinking of that time with paste in her mouth, and she wanted her mama. Her mama was there. Her mama was bumped and bruised, but she was still there. And she was hearing Penelope cry. It felt bad to cry. But it also felt good because it was something that mattered, and her mother had to pay attention.

Her mother was driving and not listening to what her daughter wanted her to hear. Stop driving, Mama! Maybe if Penelope bawled a little louder, her mother would pay attention. There, she was saying, "Shhh, sweetie pie." But *shhh* was a stupid thing to say to a bawling girl, so she bawled some more, clutching at the cat on her lap.

Finally her mother pulled off the road into a parking lot. It was daytime again, and Miss Penelope Mole wanted breakfast with milk — now! Okay, okay, she could have whatever she wanted if she was a good girl and waited in the car while her mama went into the 7-Eleven. Being good was easier than being bad. But don't tell anybody or you won't get your way. She stroked the cat hard between his ears so he would understand.

She almost always got her way, and when she didn't, she bawled. There went her mother into the 7-Eleven to keep her from bawling. It gave her a nice sense of being certain about things. She was certain that it was breakfast time. She was certain that she was thirsty. She was certain that eating paste was not a reason to be slapped.

She wouldn't be back at nursery school on Monday. It made her happy to picture the empty coat hook below her name and Mrs. Murray wondering why she was late. Never to be slapped again, ha! But *never* wasn't a big enough word to be what it meant. *Neverever* was better.

From somewhere far away behind the store came a new sound, a chicken squawking or a car honking. Then a big car the color of a water faucet pulled in a few spaces away, and a woman in a puffy brown coat hurried from the car into the store, taking quick steps, trot-trot, like a little pony.

A snowflake came out of the sky and landed on the windshield, turning right away into a drop of water. Soon there was another snowflake, but that was all.

Waiting for her mother to come out of the 7-Eleven, Penelope wondered what the letters on the sign in the store window spelled. *S-A-L-T. S* made the hiss sound, she knew. *Apple* began with *A,* and *L* was just *L.* But what was that next letter? Think, think, think, she told herself, poking at her temple to make the thoughts come. To her disappointment, she couldn't remember the certain thought about the letter. Either she'd forgotten what it was or she didn't know it. There was an important difference between the two, between forgetting and not knowing.

She'd decided to give up on trying to figure it out when she saw her mama come out of the store smiling but not really smiling, only pretending to, squeezing her lips to force them into the smiling shape and cover her broken teeth.

That mama. She wasn't very good at pretending.

But she was good at getting breakfast. *Look,* she mouthed with her pretending lips. She was on the other side of the closed car window, holding the half-pint carton of milk she'd pulled from the paper bag. Yes, look! It wasn't just regular milk, it was chocolate milk, and a package of powdered doughnuts, too!

Penelope turned the handle around and around. It was hard for her, but that was what she had to do to open the car window, and she had to open the car window to take the carton of chocolate milk from her mother.

Yum.

But oops, she dropped the milk carton when the cat jumped. Bad cat! And there he went, being very bad and very fat, dragging himself over the edge of the car window and out like a bouncing ball across the parking lot. He could go fast when he bounced, bounce, bounce, bounce, his big belly flopping from side to side.

Penelope had enough time to cry out, "Stop!" before he disappeared behind the other car. Then she called his name: "Leo!"

He reappeared beside the front bumper, blinked like the lazy cat he was, and licked his chops, as if he had just finished eating the first course of a meal and was ready to move on to the next. Penelope glared at him, telling him with her eyes that he had to come back, there was nothing else to do that would be right. But then because he was a selfish, stupid cat, he did the wrong thing, darting around the corner of the 7-Eleven and disappearing into the woods.

Penelope would mark the beginning of her new life not with the car ride but with Leo the cat running away, a terrible loss that would have broken her heart if she hadn't been so furious at him. It was horrible enough that he'd chosen the woods over their nice warm car. But even worse was the way he'd looked at her, denying that he had any reason to be grateful for all she'd done on his behalf. That was why she wouldn't let herself be heartbroken because of him, and neither would she forgive her mother for all the trouble she'd caused.

For Sally, though, her new start had begun earlier, with the fist that slammed into her mouth. That she could have had the broken teeth capped by any capable dentist didn't occur to her. The damaged face staring back from the mirror in her bathroom and from the rearview in the car and from the glare in the store window was hers to keep, and if she now resembled the Raggedy Ann she'd had as a child, well, wasn't that appropriate? She had treasured that doll for years.

Between Tuskee and the 7-Eleven along the country route, she'd covered only a little more than sixty miles, driving at a snail's pace because the curving dark road was slick with ice. And when exhaustion had gotten the better of her, she'd pulled over into the lot behind an abandoned gas station, shut off the engine, and tried to doze. She thought she wouldn't actually fall asleep, but the next thing she knew there was a pale light above the treetops indicating that several hours had passed.

She had no idea where she was heading, only that she would follow the river until there were no passable roads, and then she would find another road and keep driving, and eventually she would reach the place where she wanted to be. She would have driven straight through to noon if her daughter hadn't woken up and demanded her breakfast. To pay for that breakfast she'd taken a dollar from the purse containing Mason Jackson's money. She'd saved that money for years. She'd been planning to keep on saving it, and here she'd gone and used it to buy milk and those goddamn powdered doughnuts.

But it was Leo's escape that threatened to undo her. Frozen by panic as she'd watched the cat disappear, she felt she couldn't take any more — not another blow or harsh word, not any new expression of discontent from her daughter, not a prurient glance from a store clerk at her swollen face, and especially not such an unspeakable betrayal as this, by the same cat that had saved her life.

When awareness of the consequences caught up with her, she came to her senses and rushed after the cat. But the faster she ran, the faster the cat bolted ahead, and he reached the edge of the woods while Sally was still far behind. She crashed after him through the thicket, tore through brambles into a swampier area carpeted with moss and dormant stubs of cabbage. She shouted his name and then called him in a desperate whisper that she tried to make alluring. But the only answer she received was the hum of the wind.

She went back and found Penelope standing shivering, coatless, on the edge of the lot. She picked her up and tried to warm her in her arms while she continued to call for the cat. When she realized that the glistening dots gathering in the girl's hair were flakes of melting snow, she carried her back to the car.

They stayed parked at the store for another two hours. Sally tried to lure the cat out of the woods with bologna, and when that failed she bought a tin of sardines. By late morning the cat still hadn't appeared, and Penelope was hungry again, so Sally bought a turkey sandwich for them to split, and while they ate, she wrote out a detailed description of the cat on a flattened paper bag. She even drew a picture of him on the bag, and she wrote down the number of Potter's Hardware. With the clerk's permission, she pinned the notice to the community bulletin board by the door.

When she declared that they'd have to leave without the cat, she was surprised at Penelope's apparent indifference. Sally thought she would have been hysterical. Glancing at her as they drove north, she worried that her daughter was growing hard and unforgiving. But such a change was impossible. She decided instead that her little princess was so used to affection that it wouldn't occur to her to love anyone or anything that didn't love her back.

■ ■ ■ ■

Until she either found a job or wired the bank in Tuskee to send the money from her account, Sally would have to pay for everything in cash, with Mason Jackson's money. It had been difficult to part with the first dollar, but she expected that with every new transaction, spending it would become easier, more naturally inevitable.

Still, she felt compelled to search out the best deals possible. They stayed that night in a motel advertising rooms for $19.99, located near the entrance to the state park, registered under the name she came up with when she had the pen in hand: *Sally Bliss.* She liked the name immediately, though when she asked her daughter if she wouldn't mind trying out a new last name for a while, the girl said no way, not for a hundred dollars. But Sally had already made up her mind. Even if she didn't say this to her daughter aloud, Penelope Bliss would just have to get used to it.

They had supper at the diner adjacent to the motel. Penelope ordered a cheeseburger, and Sally chose the most inexpensive hot meal on the menu, spaghetti and meatballs, which included a basket full of soft, warm rolls, pats of butter on ice, and packets of saltines. Not only did she eat several rolls slathered with butter, but she also slipped all the saltines into her purse to snack on later.

A map of the state was printed on the place mat, and a dozen towns and cities were indicated with their first initials followed by dashes to be filled in by children and other bored customers while they waited for their meal. The whole course of the river was marked with a bold, squiggling line, and at the halfway point was a *T* for the city of Tuskee. Sally wrote out the name with a crayon from a cup on the table. She filled in the letters following the *B* in the corner of the state and the name after the *A* to the east. And though she'd learned long ago that there was no such city called Rondo along the Tuskee, that's the name she gave to the city situated on the lake at the mouth of the river, filling in *o-n-d-o* after the *R*.

The newspaper she bought was from that city, Sally Bliss's Rondo. She paged through the sections while her daughter watched *People Are Funny* on the television in the motel room. The TV audience's laughter seemed to rise in response to the stories that Sally was reading, and it made her wonder if any of it was true.

It could have been yesterday's paper or tomorrow's. But there was some useful information — a reminder that daylight savings would end Sunday at 2:00 a.m. and a forecast of wintry weather for the weekend. And look at that nice photograph of Harold Lloyd, shown seated on a hotel sofa reading a newspaper article about Bing Crosby's marriage. So Bing was getting married. Oh, that lucky duck of a woman!

There was a big ad for a men's sport hat, the Dobbs Gamebird. And under the heading of church services, the sermon that sounded most promising was "What the Bible Teaches about Demons," to be delivered at 7:30 p.m. on Sunday at the First Assembly of God on Field Street.

But really, it was the classifieds that mattered, and Sally set them aside as though they were dessert, turning to them only when she was done with the rest of the paper. And here was a whole half page under the heading of "Help Wanted: Female." One announced an opening at a downtown bank, good pay with benefits, but keypunch experience was desirable. Girls were needed for laundry work at the Star Palace, 61 North Street. Business girls who wanted to add to their present income were encouraged to write to Avon Cosmetics, PO Box 516.

She circled the notice for *Girl, general office work, 5 1/2 days/week, must be good typist.* Another ad for an *Experienced person for one-girl shop office* sounded promising: *Typing, shorthand, payroll, and clerical duties. Weddell Tools.* But she had no experience with shorthand or payroll.

There were several ads for housekeepers, to live in or out, paying up to forty-five dollars a week. And there were other, less familiar possibilities: *2 ladies to sell costume jewelry. Either home, fashion shows, or where you work. Weekly commission.*

And there was an ad for *Dictaphone operations, section ability, shorthand not necessary.* This one offered a salary of *sixty to sixty-five dollars a week.*

The ad that looked the most appealing of all was for waitresses at Neimurs Dinner Cabaret, *Cocktail girls, nice figure, talent a plus. Performance potential. 5-day week. All benefits. Good salary. Apply at box office.* She circled this one and put a star by it.

The city at the mouth of the Tuskee may not have been as far as she would have liked to go from Benny Patterson, but in the past she hadn't ever gone as far as she'd planned.

It appeared to be a big enough city where she could live without being found. And if the classifieds were accurate, there were too many available jobs to pass by. The city of Rondo it was then — her destination again, as it had been before.

She set the folded paper on the table and watched television with Penelope. By the end of the show she was convinced that people really were funny, and she fell asleep in a hopeful mood.

The next morning they both slept late, past nine. They took baths — Sally had to plug the tub drain with a washcloth because she couldn't find the stopper — and they had a big breakfast of pancakes and sausages at the diner. But when Sally tried to start the car, the engine just rattled without revving. Though she kept trying to turn the key farther in the ignition, pressed the accelerator to the floor, and even banged on the dashboard, nothing happened.

If the car had broken down the previous day, she probably would have given herself up to despair. But she felt stronger after the night's rest, better prepared for unexpected difficulties, and she had enough wherewithal to ask the motel clerk to call a towing company.

The tow truck arrived within the half hour. The driver — a polite, grease-stained teenage boy — looked under the hood of the Mercury and diagnosed a carburetor problem. He said his boss was at the garage, and they'd try to have the problem fixed by the afternoon. He apologized to Sally several times, as though he were responsible for the inconvenience.

It was a crisp day with a fresh blue sky, and after the car had been towed away, Sally tied a wool hat on Penelope and lured her into taking a walk by telling her that they were going on a treasure hunt.

They followed the winding road a short distance into the park until they came to a sign posting park rules. From there they followed a red blaze on a trunk marking the start of a trail. They walked parallel to the road for a hundred yards and then down a gradual slope through a thick pine grove, between towering trees that must have been planted deliberately decades ago, in even rows.

They passed only one person, a little man who came from the opposite direction carrying fishing gear. He grumbled a greeting in an accent that Sally thought was German, and she had an impulse to stop and strike up a conversation with him. But with

379

his shoulders hunched and his cap low over his eyes, he gave the impression that he didn't want to be approached.

They continued along the path, their steps muffled by the cushion of wet needles. For the fun of it, Penelope found a stick and began lashing it against the bushes, and the ruckus startled a doe, sending it loping across the path ahead and into the woods.

The trail grew rougher as it sloped downhill, winding from beneath the pines through a stand of birch, with yellow leaves still clinging to the branches and glittering in the sun. Beyond the birch was a meadow, and past the meadow was a wooded area cresting the steep ridge of a ravine, where, from the bottom, came a sound like a pot's lid rattling over boiling water. They climbed carefully down the path, Sally leading the way and turning at each difficult stretch to brace Penelope and keep her from slipping. Though the sun was hidden by the far edge of the ravine, the bright sky cast enough light to make sharply defined shadows that shivered and melted into new shapes with the breeze. Dampness intensified the smell of sap and pine bark, and in the deeper shade, patches of frost were visible. Crows squawked back and forth high in the trees, and one of them burst into a lengthy chatter so varied that the sounds seemed composed of words. And when Sally heard a small animal's sudden scratching through the needles, she had a flash of hope that Leo the cat had come back to them. But of course Leo had disappeared many miles away.

The river appeared suddenly in front of them as Sally pushed aside the screen of brush. A set of uneven steps carved out of the sandstone led from the path to the edge of the water, which flowed out from a cave-like opening into the broad stretch between the wooded slopes. A hawk circled high overhead. The far side of the ravine was blanketed in a solid shadow, but the water sparkled as it rushed against huge boulders, foaming and splitting into transparent cords, cascading over wide stone shelves into foaming pools.

Here's your treasure, Sally wanted to say. But the river wouldn't be enough for her daughter. They'd come all this way, walked for an hour or more, and she would be expecting a real reward, not just something to look at, but something to own.

Penelope was crouching at the edge of a graveled ridge that jutted out into the water, poking with a stick, stirring the submerged pebbles into a smoky stew. She didn't need to be warned to be quiet. She was silent, concentrating intently on the water, so Sally relaxed, closing her eyes, breathing in the rich smell of moss. She thought it remarkably strange that this was the river that came bubbling out of the spring on Thistle Mountain, the same river that crawled past Mason Jackson's house in Fishkill Notch and flowed below the Barge in Helena. It looked too pure and too contained by the high walls of the gorge to have covered that distance. But she was certain it was the Tuskee because she'd been following it the whole way north.

Pressing her tongue over the jagged edge of the broken tooth and pushing at the loose tooth next to it, she imagined that she was being healed in this remote spot on the bank of the Tuskee. And then, partly because she was curious to hear how her voice would sound in this isolated place and partly because she just felt the urge, she began to sing in a soft voice.

It's simple to wish . . .

Singing softly, eyes closed, swaying slightly, drifting through the verses, she didn't hear her daughter's sudden gasp or see her arm freeze in the air. Not until Penelope whispered, "Mama!" did Sally open her eyes and look down.

At first she thought she recognized the same kind of fish she'd seen in the shallows below the platform in Tuskee. But she was mistaken. It was some kind of water snake or maybe a salamander or a newt, yes, like the one she'd seen years ago at the spring, with the weeds clinging to it like wet hair, the sleek bronze-colored strands matted on its head and wavering below the surface. How dark and staring its eyes were — brown buttons too large for its head and heavy lids fringed with a fuzzy line that almost looked like lashes. And how human-like its tiny forelimbs were, the webbed, long-fingered hands clinging to the curve of a rock, tensing when she leaned forward, as though it were preparing to bolt.

Funny little creature, too strange to be real, and yet it was real, too real and out-landish to be any kind of animal that could be named. Why, it almost looked like it would open its mouth and talk. But it didn't want to talk. It wanted exactly what they wanted, to understand what it was seeing.

And simple to dream . . .

The murmur of song came from within Sally, but at the same time the sound seemed separate, impossible to stifle, as though she weren't responsible for it. She guessed that the music had a soothing effect, for the creature seemed to be straining to listen even as it stared at Penelope, holding the girl in its gaze as though admiring her beauty.

Either Sally was mad or there was a magical being that lived in the river. Yes, she'd decide, she must be mad to believe that she'd seen something that couldn't really exist, and she was mad to think that she'd seen its kind before, upriver, in Tuskee and Helena and even at the spring on Thistle Mountain. All right, then, she was mad, but she couldn't help it.

Her daughter shared her awe. For those few seconds they were both equally fascinated. Surely this was the treasure they'd come looking for, perched before their very eyes. Don't move. Don't startle it. Engrave the sight of it on memory — too late, there it goes, cocking its head as though hearing its name called, slipping down the rock and disappearing into the water.

Sally would always consider that day momentous because of the encounter in the park. But Penelope would mention the park only when questioned, and then she didn't remember much about it. For her, that particular day — October 25, 1957 — was significant because it was the day she and her mother arrived in the city of R.

It took them until evening to get there — to *Rondo,* as Sally would insist on calling it, though not because the city was far away. Following Route 15 along the river, it should have been no more than a three-hour drive. But Sally wasn't driving. She and her daughter traveled to Rondo in a bus that day rather than in the Mercury that Sally had bought secondhand in Tuskee. The car, she was told, wasn't worth the expense of repairing it. It was old, with corroded pipes and a worn-out engine. She had no other option, no friend who would fix the car for free, no mechanic around to offer a second opinion. The owner of the garage where it had been towed gave her fifty dollars — a generous sum, it seemed to Sally — and kept the car as salvage. When the boy in the tow truck came to the motel to deliver the money, he offered them a lift to the bus station in the nearby town of Sarabelle.

Sally heard the name of the town with an odd sense of déjà vu, though she couldn't recall ever having heard it before. Why, she wondered as they boarded the bus, did the name of the town even matter?

She'd bought a bag of potato chips for Penelope to eat on the bus and for herself, a pack of cigarettes. She smoked slowly, lazily, entertained herself by blowing the smoke through the gap of her broken tooth, while her daughter played with a pair of little dolls. Sally felt lazy, and while she regretted giving up the car, she also felt relieved to be on a bus, where she could regard with a pleasant calm the ribbon of the river on one side coming in and out of view behind a row of shingled houses.

She didn't fight the urge to doze. She closed her eyes and reminisced dreamily about her life in the city of Tuskee. She was comforted remembering that time at the Rotary Club when the audience called for an encore, and the memory revived in her the desire for success. It was a good sign that she'd thought up a new name for herself so easily, a name people would want to say aloud but that Benny Patterson wouldn't recognize.

Sally Bliss. Yes, *Sally Bliss* would do just fine.

They were both asleep as they moved through the grid of streets in the city. When Sally woke at the jerking movement of the bus turning into the station, she was startled by the different setting outside the window — a wet sidewalk; fog shrouding the street-lamps; dark stone buildings; a display window glowing, lighting up mannequins nestled in wool coats; a theater announcing showtimes for *Back from the Dead;* and a neon sign above a doorway flashing the name of the Cadillac Hotel.

The Cadillac Hotel was only a couple of blocks from the bus station, so that's where they stayed while they were looking for a permanent residence. Sally didn't much like the association in her mind with that particular make of car. But it was a pleasant hotel — a bargain at thirty-five dollars a week, with fine cotton sheets on a queen-size bed, a modern shower in each room, a fulltime attendant at the lobby desk, and a doorman who always had a lollipop to give to Penelope. And thanks to the fifty dollars from the mechanic on Route 15, Sally wouldn't have to spend any more of Mason Jackson's money.

The next day they went to the address listed in the classifieds for Neimurs Cabaret, but it was closed. The marquee announced that a new performer, Big Betty, would open the following Saturday. The poster on the wall labeled Big Betty's show "The Sassafras Burlesque," and a message posted diagonally across the poster informed the public that Neimurs was under new management.

With her daughter in tow, Sally spent the rest of the day taking care of important business. She opened a bank account and had her money wired from Tuskee, she visited the chamber of commerce, and she contacted several landlords advertising in the rental section of the paper. She was dismayed by the steep rents. But judging from the job listings, the salaries were better here than she was used to, and once she was working, she'd be able to afford lodging in a good neighborhood.

Mother and daughter went back to Neimurs the following day. A man sweeping the lobby told her to knock on the door of the manager's office, but when she did, there was no answer. They waited outside the office for half an hour; Sally was just about to leave but thought she heard a voice from behind the door, so she knocked again, and the door was opened abruptly by a tall woman, a fancy woman with a blond beehive that added three inches to her height.

Pulling her daughter close to her, Sally said she'd come regarding the waitress job. The woman declared that she didn't know what she was talking about. Sally would have left, but a gray-haired man, shorter than the woman, appeared beside her, casually adjusting his tie. He gave Sally the once-over, ignoring the little girl scowling beside her. It seemed he didn't notice the fading bruises on her face, or else he didn't care. He told Sally to come back at three thirty the next day for auditions.

It was strange, Sally thought — auditions for a job waiting tables. But the ad had indicated performance potential. If they gave her a chance to sing, why, this could be her break, she thought as they walked out onto the street, the rise from rags to riches that's described in every movie magazine. All a girl needed was one chance to let her talent shine.

They returned to Neimurs the next day, right on time, just as a pair of stately, long-legged young women left the theater. They must have been dancers, Sally thought. And she found a crowd of girls gathered in the lobby — girls wearing flowing feather boas, girls in leather boots and tight dresses, girls with false lashes and bright red lips. The manager came out and directed the group to line up on the side of the stage. Sally left Penelope at a table at the back of the theater and told her to stay there, in a voice that was more pleading than commanding. The child, too bored by the situation to do anything but accommodate her mother's wishes, shrugged and danced her dolls along the arm of her chair.

The room was dark, with cocktail tables pushed close together, but the stage was illuminated by footlights. The girls were directed to stand in the wings and, when signaled, approach the woman who was sitting at a table on the far side of the stage — the same woman who had answered the office door the day before. The manager himself took a seat in the middle of the room and folded his arms in a manner that suggested he was waiting for the beginning of a show he'd already seen too many times.

The woman beckoned to the first girl, a pretty young blonde who strode in all her high-heeled elegance across the stage, moving her hips expertly. She sat at the table and whispered excitedly while the woman took notes.

It was a quick conversation, and after the girl left, the woman at the table beckoned to the next girl. The manager said nothing.

Sally kept shooting glances at her daughter, hoping that her patience wouldn't wear out during a process that slowed as it went on, with the whispered conversations lasting longer and the girls taking their time walking across the stage. Some didn't just sway as they walked; they spun like models on a runway. One of them, an older woman, got impatient and broke into a run and then kept running past the table, up an aisle, and out the door. One girl turned silly and began squawking like a chicken and flapping her arms on stage. And one girl inexplicably buzzed like a bee and ran in spirals.

What strange world were they all trying to gain entry to? Was the whole city equally absurd? Sally started to weigh the consequences of leaving before her own so-called audition, but by then it was too late to change her mind. She was being called to cross the stage.

With her daughter watching, she wasn't about to strut in a lewd fashion. She walked firmly, businesslike, and took a seat with the woman, who asked her name but didn't bother to fill in the space for it on the form. She just rolled her pen between her fingers and with powerful indifference asked Sally if she'd ever had any experience waiting tables.

Sally already had an innocent lie prepared. She said she'd been a waitress at the Tuskee Diner. But that wasn't good enough for the woman, who lifted a shoulder to indicate the exit, and thanked Sally for her time.

That was it? Not a missed opportunity — not an opportunity at all. She sat back in her chair, stunned by the dismissal. When she asked if she had any chance of being hired, the woman gave a mocking chortle.

Sally raged inwardly. *You think you're better than me, you with that flea nest on your head.* A minute earlier she'd wanted to escape from the scene. Now she was supposed to agree that she was worthless. She'd been given the once-over and judged inadequate. Really? She didn't measure up? Oh, yeah?

In defiance, she marched to the center of the stage and cleared her throat, the sound as good as an announcement that she was going to sing. There was a giggling murmur from the girls, a snort of disgust from the woman at the table. The gray-haired man was concentrating on his cigarette, watching the smoke curl toward the ceiling.

It was a fine stage, grander than any she'd ever performed on, and she imagined the room packed with an audience of rich ladies in furs, men with gold watch chains. She would sing "Turn Around, Lou" to impress them. She would sing to court their goodwill. She would sing with a passion that anyone with any class would perceive as noble but to the girls waiting their turn would be nothing less than ridiculous. Sally was already ridiculous in their eyes. Even before she sang the first note, the girls' rumbling giggles rose to a roar.

Just look at her.

What a square.

Slut.

Who said that?

It was impossible to differentiate between what she imagined she heard and what they were actually saying.

Whore.

Who?

Sally.

Sally's gone away.

Run, Sally.

But she wouldn't run, not this time. She would walk from the stage accompanied by hooting encouragement: "Go ahead and do something, lady!"

Sure, she'd do something. She tried to convey her fury with every step, thinking to herself, oh, she'd show them, she'd show them, and at the same time feeling more humiliated than she would have thought possible, shame searing her cheeks. Mottled by her blushing, in her dull dress, with no makeup and broken teeth, she must have looked as pathetic as she felt, there was no disguising it and no reason to hope that she'd show them anything other than what a thorough fool she was.

Walking up the aisle, she noticed that the

manager's chair was empty, though smoke was still rising from the cigarette he'd left in the ashtray. Obviously, he had better things to do than to sit there waiting for Sally Bliss to sing.

But Penelope was still there, dancing her dolls across the table as though she were hearing in her mind the song her mother hadn't had the courage to sing. It helped Sally just to watch for a moment as her daughter made the funny little dolls somersault effortlessly through the air. It made her feel a little less humiliated, a little less responsible for her own embarrassment. At the same time, she didn't need anyone to tell her that out in the real world, she didn't stand a chance as a showgirl.

She was thinking expansively at the moment, desperate to ensure that she would never be laughed at again. The best way to protect herself was to give up her dream of singing in public. And at the same time she'd spite those who wouldn't experience the pleasure of listening to her. She had quit singing before; she'd quit again.

Even if she sensed that she was letting herself be too easily defeated, she had a strong pragmatic side, roused by the sting of her failure at Neimurs. As much as she'd wanted to be the next Dara Bliss, she wouldn't waste her voice on a futile fight for respect. There were better ways to earn a living.

The next day they spent three dollars on a big breakfast at the diner next to the Cadillac Hotel. They were lingering lazily at a table, waiting for their dishes to be cleared, when Sally recognized the older woman who'd been at Neimurs, the one who'd left the stage without stopping for an interview. She was at the counter of the diner, sucking on a cigarette as though it were water for her parched throat. Sally walked right up to her and introduced herself. The woman seemed genuinely happy to see her and was eager to talk.

She was named Elena, she said, and offered an incomprehensible last name. Sally asked her if she'd found work yet. In a thick accent that Sally thought was Russian but later learned was Polish, she said she wanted nothing to do with *doz Neimur bazturdz*. And she generously shared the information that Sibley's Department Store on East Main was looking for salesgirls. She'd been planning to go there as soon as she finished her coffee.

And so it was at Sibley's where both Elena and Sally ended up applying for work that day. It was as easy as filling out forms in the personnel department. Along with her invented name, Sally Bliss was able to put down Elena's address as her own. She listed Penny Campbell and Buddy Potter for references, and she said truthfully that she'd been an assistant at a hardware store for the past five years.

The personnel director hired them both on the spot. Elena was assigned to the dress department, Sally to household goods on the fourth floor. They were to start the following Monday.

So Sally Bliss would make her living in the city of her dreams as a salesgirl in a department store, fifty-five dollars per week, benefits included. It was the best outcome she could have hoped for.

All that was left was to find a place to live. It was too late in the day to look, she was exhausted, and Penelope had lost patience and was beginning to whine with hunger. Sally said good-bye to Elena and took her daughter back to the diner for an early supper before returning to the Cadillac Hotel.

From then on, their arrangements fell into place more easily than Sally could have hoped. She thought it must have had something to do with giving up her unreasonable ambitions; she was ready to accept what the world thought she deserved, to expect no more than her fair share.

They moved into their own apartment at the end of the week. Advertised as *comfortable accommodations on a bus line,* at eighty dollars a month, the apartment Sally liked best was located over a shoe repair shop, diagonally across from the municipal post office. The landlord, Mr. Botelia, the shop owner, was a potbellied, grizzled man. When he met them at the side door of the building, he was wearing an apron stained with shades of polish, he smelled of leather cream, and as he greeted Penelope, he held out a sharp-clawed bear's paw in place of a hand.

He growled, and Penelope burst into tears. No, no, that's not what he was after. It had been Halloween the day before, hadn't it, he'd wanted to have a little fun, but he didn't want to frighten the girl. He pleaded with her to stop crying, and with a swift movement he removed the bear's paw from his long sleeve and pulled from his tool belt another appendage, a mechanical contraption ending in a pair of shears, which he sliced, clack-clack, in the air. Was that better? he asked Penelope, but she hid her face in the folds of her mother's skirt and kept bawling. No? Then how about this? He exchanged the shears for a plastic arm ending in a slender-fingered hand, probably a woman's hand, he admitted as he tucked it up his sleeve, though didn't they agree that it was hard to tell for sure? He'd gotten it for free, taken it off a store mannequin that he'd found in the garbage.

In fact, he had two hands of his own. But he couldn't resist a good joke.

The apartment he showed them was more spacious than Sally expected, with a bay window and a reading nook facing the street, though the furnishings were meager — a single table, twin beds, a tattered sofa. And it was so dusty that their feet left prints across the floor. But when Mr. Botelia said he'd let Sally determine the rent she thought was fair, she replied with some awkwardness that she thought fifty dollars a month was all she could afford. Mr. Botelia offered better than that and set the rent at forty dollars a month, half the amount listed in the ad and less than the rent she'd proposed because, as he reminded her apologetically, utilities were extra.

They would get used to the mail trucks rumbling down the road every morning at four. They would get used to the smell of polish and leather, which permeated the whole building. They would get so used to the apartment above Botelia's Shoe Repair that they'd settle in and stay for many years.

They soon discovered that their newest home wasn't far from the river, less than a mile. The first Sunday, Sally took Penelope to explore the neighborhood, and they ended up on the Ford Street Bridge, where they leaned against the rail, trying to catch sight of one of the strange fairy creatures they'd seen in the state park. But this stretch of the river was the color of a rusty pipe, and the stone embankment was coated with a noxious black slime. The reality of it made the memory of their experience in the park seem impossibly distant to Sally, as if it had happened in another life.

Later in the week they followed a path leading from a warehouse to the water, and they were able to walk right up to the riverbank. But there was a strong sulfur stench coming from the mud, and the shore had served as a dumping ground for trash. Sally gave up hope of ever seeing anything alive come out of the water. Nothing could survive, she decided, not in that poisonous stew. Over time, when she bothered to look at the Tuskee at all, she saw a surface as impenetrable as the macadam of the city streets.

When Sally described this period in her life, she'd warn that there wasn't much of interest to say. Who cared that over several months she transformed that dusty wreck of an apartment on Magellan Street into a cozy home? Who cared that Penelope Bliss got used to her name, even came to like the sound of it? And who cared that by the age of twenty-nine, Sally was so proficient in her sales job at Sibley's that she'd been promoted to an assistant manager of the floor? All the mundane stuff, work, work, work, day in, day out — it might have filled the bulk of the hours of her life, but it hardly figured when she added up the years. Still, it was something when a customer came in to buy a smoking stand and she talked him into buying a brass magazine rack along with it. And there was that woman in search of a casserole warmer who left the store with a new dinnerware service for eight. And what about that day she sold seventeen Mary Proctor ironing boards in three hours!

Oh, she did work hard, and she was shrewd at gauging what a customer might be willing to add to his purchases. But she was just your average Jane, just another single mother trying to keep ahead of the game, two teeth missing after the loose one fell out and a faint pink wriggling scar poking up from her right eyebrow. It didn't matter in the larger scheme that having set herself the challenge of saving as much of her hard-earned salary as she could, she'd take a twenty-minute bus ride to the IGA instead of walking to the nearby A&P. If she was lucky, Mr. Botelia's wife, who was as plump and filthy as her husband, would drive Sally to the grocery store in their car, a battered wood-paneled station wagon that bounced her out of the seat when it hit a pothole.

And all those receipts she saved — what was the point of them other than to prove that Sally Bliss knew a bargain when she saw it? Not until 1960 did she pay more than fifty-five cents for a package of franks. She would buy frozen mixed vegetables on sale, two for one, and save ten cents. She'd buy the cheapest margarine. Blue Bonnet was her favorite, and at the IGA it usually came on sale at the first of the month.

She became fond of Dinty Moore beef stew. A twenty-four-ounce can was only forty-five cents. Penelope liked American cheese, Sally preferred pimento, and once she found them on sale together. She bought chuck roast instead of round steak. She bought canned chicken, though she would have preferred the fancy pink salmon. She invited her Polish friend, Elena, for New Year's dinner and bought a smoked ham on sale, along with an angel food cake, which she covered in an instant lemon sauce from a packet. For her daughter's fifth birthday, in March of 1958, she invited over a group of little girls from the neighborhood. She borrowed cake tins from Mrs. Botelia, bought a mix and made a cake that was a big hit. She had snapshots of the girls with their mouths rimmed with chocolate. And Sally gave Penelope a real Lionel train set, which she'd bought at seventy percent off the original price because the caboose had been damaged in shipment.

They bought a used console television, which filled all their extra time. Most nights they would turn to Channel 4 and watch Frank Sinatra. Sally loved Frank Sinatra, even if he did collect girls as if they were souvenirs. He could come along and collect her any day! And that heartthrob Senator John Kennedy . . . Once Sally had a dream in which the senator appeared on the fourth floor of Sibley's, said flattering things to her, and they made love on the red velvet sectional. And when in real life he ran for president, she wore a JFK button pinned to her lapel.

There I am, she'd say, holding up the old newspaper she'd saved with its front-page photograph of the Memorial Day Parade in 1960. She was the girl standing in back of the blurred group of faces, the one in an oversized white sailor's cap she'd bought at the five-and-dime. If she hadn't been wearing that white cap, it would have been impossible to distinguish her in the crowd.

What was there to say to distinguish Sally Bliss from thousands of others like her in America in the late 1950s? She was pert-looking, with full cheeks and rosy skin. She'd trained herself to keep her mouth closed when she smiled to hide the hole of her missing teeth. She'd put on a few extra pounds around her thighs, but wasn't that what happened to a woman once she hit thirty? She sang when she did housework but never out in public. She bought wool suits, half slips, and Dacron blouses from the sales rack. She found a fine calfskin bag on the clearance shelf for $7.99.

Correspondence with her friends in Tuskee kept her posted on the news there. None of them expressed any disapproval of her sudden departure; though they didn't admit it, Sally guessed that they knew why she'd left. She wished she hadn't had to leave. Their letters reminded her of how pleasant life had been in Tuskee. Buddy Potter wrote to say that he was thinking about retiring and selling the store. He kept on thinking about it for the next twelve years. On July 4, 1959, Penny Campbell married Arthur Steerforth from the Dockery. They had the wedding in Penny's hometown, in the backyard of her parents' house, and it poured buckets all afternoon, though at the end of the day a double rainbow appeared. And wouldn't you know, within the year Penny was pregnant with twins!

Implicit in Penny's letters was the understanding that their music, as fun as it had been, was something they'd outgrown. They both had children to raise and a home to keep up.

Sally usually ate her lunch in the store's fifth-floor restaurant. Once in a while she'd meet a friendly man, a customer or another employee. But she wasn't about to risk getting to know him better, not after all she'd been through. She felt much older than other women her age, more worldly and shrewd, and she was convinced that romance was a notion exploited for commercial appeal. If she ever got married, it would be for pragmatic reasons. She wouldn't have minded having help paying the bills. But he'd have to be high-class for Sally Bliss to be interested, a real gentleman. And that wasn't the kind of man who would go for a career girl with broken teeth.

What Penelope would remember from those first years in Rondo was the train set she got for her birthday, with the caboose that always fell off the track at the top of the figure eight. *Chugachugachug.*

She was five.

When she was six she played a mouse in the class play. *Squeak, squeak,* she said, and the audience clapped. She had a very nice teacher named Mrs. Doherty, who didn't give just stars to students when they got a perfect score on a spelling test. She gave blue ribbons. Penelope tacked her ribbons alongside her closet door, and by the end of the year there were blue ribbons going up one side of the doorway and down the other.

She was good at spelling. She was good at imitating Donald Duck. She knew she was pretty — she could tell because everyone wanted to be friends with her, even the girls who lived in houses with swing sets in their yards. And once a boy named Gregor gave her a present. It was a glass heart almost as big as a regular peach, and on it was written: Kathy and Billy, 1-1-42. She didn't have a chance to ask Gregor who Kathy and Billy were because the next day he moved to Florida, and she never saw him again. But she vowed to keep the heart forever.

The time when she hadn't known how to read seemed like a dream. It felt like something she'd always been doing. She liked reading, and Mrs. Doherty often called on her to read aloud because she was good at it. The only things she wasn't good at were singing and dancing. They were chores, like wiping the dishes dry with a towel. She even sang in the junior choir at church every week, week after week, but she never improved and she never came to like it.

Not counting singing and dancing, she was good at everything. She would never say this to anyone, but it was all right to think it, as long as the thought didn't make her vain. It was all right to be proud, but not vain. She pretended for a long time to know the difference between the two, and eventually she did know, even if she couldn't explain it.

When she grew up she wanted to be a nurse. Then she changed her mind and decided that she wanted to be a teacher. Then she changed her mind again because she had a friend named Lucy who wanted to drive a bus, so Penelope wanted to drive a bus, too. After she played the mouse in the school play, her mother predicted that Penelope Bliss would be a star of stage and screen. But sometimes her mother was wrong.

She was seven and learned to roller-skate at the rink in the park. When she was eight she borrowed a bike from the Botelias and taught herself to ride no-handed. And then everything changed all at once, between yesterday and tomorrow.

Everything changed because the lawyer representing Bennett Patterson finally succeeded in locating Sally on the fourth floor of Sibley's. It hadn't been easy to find her. Initially, Benny had hired a private eye from Buffalo, but the man turned out to be a fraud and conned Benny out of a bundle of money without providing him with any useful information. The firm of Atwell and Stevenson based in Fenton proved more helpful. They obtained records of Sally's financial transactions from the Tuskee Bank and were able to track her travels north. This was after confirming with hospital records the most relevant fact: Sally's daughter had been born on March 17,

1953, exactly nine months after Sally and Benny had had their fling in Helena.

If Benny had only had a job or a steady girlfriend, or if he'd just been interested in any aspect of the world around him, he would have long since forgotten about the tart of a girl he'd met at the Barge. After giving her a good wallop for deserting him, that should have been that. But while Benny was at the hotel nursing a headache the day after finding Sally in Tuskee, his pal went through the items in the purse Sally had left behind and found the photo of her child.

Sally Mole, formerly Sally Angel, and currently, as the lawyer for Atwell and Stevenson discovered, Sally Bliss.

So the slippery item who kept changing her name on a whim was the mother of Benny's daughter. Well, Benny surprised everyone who knew him by caring about the little girl. It mattered to him that he was her father. It mattered that the child didn't have any decent influences in her life, what with that dumb broad for a mother. He had to fix that.

He figured he could choose his role. But surely it was ridiculous for a man to presume that he could appear out of nowhere and take his place as the father of a child he'd never met, demanding a share of custody along with a say over her upbringing, her education, her future. Whether or not he really was the father — a point impossible to verify without the mother's help — Bennett Patterson had only ever proved himself a lout. That was his reputation, at least, and he'd never before evinced any interest in the consequences of his actions.

Yet a reputation wasn't the same thing as a purpose in life, and after the family farm was sold out from under him, Benny needed something to think about. A daughter was enough of a something. He was looking forward to being her father. And he was used to getting whatever he wanted.

He wanted to be a father to the girl, was all — or so his lawyer would go on to explain to Sally, having found her arranging martini glasses in rows on a shelf she'd just dusted. It was Monday morning, normally the quietest period of the week, and the employees were expected to take advantage of the time and put things back in order after the weekend rush. Sally, as assistant manager, could have ordered a salesgirl to dust the shelf, but she preferred this chore to others and was experienced in handling the glassware — though not experienced enough to keep her hand from sweeping three glasses to the floor as she turned in surprise at the sound of the lawyer's voice.

Miss Sally Angel?

While she couldn't have understood it at the time, the lawyer's tactic of approaching her from behind and using the name he knew she'd given up would herald a strategy of sneaky maneuverings. Catching her off guard, he would manage to manipulate from her concessions that only later would she recognize were unreasonable. From the start, with the three glasses lying broken on the floor, the triangular bowls snapped from their delicate stems, she would be too confused to defend herself against him.

And she was too busy gathering the pieces of glass to explain that she was Sally Bliss, not Sally Angel. All she could think to say as she pulled the wastebasket close was "Can I help you?" *Can,* she heard herself saying — not *may.* She closed her lips over her teeth.

She sure could help him, thanks very much. He introduced himself as Griffin Marcus, Esquire. Sally noticed that he was wearing a Dobbs Gamebird, the expensive hat she'd seen advertised in the paper. And here was his assistant, a young man, or a man whose real age was disguised by an abundant mustache, a head of black hair, and a wiry, short build — this was Mr. Melvin Trotter, who took off his tweed cap as he stepped forward, nodded, and then stepped back again into the shadow cast by his superior.

Mr. Marcus intended to get straight to the point. Time was too precious ever willfully to waste, he said. Indeed, he'd based his recent presentation on this point when he went to Albany to argue — successfully, he might add, perhaps Miss Angel had read about him in the news — in support of a proposal to raise the speed limit on state highways.

No, she hadn't read about him, but he didn't give her the opportunity to say so, for he was proceeding without further delay to the point of his visit. She heard the hum of his voice without hearing the words. And yet somehow she comprehended what he was saying. He'd come on behalf of Mr. Bennett Patterson of Litchfield, Prospect County, to inquire about his daughter and to communicate Mr. Patterson's concern to Miss Angel —

"Bliss."

"Excuse me?"

"My name is Sally Bliss."

Yes, of course, Sally Bliss, formerly Sally

Mole, and before that, Sally Angel. The lawyer apologized for his mistake. But surely she would be pleased to hear that Mr. Patterson was interested in the welfare of the child, *their* child, after all he was the father, of course he was the father . . . wasn't he? Please forgive Mr. Marcus for raising the possibility that such a sacred bond could be cast in doubt, though for the record, and with immense humility, it was necessary to confirm that Mr. Patterson of Litchfield, Prospect County, was indeed the father of Penelope.

Benny Patterson. Sally had escaped from him twice before, and she should have been thrown into a panic trying to figure out how she'd escape from him again. But she couldn't summon the strength to panic; she suddenly felt too worn out by the impossible predicament to feel anything with great intensity. After the initial shock, she'd begun to sense the prickling of an enveloping numbness. And deep within the numbness a wearying resentment was beginning to spread. She'd been running all her life, running, running, running from every mistake she'd ever made, and she'd run right into the trap that Benny Patterson had set for her.

So that pig had found out about Penelope. The game was up, and there was nowhere to hide. She didn't want to hide. She wanted to spit out the rancid taste in her mouth. She wanted to wake up from the bad dream. No, she didn't want to wake up — she wanted to trade the bad dream for a good one in which she could rage at Benny, and he couldn't touch her, and no permanent damage could be done.

It helped that he wasn't there in person to react to Sally's anger. She was free to despise him. He could go to hell for all Sally cared. If he came near her, oh boy, if he dared to show his ugly face around here, he'd be in for it. You tell him, Mr. Griffin Marcus, that Sally Bliss had friends — friends here and in Tuskee and in Fishkill Notch, so that Benny had better watch out and stay clear, if he knew what was good for him.

"Please, madam," the lawyer said over the sudden jingling of the phone at the service desk.

His syrupy tone incensed Sally. She'd let him know what she thought of him, in just a minute, after she answered the phone.

It was the delivery supervisor informing her that a new box spring was being sent up for a floor display. Fine, she was ready to receive it. She was ready for anything, including Benny Patterson, to whom she had nothing to say but good-bye and good riddance.

Good riddance to child support? Good riddance to a father willing to contribute on a monthly basis to ensure that his daughter lacked for nothing?

What was this all really about? Sally couldn't fathom how the man who had attacked her could reappear in her life this way, through the front of a slick lawyer who was promising her money, if only she'd agree to accept it. She could use a little extra money, but if it came from Benny Patterson, well, you couldn't pay her to see him ever again.

The lawyer explained that she wouldn't have to see Mr. Patterson if she chose not to. Checks would be drawn up and sent to her directly from the firm of Atwell and Stevenson. If she'd please write down her address on page two of the form and sign on the dotted line . . .

Oh, this man took her for a fool. She wasn't signing nothing. Anything. She would appreciate receiving a copy for her own lawyer to look over. *Her own lawyer, sure,* like she had a lawyer. But what fast thinking to pretend. She was pleased with her cleverness. How easy it proved to act as though she was the kind of woman used to doing business with lawyers, while really she was just an assistant manager who was supposed to be waiting at the service elevator for the men delivering the box spring for display, so *if you'll excuse me, Mr. Marcus . . .*

He wasn't daunted by her hesitation. He said he had come prepared with an extra copy, she could have it . . . here — the document was produced from Mr. Trotter's briefcase, and if her lawyer would be so kind as to mail it back to the highlighted address with her signature at the X, Mr. Marcus would be grateful.

Sally was surprised at how readily he conceded to the delay. If he'd been trying to trick her, he should have gone on trying. Instead, he expressed his pleasure at making the acquaintance of Miss Sally Angel —

"Bliss."

"Bliss, yes . . ." He looked forward to hearing from her lawyer. But now she'd have to find a lawyer, damn it, damn him, damn Benny Patterson for bringing trouble back into her life every time she thought she'd found peace.

As she watched them wind their way between shelves of glassware, most of it too pricey for her to afford, she thought, *good riddance* to the men, though it was a half-hearted dismissal, for in truth she longed to accept what they'd come to offer, if only on her daughter's behalf. Money was money, even when the source was Benny Patterson, who'd gone to great lengths to seek her out. If he was simply hoping to soothe his tortured soul by making amends to Sally in the form of a check in the mail, then why shouldn't she put up with him, as long as she didn't have to see him, and as long as he didn't come anywhere near Penelope?

She rushed to catch up with the men. All right, she said, she'd sign the form, she didn't need to consult with her own lawyer first. Why, she was prepared to admit that she couldn't really afford a lawyer of her own and would welcome whatever counsel these two friendly gentlemen were ready to offer her.

Fine, here was the pen, thank you, Miss Sally Angel, Bliss rather, and good day — just like that. They sealed themselves inside the elevator and were heading back down to the ground floor, for Mr. Marcus had another appointment to keep. He didn't have time to provide further advice for a lady who wasn't his client. Anyway, he'd acquired from her what he'd come for: the mother's admission that Bennett Patterson of Litchfield, Prospect County, was indeed the child's father.

What a colossal mess Benny Patterson would succeed in making, wanting merely, as he claimed, to do what was right, doling out money as a way of demonstrating his interest in the girl and then sideswiping Sally, as soon as she'd cashed the first check, with his demand for shared custody, the specific details of his plan communicated through Mr. Griffin Marcus, along with the warning that he'd take his claim to court — and Sally would want to avoid that at all costs, for she was at risk, according to Mr. Marcus. Having failed to notify the father of the girl's birth, Sally Bliss could be held liable, and a court might well see fit to award the father with full custody as recompense for the lost time, since he had missed the first eight years of his precious daughter's life.

Now that wasn't the outcome Sally sought, was it?

But didn't Sally have any rights? This was America, and a child couldn't be taken away from the only mother she'd ever known. It was an absurd notion, Sally wanted to believe. But she was wise enough to guess that absurdity was not necessarily illegal. And when she received the proposal detailing where and when the father would visit with his daughter, she decided that she would have to hire a lawyer after all, something she should have done before putting her name on any legal document or cashing Benny's check.

In a desperate attempt to find the right lawyer without the benefit of a recommendation, she called the last listing in the Yellow Pages — Zandler, Zeleny and Stilman — and asked to speak to Mr. Stilman. She was informed by the secretary that Mr. Stilman had retired eighteen years ago and was living in Florida. Sally apologized for the mistake and wished the woman a good day. She tried another firm, Youngblood and Springer, but no one answered the phone. She looked farther up the list and decided to call the office of Kennedy and Kennedy simply because of the unlikely chance that they were related to the president. A man answered, announcing the name of the firm in such a whispery voice that she almost lost her nerve and hung up. But when he murmured an inquiring hello into the silence, she blurted out that she needed legal advice regarding, as she said vaguely, a financial transaction. Without pressing her for more information, the man offered an appointment at nine a.m. the following

Thursday.

It was hardly a notable exchange. She had simply dialed a number and set up an appointment. But as she stared at the phone cradled on her kitchen counter, she felt an urge to undo what she'd just done, pack up her belongings, and leave town with Penelope. Yet flight was no longer an option. By accepting Benny's money, she'd agreed to play by his rules, and now she was in too deep ever to get out.

It was June 23, 1961, a heat wave had been predicted for the rest of the week, the flat white sky was sealing in the humidity, and oh boy, could Sally Bliss use a drink!

Did someone suggest a drink?

Someone was always suggesting a drink. Typhoon Sam's on Ivy Street was the place of choice, and Sally could count on seeing at least a few familiar faces there, Elena and the girls from Sibley's or acquaintances she'd met in the neighborhood. She didn't go there often, no more than once a week, and only when her daughter was over at a friend's house. Even then, she was usually careful to limit herself to a couple of gin daiquiris, for she didn't want to end up like Gladdy Toffit, who had lost the ability to judge when she'd had enough. Sally preferred to save her money for better uses than to watch it disappear into the cash register at Sam's. But infrequently, she'd fall into a dark mood, and she'd become convinced that the only way to shake it was to follow the second drink with a third, and then a fourth.

Cheers.

And everything would start to look a bit rosier.

Sun don't care,
blue sky won't mind . . .

That's when she'd remember how good it felt to let go and sing. Singing made it easier to accept her situation. It could have been worse here in Rondo, after all. She could have been trapped in a job she hated, or she could have been too poor to afford stylish clothes for herself and her daughter, much less a console TV. She'd started sending money to her son again. Maybe Benny Patterson was a torment to her, but she was tired of running away. Having come as far as the river would take her, she planned to stay for a while.

Left and right, day and night . . .

That sweet sound of music rising from inside her. The nice, silky coolness of cigarette smoke sliding in the opposite direction, back down her throat. Home from

Typhoon Sam's, she'd sit by the window and think about how strange it was that the sky out there was the same sky above the Jensons' pasture in Tauntonville.

Here's to the stars shining above.

And the river spilling over the Upper Falls by the brewery was the same river she'd watched flow beneath a crust of ice in Fishkill Notch. Strange . . .

Turn around, Lou, just turn around.

She'd earned the right to relax. Once in a while, alone in the kitchen, she'd open one last beer, and that's when she'd raise a toast to Mason Jackson for giving Sally her first break. And to Georgie, who probably had more children than she could keep track of by now. And to Swill of the pigsty and Erna of the beehive. To Gladdy Toffit, who had gone to Florida; to Penny, who was a wife; to Buddy Potter, who would never retire; and to her own dear Mole way up in heaven.

Nothing left of rainy-day love
But a secret memory . . .

Who could blame her for wanting to fill the silence with sound. And remember how they loved her at the Rotary Club?

It wasn't over until it was over, and still there were all those beginnings, such as the day she watched her daughter head off to school carrying a book bag — gee, that was something nice. And so much of the world waiting to reveal itself. And the clouds passing in front of the moon with or without anyone's consent —

Grinning his grin and fading away,
Grinning and fading away,
away
away . . .

She sure liked to sing, and she'd go on singing to keep from talking to herself, though only in the privacy of her own home, with just her daughter, lying awake in her bed, listening to her through the walls, and maybe Mr. and Mrs. Botelia downstairs, who probably wondered what they were hearing until they realized it was Sally, their own Sally Bliss, her tongue loosened by an extra drop. *Poor dear. But really, you don't need to feel sorry for her, it's only Sally being Sally. And won't you just listen to that voice.*

She really didn't intend for them to listen, but the way the sound seeped through dense solidity — why, it would have been considered magical if it weren't so ordinary.

So maybe Sally overindulged once in a while. So what? In her daughter's retelling of these years, she couldn't count up the many times she lay awake listening to her mother's drunken singing. It was a sound that would be mixed up in Penelope's memory, raising feelings of pride, along with plenty of lingering embarrassment. In Sally's memory, though, it was a rare exception and didn't mean she wasn't respectable. Mostly she stayed focused. She never slept through an alarm or forgot to pay a bill. She saved her money and regularly sent a portion to her son. And she never failed to provide her daughter with whatever she might need.

And since her daughter needed to be protected from her father, on the Thursday of her scheduled appointment with Kennedy and Kennedy, Sally called in late to work and made her way to the office on the seventh floor of the Terminal Building. The reception desk was in the foyer, and beside a bookcase an archway led to a hallway, off of which were several closed doors suggesting that secret proceedings were going on behind them. The man at the desk was the same who had answered the phone. She recognized his whispery voice, and even more, she felt as though she recognized his face, having imagined it with impressive accuracy beforehand. She was right about his age — she'd judged him to be between forty and fifty — and she'd been correct in picturing him with dark hair and graying sideburns, the hairline receding from the temples and the full waves in the center flattened and pasted against the scalp with cream. He was thin, handsome in a way, though his hollow cheeks made him look hungry, and even with a ceiling fan clicking above him, his face shone with sweat.

He came around the desk to shake her hand, a move that struck Sally as awkward and unnecessary. He introduced himself as Arnold Caddeau and asked how he might assist her. Sally said that she had an appointment with Mr. Kennedy. With Mr. Kennedy — really? The man seemed perplexed, as though he couldn't imagine why anyone would want to meet with Mr. Kennedy. Or with the other Mr. Kennedy, she suggested. There was no *other* Mr. Kennedy, Mr. Arnold Caddeau offered gently, almost as a question. But if she wanted to meet with *the* Mr. Kennedy — no relation to the president and his family, as she'd learn later — *then right this way, please.*

He led her down the hall, opening one door and then another, unsure, apparently, of Mr. Kennedy's whereabouts. They finally found him in the farthest room, a small library saturated with smoke from the cigar that the wizened Mr. Kennedy, in a wheelchair, held clamped in his mouth.

424

Arnold Caddeau called him *sir,* and announced that he was pleased to present *Mrs.* — he glanced toward her left hand — *rather, Miss, um . . .*

"Bliss," Sally offered. As she approached, the old man put aside the magnifying glass he'd been using to peruse a book. She saw that plastic tubing connected the tank strapped on the chair with the nasal apparatus aiding his breathing. But still he puffed on that fat cigar, the ash pulsing with a glow as he inhaled, the embers mesmerizing her for a moment, so she didn't notice when Mr. Caddeau left, closing the door behind him.

The old man squinted through the smoke at her, and with his teeth gripping the cigar, he looked like he was considering whether she'd make a good meal. And when he asked her what she *could do,* she felt sure that the question was offensive, though she couldn't tell exactly why.

She could do lots of things, she said.

That was so funny to old Mr. Kennedy that he began choking and wheezing with what must have been laughter but was nearly enough to kill him, causing him to spit his cigar onto the floor and double over, spluttering, coughing, hacking, his body contorted by the effort to take in more oxygen than he was getting. He was suffocating, right in front of Sally. He'd be dead in a minute if she didn't do something.

She could do a lot of things, she'd already indicated. For example, she could hit an old man on the back to clear his clogged lungs of phlegm. She thumped him hard between his shoulder blades, again, and with the third thump produced from him a loud belch.

Ah, that was nice, almost as good as a massage. And to the missus who could do a lot of things — would she be so kind as to pick up his Havana, before the whole room exploded in flames?

She handed it to him, even as she suggested that he should lay off the cigars for a while. He told her to mind her own business, and anyway, there was nothing like a fine Havana to lift the spirits. But oh, for pete's sake, he had work to do, he didn't have time for one more interview, so for that reason she was hired.

Did he say *hired?*

That's right — hired. And if she thought he was going to pay her more than one hundred dollars per week just to answer phones and put away files, she'd better think again.

Did he say *one hundred dollars per week?*

"Not one penny more," he insisted. She could start immediately, Arnie would show her the ropes.

"Now get out of here." He waved her away and positioned the magnifying glass over the book. Oh, and she should understand, he added, that he would appreciate being left alone. She shouldn't bother him with trivial matters.

Back at the reception desk, she cleared her throat. Without looking up at her, Arnold Caddeau asked if she'd had any success with the old man. Well, sure . . . *success* . . . it wasn't inappropriate, she supposed, to use that word to describe the outcome of her meeting with Mr. Kennedy. In fact, he'd offered her a job on the spot. But he was probably joking, she added. Oh no, the old man never joked, Mr. Caddeau said, meeting Sally's eye finally, offering her a timid grin.

Then the salary of one hundred dollars per week, it was a legitimate offer? Entirely legitimate, with benefits in addition. The office was in desperate need of a receptionist, as she could surely see for herself, and if that was suitable to her and Miss Bliss was ready to accept the terms, he'd draw up the formal contract.

With apologies, Sally reminded him that

she'd come to the office not to apply for a job but to ask for advice. She described her predicament in broad terms, without specifics. Mr. Caddeau didn't need specifics. He'd help her sort through her options and plan a course of action. In fact, though his somewhat sheepish manner suggested that he wasn't certain he had the authority, he said he'd represent her for free — an extra perk of working at the firm of Kennedy and Kennedy that made the whole offer impossible to refuse.

That same day, Sally gave notice that she was resigning from her job at the store, and by the following Monday she was working for one hundred dollars a week as the receptionist at Kennedy and Kennedy. She soon learned that the first Mr. Kennedy, the father of the second, had died thirty years earlier, and his portrait hung prominently in the hallway. Maybe it was his glowering look that kept everything hushed and tentative in the office, maybe it was the shared sense that they were all participating in a precarious venture, or maybe she'd been enlisted in the dream being dreamed by the surviving Mr. Kennedy — a dream that mustn't be disturbed.

Yet even if initially she felt the whole situation wasn't quite real, the reality of her paycheck made her eager to adapt. She began to foresee a different, more prosperous future, contrary to her expectations. All that followed because of this new position promised to unfold with a natural and irresistible logic, as if the contract included in its terms a prescription for her conduct both on the job and away from it.

And regarding her predicament, she had to admit she'd never been married to her daughter's father. She'd made the mistake of thinking she was fond of him, she said, though even that was more than Arnold Caddeau needed to hear. He gave no sign that he blamed her or thought less of her because of it. He studied the matter thoroughly and met on two occasions with Griffin Marcus. And though he didn't end up accomplishing much on her behalf, she had the impression that he could have saved her a lot of trouble, if only she'd contacted him earlier.

So here was Benny arriving like Rumpelstiltskin to make good on a contract and claim the child he was promised; there was nothing Sally could do or say to dissuade him. She'd been a fool to acknowledge her history with him, but there was no taking it back. Like it or not, Benny Patterson was inextricably involved in Penelope's life.

Since Sally was not the type to register her disappointment directly, her account of this period would tend to be terse and to begin with a bland *suffice it to say . . . Suffice it to say,* the law clearly stated that a competent father had the right to be involved in the child's upbringing. That the father had once assaulted the mother was not an issue. As Mr. Marcus pointed out, there were no existing records indicating that a complaint had ever been filed against Benny Patterson with the Tuskee police. And if Sally wanted to pursue the case in court, she should remember that she was responsible for failing to inform the father about the birth of their child.

It was agreed that they would settle the matter out of court. Mr. Patterson would get what he wanted. There was one small concession Arnold Caddeau achieved, though. He argued that the father, being a stranger to the girl, shouldn't intrude into her life all at once. Visits would be limited to one afternoon a month, Griffin Marcus agreed, until a relationship had been established and the child felt comfortable in her father's presence.

And so on September 9, 1961, Benny

Patterson arrived to wedge himself into the narrow space between Sally and her daughter. For their first visit, Benny brought along his own mother, a stout old woman draped with pearls. She was the one who came to the door to pick up Penelope. Sally sat for the entire afternoon at the upstairs window, watching for the car to return, hardly breathing. They were supposed to return at exactly four o'clock, and when they weren't back at five minutes after four, Sally considered dialing the police. At six minutes after four, Benny's Cadillac pulled up in front of Mr. Botelia's store, and Benny's mother stepped out of the car with Penelope, who was gnawing on the tip of an ice cream cone.

For the second visit, Benny arrived with his younger sister, Tessa, who came to the door holding a wrapped package. She wouldn't let Penelope open the gift until they were in the car. Again, Sally sat by the window waiting for them to return.

Eventually, she found something to occupy her during the empty hours. This was the period in her life when she began making her own bread, less for the pleasure of producing something to eat than for the satisfaction she got from handling the mound of dough. She'd pound it more than knead it, punching the bubbling surface smooth until she was worn out, and then she'd punch it some more, right in the gut of the dough. She'd go at it for close to an hour instead of the twenty minutes suggested by the recipe. It was a way to pass the time, and it helped her to be less afraid of Benny, even if it didn't help her to get used to him.

As it turned out, it was easy for Penelope to get used to a man who bought her ice cream and jewelry and, on his third visit, a fancy three-story Victorian dollhouse, furnished and occupied by a whole family costumed in velvet and silk. It was easy to like a jolly stranger who took her out to the amusement park and paid for her skating lessons and even promised to buy her a pony for her next birthday. She liked having a real granny and an aunt. She liked the feeling of being important to the whole clan of Pattersons, and she had her dad to thank for that. She didn't understand why her mother didn't like him. Her mother wasn't even impressed with that great big green car he drove. She said it was a piece of junk and more than once wondered aloud why, if Benny was really a man of means, he didn't buy himself a new car — a question that frustrated Penelope, since though she knew there must have been an answer, she couldn't think of it.

Penelope soon learned that it was easier to blame her mother than to try to argue with her. She blamed her mother for not being friendlier. She blamed her mother for scrimping on everything, even while she boasted about earning one hundred dollars a week — more if you counted the income from child support. She blamed her mother for baking bread that was inedible. And of course she blamed her mother for keeping her father a secret all those years.

It was clear to Sally that Benny had set out to buy his daughter's affection, though to what end she couldn't say. At some point in the distant future, when Penelope was grown up, maybe Sally would tell her that Benny had been the one who'd knocked out her teeth that night in Tuskee. But for the time being, she decided that she should spare the girl the truth.

It surprised Sally that Benny's presence in their lives wasn't more of an immediate disruption. His checks came in the mail as dependably as his car pulled up in front of the door. Once a month he arrived to torment Sally and trick her daughter into adoring him. The rest of the time Sally strove to forget him.

As for her job as the receptionist for Kennedy and Kennedy, it was less demanding than any other work she'd done. The phone didn't often ring at the office. Rarely were there reports to be filed or letters to be typed. Sally bought a book to teach herself dictation, but neither Mr. Kennedy nor Mr. Caddeau had anything to dictate.

In the quiet hours of the afternoon, she'd listen to the spokes of the ceiling fan click with each revolution. She'd dust the windowsills and run the sweeper over the carpet. She'd write out a list of groceries to pick up on her way home from work. But was it even accurate to call it work? Yes, if it earned her one hundred dollars a week.

Mr. Kennedy, it seemed, had long been neglecting his practice and was devoting himself to founding a company that would construct basement bomb shelters in private homes. It wasn't that he worried about the devastation of a nuclear war; he liked to say that he'd be long dead and buried before the world was blown up. But he hoped to take advantage of other people's worries. It was a get-rich-quick scheme for a sickly man who through inheritance and hard work was already rich. He was sure that bomb shelters would make him richer, and he'd been investing large sums of money to pay for advisers and architects and engineers, against his family's wishes. With Soviet ambitions escalating, as demonstrated most vividly by the wall that went up overnight, dividing East Berlin from West, he insisted that there wasn't any time to waste. He had to hurry and put the pieces in place before some other canny entrepreneur beat him to it.

But Arnold Caddeau, who was married to Mr. Kennedy's daughter and had four children of his own at home, didn't show the same enthusiasm for Shelters, Inc. Sally had the feeling that he was just waiting for his father-in-law to die so he could lure back the business they'd lost through neglect. In the meantime, he stretched out his work on a single ancient insurance case to fill the hours.

As long as Sally arrived by nine and didn't leave before five, she proved her worth to Mr. Kennedy. But whether or not she'd keep her job after he was gone, she wasn't so sure. Through that first summer, as the old man grew more feeble and more certain that the Soviets were plotting to blow up the world, Sally came to realize that her future at the firm depended upon Mr. Arnold Caddeau, and she set out to make herself indispensable to him.

He always arrived before her in the morning. For a couple of weeks she took to picking up an extra coffee and a cherry Danish at the stand in the lobby of the building, until she discovered all ten of the uneaten Danish wrapped in cellophane, tucked away in the fruit drawer of the lunchroom refrigerator. She didn't know whether he drank the coffee or just poured it down the sink. She tried tidying up his desk while he was away at lunch, stacking his newspapers and returning reports to their folders, but immediately upon his return he would take out the reports and scatter the papers. She offered to pick up his dry cleaning for him; he'd always say that he could pick it up himself. She offered to mail any packages on her way home from work; he had no packages to send, nor did he have prescriptions for her to collect at the apothecary or maintenance issues to convey to the building supervisor.

While Mr. Kennedy puffed away in his frantic effort to smoke as many Havanas as he could and at the same time get his bomb-shelter business rolling, Arnold S. Caddeau sat studiously at his desk, poring over briefs, taking meticulous notes, making lists, and preparing for an outcome different from the one his father-in-law foresaw. Rather than becoming more informal in his dealings with Sally, as she would have expected, he seemed to grow more distant, more timid in the few requests he made. She wondered if he blamed himself for failing to do more for her in her battle with Benny Patterson. He'd gone out of his way to help. There was nothing more he could have done, and she would have told him this, repeatedly, if their rapport allowed it. But they had no rapport beyond perfunctory courtesy. Increasingly, Sally worried that he didn't like to interact with her. His timidity hardened to outright coldness, even as the weather turned cold and the fall rains changed to snow. He declined her help with a brisk wave of his hand. Though he always left his office door open, he was too absorbed in his reading to look up when she appeared on the threshold. She'd have to announce her presence by clearing her throat before he'd acknowledge her.

At home, her daughter grew prouder as she grew taller, her legs stretching into stilts, adding three inches to her height in a year. Nothing Sally did was right in the girl's eyes. She overcooked the hamburger, she undercooked the peas, she rode the bus to the grocery store, she drank too much and sang too loudly.

At work, Arnold Caddeau was so aloof that Sally gave up trying to anticipate his few requests; if there was something he needed her to do, he'd have to ask. The tension became so great that after almost a year of working at the firm, she began reading through the classified section of the newspaper again. She wasn't ready to leave her job for any of the available openings, all of which paid less than half of what she was currently earning. But she wanted to be prepared, in the event that she was fired.

From the time she started working for Kennedy and Kennedy through most of the following year, Sally went about her duties with an increasingly pessimistic diligence, expecting her fragile situation at any moment to take a turn for the worse. If she wasn't fired outright, then her hours would be reduced, along with her salary. If Arnold Caddeau didn't recognize that she was being paid for doing close to nothing, then Mr. Kennedy would catch on. Or else the whole office would shut down, driven into bankruptcy by Shelters, Inc. Or else Mr. Kennedy would drop his cigar one too many times.

The clouds were gathering, thunder rumbling in the distance, the air was thick with premonition, the tension high not just in the offices of Kennedy and Kennedy but around the world. How easy it would be to lose everything all at once. The story could end here, in 1962. Something terrible and final could happen, and Sally, along with everyone else involved, would never get to experience the unlived portion of her life.

Finally, Mr. Kennedy gave her a letter to type. It was to be sent out to residents of the city's and suburbs' upscale neighborhoods, advising them how to survive through the coming Armageddon and reminding them that the fifteen kilotons of explosive in the Little Boy bomb dropped on Hiroshima was nothing compared to the newest state-of-the-art weaponry. *Let all souls here rest in peace, for we shall not repeat the evil.* God, Sally didn't want to think about it. The Russians were coming. The Cubans were angry. On the twenty-first of October, President Kennedy declared a naval blockade. Americans were glued to their radios and televisions, all except the singular Mr. Kennedy of Kennedy and Kennedy, who was holed up in an office on the seventh floor of the Terminal Building, busily composing the line items to include in the contract he'd ask his clients to sign.

See you when the world ends.

Oxygen diluted with smoke, smoke mixing with blood, grime mixing with mucus until the goddamn body can't take it anymore. Cough, cough, sputter, retch, gulp —

"Mr. Kennedy, are you all right? Mr. Kennedy?"

Sally was knocking at the door, Arnold Caddeau right behind her. But earlier that morning the old man had gone to the trouble of locking himself in the room, probably to shut his own son-in-law out of his scheme. He meant to keep the wealth to himself and destroy the firm while he was at it.

"Mr. Kennedy, won't you open the door?" No, he wouldn't open the door, he couldn't open the door, and by the time his son-in-law had found the key and turned the lock, ancient Mr. Kennedy couldn't even open his mouth to tell those entering the room to go away.

Though it was actually the third stroke he'd suffered in the past decade, it was the most severe; he lived for another day and a half but died before Khrushchev announced that the weapons in Cuba would be dismantled. Shelters, Inc., would never open for business, and the letters advising residents to prepare for the end of the world would never be sent out.

To Sally's surprise, his son-in-law seemed genuinely moved by the old man's death. At the funeral, Arnold Caddeau delivered a eulogy describing Mr. Kennedy as a great man who never failed to deliver on a promise. Back in the pew, overcome with grief, he covered his face with his hands, and the regal, broad-shouldered, iron-haired woman who Sally guessed was his wife bent toward him to whisper comfort.

But it turned out to be a brief period of mourning. One day, a week after the funeral, Sally caught him going through the papers Mr. Kennedy had left on his table. As she approached, she noticed that he was blinking rapidly, blinking back tears, she thought. She had already, repeatedly, offered her condolences, and she offered the same again, expressing her appreciation for Mr. Kennedy's courage and vision, thinking that this was what her employer wanted to hear. Arnold Caddeau thanked her, but he wasn't persuaded by her praise.

"Maybe he had courage," he said with unusual bitterness, "but he didn't have much vision. He couldn't see that he was driving us into bankruptcy."

"Gosh, I think he had plenty of vision," Sally blurted. "He could imagine surviving an A-bomb. That's something."

Arnold Caddeau was still blinking, but not because he was pained by the loss of Mr. Kennedy. He looked as though he hadn't expected his secretary to have a thought of her own. She worried that she'd been too forward and started to apologize, then let her voice trail off. What should she say next? She wanted to be solicitous. Was that what he wanted? The silence in the room was heavy with possibility, but Sally couldn't decide whether to be afraid or intrigued.

How strange it was that they both went for so long without saying another word. How strangely mesmerizing, this feeling of uncertainty. They neither spoke nor made a move that would stir them from their absorption in each other. She had thought he was a man whose character was superficial and easy to grasp, a man defined by his work and family responsibilities, but all of a sudden he seemed no worse than shy, and capable of surprising her in innumerable ways. Everything seemed strange right then: Arnold Caddeau's habit of blinking rapidly, as though at a light too bright for him to tolerate — that was strange, as was the slight purplish tinge at the edge of his lips. And how strange it was to feel a sudden desire to touch the tinged part with her tongue. It wasn't that she wanted to kiss him, she just wanted to see if his lips tasted of plum. Strange, this urge rising as a logical response to a color rather than as a symptom of desire. She wouldn't have thought she'd be drawn to him. He was too old, too dull, and obviously too attached to his wife. Whatever other rules Sally had broken, she'd never cheated with a married man. But wasn't it strange that she would be standing there secretly thinking about cheating even if she wasn't truly considering the prospect? It was strange that they both were unable to break the spell that kept them locked in each other's gaze. And the strangest thing of all was that though old Mr. Kennedy had been dead for more than a week, the faint smell of smoke from his cigar still hung in the air.

Arnold Caddeau was the one who finally summoned the will to speak. And how tender his whispery voice seemed as he said, "Indeed," and added, "That's something," in echo of Sally.

It was something, the tension that had held them rapt for a few long moments. It was more than something. But right then, they both had no choice but to decide the experience had been insignificant. In their conviction that they had to defend the arrangements they'd worked so hard to establish, they were identical. After struggling to get to where they were, they weren't going to put their successes in jeopardy. And while Sally was far less affluent, she believed that she had more to lose. A man in Arnold Caddeau's position, with all his education and advantages, would never be as poor as Sally Bliss would be if she lost her job and couldn't find another.

Indeed, *it was something,* but not enough to change much. She'd keep her job, and the two of them would settle into a comfortable, professional relationship. He'd take to calling her Sally; she'd call him Arnie. His wife, a cipher behind her dark glasses, would stop in occasionally, and she'd give Sally expensive hand-me-downs — Chanel purses and Mr. John hats, along with clothes for Penelope that her own children had outgrown.

Through the next year, Arnie would rouse the firm from stagnancy, steadily luring back clients, adding an attorney, then another attorney, and then a fourth, plus a secretary for each man, so by the summer of 1963 all the rooms would be bustling with activity, the phones would ring constantly, and Sally, as Arnie's personal secretary and the main receptionist, would be at the hub of it all, forwarding calls, sorting correspondence, and greeting every visitor with a smile that conveyed her dedicated pride. She was proud to be working for Kennedy, Kennedy and Caddeau, proud to play an essential part in the firm, and proud, most of all, to see how Arnie would blush when he dictated a letter, or maybe he'd forget his hat on his way out or trip as he entered the office, proving that no matter how hard he tried to hide it he couldn't get used to her presence, and just the sight of Sally, day after day, month after month, was enough to fluster him.

November 22, 1963.

There they were, the both of them, thirty-three years old, *impossible!,* Sally posing inside the mirror, and Sally on the outside, observing.

Good morning to me.
Good morning to you.

Touch of eyeliner on the top lid, curling up, *like this,* whiskery tip at the edge, and mascara, then puff-puff of rouge over the foundation, coat of hair spray, *that's nice,* lipstick on pouting lips, *mmm,* slip on that plaid kilt, white blouse, a Mr. John hat in pink felt wired into a narrow dome and topped by an ivory button. *Flash a smile, that's good,* and tug on the chain to turn off the light.

"Come on, Miss Penelope Bliss, we have to go!"

"I'm not ready."

"Well, get ready!"

"You get ready."

"I am ready. Now hurry up, you're going to make us late."

"Just stop bugging me."

Of all the young girls she'd ever met, she'd never known one to be as hotheaded and stubborn as her own daughter. Tap, tap, tap, one minute, two, five minutes . . . finally, now scurry along, hurry up, hop-hop down the steps and rush the seven blocks through the cold drizzle to Penelope's school, but the doors were already closed, she'd have to sign her daughter in again and come up with a new excuse, the second time this week they were late. And then she missed the 8:11 bus and had to wait in the cold.

Damn that bus. Damn the rain. Damn time for passing too fast for her to keep up with it.

She resigned herself: it was going to be one of those days. As she spun through the revolving doors into the lobby of the Terminal Building, she imagined the onslaught of fresh inconveniences awaiting her. She heard the echo of her own heels clacking

446

over the marble tiles as an annoyance, and she was so absorbed by her irritation that she forgot to say hello to Freddy Balin, the Terminal's janitor, passing in wordless concentration right beneath his outstretched arm as he fluffed a feather duster across the elevator's dial.

Good morning, you've reached the offices of —

Say *Kennedy, Kennedy and Caddeau* five times fast, and it becomes *Kendycandyc'doo.*

And how may I direct your call?

She fielded a call for Arnie from an executive at the Union Trust. The name of the bank reminded her that she was two days late with her rent. Funny how she had more money than she'd ever had in her life, and it wasn't enough. The more she had, the more she saved, and the more she wanted to spend. She wished she had enough money to make both her offspring rich — the daughter she was raising and the son she'd left behind. And she wouldn't mind earning extra cash to spend as she pleased. At the same time, she wished she'd never revealed to Mr. Griffin Marcus that Bennett Patterson was her daughter's father.

The phone was ringing. The newest associate, Mr. Lipton, was standing at her desk. His own secretary had called in sick, so could Sally type a letter for him? Could Sally make the coffee? Could Sally find the report that the other associate, Mr. Tweet, had mislaid? Yes and yes and yes, Sally could do lots of things. But goddamn it, would you look at that! The carbon paper ripped when she pulled it from the typewriter, and she had to type the letter all over again. And then the paper wore through beneath the pressure of the eraser's wheel. And then it was lunch break, rain beat against the windows, and the two other girls in the office both had appointments, so instead of fighting the weather and going alone to one of the diners along Court Street, Sally ordered a pastrami sandwich and ate it at her desk, paging through an old copy of *Life,* pausing over the travel ads with their photographs of white sandy beaches fringed by palms.

Wouldn't it be nice to spend a week in the sun with a darling beau? She was thirty-three years old, an old hag with missing teeth, men didn't even look twice at her anymore, construction workers didn't whistle, and she hadn't been on a date for so long she'd lost track of how much time had passed. Poor Sally. Lonely Sally. How did she come up with that stupid name *Bliss* anyway? For a moment she couldn't remember. Was it even worth remembering? Her own insignificance felt immense right then. She was notable for her high-speed typing, for ripping the carbon paper when she lifted it from the typewriter, for making coffee that others found weak. She was one of a kind — hardly. Obviously, she was replaceable. Even her daughter, now that she had a doting father, could have managed without her. And her son, wherever he was — to him she would never be more than the absent benefactor who kept adding to his college fund. Did he have a college fund? It was unbearably sad not to know what her son was doing with the money she sent him regularly. Everything was unbearably sad — the unforgiving light of the ceiling bulb, the rain beating against the windows, the greasy pastrami, the crumpled paper in the wastebasket representing all the dull letters she'd had to type twice.

How sorry for herself she felt. And wasn't self-pity a comfort in itself? Just to think about how she deserved more than she had — this was something. She'd been through it, that's right, ever since way back when Georgie of Fishkill Notch had told the truth about her. But who would have guessed that having a baby and running away from home was only the beginning, and the story would go on and on, until she couldn't take it anymore, and then —

And then?

Then she would humbly beseech the Lord to comfort her and pardon her iniquity and bring good tidings and subject her not to diverse temptations in all Thy grace according to the measure of the gift of Christ. Amen.

Whatever that all meant.

It meant Sally was looking for love.

Sally was looking for a man. A nice man. Mr. Right.

There he was.

But that wasn't Mr. Right. That was just Mr. Caddeau returning from a late lunch —

Coming through the door, rushing rain-drenched and red-faced, slurring, stuttering, mashing words into a pulp of garble as he tried to say, he was trying to say, to tell Sally, to convey the news with the correct words, simple words, just say it: "They've shot Kennedy!"

Kennedy? As in Kendycandyc'doo? That's all Sally could think of right then: Arnie was announcing that ancient Mr. Kennedy, son of the firm's founder, had been shot. But wait a second — wasn't Mr. Kennedy already dead?

"What did you say?"

It would be understood only as a simple

declaration: "President Kennedy has been shot!"

President Kennedy, the perfect lover of Sally Bliss's dreams, shot on a Dallas street and soon to be declared deceased over national news. What did it mean? It meant, didn't it, that the Soviet armada was afloat, the Cubans were angry, and missile silos all over the world were opening their hatches to the sky? Stop! Say it's not so. Please, hold Sally, take her in your arms, let her indulge in the luxury of fear for a moment.

"That beautiful man. It's unbelievable," Sally whispered. Yes, Arnie agreed. It was unbelievable. There was a tremor in his voice, and even as he blotted the tear on her cheek with his thumb, she saw the swell of tears in his eyes. He had never seemed nobler than at that moment. Despite his shock, he was steady enough to support her as she folded all her weight against him. What a comfort he was, this good man, her boss, offering solace that was more affectionate than Sally would have ever allowed herself to expect, offering a hint of intimacy as if it were a natural response, brushing his lips against hers, pressing his lips more firmly in an effort to tell her that it would be all right, they'd get through it, the nation would recover from the blow and the two of them, why, they'd have each other from here on in, so kiss him back, Sally, go ahead, lock your mouth to his and become familiar with the taste, to savor later.

After the others had returned to the office bearing the news that the president's injuries were catastrophic, after it was agreed that they should all go home early and Sally had started walking to the bus stop, she thought about the meaning of that kiss. The crackling from a transistor radio at a corner newsstand was the sound of chaos. The president was dead. What the consequences of the assassination would be for the country and the world, Sally didn't want to contemplate. On the other hand, she was sure that she could predict what would follow from the moment her lips touched the lips of Arnie Caddeau.

There had been more to it than his attempt to comfort her. She'd understood this in a vague way even as she had clung to him, and she experienced a more expansive realization as she walked along Court Street. She pictured how he'd come rushing into the office; as she rehearsed the memory, it seemed that he'd chosen her to hear the awful news. He'd plunged breathlessly through the door and toward her as though, at that moment, she was the only one who mattered to him. And now, because of the subtlest communication they had shared in each other's arms, they were in agreement about something that they didn't dare put into words.

Oh, but look at her crossing the Court Street Bridge in the drizzle, floating more than walking, not noticing the sidewalk stained with mud, the flattened cigarillo holder on the curb like the crushed carcass of a white beetle, or the river flowing below with a deceptive sluggishness toward the lip of the falls, its surface rust-tinged, as though there were a powerful flame burning in its depths. Strange to think that this same dirty, dreary river that she had followed from its source had led her to the place where she finally belonged. After all the false starts and losses and mistakes of her youth, she was embarking on a new beginning, one paradoxically generated by that awful ending recorded with fresh blood and brain on a convertible Lincoln Continental in Dallas.

The president was dead. The fixed certainty of that fact stood in contrast with her evolving impressions of the man who had been her boss for two years. Mr. Arnold Caddeau. She never would have guessed he was such a romantic. It was terribly wrong to think of him this way at such a time, when the country was in shock. But she couldn't stop from imagining the next encounter that would follow from the first. The touch of his lips on hers, the scent of lavender on his skin, his silky sideburns, his peppermint teeth. She knew she should proceed cautiously, since she really couldn't be sure that her interpretation of the moment was absolutely correct. Had they really experienced something crucial together? Well, she knew what she'd felt. She didn't doubt that she found him alluring. He wasn't the kind of man that other women would have identified as irresistibly attractive, and yet she was finally ready to admit to herself that she'd been attracted to him for months. Maybe she had sensed, without quite being conscious of it, that he was attracted to her. Maybe they'd been looking for an excuse to move beyond their routine formalities. Any intimacy could be only hurtful to others, dangerous to themselves. But maybe they couldn't help it and were already in love.

The president was dead, long live the president. Who killed JFK? Hum, buzz, whisper of conspiracies. It was the Reds, people said. It was the CIA. It was the

Mob's own Murder Inc. Once ignited, the lust for revenge is an eternal flame. A great man's death deserves to be honored by another great man's death, so the story goes. That and the concoction of poisons mixed in fifty-gallon tubs and deposited in the empty carcasses of B-52s, to be dispensed when the need arises. The world is too much with us. Who can blame those tender souls who stop buying newspapers because the headlines are just too damn depressing!

Sally registered the news items as a set of symptoms that could be ameliorated with love. In the midst of the country's turmoil, she felt as though she'd discovered that she had a secret ability to walk on water. And as if in an effort to record her happiness, she took to saving the receipts for all the bills paid by Arnold Caddeau on her behalf. Twenty dollars and change for a whole night's stay at the Cadillac Hotel, though the room was used only for two hours on the frosty afternoon of December 10, 1963. Thirty-two dollars for a silver bracelet purchased from Foster's Boutique. Sixteen dollars for an elegant lunch at the Bonville up by the lake. Another twenty for a second stay at the Cadillac Hotel, paid in full January 15, 1964. Twelve dollars for a rhinestone chameleon brooch purchased at the Art Gallery, March 3, 1964, intended as a birthday present for her daughter, with happy birthday wishes from her mother's boss.

A present for Penelope from Mr. Caddeau? Really? From that disgusting man? Penelope, age eleven, wiser than her years, knew up from down. She may not have clearly understood the nature of the affair and didn't suspect that her mother occasionally took an extra hour for lunch in order to strip off her clothes and climb into bed with Arnold Caddeau. But Penelope was sharp enough to guess that her mother's boss was responsible for her mother's happiness, and her mother's happiness was making her flighty and selfish. Sally didn't bother to prepare a proper dinner. Either they'd go out, or she'd bring home a bucket of fried chicken. Sally didn't bother to come watch Penelope play shortstop in the girls' softball league on Saturday afternoons. Sally missed the teacher-parent midyear conference simply because she forgot. She forgot everything that mattered, all because her head was stuffed with thoughts of her lovey-dove boss. That disgusting man. Penelope had no use for his gift of a rhinestone-studded chameleon. Into the wastebasket it went.

"Baby, don't do that!"

"Leave me alone!"

Sally's darling child, her purpose in life, her little princess — she hadn't been brought up to become a spoiled little brat. But who was really the spoiled brat! Go look in the mirror, Sally Bliss.

All right, she'd look. There she was, lashes extended with a fancy new mascara, lips a nice ripe ruby red, no wrinkles yet other than the laugh lines at the corners of her twinkling eyes. She looked better than she had in years, as long as she didn't open her mouth wide enough to display her broken teeth. She couldn't help it if she was happy. She who had lost so much through her first three decades of life had finally found a point of stability. Too bad that Arnie was already married and would stay married, not because he loved his wife but because he was a good man who honored his commitments. And consider that the poor woman had been diagnosed with some terrible degenerative eye disease. There was nothing to be done about it, no prevention or cure. Arnie and his wife had decided to keep the matter to themselves. Not even their children knew about it. But Sally knew. After their first rendezvous at the Cadillac

Hotel, Arnie revealed to her that his wife was going blind. He loved Sally, he really did, but she couldn't expect him to leave a wife who was going blind.

Of course not. He loved her, and she loved him. She didn't think of herself as his mistress; rather, their relationship was a secret treasure to protect, for others would covet it. Sally deserved Arnie, Arnie deserved Sally, and they never ceased to be grateful for the affection they shared.

Over the course of several months they established a comfortable routine. They learned to communicate their intentions through glances and scribbled notes (*meet me at . . .*) and took delicious pleasure in the subterfuge. They made sure to give no reason for anyone in the office to suspect what they were up to. In public, they were convincingly indifferent to each other. But oh how that man adored her, he couldn't contain himself, whenever they were alone he grabbed her, spun her toward him, kissed her, told her she was beautiful. This woman who stared back from the mirror: this woman was beautiful, and she stirred in Sally a distracting pride.

Who could blame her for forgetting the conference with her daughter's teacher? She tried to make it up to Penelope by ordering a banana split for them to share.

But Penelope hated bananas.

Since when did she hate bananas?

Ever since right now.

Ever since she was eleven years old and one week. At eleven years and six months, she still hated bananas and would not forgive her mother for forgetting to pick up fresh milk at the store. By her twelfth birthday, she was even angrier. Sally kept trying to pretend that she was a devoted mother, though she was always late coming home and when she was home she was either vacant-eyed or absorbed by some soap opera magazine, leaving her daughter to sit in front of the TV watching show after show — that's if Penelope wasn't banging on the top of the old black-and-white RCA, trying to stop the spill of horizontal lines that kept filling the screen. Nothing worked properly anymore; her mother couldn't be bothered to repair anything that broke because her head was stuffed with thoughts of her lovey-dove boss, who wouldn't marry her or even come visit her at home. And now and then there were those embarrassing nights when Sally couldn't stand being alone in her bed. She'd go out with her girlfriends and come home drunk and belt out those syrupy songs for all the world to hear. Such a foolish mother was hard to endure month after month, year after year, and by the time she was thirteen, in the summer of 1966, Penelope Bliss announced that she couldn't stand it anymore and was moving to Litchfield, Prospect County, to live with her father.

Penelope's dad had a color TV. He had a big plastic bowl of a swimming pool in his backyard. He liked fried foods, hot weather, and arguments. He hated Commies and David Frost. But the worst was that pussy heavyweight Muhammad Ali, who was too much of a coward to put on a uniform. This grand old U.S. of A. was going to the dogs. And for those in doubt about the merits of the electric chair, let Benny point out that taxpayers would be covering the Boston Strangler's room and board through his life sentence — and he was only thirty-five!

But gosh he loved his little girl, *Benny's Penny,* as he called her when he was introducing her to his friends. He had a bedroom done up special, painted pink, with stenciled ponies on the walls. So what if she considered herself too grown up for stenciled ponies? He was glad she'd chosen to live with him. He'd bring her out to dinner, and boy oh boy would the waitresses fawn over them both. He even took to going to church once in a while so he could show her off. That's how he met Harriet Sullivan, who worked as an aide for an elderly woman. She was wheeling the old woman into the sanctuary, the front wheel of the chair got stuck, and Benny was there to lend a helping hand.

Maybe it was having his daughter in the house that prompted Benny to decide that it was time to settle down, or maybe he just realized he was getting old. He courted Harriet Sullivan and early in 1967 asked her to marry him. She was eager to escape the irritable old woman she worked for, and she accepted Benny on the spot. They were married within the month at the church where they'd met, and after a two-day honeymoon in Niagara Falls, Mrs. Patterson arrived in Litchfield with just three small suitcases, which she unpacked slowly, over a period of several weeks, sorting into piles the clothes she wanted to keep, to store, and to give to the Salvation Army. And once she calculated her wardrobe needs, she began to shop.

It was shopping that Penelope would remember best from these years she lived in Litchfield — shopping by mail order with a checkerboard of catalogues laid out on the kitchen table. Shopping in Fenton, until her stepmother decided the stores there weren't ample enough. And then driving the whole long way to shop in the city of Tuskee.

Thanks to her stepmother, who needed to shop, fourteen-year-old Penelope returned to the city where she'd been born. Though her memories were vague, she hadn't forgotten how her mother would just start singing in public wherever she was, and people would gather to listen. She remembered feeling that she could never get enough of her mother's singing, and the memory of her pleasure made her wistful as they drove into the city center.

Trailing behind her father and his new wife after they'd parked her car, she studied the face of every passerby wondering if she'd once known them or if they'd possibly remember her. She thought she recognized a smell in the damp air similar to the fragrance she imagined burning raisins would give off. She wondered if she should try to find the woman she'd been named after, her mother's friend Penny. She only vaguely remembered her and didn't even know her married name. Anyway, it would be awkward to appear at her door without notice. The premonition of awkwardness, once it came to her, became more insistent with every step she took. She'd never understood why they'd left Tuskee in such a hurry, but now, knowing her mother as she did, she could fairly assume that Sally had been involved in some kind of foolishness. Her mother couldn't help but make a mess of things. Her mother had dropped out of school at the age of twelve. She had never heard of Boris Pasternak or Fletcher Knebel, and she was amazed that Penelope could count to ten in French. She shamelessly wore hand-me-downs given to her by her boss's wife. She hadn't been able to keep straight where her daughter was supposed to be and when. They might have had a nice life for themselves in this sweet river city of Tuskee if her mother hadn't been so foolish.

And here was Penelope retracing her mother's path, walking in her muddy tracks, returning to the place of her humiliation. Suddenly the air seemed unbearably thick at the furrier's where Harriet wanted to browse. Everywhere you looked there was a dead animal hanging from the rack. Harriet went ahead and picked out a fox stole, one with its silver tail jammed between its teeth. *Please please please couldn't she have it?* Benny grudgingly obliged, and while the proprietor was drawing up the bill, Penelope snuck away to wait outside.

The first thing she noticed was a large spotted cat sitting on the windowsill of the brownstone next door. The cat's spots were uneven, pumpkin-colored, and blended at the edges into darker fur; he rested on the excess of his body as if on a cushion. He blinked slowly, with obvious arrogance, when Penelope approached. Why, this cat reminded her of the cat she'd once had named Leo, a fat cat with orange spots and a superior manner, yes, just like this fat spotted cat.

As she reached out to pet the cat, she was jostled accidentally by a woman hurrying past, who offered a quick *pardon me.* But then she was jostled again — deliberately this time, with a jam of an elbow — by the small boy the woman tugged along. The child smiled wickedly at Penelope and then broke into a trot to keep up with his mother, who yanked at his hand. But it wasn't the boy's malice that surprised Penelope. It was the song he sang, a loud, almost tuneless song.

Grinning his grin and fading away,
Grinning and fading away, away, away.

Penelope stared at him in furious shock. She knew that song he was singing. It was her mother's song. It belonged to her mother, only to her mother, not to anyone else in the world. How did the boy know it? He might as well have snatched her mother's purse from out of Penelope's hands. The little thief. She wanted to give him a good slug, but he was gone around the corner, and when she turned back to the brownstone the windowsill was empty, the cat had disappeared into thin air, and there were Mr. and Mrs. Patterson coming out of the store, holding hands, Harriet already wearing that stupid fox stole, Benny trying to fold his wallet around a wad of bills.

Seeing how smug he looked with his overstuffed wallet and a fancy new wife at his side, Penelope wondered if she'd made a mistake choosing her father over her mother. Secretly, she was angry at both her parents for making it necessary to choose between them. She wanted to go home, but not to either of the homes available to her.

She felt better after her father bought her a new pair of pink Keds sneakers, and she felt even better when he bought a phonograph for her to keep in her room. She was in a good mood up until the end of the day, when they were driving back to Litchfield and she asked how much Harriet's fox stole had cost. Instead of answering her question, her father instructed her to call Harriet

Mom. She refused, of course. She already had a mom. Think again, Benny's Penny. As long as she was living in her father's house, her father's wife would be her proper mother, with all the authority that went along with the title. Harriet tried to be gently encouraging and promised to spoil her stepdaughter rotten. Benny promised that there'd be no spoiling if Penelope didn't do what she was told. He searched the rearview mirror for her response. It was then that she experienced the faint awareness of his potential for meanness. But she would have to wait several years before she could come right out and accuse him of trapping her.

Penelope lived in Litchfield for three years, convincing most everyone that she was as average as the next girl and could fit easily into small-town life. She played first string on the girls' field hockey team at her junior high school and second string on the basketball team, she sang in the school chorus but was never chosen for a solo, she earned a solid B in all her classes, she auditioned and got the part of one of the dancers in the high school's production of *Oklahoma!* but missed the performances because she fell and sprained her ankle during dress rehearsal. She had friends and went out on dates with boys, she babysat for her half brothers, a pair of twins born in 1968, she talked on the phone for hours while her father and her stepmother shouted at each other in the kitchen, and on her sixteenth birthday she got her driver's license. It was her stepmother who drove her to the county motor vehicles bureau, not her father, because by then, the spring of 1969, Penelope and Benny could hardly stand talking to each other, having learned through their three years in the same house that they disagreed about any subject that came up, from the bombing of Hanoi to the message of the book of Revelation. They got worked up before anything was even said, so useless and idiotic did each find the other's opinions, with Benny increasingly convinced by his daughter's leather skirts and low-cut blouses that she was just like her mother — *that goddamn whore,* as he didn't hesitate to point out — and Penelope recognizing that with the birth of his two sons, her father didn't want her around anymore, she was just another mouth to feed, *no more the cute little girl who idolizes you, nope, she's all grown up, a young woman now and you don't know how to talk to a woman, not even to your wife, all you do is yell at her like you yell at me, you can't stand it when anyone gives you shit, you and your fancy car and your Brylcreemed toupee, you hate it when I won't do what you say, you hate it that you can't get a decent job without a college education and now with money drying up you hate it that you have a daughter to support, you hate having to do anything for me, you hate watching me go out the door with my friends while you sit around doing nothing, you won't even change a diaper, that's woman's work, isn't it, you hate women, you hate your wife, you hate me and I hate you so there's no reason for me to hang out here for another fucking minute, keep my stuff, you paid for it, it's yours, so long, and I'll see you in another life.*

The first time he slapped her for her insolence was at the dinner table; in a fury, she knocked over her chair as she stomped from the room. The next time he slapped her, she warned him that she'd kill him if he did it again. So he did it again, right there standing in the kitchen, boxed her hard on the ear before she could stop him. Instead of killing him, she walked out of the house.

Penelope was sixteen, it was the summer of 1969, and she believed not only that she bore no resemblance to the sluttish girl her father made her out to be but that she could be much better than she already was. She agreed with her friends, who in the spirit of the times insisted that they had infinite freedom to choose their own fate and liked to sing together —

Mystic crystal revelation
And the mind's true liberation . . .

She wouldn't let the fact that she had no money of her own deter her. She walked along the shoulder of the road, turned when a car approached, and stuck out her thumb. She ended up hitching a ride with Mrs. Peabody, the cafeteria aide at Litchfield High School, who was driving up to visit her daughter in the city of R.

"That's funny. You're going to visit your daughter, and I'm going to visit my mom," Penelope said. She'd slipped her feet out of her sandals and was resting them on the dashboard, absorbing the coolness from the vinyl.

"We can keep each other company," Mrs. Peabody said. She lifted her sunglasses and gave Penelope the same look she offered when she ladled out soup.

Penelope lowered her feet back to the floor of the car. "Thank you so much," she replied, trying to say it in a way that would let Mrs. Peabody know that she really meant it.

■ ■ ■ ■

And so she came home, returned to the place where she was wanted, where she'd been sorely missed, where she belonged. During their brief visits together over the past three years, Sally had continued to think of her darling daughter as a hot-headed, irresponsible child. But now it was impossible for her to ignore the fundamental changes: Penelope had transformed from a willful little girl into a young lady eager to find a purpose in life. She was as pretty as ever, a natural beauty, though not as eye-catching as she could have been since she refused to wear makeup or the kind of clothes that would have accented her good looks. If anything, she seemed to prefer to mask herself in plainness. But there was something else that made her stand out. She seemed to notice more and to appreciate experience with a great depth of feeling, as though she'd just been released from a long incarceration.

Three long years. Was Sally still hot on that boss of hers? Penelope wanted to know. Well, if *hot* was the best word . . . all right, *hot* would do, sure, that described how Arnie made Sally feel, though really they were like an old married couple by now. He even came by for a visit once in a while and was planning to come for lunch on Sunday, if Penelope didn't mind.

Of course she didn't mind that her mother was in love! She'd come home three years older and more capable of sympathy, and with her return she offered her mother a satisfying sense of completion. Penelope was three years taller, smarter, curvier. Three years wiser. Three years closer to being a full-fledged adult. Three years stronger and more desirous of a certain kind of attention. Three years toughened by her father's insults, and she was ready to take on the world.

She was still young enough to be uncertain about how to focus herself. She tried out different crushes on boys in the same way that she tried out new foods. She worked to make up for her slack habits in Litchfield and took to studying late into the night, long after her mother had gone to sleep. She started drinking coffee and reading the newspaper in the morning before school. She became increasingly absorbed by political causes and helped fellow students draft speeches against the war. Soon she was giving the speeches herself at rallies, standing on the platform in Crescent Park and listing the benefits of peace.

Why, look, that was Sally's darling girl shouting into the megaphone, making sure that her appeals would be heard above the sounds of wind and traffic. She spoke with passion and eloquence. Why, that was Sally's daughter stealing the show! So what if the show didn't involve singing and dancing? It was a start, wasn't it? You didn't have to be a fortune-teller to predict that this hometown girl would enjoy a life of renown. Sally, front and center, led the crowd in the applause.

Penelope Bliss. She was Sally's daughter, yes, she belonged to Sally. She'd been away, but she was back again, and wow, just look at her. What a beauty, what a sweetheart, the boys would go mad for her, she'd have her pick of the crop. First, though, she wanted to go to college. What a good girl, a bookish, determined girl. Sure, she should go to college. She should learn something useful as a fallback, Sally advised. Even though she wouldn't need a fallback. When it came to the qualities that would earn her the kind of prominence Sally dreamed of for her, Penelope had a surfeit. She was lovely, poised, and articulate, and she had made up her mind to flourish. And though she hadn't inherited the special quality of voice that distinguished her mother's singing, her confidence and determination more than compensated for her lack of musical skills. She was born to be a star.

Except she didn't want to be a star. It was no secret that Penelope didn't share her mother's aspirations for her. After all the years of sullen moods and sudden rages, she'd become a girl empowered by her sense of her own moral conviction. She'd grown independent under her father's jurisdiction. It followed that she didn't need him anymore. Soon she wouldn't need her mother. She already had all those boys to flirt with, a Will, then a Jessie, and then an Abe, all of them with stringy hair down to their shoulders. Sally would have liked to recommend a good shampoo, but she kept her mouth shut. The joys she'd assembled in her life were delicate, and she had learned the hard way that a harsh word could be enough to disrupt everything.

How pleased she was that her daughter had decided to come home. While Penelope figured out how to put her God-given talents to good use, it was Sally's task to make sure that Penelope understood how deeply she was loved.

Time passed too quickly, and before Sally

could catch hold and yank it back, it was January 1974. How did that happen? Penelope had been awarded a scholarship to attend a college downstate, Arnie and Sally were still having their affair, Arnie's wife, the poor woman, was stone-blind, and Mr. Botelia, Sally's landlord, became ill with pneumonia and died at the end of the month. When his wife sold the building to a real estate company, Sally was forced to move.

She bought a ranch house a few blocks away on a side street — a small house, just two bedrooms, no garage, and it needed a new roof. Still, it was snug, with an efficient furnace. Sally appreciated her good fortune and never complained. She liked the way the morning sun came into the bedroom and woke her up. She liked the way the cardinals hopped from one branch of the forsythia to another, knocking off the wet clumps of snow from a late winter storm. She liked getting dressed and looked forward to seeing Arnie at the office. She liked the soaking rains of spring and the thunder in the summer.

La-di-da . . . walk with me . . . It's simple to wish . . . I got you good. She would never stop taking pleasure in the action of singing, even if there was nobody listening. *Turn around, Lou, turn —*

Hey, Sally, don't you hear the doorbell? Someone has come calling. Yes, you have a visitor waiting on the stoop, a pale woman standing at a slant, wearing a boxy plaid dress with a green shawl draped over her shoulders, her brown hair streaked with silver and pulled back in a tight bun. Her lips were thin, unpainted, and they stretched like elastic as she blurted, "Sally Werner!"

Sally didn't mean to imply with her stunned silence that she didn't recognize the woman standing there. She didn't mean she wasn't glad to see her. She wanted to say . . . she didn't know what she wanted to say and couldn't utter a word, she was so perplexed, as though somehow she were suddenly cognizant of an omen's import even while she was still unaware of its message.

It was June 3, 1974, twenty-seven years to the day since Sally had run away from her childhood home, and Trudy was standing on the doorstep asking her sister, "Don't you know who I am?"

November 6, 2007

It turned sharply colder last night, and when I went back to the gorge this morning there were wet flurries blowing through the channel. Steam from the brewery smokestacks hovered below the ceiling of gray clouds. The wind came in chilly gusts, and I had to cover my ears with my hands to warm them so at first I didn't hear the tapping, not until it was close behind me. I turned to see an old man approaching, a little bald man dragging his plastic cane to the side, bouncing the tip against the metal spokes of the rail. He nodded in greeting as he passed me and continued along the bridge. His tight-lipped smile gave me the impression that he was holding back a guffaw, as though he were absorbed by some hilariously impolite thought.

I shifted my gaze back to the gorge. I had no loose change in my pocket, so I couldn't toss a coin into it as I like to do. But after a quick look around I found a gull feather beside one of the benches. I threw it into the air, but the wind blew it right back onto the bridge. I tried again, dropping it from the far side of the bridge this time, and watched as the feather flew skyward and spun in the wind. The barbs seemed to turn around the axis of the shaft that hovered magically, as though submerged in water, like a sprig of seaweed turning with the force of the current.

After a moment a strong gust blew the feather farther away from me, tugging it in one direction and then another and eventually dropping it onto the surface of the river.

The water level is low after a summer of drought, and the mossy sheen that's usually visible toward the bottom of the gorge walls has long since dried up, leaving its dusty imprint behind. Only a thin thread of water streams down the cliff face of the falls. The gorge looks emptier than ever, too vast to fill up. It doesn't seem possible that the river could have risen high enough to reach the embankment wall at the Beebee parking lot. But I've been reminded that what is hardest to explain can be easy to imagine — and this morning, even with the flurries blowing and the rocky borders of the riverbed peeking out through the shallow water at the bottom of the gorge, I imagined my father spinning in the river like that feather spun in the sky, propelled upward by the river's back surge.

Until her death my grandmother maintained that a miracle caused the strange flood that saved my father's life, and in her last months she became increasingly absorbed by the superstitions that supported this belief. It was the river angels who made the Tuskee flow backward that day, she said. God summoned them to do His will.

Psss, shhh, come here, my grandmother would say, motioning to me even if I was already sitting close to her bed. *I want to tell you something,* she'd say. *The little angels in the river, they only pretend to be a legend. They are really very clever. Oh yes, sure, they know what's what. They know what would happen to them if word got out. The race to catch them would be on. They'd be caught, they'd be sold, and yes, sure they'd disappear. They'd all disappear.* She told me that I should never let anyone know that there were tiny angels in the river. It would be all right for me to write about them, she said, but I must give the impression that they don't really exist.

In the last days of her life, I'd sit by my grandmother's bed and listen to her speculate about the miracle that had saved my father's life. Sometimes she'd speak matter-of-factly, as if she assumed it wouldn't have occurred to me to doubt her. Other times she'd ramble, or speak with bemusement, as if she were recounting a dream. But she'd always end up acknowledging that there was much she didn't know about the legendary creatures the native people called Tuskawali, and she left it up to me to find out what I could. She wanted me to trace their route from the source, to locate the spring that bubbled up from the aquifer on a slope in the Endless Mountains and to follow the creek as it spread through the meadow flats. I was supposed to look for the Tuskawali in the clear pools or basking on sun-warmed rocks. If I was persistent, I'd find them. Sure. I'd find them if they let me find them. My grandmother wanted me to study them and figure out how they survived beneath the winter ice. Maybe they hibernate in the mud, my grandmother suggested. Or maybe they swim out of the river, across the lake, east through the seaway, and into the Atlantic Ocean, and there they head south, journeying to some secret coral paradise. How long do they live? she wondered. Do they live for all eternity, like true angels? What do they do as the river picks up sewage and chemical waste? How do they protect themselves against pollution? Maybe some of them grow extra hands and legs, maybe they go blind as they make their journey down the Tuskee, or maybe they never even make it to the lake. *Those poor creatures,* my grandmother would say. *What did they do to deserve us?*

The truth is, I've never found any Tuskawali, though not for lack of trying. I may not ever know for certain why the river ran backward that day my father tried to drown himself. I really can't verify that the river ran backward at all, since all I have to go on is my grandmother's questionable account. My father himself doesn't remember the flood. He doesn't even remember falling from the bridge through the chasm of the gorge. From the moment when he slipped off the rail until less than a minute later, when he awoke in a puddle across from the brewery, he has no recollection.

I do know what happened to him subsequently, though. Since I first heard from him, I've probably come to know more about him than I would if he'd been there while I was growing up.

Now that I understand the reasons for his absence, I understand why it took him so long to get in touch. There was no question in his mind that he was sparing my mother and me more turmoil by staying out of our lives. Thanks to my grandmother, he was convinced that nothing would be gained by trying to repair the damage he'd done.

My grandmother hadn't wanted to drive him away. She did her best to resist her initial suspicions about my father. Yet she couldn't keep herself from following the trail of clues that led to the truth. And of course once she had proof, she was obligated to tell Abe who he really was.

When he fled the city of R, he left behind his own reckless ways. He moved to Michigan and then Illinois and took on new responsibilities that would distract him. While he worked at night as a bartender, he enrolled in education courses and earned his certification. He ended up marrying a woman from Evanston, and he taught in a middle school. For years he stayed focused on his life in Illinois, on his growing family and students and friends. But as he would eventually confide in me, *Penelope Bliss isn't easy to forget.*

Long after he'd fled from my mother, he found himself reviving the same memories he'd tried to erase. He decided that he wasn't to blame for becoming entangled in a doomed love affair. And why was he the one who had to run away? He tried to remember how he had met my mother in the first place, how one thing had led to another. He began writing to people he'd known in his childhood, friends and relatives he hadn't contacted for years. He'd been out of touch for so long that he had difficulty tracking down addresses. The process was slow and often unproductive. Eventually he had some success, once he figured out the right questions to ask. And among the people who responded to his queries were two women from the town of Tauntonville, Pennsylvania, who had astonishing information to share.

After my grandmother's death, he considered getting in touch with me directly, but he kept talking himself out of it. And as he became increasingly active in local protests against the war, he hardly had time to think about personal matters. Then one October day in 2005, he came away discouraged from a lunchtime peace rally. Nothing he'd said had an impact. He'd been heckled and then ignored. The few students listening to his speech knew as well as he did that the war would go on regardless of anyone's attempt to stop it.

He taught his afternoon classes with extra

vigor, as if to prove to the world that he had a purpose, but at the end of the day he felt more dispirited than ever. He decided to skip the faculty meeting after school and instead shut himself in his classroom. With nothing else to do, he pulled out the tape recorder he kept in his desk drawer and started talking to me.

I was thirty-one years old — old enough to be skeptical. I couldn't help but assume, upon opening the box of cassettes, that I'd been targeted for an elaborate hoax.

Dear Sally

Hello from outer space. This is Abraham Boyle attempting to establish contact. Wait, don't throw this tape away yet, please keep listening, for I think that what I have to say will interest you. You don't even know me, not yet. But you will if you keep listening. So, um, what can I offer by way of introduction? Let's see. I teach science in a middle school. I was married for twenty-two years. My wife and I divorced in 1999. The kids shuttled between our homes, but now the kids are grown. What else? I would be a vegetarian but can't resist a cheeseburger from time to time. Uh, I like to read, yeah, I'd read more if I had more free time, but what with preparing lesson plans and grading tests, well, you know, when I do open a book I like to return to old favorites. I've read *Great Expectations* twice all the way through. Have you read it? Play for me, Pip, play. Another favorite of mine is *The Descent of Man.* Now have you ever read that cover to cover? All animals feel wonder, and some feel curiosity, that's what Darwin said, that's what excited him. To prove it, to prove that animals feel wonder and curiosity, he put a stuffed snake in the monkey house at the zoo. What a mind he had, always turning . . . the way I see it, he turned by the force of logic toward the unexpected. Gee, well, it would be nice to sit and talk with you about books. Or about the weather. Or about this goddamn war and the shits who duped us into it. Oh, don't get me started. I spent my lunch break at a rally and, you know, huh, hardly anyone showed up. My students baked cookies and painted peace signs on them with icing. Listen, I'm taking a bite . . . of peace. Mmm. You must think I'm a kook. I *am* a kook. But you wouldn't exist if I didn't exist and that's a fact. So anyway, why am I contacting you out of the blue? Maybe I haven't contacted you. Maybe you'll never receive these tapes. I found an address for you in the phone book, but for all I know I'm contacting another Sally Bliss who is not my daughter. I'll keep my fingers crossed that some kind soul will forward your mail. Or maybe not. Maybe you don't ever want to hear from me. I don't blame you. But if you'll just be patient, I might convince you to change your mind about me. Are you listening? Here I am: Abraham Boyle, your delinquent dad. How do you do? I understand why you wouldn't be ready to meet me in person. I wanted to pick up the phone and call, but I was worried you'd hang up on me. I could have sent an e-mail or a letter, I know, but I wanted to talk to you. So this is a way of talking to you. What? Okay, just sign it out, hey, sign it out, please! That was one of my students borrowing a calculator. Between you and me, I'm skipping a faculty meeting right now. Any excuse, you know. What was I saying? Um, I apologize for my mistakes. I'm a bungler by nature. Earlier today, I was demonstrating an experiment, I was using a carrot, a cork, and a sugar solution, and I knocked over the beaker, knocked it right over, of course it broke. You'd think I'd be more careful than that, seeing as I've done the same demonstration for twenty-five years. Twenty-five years plus five. In that time you grew up, went to college, and then what? I don't know. Maybe you'll tell me about yourself someday. You were still cooking inside your mother when I left town. I'm sorry you had to spend your childhood without me. You have every right to blame me for all that's wrong in the world. But,

486

ah, let me take this opportunity to explain why I did what I did. It's hard to decide where to begin. Well, no it's not. A story should begin at the beginning, so that's where I'll begin. It will take some time to get to the point, but bear with me. I have a lot of material to cover. Here we go, then. I'm fifty-eight, or thereabouts. It could be that I'm fifty-seven, depending on the month of my birth. As you can see, I don't really know much about my beginning. I don't have my original birth certificate. I don't . . . I don't know my precise birthday, though for most of my life I've celebrated it on the ninth of September, that's what I put down on forms. September 9, 1947, a good date, as it turned out, because during Vietnam, men with this birthday were issued a draft number that was never called. So even though I don't know the exact day when I was born, it's a good thing I always put September 9 on forms instead of, say, September 5. September 5 was not a lucky day to be born when it came to the draft. Of course, maybe I really was born on September 5. Or not. Maybe I was born in August, for all I know. What do I know? Um . . . as you can see, I'm not very good with words. They're like, like, like flies just sitting on the counter, and then they take off before I can swat them. Well, it's later than I thought. The overhead light above my desk is flickering. The orbital electrons, as we say, are in an excited state. By the way, I teach at Vergonia Middle School in Vergonia, Illinois, in case you're interested. I have two daughters, Marcia and Tracy. Plus you. I'm going to explain everything, I promise. Believe me, I have lots to say about how you came about, but it's late, I have to go, I have a stack of papers to grade. I hope what you've heard so far serves as an, um, adequate introduction and that you keep listening. And you'd better not tell your mother that I've contacted you just yet. She wouldn't approve. Maybe later, when I'm done with my story, maybe then you can say something to your mother about me. But not yet.

Dear Sally, hello again, it's your favorite Martian. How are you? I'm sorry I'm not even giving you a chance to respond. I admit I'm nervous that you wouldn't want to respond. So I'll just keep talking to you, if that's all right. Talking and talking. Anyway, I promised to tell you my story from the beginning. I apologize if I get sidetracked. I wonder if it would help to start over. Yes, I'll do that. All right, here goes. There was my birth, and . . . and there were two years I can't account for. I was sent to live with the Boyles around the time of my second birthday. The Boyles were an older couple from Pittsburgh. They had one son, Philip, and since his birth they'd tried and failed to have another child. All my parents ever told me was that I'd been adopted through the Catholic Diocese of Pittsburgh. My adoptive mother's name was June Henrietta McAllister Boyle. My father had been named Redding in honor of his maternal grandfather. He was called Red Boyle, and, you know, that's a problem, to be called Red Boyle. So when he was still young he changed his name to his initials, RB. But you say RB aloud, of course you think of rhythm and blues, and that's what some of his friends called him. Blues for short. He grew up in Pittsburgh and went to the university there. He'd risen up in the ranks of the accounting department for WESCO. Shortly after I joined the family, RB was transferred to the New York office. We lived across the Hudson River, there in Jersey City, for a year. Then, then we moved to Long Island because that's where the executives in the office lived. My parents took out a big mortgage to purchase a fancy house, it was a modern house, floor-to-ceiling glass walls, out there in Oyster Bay. They joined a country club and also the local Episcopalian church, though they'd both been raised Catholic, actually. They sent my brother to a boarding school, I can't recall the name of it, and then he went to Dartmouth. They sent me to a private day school. Those were flush times, with June and RB thinking that the way to get ahead was to act like they were stinking rich. But they weren't stinking rich enough to afford the monthly payments on the loans they'd taken out to cover their expenses. They fell behind on payments. And they lost money, they lost a ton on bad investments. When the plate glass in the kitchen was shattered by a tree during a storm, they replaced it with plywood. They couldn't afford my brother's college tuition, so he dropped out, he never finished his degree. Just when they thought it couldn't get worse, RB lost his job over a fellow accountant's embezzlement, or I guess it was an attempted embezzlement thing. Though RB swore he wasn't involved in anything illegal, the company blamed him for failing to expose the scheme and fired him. So there he was, fifty-six years old, broke and unemployed and without the references, you know, that would have helped him land another job.

He'd take the train into New York each day to look for work. I'd go with my mother to pick him up at the station in the evening, and I'd watch him follow the other men, the other commuters, off the train. He wore a suit and carried a briefcase like, oh, I don't know, like he was just a normal businessman, but I tell you, he looked more worn out than the others. When he got into the car he wouldn't say a word about how he'd fared that day, and my mother wouldn't ask. Those were tough times, sure. But you know, it wasn't all bad from my perspective. I liked the public school I went to much better than the private school, where I'd had to wear a tie every day. We always had plenty to eat at home. And RB and June stuck it out together. They really shored each other up. They'd nuzzle on the couch in front of the TV at night, ha, and sometimes they'd go shut themselves in their bedroom even before the TV show was over. We didn't hear much from my brother, Phil, in that time. All my parents knew was that he was up in Buffalo, living with friends and working for, I think it was a roofing company at first. Phil got the short end, really. Anyway, the bank was threatening my parents with foreclosure, so they had to put the house up for sale. It took nearly a year to sell and only then for, what, a lot less than what they'd paid for it because it was in such poor condition. We moved into a two-bedroom bungalow in Roslyn, behind the YMCA. My mother got a job waiting tables at the IHOP in Roslyn, and my father kept on taking the train to New York and looking for work. I guess we were strapped for cash, yeah, we must have been, but I thought we were managing just fine. I'd spend my afternoons shooting baskets with friends at the Y. My mom would bring home sausages wrapped in pancakes, the IHOP special, pigs in blankets. I named my dog Pig in honor of that dish. I found him one day on my way home from school, or I guess I should say he found me. He came out of nowhere and began bouncing on his hind legs and licking my hand until I gave him the rest of the roll I was eating. He was some kind of terrier mix, a scrawny mutt, he hardly looked like a dog at all, more like a wet rodent. I brought him home and wrapped him in an old blanket. He stopped shivering, and I named him Pig. My mother let him stick around. You see, there wasn't too much unusual going on, the way I saw it. I was a kid like other kids. Then what happened was one day, uh, we went to pick up my father at the station, and, well, he didn't get off the train. We waited for the next train, but he wasn't on it. We waited in the car until long past dark, I remember I was so bored and kept complaining and June told me to shut up. Finally we went home and waited for him to call. I fell asleep waiting, and when I woke up it was morning, I was on the couch, and Pig, uh, Pig was barking at a sheriff's deputy, who for some reason was knocking on the back door instead of the front. Yeah . . . well. . . . Listen, I'm going to stop here. You can fast-forward over the pause. Good-bye for now, dear Sally.

Are you still with me? It's dark out. I'm back from basketball practice. I've been coach of our JV team for twenty years, and we've never won a game. Ha. But we have fun. And I always make sure that my players understand why gyroscopic forces help a body in motion maintain its original direction. I like to sneak in education when I can. I was thinking about something earlier. Today I talked with my students about the 180th meridian of longitude, you know, the international date line. I explained that if we cross the date line heading east, today changes to tomorrow, but if we head westbound, we go backward, back to yesterday.

One student asked if that means we have to do everything we did today all over again. I said no, the day is new, even if we've already been through it. I didn't say that I like to imagine what would happen if we really did get the chance to avoid making the same mistake twice. Since I started talking to you, I feel like I'm heading westbound over the 180th meridian. Just by putting down in words what I remember, I can almost convince myself that I can change what happened, you know, turn left instead of right after the intersection, and save everyone a lot of trouble. If only I'd known then what I know now, to borrow that cliché. Except in my case, there's nothing I would have done differently. Well, almost nothing. But it will be a while before I get to that part. I hope you don't mind that I spend some time filling in my background. So yesterday I'd begun telling you about the day my father died. That morning he'd been found washed up on the beach, and the sheriff's deputy arrived at our house to break the news to my mother, then asked her to come with him to identify the body while I waited at home alone. I was telling you about that. I, um . . . hey, did you know that a walrus sleeps in the water in a vertical position, with its head floating just above the surface?

I always thought this was interesting. In the first dream I had about RB after his death, I saw him floating offshore, his head bobbing above the surface. I jumped in and swam out to him. He was asleep when I got there, and I had to shake him to rouse him, to wake him up. I wanted him to tell me what he was doing there. But all he did was give a great big yawn and go back to sleep. He wouldn't wake up, but I did, obviously, I woke up. We celebrated my twelfth birthday the day after we buried him. It was June and me, along with the waitstaff at the Roslyn IHOP, who stopped what they were doing and gathered around my table to sing. There were burning candles stuck in the bundled pigs in blankets. I remember that they were the trick candles, you know, the kind that flare back up after you blow them out. Funny the things we remember. And do you ever stop and wonder about things you've forgotten? Wonder and curiosity, yeah, they're important. I've forgotten whether I ever saw my mother cry. She must have been broken up by my father's death, I'm sure, but what I remember is coming out of my bedroom into the kitchen and watching June pounding on my father's portable typewriter, his old Smith Corona. I asked her if she was writing a book about

RB, and she nodded without looking up, I remember. But it turned out that she was writing letter after letter in an attempt to cash in on RB's life insurance policy. The initial inquest, you see, ruled that my father had drowned himself, so June didn't have a legal right to the insurance money. But she demanded a review of the inquest, and, and the original ruling was overturned, and my father's death was ruled accidental. Even then, the life insurance company kept stalling, yeah, it took three lousy years for them to pay out the claim, but when they did, wow, a hefty fifty thousand dollars came to us as a single check in the mail one day. Geesh. My mother opened the envelope and held the check up to the light and said here's the book about RB, here's the story of his life. I was fifteen years old by then, and I just thought the whole thing was a joke. I have a clear memory of that moment, with my mother bending toward the lamp like a plant toward light while I was sitting there, I happened to be watching an ice cube melt in my water glass. I remember thinking there were two things that were impossibly strange, my mother and the ice cube. June was strange because she thought my father's whole life would fit on a small piece of paper, and the ice cube was strange because it didn't raise the level of the water as it melted. Um, so, well, anyway. I didn't understand my mother. She'd kept herself busy since RB's death. Between her job at the IHOP and her wrangling with the life insurance company, she hadn't had a spare moment to think about anything else. She hadn't taken the time to miss RB. She hadn't noticed that I was growing up. And she didn't realize that she had exhausted herself. I was plenty angry with June, and for years I figured she was a money-grubber out to make good on RB's death. I've since come to understand that her fight with the life insurance company was not about the money. It was her attempt to honor her husband. You see, she discovered that he had life insurance only after he died. He'd taken out the policy and made the payments in secret during the last five years of his life. It was his plan, I guess, to provide for his family, and in this sense June felt an obligation to get the insurance money. But when the check finally arrived, it didn't come with RB alive, of course. The check had been drawn because RB wasn't alive. RB was dead, and the check announced the eternity of this fact. In place of RB Boyle, we had fifty thousand dollars. That was the value of RB's life — fifty thousand dollars. Really, he'd earned the money in a wily scheme. With June's help he'd played one last trick on the system by dying. This was his big ha-ha, his revenge for the injustice dealt to him in life, and now that it had all played out, RB was gone forever, and June's work was done. Well, what do you think of this story so far? I'd promised to explain why I did what I did to your mother, why I left her in the lurch. Given my stated purpose, all I've told you so far probably seems irrelevant. But I think it's important for you to know how I spent my early years, if only to help you understand the man who would go on to fall in love with your mother. Does this make sense? Are you still with me? What happens when you tell a story that no one hears? It's like blowing air into a tire. You inflate the tube with gas, the molecules pelt against the walls of the tube, the pressure inside the tube exceeds the pressure outside the tube, and yeah, the tire is inflated, ready to turn. Or not to turn, if it's never used. Those restless molecules just keep on with their crazy pelting dance. Listen to me, I'm rambling, it's late, and I have to grade papers and catch up on the news. Maybe I should remind you that you can turn me off whenever you feel like it. You can decide whether to keep listening.

■ ■ ■ ■

Dear Sally, I can't tell you how much it means to me that you're still listening. I feel *emboldened.* That's a word I've never used before, not aloud, at least. But I'd convinced myself that you would only ever despise me. You know, your grandmother liked to tell me about you, and before she passed away she told me that you want to write, she said you're trying to write a book. I wonder what it's about. Huh, I passed a bookstore yesterday and saw in the window a pile of copies of a book called *Drop Those Alfredo Pounds.* If you want to write a bestseller, write a diet book. Or how about a book called *The Germ Police*? I could help you with that. People are concerned about germs these days. This hasn't always been the case, you know. Oliver Wendell Holmes wrote an essay ascribing fever to an invisible something, and he was ridiculed. But that was the nineteenth century. I like to look for any evidence that we've made progress. And then I see the latest statistics about endangered species, and I despair. Well, we could write a book together, you and I, about how to fight germs. Or maybe we could write about building a greenhouse. I don't know, that's always seemed to me a topic that would interest people. Either way, we'd make a bundle! Okay, I'm kidding. Anyway, I was telling you about what happened after RB died. Mmm, well, I hung out with my friends Deano Colletti and Tony Minastronti, we called him Minestrone, Stroni for short. We were a bad lot. While other boys our age were conditioning themselves for the football season, we were smoking pot and getting drunk. Once when I was fifteen I spent a night in the holding cell at the police station — this was shortly after June got the check from the life insurance company. We'd stolen a case of beer out of a garage and set out walking down the street. I know, we weren't the brightest bulbs. A cop pulled up, just our luck. Deano and Tony were bailed out by their parents that night, but June didn't come get me until morning. She wanted me to spend the night in the holding cell in hopes of teaching me something about the consequences of my actions. I didn't learn much. My poor mother. Well, to move on, I turned seventeen in 1964. I hardly saw June. She'd quit her job at IHOP after the insurance claim paid out. But she had to use a good chunk of the money to pay our debts. And anyway, she couldn't stand sitting around the house doing nothing, so she got a job as a waitress at the Red Lobster in Huntington. She took every double shift they gave her. She was so busy she didn't even know that I'd stopped going to classes. When the school sent a letter home, I forged a letter back from June that explained I'd been diagnosed with mononucleosis and could my teachers please send a list of homework assignments for the month, which they did, and which I didn't bother to complete. I don't know why they let me graduate. For Christ's sake, I graduated early, a semester early! And then in January of 1965 I took Pig and visited my brother, Phil, in Buffalo. June didn't mind me going, or she didn't let on if she minded. She gave me a load of money to share with Phil. She said we should live it up. So that's what we did. Phil already had gone through the money June had sent him the year before. He'd bought a truck and a snowplow for himself and was trying to get his own plowing and hauling business up and running. Plus he'd been getting ready to marry a girl and had put a down payment on a house. That's where he was living when Pig and I arrived in Buffalo, in a rotten little ranch house on Tonawanda Street. His fiancée had broken off the engagement, and he'd sunk pretty low by the time I arrived. When it snowed he'd go out to plow, but the rest of the time he sat in front of the TV. I sat with him the first month I was there. We drank beer and watched TV, we ate pizza and wings and fed the leftovers to Pig, we got fat, we got depressed, we went through the money from June. She wired us five hundred more, we went on drinking beer. In March there was a storm, we must have gotten three feet of snow over a weekend, and Phil was too lazy to take the truck out, so I did it for him, I followed his map and plowed all day Sunday and into the night, and at two in the morning I came back and Phil was gone, I mean really gone, along with his clothes and his radio. He'd left the TV and the stereo behind for me. There was a note on the kitchen table explaining that an old girl-friend had stopped by, not his ex-fiancée, another girl, she had a car and invited Phil to drive with her to California, and he said sure, he was ready for adventure, and as soon as he'd settled I could come and join him. I remember Pig had eaten too much of the leftover pizza and thrown up on the couch, so I had to clean that up, and then I went to bed. I was exhausted. I was woken the next day by the phone ringing, it was June, even before I answered she was yelling in my ear that they'd found Phil, they'd found Phil, but I didn't understand, I, I, I didn't think Phil was lost, I'd seen him the day before, Sunday morning, sitting at the kitchen table drinking coffee. Hmm. I think that was the only time I heard June raise her voice. What she meant was that the police had found Phil's body, along with the girl's, in their car at a rest stop on 90, both of them shot up, shot in the head from behind and in front, like they'd been surrounded and executed at close range. No one was ever charged with the murders, but my guess is it was the girl's boyfriend. It turned out she had a boyfriend, and what I still believe is that she was running away from him, that's why she came to Phil, so she'd have someone to run away with, but they only got as far as the rest stop on 90 just east of Erie, Pennsylvania. That boyfriend, in case you're wondering, he's some bigwig, works in the banking industry. Well, thanks to him, it was my turn to go to the morgue. While June headed to Erie in a bus, I went to confirm that the male victim found in the Mustang along Interstate 90 was indeed my brother. You know, I remember watching a TV show later that day, a documentary about, about of all things a juniper tree, a six-thousand-year-old juniper tree that had been found growing on a ridge in the Sierras. Now whenever I think about my brother, I think about that tree. This was '66, I mean '65. After we buried Phil, I stayed on in Buffalo while June went back to work in Huntington. I didn't get around to selling the house for a while. I enrolled as a part-time student at Buffalo State, and I supported myself with my brother's truck, hauling in the warm months, plowing in the winter. It would be a long time before I met your mother, nearly nine years before I met her and fell in love. Those nine years, there's not much to say about them. It took me nine years to graduate from college, I graduated with a degree in biology, with honors, summa cum laude, if you can believe it. I had an idea I might go to medical school, but no, it didn't work out. I got a job driving for a moving company. I saw every state in the Union, except Hawaii, Alaska, and, for some reason, Kansas. I never drove through Kansas, I don't know why. So anyway, the company ended up moving its headquarters an hour east, to the city you call home, and since that was my base I spent more time there than in Buffalo, though I wasn't happy about it, since I had friends in Buffalo, but that's how it was, a few years after the headquarters moved I

504

decided to sell my brother's house. There wasn't much to take in after the mortgage was paid off, but by then I'd graduated from college. I signed up for the long hauls and crisscrossed the country in my rig, and when I wasn't driving I was living in rented rooms and hanging out at Jeremiah's on Monroe Avenue, you might know the place, that's where I met Larry, who knew Tom, who was the boyfriend of Phyllis, your mother's friend. That's where I met your mother, at Jeremiah's on Monroe. I remember, I remember there was a thunderstorm while we were driving down Monroe. By the time we got to the bar the rain had stopped, but the trees were still dripping, and the gutters were running. I remember listening to the sound of water running through the gutter as the door opened and out of the bar came Penelope Bliss. I'll tell you about falling in love with your mother, but now, it's late, I've gone on, haven't I? I'll close here, but I promise to follow up, you'll hear more if you keep listening.

Dear Sally, I had a dream last night, I dreamed of you, I dreamed I saw you crossing a hotel lobby, you were pulling a suitcase, and I asked if I could come along on your trip with you, wherever you were heading. You didn't know me from Adam, but you said sure, why not, come along. But then the lobby was suddenly full of people milling around, and you disappeared in the crowd, I couldn't find you anywhere. I woke up feeling lost. You know, it makes me think of the common advice that following a stream downhill will eventually lead you back to civilization. Yeah, you can follow the stream through marshlands and forests, you can batter your way through alder and willow, and then, surprise, the flow might very well end in an isolated pond and you're still lost, you're lost worse than ever. Well, that dream last night, it was only a dream. I'm in between classes right now, I'd better get ready, so you'll find a pause in the tape. I'll be back later in the day.

I was telling you about my dream, and before that, about your mother. The way life changes, think about it, think about that feeling on a roller coaster when you're barely moving at the top of the rise and then you surge toward the bottom of the down-grade. That pit in your stomach, you don't feel it because your speed is so fast but because your speed is changing so fast. You're at the age where life changes fast, it's thrilling, isn't it, you don't have time to worry about the future, you just go and go, chugging up to the top of the hill. I used to love that roller coaster there by the lake. You must have ridden on the Rabbit, the Jack Rabbit, if it's still in operation, though it might not be, it was a rickety wooden thing when I was young and that was thirty years ago, more than thirty years. I remember the first time I rode on it, I was with friends, there were five of us and I ended up being the odd one out, so instead of sitting with one of my buddies I had to sit with an old lady, my God, a very old lady, she must have been ninety, and she said she had been riding the Rabbit once a year every year, ever since its first year in operation. That first year a fireman stood up in his seat and was killed when the train went through the tunnel. The old lady told me about that, I remember, just as our train started to move, she told me about the fireman getting killed on the Rabbit, and then she said, I'll never forget, she said, I hope you don't mind if I scream. And boy did she scream. We both screamed. Ha. The next time I rode on the Rabbit was with your mother, that same summer, the summer of 1974. I was going to tell you about meeting your mother. I met her that summer at Jeremiah's. Ask her if she remembers meeting me. Don't tell her I told you to, but go ahead and ask her, see if she remembers. Maybe she won't want to remember. Does she ever talk about me? God, she was gorgeous, with her eyes, her blue eyes beneath the domes of those wide lids, and her hair, it was the early seventies and she had long hair, she wore it with the front ends pulled back and held in a clip. She was nearly as tall as me, I'm five nine, she was, she must be close to that, I think. What can I tell you about your mother that you don't already know? I wonder if you find her as hard to describe as I do? Well, it's no secret that she was a real beauty with those silky curls, red curls, and her blue eyes always open so wide, as if she were trying to see everything at once. I used to like to watch her watching others. She paid attention, she looked at the world with interest, with wonder, that's a better word, with wonder and curiosity. And when she found a worthwhile cause, she'd throw herself into it. Don't get me wrong, she wasn't a saint, she had her own streak of wildness, yeah, she liked a good thrill. She liked to ride on the Jack Rabbit. She had a quick temper, it's true, but she was just as quick to laugh. Does it ring true to you if I say of your mother that she seemed to experience life with more intensity than most? Honestly, the only time I remember seeing her bored was once in front of the TV during a sportscast of a golf tournament. She had no patience for golf. I remember she balled up her sock and threw it at the TV, at the sportscaster. And I swear that guy looked surprised when the sock bounced off the screen, like he could feel it, he could feel the sock hitting him in the face. We laughed so hard, we couldn't stop laughing. When she laughed, I remember, she used to thrust out her tongue, she'd squeeze the tip of her tongue between her lips. We spent a lot of time laughing together, your mother and me. I can tell you it felt good to be with her. But how to describe what good means? I'd never felt it before and never since. Your mother was the love of my life. Maybe I shouldn't admit that. I had a decent marriage, more than decent, I loved Donna, it was a different kind of love, but I loved her. And I have two wonderful daughters from that marriage. I wouldn't trade them for the world. Your mother, though, she came into my life at a time when I expected nothing. I'd lost so much by then, my father, my brother, and that spring my mother got sick. I didn't realize how sick she was. I think she was worn down, worn out. She'd told me she had the flu. When I talked to her on the phone she'd start coughing, sometimes she couldn't talk through her coughing and would have to call me back. When I saw her in May, she looked okay, she was still working, but she had that cough, and then in July I got a call from her friend, who told me she was in the hospital. Your mother came with me to visit her. Your mother. Penelope. Penelope Bliss. I don't know how I would have gotten through that summer without her. I don't know how I've managed without her for thirty years. More than thirty years. Ask her, will you, if she ever thinks about me. Don't tell her why you're wondering. Is she still so angry with me that she would refuse to let me speak directly to her? I wouldn't blame her. No, I wouldn't blame her. Well, I'll stop here. There's more to say, of course, but I'm late for an appointment. I'll be back soon.

Dear Sally, here I am. What a day, oh, it's not worth going into, suffice it to say that it took a bad turn when I spilled my coffee in the car on the way to school. From then on, everything that could go wrong did go wrong. When the bulb on the overhead projector popped, I knew it was time to give up. Why are we still stuck with projectors in this school? I have friends teaching in the town next door who have smart boards in their classrooms. How about that. And then I had to go and ask one of my favorite questions. I like to ask my students to explain why spiders don't get stuck in their own webs. You know what one said? One boy, he said they don't get stuck because God doesn't let them get stuck. Well, okay, let's pack up our books and go home, there's nothing to learn, everything's the way God made it so what's the point of scientific inquiry? What's the point of this question? Of all questions? I tell you, there's a large portion of the population of this country who believe a question is in its very nature Satan's work. Don't get me going. So the spider, what he does, do you know what he does? He spins his original web of dry threads, threads that aren't sticky, and then when he's almost finished he weaves in a gummy silk, and it's this silk that catches the insects, this gummy silk that's only in certain places on the web. If only we were as intelligent as spiders. Well, anyway, how are you? I hope you're in love with someone who loves you. I hope nothing comes in the way of your love. I was listening to Johnny Cash on the drive to school this morning, I was listening to him sing about love. You are the rose of my heart, you are the love of my life. . . . Oh, what slush, but I tell you, more and more, I like slush like that, as I get older, I can put up with slush. I think if I ever tried to write a song, I'd write a slushy song. You are the rose of my heart, like that. Did you ask your mother about me, by the way? But I guess it would be better for you to listen all the way to the end of this story before you speak to her about me. By the time you get these tapes, it will be past Christmas, though right now, Christmas is next week. I have a gift I wish I could send you, but I don't have the nerve. I was surprised to find it at Marshall Field's downtown, the old Marshall Field's, it's Macy's now, but they had the perfume your mother used to wear. Ah, it takes me back. It takes me back. This takes me back, just talking to you about her. I'm going to stop now. I'm not in the best frame of mind to continue. This is the first Christmas in twenty-eight years that I'll be alone. The girls aren't coming home. My daughters, my two younger daughters, are out west. You'd like them. They'd like you. Marcia, she's the serious one, a whiz at math, she's in an engineering program at Caltech now, and Tracy, she wants to be an actress, she's waiting tables in LA and trying to get auditions. She's been in one TV commercial so far, a local commercial for, um, it was for pet food, and Tracy is on a beach throwing a ball to a dog. The dog is the one mostly in the commercial, Tracy's only on for a split second. I don't know, I don't think LA is the best place for her, but I can't tell her that. Maybe you could tell her that. Someday you'll meet the girls, you're half sisters, after all. Well, Merry Christmas to you, and Happy New Year.

Dear Sally. I appreciate your patience and hope you will bear with me a while longer. I was remembering when I heard from your grandmother, when was it, back in 2000, that your mother's second marriage had ended in divorce, I was sorry for her. No, I wasn't. Well, you could tell her for me, tell her — no, I guess you shouldn't tell her that. Forget it. Let's wait. Maybe you can coax her to reveal things to you without admitting that you've heard from me. There's her side of the story, there's mine, we're lichen, our stories, the way they relate, they remind me of lichen. Lichen, you know, is made up of fungus and algae, it's really two plants in one, the fungus is a parasite, it draws the carbohydrates from the algae, but the algae don't seem to mind.

I like to cite lichen as a prime example of symbiosis. Doesn't every story involve symbiosis in a way, a relationship of dependence between parts? Your mother's story, what she knows, it's a partial version, but so is your grandmother's. The story your grandmother believed, well, it's not all true. It's true that she thought it was true. What I mean is, oh, I'm getting all bollixed up. Your grandmother. Okay, so this is where it gets complicated. Are you sitting down? I'm standing, looking out the window of my condo, looking at the parking lot. It's unseasonably warm today, it's been warm for weeks here. How about there? But why am I stalling? I'm going to tell you, I can begin to get into the details. Let's see. In the summer of 1974, your mother and I fell in love. By August, she was pregnant with you. That November, I abandoned her. I never wrote to her, never explained anything. I left her to conclude that my disappearance was an act of, of profound betrayal. And that's what you were brought up to believe, I assume. Right? How would you ever know different? The real reason I left was a secret I was obliged to guard for the rest, I thought for the rest of my life. There was only one other person in the world who knew the truth, what I thought was the truth, and that was your mother's mother, your grandmother. But wait, let me back up, I'm getting ahead of myself. I could use a sip of water.

All right, I was telling you about that summer. Your mother worked during the day as a lifeguard at a country club, and after work she'd come to my room, when I was in town, that is, and not out on some highway in Minnesota or Missouri. It's strange that I drove through Missouri but not Kansas. I don't know why I never drove through Kansas. I was away more often than I was home, but when I was home I was with your mother, she came over every night. We'd listen to music and take off our clothes and lie with each other. But maybe I shouldn't be telling you the details. Is a father supposed to talk to his daughter about her conception? It was in one of those old houses by the train tracks, those shingle houses in Maplewood, or maybe it was in the Edgerton neighborhood, or Dutchtown, it could have been Dutchtown. I was renting my rooms by the month back then, and I lived in three different rooms that year. I was in search of the best room I could get for the money. I wanted a nice room where your mother and I could listen to music and make love. We were so caught up in each other, we didn't think about birth control at first, and when we did, well, it was too late. In September your mother went back to school, but I'd visit her on weekends whenever I could. And she came home and surprised me one evening in October. As I opened the door to let her in there was a rumble of a train in the distance, I remember hearing a freight train. And then when we were inside together, the overhead bulb went out suddenly, just for a second, and then blinked on again. I remember Penny, I called her Penny, you know, I remember she became vivid with the light, her face was suddenly vivid, and I saw that she was struggling to speak. She wasn't upset, though. Not exactly upset. She was frowning, like she was trying to think up a word to a crossword clue. Does she still love crossword puzzles? There was one time, I remember, when she would do nothing else until we came up with the answer to a difficult clue. I don't, I don't remember the clue, but the word, it was *elaborate,* I mean *e-lab-orate,* we figured it out together. Well, that was a different time. The time she came over to tell me she was pregnant, all she said was I have something to tell you, and I knew, I . . . I knew what she had to tell me, and without asking what, exactly, she had to tell me, I said, We'll get married, let's get married. We really loved each other, we wanted to be together forever, we wanted to have a family together. We weren't expecting to start so soon, but we figured, we thought we were ready. And when it came to committing ourselves to each other for the rest of our lives, we didn't hesitate. We were in complete agreement that we belonged together. We started to plan a wedding, and then we decided it would be better to elope. You see, your grandmother had taken a dislike to me, or that's the impression she gave. I thought she'd decided that her daughter deserved better than me, and she didn't want me around. But it turned out she had another reason for wanting to keep us apart. My own mother was dead by then, she died in July. June was over in July, there's the irony. Anyway, I was all alone except for your mother. We were having a child together, we'd marry and start a family. You have to understand, I would have been totally alone without your mother. I was alone after I left her. I couldn't bear being so alone. I remember reading a statistic in a magazine around that time, I remember it said that one in every four Americans will develop a physical, a physical ailment attributed, attributable, to emotional causes. I don't know if that was an accurate statistic, but I thought about it, I was thinking about it when I was driving to Detroit. But here I've gone and gotten ahead of myself again. Let's see, I was saying that we knew by September, no, by the beginning of October that your mother was pregnant. And we let, gee, it was nearly a month, we let about a month go by, we kept it a secret while we planned our future together. We were going to elope to New York City, we were going to drive to New York City and get married and then spend the weekend in the Catskills. We talked about this all month. We spent every weekend together all through that October. I'd go to see her at school, and we'd stay in a motel. We lived together on weekends like a married couple. We were going to be married. We were going to be together forever. It seemed, the way I remember it, when your mother arrived that day to tell me she was pregnant, we planned what we were going to do in an instant, before we even spoke, in that instant when the bulb went out and then lit up the room, like lightning. Did you know, by the way, that one of the by-products of lightning is nitrogen, that lightning causes atmospheric nitrogen and oxygen to unite, forming nitric oxide? I like to talk with my students about this, about how the nitric oxide compound picks up another, an additional oxygen atom, and forms nitrogen dioxide, and this dissolves in rainwater and falls to the earth. The earth is bathed in nitric acid, dilute nitric acid, which then unites with chemicals in the soil to produce calcium nitrate, and, and calcium nitrate, you probably know, is a nutrient for plants, it's a good and essential nutrient. So during a thunderstorm, the soil is being enriched. When I think about that moment with the light, the vivid glow of your mother's face in the sudden light, it's like, it's like my awareness of her was being enriched, I understood her deeply, and I knew I couldn't live without her. I mean, I'd already decided that, but I knew it in an absolute way right then. Huh, I never guessed what lay in store for us. I never guessed. It's hard to speak about your mother like this. About the two of us together. I think, I think I'd better stop here, if that's all right. I'll say good-bye for now.

Dear Sally, I wonder if you're making progress on your book. You know, I'm proud of you. Even though we've never met, I'm proud that you are willing to make yourself vulnerable by putting your name on the cover of a book. I'm sure you don't need me to warn you to be prepared. I just read a piece in which the reviewer declared it a shame that so many trees were sacrificed for such an awful book. And how about all the insults floating around in cyberspace, the complaints, the stupid rankings. I need a refrigerator, it's time to replace my old refrigerator, so I've tried checking on the Internet to see what is available, and you know, every model has its critics, loads of dissatisfied consumers who take revenge by denouncing their purchase on one site or another. Those anonymous evaluations are probably all scripted by the competition. It's impossible to sort out the judgments. We're going to wake up and there will be no reliable source of information left, we'll be asked to cast our vote for every fact to establish its veracity. Forget research. Forget rationality and evidence. It reminds me of the woman who wrote in to our local paper this week, she took the time to write to the editor and hold forth on intelligent design. She believes in intelligent design, she says, because she wants to believe in intelligent design, because believing in intelligent design is better than not believing in intelligent design. Such profundity is worth a place on the editorial page of our local paper. Meanwhile, no mention is made about the conditions at Guantánamo. And in the *Times,* the *New York Times,* did you see the article on evolution? Research shows we're still evolving, that's the gist of it, nothing unexpected there, but oh boy did it raise hackles on, on creationism.org. Check out that site if you're interested in seeing a blueprint for ignorance, creationism.org, which is full of rants against atheist science teachers who dare to introduce students to Darwin. Instead of Darwin we're supposed to teach that protein formation was intelligently designed from the very beginning, we're supposed to be sure of life's origins, and there's the difference, scientists offer theories which are tested with evidence while fanatics offer pronouncements that we aren't allowed to question. Don't get me going. I'm already going. Going and going. Listen to that, my neighbor is home from work, I know when she comes home because she turns up the volume on her iPod speaker. You can't hurry love, oh, you just have to wait, yeah, yeah, mmm. The walls are thin around here. But I don't mind. I like hearing evidence of people living their lives with enthusiasm. You can't hurry love, uh-huh, mm-hmm, it's a game of give and take. I like evidence in all forms, new evidence on top of old, and not because I need to know things with certainty, really, it's just the opposite. Don't we appreciate the complexities of life better when we look hard at the world and at ourselves? Doesn't education teach us a respect for mystery? I hope so. That's what I believe. And I'd meant to add, when I was telling you about watching your mother's face in the flash as the lightbulb blinked back on, I was telling you about that, and I said, I think I said I was sure I understood her. But understanding, real understanding, involves an awareness of our limitations, the limitations of our knowledge. There are things we can't know, and the deepest knowledge makes us more aware of this. When I said that I came to understand your mother, I wasn't trying to suggest that, that there were no surprises left. No, not at all, I knew she wouldn't stop surprising me, I mean, if we'd stayed together, if we'd lived our lives together, she wouldn't have stopped surprising me. It was an understanding of that, a perception of a quality of being, a . . . I guess I can't explain it adequately. Well, the point is, we didn't stay together. I loved her. She was pregnant. I deserted her. And now I'll tell you why.

All right, here we go. In November of that

year, early in November, November 5, 1974, to be exact, your grandmother Mrs. Sally Bliss, Sally Bliss Senior, she was waiting for me on the porch of my apartment when I came home from a two-day haul. She was standing on the porch. It was raining hard. Rain was streaming between the shingles of the roof and forming a sheer curtain around the front and sides of the porch, I remember, so I didn't recognize your grandmother at first. I saw the shadow of a person there as I walked up the front steps, and I smelled cigarette smoke mixed with the rain. I knew it wasn't Penny because Penny didn't smoke, but not until I stepped under the cover of the porch roof did I recognize your grandmother standing there. She was holding a cigarette, sucking on the stub of a cigarette, taking one last drag. And of course I thought that we'd been found out, she'd discovered that her daughter was pregnant. She wanted Penelope to finish school, to graduate with a degree in theater, and then it would be a short step either to Broadway or Hollywood. That was your grandmother's dream for your mother. She wanted Penelope to be a star. She was convinced that it would be easy for her, all Penny had to do was bring her college degree along with her talent and beauty to her first audition. Sure.

That's the way it works. Huh. Anyway, it wasn't in the plan for her to get pregnant, not in Sally's plan for her daughter. I'd come along and messed things up. But your grandmother wasn't waiting on the porch to blame me for messing things up. There was another reason for her visit. I remember when I moved under the cover of the roof, I said, Hello, Mrs. Bliss. I always called her Mrs. Bliss, though I knew she'd never been married herself. And I invited her to come inside, to have a cup of coffee. The rain was dripping and hissing and splashing, what a downpour, I don't think I've ever seen it rain as hard as it was raining then, that day your grandmother appeared on my porch. I remember the cigarette seemed to fall out of her hands, I don't think she'd meant to drop it, but she went ahead and ground it out with her heel. And as she stepped inside, she tripped over the lip of the doorway, I recall. She managed to catch herself, to grab the pole of the coatrack and keep herself from falling flat, luckily. This part of it is still clear in my memory. But, um, what follows, I . . . I don't know, it's hard to remember the sequence, exactly as it happened. I had an electric burner, and at some point I put the water on to boil, though I'm not sure if this was before or after your grandmother spoke. I really don't know whether she was holding her cup of coffee while she announced to me . . . but maybe *announced* isn't the right word. I mean, she spent a while with me in the room that evening. She talked about how she'd had a baby when she was sixteen. She explained that she'd left the infant with her family and run away from home. She told me everything, but in what order, I'm not sure. She told me about her sister, your great-aunt Trudy. She'd been searching for Sally and had finally found her that summer. Whatever her sister said was enough to arouse her suspicions, your grandmother's suspicions. There was money involved, some sizable amount of money. Your grandmother had been under the impression that money she'd been sending regularly over the years had been given to her son. But her sister appeared early in the summer and told her that the money Sally had been sending had never reached her son. It was because of her sister's visit that your grandmother decided she needed to know what had happened to her child. So for the first time in several decades she went back to visit the town in Pennsylvania where she'd grown up. Her own parents were no longer living, and she couldn't track down her cousin, the one, his name was Daniel, Daniel Werner, who was the father of the baby. He had disappeared, and no one knew or was willing to say where he'd gone. But it was communicated to Sally that Daniel Werner had taken the baby after Sally left home, he'd tried to raise it, but he couldn't do it, he couldn't handle a baby on his own, and after two years, less than two, he gave the child up. The Werner family maintained that Daniel Werner put the child up for adoption. And that's the point where Sally managed to connect her story to mine. Is this all making sense? What your grandmother came over to tell me that night made it necessary for me to leave. But please understand that this isn't about blaming her. It wasn't her fault. She didn't invent anything. She received all her information from sources that should have been absolutely reliable. She was persuaded to believe . . . now it's going to sound absurd, I know, but back then, the discovery was presented as incontestable. You see, she became convinced, and she convinced me, that I was her son, the son she'd left behind. It's unfathomable, really. But she believed, and she persuaded me to believe, that I was her firstborn child. Well, maybe I should give you a moment to consider it.

■ ■ ■ ■

Okay. So your grandmother, she'd gone out of her way to collect the facts. She'd spoken to a sister of Daniel's, her cousin, that's who first gave her information about her son. She'd asked her cousin if the child had been adopted by a couple from Pittsburgh named Boyle. Her cousin wasn't sure about the name, but she said it sounded familiar. Sally went to the county clerk's office the next day and talked to a woman who worked there. She was a sister-in-law of your grandmother's cousin. This, I think, is significant, that there was a family connection to the county clerk's office. The woman promised to find the relevant documents for your grandmother. She said there had been a fire in 1957, some of the county's documents had been destroyed and others moved to another storage area. You know, I've since found out that there was no fire in Peterkin in 1957. But I'm getting ahead of myself. The woman, the sister-in-law of your grandmother's cousin, said she'd search for the documents relating to the adoption of Sally's son, and she'd contact Sally as soon as she found them. There was no point in Sally hanging around. She returned home and waited to hear from the woman. She waited several weeks. Though she suspected that I was her son, she had to confirm it. She was finally able to confirm it when her cousin's sister-in-law sent her an official letter verifying that Daniel Werner had given up custody of the child. And she sent her a copy of my adoption certificate from the diocese in Pittsburgh. I'm not sure how the woman got a hold of that. Anyway, your grandmother had no reason to doubt the authenticity of these documents. Still, she took the trouble to collect even more proof. She drove to Pittsburgh, where she spoke with an administrator in charge of the records of the Catholic Diocese, and though your grandmother wasn't allowed to see the original papers, the woman there was willing to assure your grandmother that the adoption certificate she'd received was accurate in all regards. Well, there was no two ways about it, your grandmother was convinced that the child she'd left on the kitchen table in 1947 was me. How could she not be convinced? The evidence seemed indisput—, indisputable. She'd be convinced of it for the rest of her life. I have to say, as absurd as it sounds, I mean, me being her son and falling in love with her daughter, a coincidence like that might be acceptable in a bad movie but not in life, in modern life, in my life, in your mother's life. A coincidence so outrageous, you can be sure I doubted it. Everything your grandmother told me, I said it couldn't be true. But she kept adding up the facts for me. Her certainty about the matter was overwhelming. I watched her sip her coffee from one of my old chipped mugs. Or maybe she'd already finished her coffee by then, I don't know. Maybe I hadn't even prepared her coffee yet. What I remember most is being engulfed by despair, a sickening despair. Oh, can you even imagine what it was like for me to hear your grandmother sit there and tell me that your mother, the woman I loved, was my sister? My sister. I'd come home from a two-day haul only to discover that I'd been thrown into the midst of an incestuous epic tragedy. What could I say? Your grandmother had a story to tell. It was a convincing story. She told it to me, and then she asked me what I would do. I said I'd leave, I promised to leave the city the very next day. She agreed that there was no other option, and she advised me not to contact Penelope. I don't think she knew at that point that her daughter was pregnant, or if she did she didn't want to talk about it. She asked me to stay in touch, to address my letters to a PO box. And she said, can you, can you believe it, she said she loved me. She was my mother, and she loved me. She made me promise to write to her as soon as I'd settled again. And then, and then, geesh, she gave me a manila envelope. It was sealed, no, it was clipped shut but not sealed, as I recall. I opened it after she'd gone, and it turned out to be stuffed with money, with hundreds of dollars, hundreds and hundreds of dollars. There was a fortune, more than two thousand dollars in that envelope, and your grandmother left it with me as a parting gift. She told me that long ago an old man she'd known, a good man, she said, had given her the money, and she'd been saving it for something special. Well, I was something special. She wanted to make up for . . . for not taking care of me during my life. It all made too much sense. Even in the downpour I could hear the engine of her car as she drove away. I just stood there, dumbstruck. I was impressed by her conviction. What do I remember about that moment? I remember that satyrs and nymphs filled the room, dancing around me, taunting — taunting me with laughter. Sure. And flames, red-hot flames flickered around my feet. I went running into the storm and tore out my eyes and howled at the gods. No, I didn't. I spent the night emptying a whole bottle of Smirnoff, I drank and drank and with each bitter gulp I became more comfortable with my despair. It suited me, I thought. I was a loser, of course I was a loser, I lost everything that mattered, I'd always been a loser, and I didn't deserve to live. So early the next morning, in a drunken stupor, I followed what seemed the inevitable course. I headed over to the pedestrian bridge, the one, you know it, I'm sure, the one that spans the Tuskee gorge. It was just a few years old in 1974, that bridge. I went there, and, and I jumped into the river. Well, I kind of jumped and kind of fell. It was as much of an accident as it was intentional. I didn't really want to kill myself. Truly, I don't welcome pain in any form. But I was close to incoherent while I was hanging on to the rail. I was thinking that a man in my situation was supposed to jump. I was thinking about how I could put an end to all my troubles by jumping. And then I slipped and fell. I fell and plunged into the river. The thick, red, cold soup of the Tuskee. Does it still glow in the dark? It's a long way from the bridge to the river, isn't it? The Tuskee, the icy, red Tuskee. But here's the thing. Unbelievably, the river didn't like the taste of me and spit me out. It spit me right out, puh, over the wall into the parking lot of the utility company. One moment I was drowning, and the next moment I was sputtering on the pavement. Somehow I survived my own foolishness. Your grandmother insisted it was a miracle that saved me. I think it was the rain. It had been raining for days, the river had backed up and started to flood the gorge. Whatever. The river made it impossible not to survive. And here I am, after all these years, still alive to tell the tale. To be truthful, I remember climbing over the rail, and then I remember waking up in a dirty puddle in the parking lot. I don't remember falling, actually. I don't remember hitting the water. But I do remember coming to my senses and recognizing that my life was over, though I was too much of a loser to succeed in dying. So I did what I'd promised your grandmother I'd do, and I left the city. I drove to Detroit. And I . . . I lived in Detroit for a year, nearly a year, working as a dishwasher. Then I moved to Chicago. There's more to tell, I want to fill you in on the rest of it, the years between then and now. This story continues. But it's late, I'm exhausted, and I see I'm almost at the end of the tape. Well, good-bye for now.

■ ■ ■ ■

Without the letters from your grandmother, my dear Sally, I get no news of you. Not that I'm fishing for an invitation. Given what you've heard from me so far, I wouldn't expect you to want to meet me. You must think I'm a creep. Or at best, a clown. My students think I'm a clown. I've just come from class, my last class of the day. I'm covered with mud. I went and slid into the gully behind the parking lot this morning, intentionally, I slid down a mud slick on an inflatable tube, a snow tube, you know the kind, and I asked my students for help getting out. This was the day's problem: to find the easiest way to pull Mr. Boyle out of the mud. I do this annually in my study of forces. I begin with a marble, I roll a marble down an inclined plane of cardboard and we discuss why the marble rolls straight and not to the side. We talk about how force can be divided and the components can be added together to equal the original force. And then I take them outside and ask them to pull me out of the mud. They talk about pushing me from behind, that's always the first idea, they want to get behind me and push. But then I remind them to consider how a force can produce components in useful directions. And sooner or later someone notices the rope I've left at the top of the slope. They always figure it out. We talk about the amplification of force. I ask them how we might use the rope. Someone is bound to suggest tying one end of the rope to the tube and pulling me, so they try this, but it's not enough to get me moving. What they have to do, the solution, is for them to tie one end of the rope to the trunk of a tree and a couple of them take hold of the rope in the middle and walk to the side. It works every time, the pressure on the rope moves the tube forward a few feet, then they tighten the rope again and do the same thing over, the tube moves forward, they tighten the rope, and so on. I can tell the kids really learn the concept, but I always end up covered with mud. There's a new physics teacher in the high school, he has promised to one-up me and demonstrate the same concept in reverse by walking on a tightrope. He says he's going to walk on a rope stretched between the school and the garage, but you know, he has yet to do it, I think it's all bluster, he prefers to teach his students with textbooks and study packets. But you're probably wondering what any of this has to do with the story I've been telling. I guess I just feel like spinning wheels in the mud today. That's what I was doing for a couple of years after I left your mother. Wherever I went, I couldn't really move on. I was stuck, I couldn't stop thinking about her. And then about you. I knew I had a daughter, your grandmother wrote to me about you after you were born. She went to great lengths to assure me that you, her namesake, were normal and healthy. She'd clearly been afraid that you would be born deformed as punishment for your parents' sins. It hadn't occurred to me to have that fear. You know, your grandmother sent photographs of you over the years, the first one was your birth announcement, another when you're two and sitting on a pony, another one, let's see, you must be about five, and you're holding some flowers. I have all your school pictures from first grade to twelfth grade. I know that you had braces for two years. I know you wore your hair long for a while, then shoulder-length and parted in the middle. You got glasses at the age of ten, and then you must have gotten contacts, or else you just became self-conscious and took off the glasses for the photographer. But maybe it's uncomfortable for you to hear that I have pictures of you. I'm a stranger, after all. You have a right to be uncomfortable. You should feel free to stop listening at any point. That's the way to shut me up. Just stop listening.

Dearest Sally, I was telling you about how I jumped from the bridge. Or fell. I guess the image of the gorge was in my head from talking about it the other day. Last night I dreamed that I was walking on a tightrope over the Tuskee gorge. I dreamed that it was snowing, and I was trying to walk from one side of the gorge to the other, and your mother was there, she was standing on the bridge watching me. And she was holding a baby. I was on the tightrope in the middle of the gorge, and I saw your mother waving at me, and I tried to wave back, and I slipped. I slipped and I fell, and you know how it sometimes is in dreams when you're falling, you keep falling for a while. I was falling through the gorge, and I was think-ing to myself, what an idiot I am, what a fucking idiot to think that I could try to impress your mother by walking from one side of the gorge to the other on a tightrope. I woke up, I was awake before I hit the water, but all today I've had a heavy feeling from the dream. I guess what I want to tell you is that it breaks my heart to think about all the lost years when I was too afraid to contact you. I'm still afraid. Time is passing. It's ten past four and ten seconds, eleven, twelve. But, but, okay, there's nothing to be done about it, we can't relive our lives, that's spilled milk. And I wouldn't choose to give up the part of my past that produced my two younger daughters. Hey, did you know, by the way, that homogenizing milk adds, adds nothing to its nutritional value? People get confused about that. They tend to think the vitamin D comes from the process of homogenization. It's easy to be confused. In general, I mean, it's easier to be confused than not confused. I was confused, obviously, when I jumped off the bridge into the river. I haven't made the extent of my confusion clear yet. What I mean is that there's more to tell. I came to realize that I'd been wrong, I'd been misled. I don't blame your grandmother, I mean, she was trying to help, she was trying to do what she thought was necessary to save me, to save us, your mother and me, from worse torment down the line. To her the horror would have been discovering the truth, what she thought was the truth, ten years later, after we'd been comfortably married and had established a life together. Imagine that, imagine if your grandmother had found out about me in 1984 instead of 1974. By 1984, of course, I was long gone. Let's see, by 1984 I was married to Donna, and we had the two girls. Oh, it occurs to me I'd told you about the dog, my dog Pig. I forgot to mention that he died when I was living in Buffalo. He was old, I don't know how old since I didn't know his age when I found him, but he just faded, faded away, he got weak and bone-thin. He slept at the end of my bed, and one morning I woke up and he was as stiff as a board, he hadn't made a sound during the night, he hadn't suffered at all. That's the way to go. Much better than drowning in a freezing river. Well, I think I'll stop here for the time being, I have a stack of tests to grade, but I'll be back.

And here I am again, it's Tuesday, and the crocuses are blooming out front. They're mostly the variegated kind, purple and white. I've lived in this complex for two years. I bought a house after the divorce, a little Cape, but I sold it when my youngest daughter moved out to California. I think I prefer having neighbors on the other side of the living room wall, it makes me feel more a part of the world. It's easy to grow isolated, I find, to go to work, come home, and turn on the TV. I know I have a tendency to get comfortable with isolation, too comfortable. But on the other hand, I know complacency's a danger. I'm not going to sit around and yell at football players on the screen. Did I tell you about that peace rally I spoke at a few months back? Did I mention that some men, they were probably fathers of my students, shot me with a paintball gun, a red ball, as I was walking back to school? Did I tell you about that? I still wear the coat, and it's still stained with red, red paintball paint. Isn't that appropriate? On the other hand, there's the danger of self-righteousness. Like I was saying earlier, it's easy to be confused, what with all the invitations to believe. What do you believe? I'll tell you, I've decided that what matters is how we believe rather than, than, than what we believe. I mean, how we believe matters more, whether we believe fanatically or flexibly, or, or absolutely or uncertainly. I've learned this, you know, in part because of your grandmother. She believed that I was her son, and I believed her. Why shouldn't I have believed her? She had evidence. And if the evidence hadn't convinced me, she demonstrated her certainty with the money she gave me to get lost. And so I went on and made a new life for myself. I was telling you, wasn't I, about

Detroit? For a little more than a year I worked in Detroit washing dishes in two businesses, I worked a double shift every day, seven a.m. to three and five to midnight, and on my pay I wouldn't have even been able to afford the rent. But I had the cash from your grandmother. This helped cover the bills. And when my car died I bought another one, a snappy '67 Bel Air convertible. I remember the roof was ripped and every morning in the winter there'd be an icicle hanging inside. I'd always forget to look for it, and I'd take my seat and bump my head against the icicle, and it would crumble and fall inside my collar, down my neck. Ha, that's a memory I haven't thought of for a while. I lived in Detroit, spinning wheels, as I said, and then I decided to go to Chicago. One of my friends from Roslyn, Deano Colletti, he lived in Chicago, he had a job managing a trade show venue, and he invited me to come visit. So I visited, and I ended up staying there. I met Donna at a party, she was a friend of a friend of Deano's. Donna was studying nursing when I met her. Gee, I don't think we'd dated for more than a month when we started talking about marriage. She was eager to settle down and have kids. And she got me thinking about a career for myself, a real career. I told you I took night courses, I got my teacher certification in 1977, and Donna and I were married that same year. I worked as a substitute for a while in the Chicago schools. Marcia was born in 1978, Tracy in 1980, and in August of 1980 I was hired by the Vergonia district. And here I still am, looking at the swollen buds on the sycamore tree outside my window. My hair is gray. I have arthritis in my knees. I have to go to my doctor twice a year to have my earwax flushed out. I wonder if that's relevant. Do you want to hear about my life with Donna? I don't think I need to go into detail. I'll just say that we were content with each other, but I could never shake the feeling that we'd come to each other on rebounds from failed relationships. In the year before we'd met, she'd been in love with a med school student, they'd had an affair, but he was already engaged to someone else, which Donna found out only after he went away for the week and came back married. She was still reeling from the humiliation when we met. She thought marriage would make her forget her true love. I thought the same thing, I guess. It worked for a while. But what happened, what made it all go sour for us, was the med student, now a doctor, a very successful neurologist, he divorced his wife and, and I guess it was early in 1998 when he contacted Donna, and she, well, she was still in love with him, despite how he'd treated her way back when. She'd forgotten about the humiliating part of it. She got all tangled up in another affair with him. She couldn't keep her secret for long. I found letters she'd written to him, I found a necklace he'd given her for her birthday. Donna and I were divorced in 1999. She's all right now, but she had a hard time, I'll tell you, when the doctor ended their affair abruptly again, for the second time. He'd met another woman, a younger woman, and Donna was just devastated, you can imagine. Donna and I, we're good friends now, but we'll never get back together. That's just not something that interests either of us anymore. Too much has changed. Rather, too much has been revealed. We know each other too well to think we could live together again. It was hard on the girls, yeah, but, but they're doing fine, I guess. And I've had time to think about other things. I've had time to think about your mother. Even before your grandmother's death, I realized that I had some lingering questions. I couldn't bring myself to ask her directly. We exchanged letters, your grandmother and I, just to communicate the basic news of our lives. We rarely mentioned your mother. And I never asked your grandmother about my father. I knew only that he was her cousin. Her cousin, huh. That's not as bad as a brother, is it? Well, I wanted to know more about him. I needed to put the facts in order so I'd be sure of my past. I started by contacting old friends from Long Island. And one thing led to another. It took me a long while, several years, to piece together the truth. I'm going to tell you what I learned. But I don't have the time now to go into detail. I'll pick up where I'm leaving off.

It's the fifteenth of September 2006. Dear Sally. I'm beginning a new tape. Do you recognize my voice? Do I sound the same? How long has it been since I last spoke into this machine? Too long. The trouble began with a migraine I couldn't shake. I even ended up in the emergency room for a night back in the spring. Then a few days later I had a setback. The doctor sent me for tests. And then while I was waiting for the results from the tests, I got a call from Marcia. She'd been in a car accident. She wasn't badly hurt, thank God, only a broken wrist, but it was her left wrist, and she's left-handed, and she needed surgery. I flew out to LA on a Thursday and stayed with her for two weeks. I told her about you. I'd never told Donna or anyone else about you, and in the spring I told Marcia and Tracy that I have another daughter. I said that I'd been thinking about getting in touch with you, though I didn't tell them about these tapes. They'd think I was crazy, making tapes for you. I am crazy. But they said they want to meet you. Anyway, Marcia's doing fine now, the cast is off. My migraines, well, they weren't migraines, it turned out. I thought they were migraines. There were some days when I was out in LA when I'd close my eyes, and I'd see, I'd see the northern lights. I'd see quivering flames of light, violent, I mean violet-tinted light. I'd see electrons colliding with air. There's a video I show my students about auroras. I call it the northern-lights-in-a-tube video. It shows scientists making auroras in miniature, in a tube in a lab. Anyway, it wasn't migraines making all the trouble, as it turned out. I had a tumor, a small tumor lodged right behind my optic nerve. I tell you, hearing news like that. . . . Well, I came through the surgery, and the tumor, the biopsy was clean, there's no malignancy to worry about. But what a summer. Tracy and Marcia helped out, they took turns staying with me. And at one point I realized that I'd missed your birthday. I'd been hoping to finish these tapes and send them to you by your birthday. Here's a late happy birthday, dear Sally. Happy birthday to you, happy birthday to you. A day to make a wish, a whole year to make it come true. I'm sorry I couldn't give you the gift of this story for your birthday. I had to go on sick leave in the spring, I couldn't finish the year. You know what I heard when I saw my students last week? They said that the substitute for my classes told them that girls don't have an aptitude for science and math because of, because of hormones. The boys got a kick out of that, for sure. And one of the girls asked me if she could have special privileges for her learning disability — the disability of being a girl. It will take me a while to undo the damage. But, well, here I am, back on my feet, talking to you again. I'm alive. For a while there . . . I'll say simply that I'm glad to be alive. Alive, alive, alive. There's much to add to the earlier segments of this story. But, you hear that? There's the doorbell. Wouldn't you know.

It's the twentieth of September. I've been absorbed with a friend's troubles. It's a terrible situation. His wife died of ovarian cancer last spring, and his son, his son has a drug problem, he's been in and out of jail. And now my friend thinks he's going to lose his job. He works for a nonprofit foundation, and because of cutbacks . . . oh, if I start telling that whole story I'll never stop.

Where was I? Let's see. Way back in the spring. I'd better look at my notes. I don't have notes. I mean, I'm not following a script here, believe me. Okay, okay, I need to get back to the point where I'd left off. I've listened to the tapes to catch myself up. It's true, huh, that I'm not so good with words, am I? But I'm more comfortable speaking aloud, that's a plain fact. I like to say something as it comes to me and not think about it twice, not stop and think about how there might be a better way to say it. There's always a better way to say it, isn't there? I hope that doesn't keep you from making progress on your book. I sure look forward to reading it, you know. I'm looking forward to most everything these days, after this summer. It's good to be able to finish what I'd started. The thought occurred to me when I was in the hospital . . . if I couldn't reach you, if I couldn't tell you the truth about me . . . I almost picked up the phone and called you. But I thought it would be too hard to make you understand. Do you understand why I'm telling you the truth this way, the way I learned it, and not all at once? I told you why I left your mother, yeah, and went to Detroit. I told you about Donna and our divorce. I'll tell you now about how I went back to Long Island early in 2001. At that point, I thought I knew what was what. I thought I knew that I was your grandmother's son and had been adopted and raised by June and RB, and I'd grown up and unwit—, unwit—, unwittingly, excuse me, I'd fallen in love with your grandmother's daughter and, ha, knocked her up. For nearly thirty years, that's the story I thought was true. So anyway I was back in New York for a conference, and I took the train out to Roslyn and had lunch with the sister of one of my childhood buddies, Tony's sister. Tony lives in Florida, but his sister Angela still lives in Roslyn, so we had lunch. We were talking, and I said something about my parents, and she reminded me that June and her mother had been friends, good friends. Well, we talked, I joked about the way we called them, called her family the Minestrones. Then she said she was going to visit her mom, who had Parkinson's, she was living in a nursing home at the time, but she was still lucid, as clear as a bell, Angela said. I asked if it would be appropriate if I went along and said hello to her mother, and Angela liked the idea. So she drove us over to the nursing home, and it was nice to see her mom, I remember that theirs was always the house with a sauce simmering on the stove, and I told her that, she liked hearing that. We talked about Tony. We talked about my parents. She was real friendly with June, especially after my father died. They used to go out to dinner and a movie once a month at least, June and Mrs. Minestrone, Mrs. Minastronti, I mean, they used to go out with some other ladies. Well, I mentioned then that I'd met my birth mother a while back. Mrs. Minastronti looked at me in a strange way, with her head shaking like a bobbly doll. I could tell I'd surprised her. I asked her if she'd known that I was adopted, and she said sure. And then the nurse came in with medicine for her to take, and I had to catch a train back to New York, so I didn't get to follow through. It seemed that there was something she'd wanted to tell me, but she didn't have time to go into it. I went back to New York, and then I went home to Vergonia, and soon after, you know, September eleventh happened, and I gave up wondering if there was something important Mrs. Minastronti had wanted to tell me. There were other stories to hear, more important stories to hear and tell. I didn't think it would do any good to know more about where I'd come from, to clear up my own personal history. But that's not exactly true. It was gnawing at me. I mean, the sense that there was something hidden, something I needed to look for in the rubble of the world. And it was more than that. I'd been thinking about your mother, and I found it impossible to think of her as your grandmother's daughter. I got used to thinking of myself as your grandmother's son, but your mother, she couldn't have been my sister, not the woman I remembered loving. Therefore she couldn't have been your grandmother's daughter. And my resistance to the truth left me with a vague doubt, a haunting doubt that there was something I didn't know. Then in October of 2002 I got the notice from Tony and Angela that their mother had died. I was on a field trip with my students that weekend, so I missed the funeral. But in the months that followed I found myself remembering our conversation in the nursing home and I felt an awful sense that I'd missed an opportunity. She'd wanted to say something to me, to correct me. That's what it was.

She'd wanted to correct a misperception, but I hadn't given her the chance. And then it was too late. Speaking of late, look at the time. My eighth graders are in the bacteria unit. I'd better brush up on my knowledge of the bubonic plague. That's usually their favorite slide, the plague bacteria. I'll sign off for now.

I learned today that my name is on a list at a foundation that funds teachers in space. There's a group trying to buy seats for teachers on suborbital flights, and I'm on the list, so maybe someday, someday soon, I'll be looking down at our steamy planet from space. And there's another organization I've been in contact with. They have a proposal in at the NSF to fund trips to the Arctic. They want to bring middle and high school teachers to the Arctic as part of an effort to educate Americans on global warming. Speaking of, will summer never end this year? I couldn't keep up with the watering, I let the impatiens in my window box dry up. Here we are in early October, and there's no rain in the forecast. When the rain comes, they run and hide their heads. They might as well be dead. By the way, I hope you're a Democrat. I can't imagine that a child of mine would be anything other than a Democrat. Really, that's a quote from your grandmother, from a letter she wrote to me a while back. She was asking me about the election, about who I was supporting. It was Bush, the senior Bush against Dukakis, and your grandmother wrote to me, I can't imagine that a child of mine would be anything other than a Democrat. I still have the letter. I miss her letters. I could tell I made her happy with any good news I sent along. The only wrong thing I ever let myself tell her was to admit, to admit that I'd jumped off the bridge. I wrote to her, in my first letter to the PO box address she'd given me, I wrote to her to tell her that I had nothing to live for, I told her that I'd tried to drown myself in the river. You can be sure that she didn't like that. She wrote back to me about God and angels and miracles, she came up with some wild explanation, a bizarre con-coction of a story about how angels hadn't let me drown because I was supposed to live. I realized that she couldn't stand hear-ing about my despair. I never could bring myself to write to her with any news about my troubles from then on. Once I was settled in Detroit she sent me more money, a check for fifty dollars each month. The checks kept coming, but after I started teaching I really didn't want her money, it didn't seem right to accept her money, so I told her to save it for you. Every time I wrote to her I assured her that all was well. Sometimes, you know, I, I'd make up the news, I'd tell her I got a raise, or my students had won awards, or the girls had done something spectacular. She never knew that I got divorced. It was important for her to think, or at least I assumed it was important for her to think that I would always be happily married. She wanted me to be happy. If I wasn't happy, she was to blame. You can understand that when I started to feel an urge to find out things, I wasn't about to ask your grandmother. Here's a secret: I saw her once toward the end of her life. I snuck into town and came to visit your grandmother when she was in the hospital with pneumonia. She was sleeping. I never spoke to her, and she never knew I was there in the room with her. It was a risk to visit, for if I'd run into your mother there . . . what would I have said? But I stayed for just a few minutes, I gave your grandmother one last kiss on the forehead, and I left. I didn't have any way of checking in on her, since I was her big secret, the son who wasn't supposed to exist. Back home, I wrote to her and waited, hoping to hear that she'd recovered. Eventually my letter to her was returned. At some point she'd stopped the payments for her PO box. I had no other address for her. I started checking online for news. You know, you can find information about anyone, and eventually, well, there was her online obituary. Sally Bliss, 1930 to 2003, born Sally Werner of Tauntonville, Pennsylvania, survived by her daughter, Penelope Bliss. I was pleased to see your mother had gone back to using her maiden name, and also her granddaughter, she was survived by her granddaughter, you, Sally Bliss. Your mother couldn't give you my name, so she gave you your grandmother's name. Sally Werner Bliss, her namesake. Sally the second. Dear Sally. To your grandmother, you know, you were an angel, perfect just by virtue of the fact that you were normal and healthy, despite, despite, you know, your parents, your mother and father being brother and sister. I'll tell you right out that we — no, I won't, I'll disclose what I came to learn by telling you how I learned it. The truth is sturdier when it comes with evidence. Just keep listening.

Hello, hello, here I am, your favorite Martian, alive, alive, alive. It's raining finally, a glorious rain. Don't know why there's no sun up in the sky. Stormy weather, uh-huh. I bought a box for these tapes. A box and some packing materials. It won't be long now. Are you still listening? If you're hearing this, then yes, you're still listening. Good. Are you ready? But, oh fuck, there's the doorbell.

What trouble. First it was Harry, my friend, the one with the son in jail, he came over to tell me that he'd lost his job, he'd been let go from the nonprofit. He doubts he'll find another job. He has practically nothing saved up for retirement. I told him he can use the back bedroom of my condo. But no, he said he's not ready to sell his house. Oh, and then Donna called. She's upset. Her brother-in-law, her younger sister's husband, dropped dead of a heart attack. He was only fifty-seven and had no previous heart trouble. Life is delicate and brief and we must take advantage of our time here on earth, we must live fully, generously, productively, and leave the world in a better condition than it was in when we arrived. There, that's a father's sentimental advice to his daughter.

I dreamed last night that I was in a race.

Oh, it was one of those classic dreams, a textbook dream. I was in a race, but my legs felt like lead, I couldn't make them move. I woke up in a sweat. And all day long I've felt an urgency to hurry up, to get going, to finish what I'd started. All right. Dear Sally. Sally Werner Bliss. Here's what happened. After I learned about your grandmother's death from the online obituary, I decided to take a weekend's trip to Tauntonville. I wanted to find out something about my father. I wanted to meet the Werner family. I waited until the end of the school year, and then I got in the car and drove to Pennsylvania. My daughter Tracy was home for the summer, dividing her time between Donna and me. I told her, I told Tracy that I wanted to find my mother's family, and she offered to come with me. Together, we drove from Vergonia to Tauntonville. It took us three days because we went off the route and stopped to see the sights. The Rock and Roll Museum in Cleveland. Niagara Falls. We reached Tauntonville on the Fourth of July, pulled into town just when the parade was passing along the main street. We sat on the hood of the car and watched the parade. There was a fire truck, a school band, a couple of floats, 4-H girls on ponies. Let's see, what else? A contingent of beagles, half a dozen Shriners driving miniature cars, the county beauty queen. The parade passed slowly, but it wasn't more than a couple of blocks long. We sat on the hood of our car and watched, and I wondered if I was related to anyone in the parade, if I was looking at cousins and second cousins. I looked for redheads. I thought that maybe the beauty queen resembled your mother when she was young. I thought that the selectman who passed by, he looked like William Randolph Hearst, like pictures I've seen of William Randolph Hearst, and those pictures have always reminded me of RB. But that didn't make sense, RB wasn't related to anyone in Tauntonville as far as I knew. Okay, Tracy and I, we watched the parade, then we went to a coffee shop for lunch. And in the coffee shop, it was Tracy who took the initiative. She was into it, she was on a mission to find our family relations. She asked the waitress if she knew any Werners. The waitress said no, but she'd ask the owner. When she brought our cheeseburgers, she said that the owner didn't know any Werners. But then when we were paying the bill, Tracy asked the woman tending the cash register if she knew the Werners, and the woman, she was about seventy or so, with a thick German accent,

she said sure she knew that name, da Verners, she called them. Were we looking for
da Verner family? I didn't hear her correctly,
so I said no. Tracy said yes. The woman
said, Gud, gud, there was Loden Verner on
County 34, and Clem Verner on Mosshill
Lane. I wasn't sure she was talking about
the same family. But Tracy thought she'd
given us useful information. And she was
right. We followed the woman's directions.
We must have taken a wrong turn, we ended
up at a dead end, at a gate for a salt mine
company. It took us an hour to find Mosshill
Lane, but we found it, we found the house.
It was a run-down place, a two-story
shingled house blotted with chipped blue
paint. Well, we rang the doorbell, we rang it
several times, and no one came, no one
answered, though we heard a dog barking
inside. So we decided to try the other address. It turned out to be a farmhouse surrounded by barren fields. When we drove
up, a woman hanging laundry on the line
looked at us and went inside without bothering to say hello. We knocked on the door.
There was no bell. I started to walk back
down the porch steps, but Tracy grabbed
my arm because a man had appeared behind
the screen door, a heavy man, bald, with a
gray beard. He looked grim. It was easy to

guess that he viewed us as intruders. But he was polite enough at first. He asked us if he could help us. Tracy spoke. She asked him if he were Mr. Loden Werner. She said Werner, not Verner. And he said yes. And she said, she asked, the brother of Sally Werner? The man didn't answer. He still hadn't opened the door. And so Tracy went on in a friendly way to explain that Sally Werner was her grandmother, and here was Sally Werner's son, the son that had been adopted in 1949. She pressed the man in her friendly way to answer. Right? Right? she kept saying, to get him to confirm the fact of our connection. The son that Sally Werner left behind in 1947 had grown up, and here he was, and Tracy was Sally's granddaughter, and we'd come, she said, to meet our family. But the man, Loden Werner, your grandmother's brother, he eyed us from behind the screen, he wouldn't open the door. And I noticed he was shaking his head slightly, like he didn't believe us. The woman we'd seen in the yard, I thought she was his wife, she moved up beside him. I guess she'd been standing in the foyer listening and she came up beside Loden, who was still shaking his head. But he wasn't speaking, and he wasn't opening the door, and for a while, after Tracy had finished explaining who we were, we all stood there in silence. I remember hearing chickens in the area, the squawk, squawk of chickens. It felt like that was the only sound left in the world. Squawk, squawk. Until the woman said softly but clearly, Why, that's impossible. You couldn't be Sally's son, she said. And the man, he said, That's right, good day. And he closed the wood door over the screen. Well, that wasn't the reception we'd expected to get. We went back to the car. We sat in the car for a while. We sat there looking at that tired farmhouse with its lopsided chimney, and I thought, This is what my mother ran away from. But then I'd just been told she wasn't my mother. And I thought, I knew that. I'd known all along that she wasn't my mother. Sally Werner wasn't my mother, and she wasn't Tracy's grandmother. We sat there thinking about this and looking at the house. We sat there for a long while. Finally Loden Werner came out and stood on the porch, and he waved at us, he was waving at us to get out of there, to get off his property. Well, I put the car into reverse, and I pulled out of the drive and started heading down the road. We hadn't gone more than a short ways from the driveway, when at a bend in the road we saw the woman, the same woman

I'd thought was Loden's wife. It was like she'd transported herself, zapped herself in an instant from the house to the road. She must have come running through the corn-field in order to catch up with us. We pulled up beside her. We had the air conditioner going, and the windows were closed. Tracy opened the window, and the woman, she finished what she'd been trying to tell us through the screen. She said, You couldn't be Sally's son. Sally's son is dead, she said. She whispered it, as if she were afraid that Loden Werner would hear her all the way across the field. Sally's son, she whispered, Sally's son has been dead for fifty-four years. That's what she told me.

Did you ever hear the one about the chem—, the alchemist who came up with a recipe for making gold from eggs? What you had to do, he said, the secret was to beat the yolks of three eggs, to keep beating them for an hour without thinking of the word *hip—, hippopotamus.* Ha. I've been talking to you, all these months I've been talking into this machine as a way of talking to you, Sally, and I've been trying not to think of what might be changed, what will happen when you listen to this story in its entirety. I've been trying not to hope for anything.

But I'll tell you, Sally, Sally Junior, that I can't stop hoping that I'll convince you not to hate me. And maybe your mother might forgive me, if she knew the mistake that was made. And you know, when you hope for something to be accomplished, it's impossible not to think of that hope. I'm beating the egg yolks, beating them and beating them and hoping. Yes. Hoping. Okay, but I should finish what I've started, shouldn't I? Unless, maybe you're fast-forwarding through my ramblings, my babble, all the tangents. That's fine. I'm not in the habit of making every word count. And I've discovered over these past months, I've learned something about myself. Even if I'm not good with words, I, I like the sound of them. I like arranging them and hearing how they work in combination. And just the beat of thought when it's given speech, dah da-dum, da-dum, dah da-dum. You probably think that's pretty da-dumb. But still, let me get on with it. Dah da-dum, da-dum. When you're told something shocking, and you're thinking about it, when you're reflecting upon the shocking revelation, thoughts have that rhythm, don't they? Dah da-dum, da-dum. Yesterday I told you how I learned that I wasn't, after all, I wasn't Sally Werner's son. I was not. Her son. I. I was not her son. As much as I wanted to hear that, as much as I'd always known it in my heart, when I heard it, I didn't believe it. Funny, the way it is. I believed your grandmother when she was wrong. I did not believe this stranger when she spoke the truth. Dah da-dum. It took us a while even to begin to figure out the right questions to ask. The woman, after she'd come to tell me that Sally Werner's son had died fifty-four years earlier, she kept looking across the field. We couldn't see the house from there, but I thought she was trying to see if Loden was following her. I was leaning across Tracy from the driver's seat, trying to talk to the woman. I asked her, because I didn't believe her, I asked her what turned out to be the wrong question. I asked her, If Sally Werner's son was dead, then where was he buried? I said I wanted to pay my respects, and could she tell me where he was buried? Well, that was enough for her. She said, she hissed it, Ssss, I have to go back. I'd made her angry with my question, and I'd lost her confidence. And as I watched her hurry away, I thought that she must have been much younger than Loden Werner, at least twenty years younger. It turned out she was his daughter. You see, back at the coffee shop in town for dinner, we got to talking to the woman there, and we described the woman at the farmhouse, and she said for sure dat vas Loden Verner's daughter, not his vife, since he vas a vidover. We asked if there were others who might have known Sally Werner. Rather, Sally Verner. The woman, huh, I don't recollect her name right now, she'd never heard of any Sally Verner. There vas no Sally Verner, she said. I thought to ask then about the other Verners, the other side of the family, Daniel Werner's, Verner's, side. She said she'd never heard of dat Daniel Verner eider. Okay, we thought we were at a dead end again, like the dead end we'd come to at the gate of the salt mine. I was perplexed, let me tell you. But Tracy, she likes detective work, she was ready for the hunt. I wanted to go back to Illinois, but she insisted that we stay another couple of days, at least through the next day, so she could check with the local library and see if there was anything to dig up in the archives. Leave it to Tracy. So we got a motel room one town over, and the next day we went to the county library in Peterkin. We stayed there all day looking through microfiche, microfilm, whatever, of the local newspaper. We came up with nothing but stories of foreclosures and petty thefts. I remember reading a story about a windstorm that blew through one August afternoon and lifted a cow up and over the power lines. I should mention that though we searched, we failed to find any notice about a fire in the Peterkin county clerk's office in 1957. Huh. Well, at dinner that night, at a strip-mall Applebee's in Peterkin, Tracy suggested going back to talk to Loden Werner's daughter, but I wouldn't do it. I figured they'd pull a shotgun on us next time we showed our faces. So she said we should go back to the other house, Clem Werner's house. No one had been home before. We should try again, Tracy said. I ended up agreeing, but that would be our last effort, and then I wanted to go home and forget about it all. The next day, we were looking for Mosshill Lane, and we took the same wrong turn, and ended up at the salt mine. We turned around and found Clem Werner's house again, and we went up to the door and rang the bell, and this time a woman came out, an old woman with a friendly, wrinkled face, with two bright blue eyes buried inside the folds of skin. There was no screen door at this house. The woman opened the door and stepped out on the porch, along with her dog, a fat blond Lab with a stub of a tail that never stopped wagging. I let Tracy do

the talking. She explained that we were trying to find out about our family history.
We'd thought we were related to the Werners, but based on what we'd heard up at
Loden Werner's house, we weren't so sure.
What had we heard? the old woman wanted
to know. Tracy came right out and asked,
Was it true that Sally Werner's son had died
fifty-four years ago? The old woman, her
eyes were so bright and piercing, it was like
there was a light shining through them and
into us, like she could see into us, and she
was trying to decide whether we were to be
trusted. She didn't make a decision right
away. She told us to wait on the porch, and
she brought out two glasses of lemonade. I
remember that it was a hot day, and the
lemonade was fresh, full of pulp, and very
sweet, but not cold enough. Anyway, we sat
on the porch sipping lemonade, with that
dog at our feet, his tail thumping the whole
while, and the old woman introduced herself. She was Clem Werner's wife. And
where was Mr. Werner? Mr. Werner was no
longer. That was the way she put it, in
response to Tracy's question. Mr. Werner
was no longer. Huh. It seemed she was offering that as a way to end the conversation.
But Tracy kept at it. She asked if she'd
known Sally Werner, Mr. Werner's sister.

Mrs. Werner was silent, but we knew she had more to tell us. And she did tell us more. She said, Yes, she'd met Sally just once, when she came for a brief visit. I asked her if her husband ever spoke about his sister. She said he'd mentioned that his big sister had gotten into trouble. Clem's big sister had gotten into trouble. What kind of trouble? Tracy asked. The woman answered by staring across the road, at the slope covered with pine trees on the other side of the road. It really seemed like there were little sparks of light in her eyes. I said, Sally had a baby when she was sixteen. The woman said, Oh? First she said it as a question. Oh? And then she said it as an answer. Oh, yes. I started to say then, I was that baby. But Tracy stopped me. She touched me on the arm, I remember, to shut me up. And she asked, How did the baby die? Well, I could see then that Loden Werner's daughter had been telling the truth. I could see from the way Clem Verner's, I mean Werner's, Clem Werner's widow flinched that Sally Werner's baby had died, that was the truth. He had died, and no one wanted to talk about it. They sure didn't want to talk about it with your grandmother back in 1974 when she'd come looking for her son. They couldn't, no, they really couldn't admit to your grandmother that they had let her baby die. Once they figured out what she expected to hear from them, that's what they told her, they gave her what she wanted. They gave her back her son. But they had to tell the truth to Tracy and me or otherwise they'd have to pretend that we were family. We weren't family, they knew it, and these women, the daughter of Loden Werner and the widow of Clem Werner, they didn't want to pretend. They were sick of pretending. Well, that day on the porch drinking warm lemonade, we heard again that the baby Sally had left behind had died. Mrs. Werner couldn't say how it had died. Daniel Werner had been raising it, but the baby died. There was talk that he had been rough with it. No one could say for sure. There was no official announcement of the death and no funeral. Daniel Werner went away, and most people figured he'd taken the baby with him. He left the area and never came back. But the family knew the truth. The family knew, was what old Mrs. Werner told us. She didn't use the word *truth.* The family knew, was what she said. The baby disappeared, and so did Daniel Werner, and after that no one ever mentioned him, or mentioned Sally. Everyone got on with their lives. But I guess it bothered some of them, living with that secret. And after Clem married, he told his wife about it. And one day his wife told the daughter of Loden Werner. And one day she told us, too. She told us that I couldn't be the son of Sally Werner because that son was dead and buried somewhere on the mountain, whatever mountain she was talking about, I don't know. But that's how it was. And after she told us this, we just said thanks and got up and drove away. I mean, what could we do? Your grandmother was gone. Her son was gone. Daniel Werner was gone. And there were only a handful of people in Tauntonville, Pennsylvania, who remembered them.

It's November the first, 2006, and I'm done with my story. Well, not quite. There are some loose ends. I could tell you how I went back to Long Island that summer and found out who my mother was. My mother, the woman who'd given birth to me, was June's sister, June Boyle's younger sister. She lived in Florida, though officially the adoption in fact did go through the Diocese of Pittsburgh. My parents felt they needed to keep this information from me. June's sister had troubles of her own. But that's another long story for another time. I wanted to tell you that I'm not really your grandmother's son, and now that I've told you, I'm done. I'm going to put these tapes in a box and take the box to the post office. I'm not even certain if the address I have for you is correct. Well, I hope, I hope the box finds you, one way or another. Did you know, by the way, that the speed of sound at sea level is — I think this is right — it's seven hundred and sixty miles per hour. But at an altitude of thirty-six thousand feet, up that high in the sky, sound travels at, what is it, sixty, I mean six hundred and sixty miles per hour. That's why you hear the sonic boom. The boom is the shock wave produced by the jet, by a fast jet flying nearby, when it passes through the sound barrier. Why am I telling you this? Why have I told you any of this? I have no expectations. I'm not fishing for an invitation to come meet you. I wouldn't expect either you or your mother to want to have anything to do with me after all these years. But you're my daughter. If you feel inclined to reply, my address will be on the front of the box. Or you can contact me at the Vergonia Middle School, Vergonia, Illinois. Good-bye, Sally. Good-bye.

January 16, 2008

Posturepedic queen-size mattresses are on sale, Dorschel Dodge is the one you turn to, what a difference a beautiful smile can make, and if you don't happen to win the lottery, then call Bellino and Charms, personal injury attorneys, two-four-three, twenty-twenty . . .

I'm at the café at Twelve Corners right now. It's a nice change from my desk at home. I'm supposed to meet my mother here, but not for another couple of hours. I came early to wait for her. She's with the mayor, who is announcing tomorrow that the state legislature has approved a billion-dollar economic revitalization fund for our region. My mother has been appointed to head the committee that oversees the distribution of aid.

She keeps herself busy. First as a lawyer, then as a family court judge, then at the level of the state supreme court, and finally as a government official, she has always had plenty of people demanding a piece of her time. It's not the career my grandmother had envisioned for her, but, as my mother puts it, she's found a way to make a difference. The past few weeks have been more hectic than ever for her because of her new position. Just to get her over to this café in the middle of the morning is something, especially now that she's in charge of a billion-dollar fund. We'd tried to set up a time to have dinner, but twice she had to cancel.

I bet she thinks that I'm going to tell her that my boyfriend, Sebastian, and I are engaged. Well, she's right about that. We've been talking about it for a long while and finally set a date. We've already started drawing up a guest list. My mom won't be surprised by this news. She will be surprised, though, to see that we're inviting Abe Boyle to the wedding. What form her surprise will take, I can't predict. That's why I thought it best to tell her about my father in a public place. She's always been a passionate person, and though she's in a line of work where she definitely needs to keep a lid on her emotions, as one male colleague once informed her, I've seen that lid go flying off in the privacy of home. Her voice gets loud when she's overjoyed. Or when she's furious. She doesn't lose her temper to the point of violence, but she does tend to overreact.

Here in the crowded café at Twelve Corners, she'll have to stay composed. People recognize her; she's often in the local paper, especially recently, and is almost as much of a celebrity as our popular mayor. And though even to me she keeps professing reluctance to get involved any further in the dirty business of politics, I know that she's keeping her options open and isn't completely against the possibility of running for office. Her friends in Albany are hoping that she'll make a bid for the state senate next election.

While it's been hard to pin my mother down in the last few weeks, it's been over a year since I first heard from my father. I wrote to him shortly after I listened to the tapes. Since November of 2006, we've been corresponding by e-mail, we've had several phone conversations, and we're planning to meet for the first time when I fly through Chicago next week, on my way to visit Sebastian's family in Oregon.

There were plenty of occasions in the last year when I could have told my mother about my father. But I didn't want to reveal anything to her before I understood how the many mistakes and corrections were connected. I needed to have the whole story in place and be sure of the sequence of events.

My father, in the course of recording his version of the story, never guessed that I already knew why he had been obliged to abandon my mother. Without having any contact with me, he had no way of knowing that I'd already heard the explanation from my grandmother. Shortly before her death, she had told me, as long ago she'd told him, that he was her son. And for a long while I'd believed her.

I'd promised my grandmother that I wouldn't repeat what she told me to anyone. It was important to her that my mother never learn the truth about Abe Boyle. Perhaps she was worried that my mother would be so repulsed by the knowledge of her family connection to the man she'd loved that she would be repulsed by me, the product of that love. Or else — I think this was the real reason — she was afraid that my mother had never really fallen out of love with my father, even after thirty years. If she ever discovered the truth, or what my grandmother thought was the truth, she might take desperate action. And the easiest place to act on desperation in this city, as my father demonstrated, is the pedestrian bridge spanning the gorge.

In the last months of her life, my grandmother set out to tell me as much as she could before she was gone. She'd been fighting lung cancer, and while the prognosis was encouraging after her last round of chemotherapy, she sensed that time was running out. We'd noticed that she'd begun to get names and dates mixed up, and she'd lose her way on simple drives from the store to her home. But even in those last months, before pneumonia ended her life, she was still sharp enough to describe, as she put it, *how one thing led to another.* She remembered the details of experiences from the distant past with a vividness I wouldn't have thought possible. And she could answer almost any question I asked her.

After her death, I went through her letters and receipts, the photographs, postcards, newspaper clippings, even the old coupons she'd never used. Everything I found substantiated what she'd told me. I couldn't prove the most remarkable part of the story — that the river ran backward through the gorge, thanks to a legendary creature called the Tuskawali. But I know something like this happened because my father managed to survive an ordeal that should have killed him.

As my father believed for thirty years, I believed what my grandmother believed to be true. Now I know that she was wrong, and her mistake kept my parents apart. But she can't be blamed for this. She'd done her best to sort out the facts. The Werners had deliberately misled her. The challenge, as she saw it, was to verify something that she already knew. She thought she already knew the truth when she asked her family to confirm it. She thought that the direction of her life was as inevitable as the direction of the river she'd followed, and all along she'd been destined to land in a new fix shortly after she'd left behind the last one.

And yet she was the one who insisted that the river has secrets of its own. She believed that there was a strange magic in the Tuskee, and she warned me to be ready, for the river was full of surprises. I think about this, and I wonder if she was as certain as she pretended to be that the river was leading her where she was meant to go.

Of course she was certain. She wouldn't have sent my father away if she hadn't been certain. But certainty was a choice for her. She chose to be certain that her past actions had led to trouble that only she could resolve. She couldn't bear to hear that the baby she'd abandoned in 1947 had been killed by Daniel Werner, so she made sure to hear only the lie that her family told her. She kept her son from suffering what he'd already suffered. She went back to the start and changed the story. This was the real miracle of her life, the one that trumps that flood in the gorge. And as sensible as my grandmother grew through hard experience, she couldn't help but believe in miracles.

Wednesday morning, at eight minutes past the hour. Outside on the sidewalk in front of the window a woman is leaning over a stroller, tying the strings of her baby's wool hat. Two women at the table to my left are talking about an upcoming bat mitzvah. Local high school kids on their morning break are draped over the arms and backs of the lounge chairs by the counter. A white-haired man in the middle of the café is reading the Science section of today's *New York Times,* mouthing the words. I read the same article this morning and know that among the questions it asks, three stand out: What's the probability of being born compared to the probability of being reincarnated? How do we think about probability in an infinite universe in which everything that can occur does occur infinite times? And why can't we unscramble an egg?

It's twelve minutes past the hour. I still have more I want to write, but my mother will be here soon. She is usually about fifteen minutes late for any appointment. She likes to call herself an old hippie, and though she lives a life where she's expected to be responsible, she never passes up an opportunity to be carefree and resist the tyranny of the clock. And here she is, right on time, her own time, here she comes across the parking lot.

SALLY WERNER

Penelope Bliss, at the age of twenty-one, was home from college, working as a lifeguard at a local country club, and she'd finished her shift, hitched a ride from a friend, and was stepping out of the car just as Sally was inviting her sister Tru to come inside to have a cup of coffee and share a smoke.

Tru Werner didn't smoke; of course she didn't smoke. That's what she was telling Sally as Penelope crossed the lawn. And without saying it directly, she was conveying that she'd been a good Christian, unlike poor Sally, who had gone astray. Trudy Werner had always stuck to the straight and narrow. She worked as a nurse at the hospital in Lafayette and sang in the choir at church. She would go on to tell Sally this, and more — that she'd never married, never had children. Sally's other siblings had families of their own. As did Sally. Sally

Werner was the mother of two children. Two. All this information would be exchanged, but first, there came Sally's daughter, Penelope Bliss, wearing jean cutoffs and a tank top, feet in flip-flops, hair stringy from air-drying on the way home from the pool.

Sally said, "Penelope, say hello to your aunt Gertrude."

Who's Aunt Gertrude? Of course Penelope didn't say this aloud. But she couldn't be blamed for being puzzled. Her mother had spoken of a sister, sure. She'd reminisced about her childhood. But had she ever mentioned that her sister was named Gertrude? Penelope had to think about this for a moment: Gertrude? Aunt Gertrude?

Sally had a sister. True. For some reason, Penelope had heard it as an adjective. Sally's sister-true. True, she was her sister. Trudy the True, whom Sally had always cast as the one Werner with an unblemished soul. But even so, she had seemed as unreal to Penelope as any dream Sally had recounted over breakfast. The True Dream, here in flesh and blood. Oh, that Aunt Gertrude. Of course. Hello.

A late spring afternoon in the city Sally Bliss insisted on referring to as Rondo, in the year 1974, and Penelope was meeting her mother's sister for the first time. Her aunt was a tall woman, a few inches taller than Penelope, who was taller than Sally. From the heights, Trudy looked down on her sister and niece, perused them, compared one with the other, and with obvious bewilderment pronounced Penelope a beautiful young lady.

It must have been a shock for Trudy to consider how much time had passed since she'd last seen her sister — enough time for Sally to have a grown-up daughter. So little had changed in Trudy Werner's own life. She lived within an hour's drive of her hometown. As a nurse she'd witnessed so many passings that death hardly seemed remarkable anymore. She went to work and came home, watched television, and fell asleep. Meanwhile, a girl named Penelope had been born and grown up into a beautiful young lady. How did that happen?

To understand better, she asked Penelope a set of questions. Was she in college? Could she drive? Did she have a car of her own? And had she ever considered nursing as a career? Sally volunteered her own ambitions for her daughter: Penelope was going to see her name in lights someday. Penelope could only roll her eyes in response to Sally's prediction. *Yeah, right.* She had other plans for herself. She'd just finished her junior year, she explained, and she was majoring in history. She didn't say that she was in love with a young man named Abraham Boyle. She did say that she was thinking about going to law school.

Law school? Why, this was the first Sally had heard her daughter talk about law school. What was the point of law school? Penelope was too beautiful and talented for law school. Trudy should see her dance.

Darling, dance for your aunt.

But Penelope wasn't going to dance right there in the foyer. If Aunt Gertrude would excuse her, her date would be here any moment.

"Yes, go." Tru waved her away. She seemed genuinely glad to meet her niece, but she needed some time alone with her sister, who definitely would want to hear what Tru had to tell her.

In the living room, sitting at opposite ends of the sofa, the sisters balanced their coffee cups on saucers and traded a few niceties. Tru complimented Sally on the décor of the house. She especially liked the printed upholstery of the chair in the corner. And the flowered wallpaper in the hall was an unusual pattern, with rose blossoms that seemed about to spill onto the floor. The mirror above the sofa — why, that was an expensive-looking item. Sally admitted that she'd bought it at a yard sale. Her sister praised her for finding a bargain.

"You look swell," her sister said.

"So do you," Sally offered. "You look youthful," she added, a comment that provoked Tru to touch her hair, as though by feeling it she could remember that it was starting to go gray. Sally said that her own was a box dye job, Clairol's Desert Dawn, on sale, she added, two for the price of one.

They laughed together at that, and Tru let her cup tip, spilling coffee onto the saucer.

"Oh, you're still a klutz," Sally said. "I'm glad to see that some things don't change. Remember how you used to flap your arms and try to fly? Gee, sis, it's good to see you."

"It's good to see you, too." Tru set down her cup, and she rolled her shoulders as if to loosen them and get ready for the effort ahead. "I'll tell you," she said, "it sure was hard to track you down, Sally Werner."

Sally didn't correct her. She'd been Sally Bliss for many years, but it would take some doing to explain to her sister why she had a different name but didn't have a wedding ring. Unmarried, she could only be Sally Werner, and so it was as Sally Werner that she listened to her sister tell her what had gone on in Tauntonville in her absence. It was as Sally Werner that she was brought up to date.

First of all, Tru regretted having to share the news that their father had departed from this world on June 12, 1970, and their mother had followed him two and a half years later. As gently as this news was delivered, Sally felt it as a slap in the face, for it forced her to give up the last shred of hope that she'd ever earn her parents' forgiveness.

After giving Sally a moment to absorb the news, Tru resumed her account. She explained that their mother, for the last four years of her life, refused to speak anything but German. But none of her offspring or grandchildren spoke German, so her conversations were limited, especially after Dietrich Werner passed away. Tru went on to explain that Loden and Clem and Willy had married and moved into houses of their own by the time of their father's passing. Laura had married a city man and was living in Philadelphia. They all had children. Loden had a daughter, Clem had three sons, Willy had a son and twin girls, and Laura, at the age of thirty-eight, was pregnant with her fifth child. She already had four boys and was hoping for a girl. Tru had her worries about Laura, whose husband was, as Tru said, *severe.* And one of Laura's sons had been born deaf. But Tru promised to tell Sally more about that situation later. First, she wanted to tell Sally about their mother, who in her widowhood could not take care of herself, so Tru made the sacrifice and moved back home in the summer of 1970.

It wasn't hard for Sally to imagine what her sister's life must have been like in that crumbling farmhouse. She pictured their mother sitting on the frayed sofa, maybe with dentures in a glass beside her and one of the barn cats who'd found refuge in the house dozing on her lap. The old woman would have been in a sour mood by the time Tru put dinner on the table, railing at her daughter in German, the pitch of her voice expressing better than the words that Tru didn't understand the rage her mother must have believed was the best way to honor her righteous husband.

How do you say in German, *Woe to the forsaken, they shall be bruised with a rod of iron and broken into pieces like a potter's vessel?*

Or, *O come hither, and behold the works of the Lord, what destruction He hath brought upon the earth?*

What Sally heard in her sister's description of their mother's last years was that she herself was to blame. Tru didn't say it, not aloud, but Sally could guess that it was the shared opinion among the Werners that the oldest daughter had ruined the family. Sally Werner had seduced her cousin and then refused to marry him. Sally Werner had saddled her parents with an extra mouth to feed and then gone off to enjoy herself. Now her parents were both dead, and there was no chance of ever reconciling with them.

"I wrote to Mama and Pop," she said. The words sounded pathetic to her. She tried to explain: "I wrote to them, to all of you, year after year." But Tru couldn't have known that Sally had written to the family. If she had known, she would have written Sally back.

"I know," Tru said.

"You knew?" Sally must have sent more than one hundred letters over the years. Her sister had chosen, along with the rest of their family, to ignore them.

The sense of betrayal was so overwhelming to her that Sally stopped hearing what her sister was telling her. And when she stopped hearing the words with their separate meanings, she began making up her own story — she told it to herself in a rush

— about how Tru never had a chance to read her letters because they were never opened. They were saved, yes, they were saved and shoved in a drawer and periodically the bundle of them was produced by her parents and burned ceremoniously in front of the rest of the family, thrown into the fireplace because *we must rise up against the wicked and wipe them out for their iniquity, yes, with the help of the Lord our God we will wipe them out.*

She could guess what her mother and father had to say about their eldest daughter. Sally Werner was nobody's fool. Though she wrote to them regularly for several years, she hadn't expected to be reconciled. Say what you will. Even while they burned her letters, she'd been living the high life. Oh yes, they were right about her. While they were sitting around watching her unopened letters burn, she'd been making friends and making money, raising a child, falling in love. She'd done all right. She didn't need nothing. *Anything.* How could she make a mistake like that?

"How much money did you send, Sally?"

"What?"

"How much money was in those letters?"

"What letters?"

"Excuse me?"

"I mean, you said, what? Could you repeat that?"

"I was talking about your letters. You did write those letters, didn't you? I'm not mistaken, am I?"

Sally gave up trying to hide her confusion. "Please, start from the beginning, Tru."

"You poor dear. It must be hard to hear it all at once." With more pity in her voice this time, Tru explained again: Their mother had been taken by the good Lord on the day after Christmas in 1972. The following October, while Tru was cleaning up the house and getting it ready to sell, she'd been sorting the linens in her mother's cedar trunk and had found the letters. "Your letters, right? You did write those letters."

"Yes, yes, of course." She was following Tru's version now, and she felt a new urgent worry in response. "There was money," she said. "I sent money for my son."

"I know, I know. I read the letters. I don't know what happened to the money, Sally. I'm sorry, I just don't know."

If the money had disappeared, what had become of the child? It was possible that the child had died. Suddenly it seemed that her sister was preparing to announce the fact, and Sally, in anticipation, briefly pictured the infant's waxen, lifeless face.

She wished that the means had been available to her back then so she could have ended the pregnancy. But the means hadn't been available, and the pregnancy had resulted in a child, and she'd abandoned the child to a fate that revealed itself to her in a flash of a possibility that was too intolerable for her to ponder at length, so she cast it from her mind, and all that was left was a powerful unwillingness ever to consider it again, along with the residue of guilt.

"I know what you're thinking," Tru said.

Sally felt herself flinch. It struck her as inevitable — unbelievable but inevitable — that her sister could read her mind.

"You're thinking that I can tell you what happened to your baby. But I can't. Daniel had him for a while. But that baby was a handful. The cutest thing, but what a handful! Sometimes Daniel would leave him with us for a day or two, and I tell you, that baby had more spirit — I mean, the way he could howl. Daniel couldn't handle him. I would have raised him myself, Sally, I swear I would have taken good care of him. But I thought Daniel was raising him. Daniel moved from Tauntonville, you know. He traveled around for a while. I figured he had the baby with him. That's what we were told. That's what I thought. Daniel didn't even come home for his mother's funeral. Aunt Lena died of cancer, you know, and Daniel didn't come home for the funeral. Our uncle sold the farm to Loden and moved away. I don't know why, but none of those Werners have wanted to be in touch with us. I haven't seen any of them for years, not even our cousin Myra, though she still lives in the area. But I've worried about that little boy, Sally. Daniel just couldn't handle him. That's the way it was. I'd have raised him myself. But I wasn't given the chance. Once I read your letters, I realized that you'd been sending money. Loden and Clem and Willy and Laura — I asked them all, and none of them could say what happened to that money. Honestly, I've never been convinced that Daniel Werner raised that boy on his own. He named him after himself, you know, but I only ever heard him call the boy with curses. He couldn't handle him. I wouldn't be surprised to find out that he'd given the boy up for adoption. I like to think that some nice family took him in and raised him. But I can't find anyone who will tell me for sure one way or another."

Tru the True. Bless her. She would never guess that despite the bleak news she was bearing, she'd given Sally reason to hope. She could hope that her son had survived and found a good home with strangers. She might never know for certain what had happened to him, but she could indulge herself imagining what he'd become: a handsome young man with a red scruff of a beard, not unlike the young man who right then was opening the front door of his own accord and calling, "Hello? Hello, Penny?" into the house after his gentle knocking had gone unanswered.

Though he hadn't been involved with Sally's daughter for long, he was already in the habit of letting himself in when no one came to the door. Penelope encouraged it. And really, Sally didn't mind. She liked knowing that she made it easy for her daughter's friends to feel at home. She remembered, long ago, being welcomed by the Campbell family in Tuskee, and she was proud to think that she'd reached a point in her life when she could offer the same sort of welcome to others. Still, she was surprised when he suddenly appeared like that, out of the blue.

"Tru, this is, this is . . ." Sally knew his name, but for some reason her memory of it went blank right then.

"Abe," he offered. Before thrusting out his hand in greeting, he wiped it against his pants leg to blot the sweat from his palm. His strained smile suggested that he realized too late that it was a crude thing to do. Sally's surprise melted to amusement, and she suppressed the urge to laugh.

"This is my sister," Sally said.

Abe's response was a jovial *howdy* — not a word Sally would have expected from him, and she wondered if she was right to sense that he regretted using it. And now that she was paying attention to him, she noticed that his face, while mature with its beard following the line of his strong jaw, had a striking childishness, with wide, relaxed eyes expressing a boyish lack of guile. She could see why her daughter found him attractive. She herself was charmed by him, and puzzled at the same time, and embarrassed that she hadn't come up with his name on her own. If she'd been a more attentive mother, she'd have recalled the name of the fellow her daughter was dating.

"Are you Jewish?" Tru asked abruptly.

"I'm nothing," Abe replied. Well, he wasn't just being awkward, he was revealing himself to be more awkward every time he opened his mouth, and Sally appreciated him for it. He was nothing. Really? That's correct.

Abraham Boyle, Mr. Nothing.

Sally let out a chuckle, but it came out more like an exclamation of discovery: "Ha-ha!" Abe blinked back his startle.

"I only ask," Tru continued, as if in response to a question, "because I was engaged to a Jewish man. I was preparing to convert. If either of you know anything about the process of conversion —"

"Good God!" Sally's shock was expressed in a whisper. "You were engaged?"

"For three days. Pop chased him away. I mean literally, he grabbed the knife Mama had been using to bone the chicken, and he chased him from the house."

"Why didn't you go after him, Tru?" Sally asked, but she knew why, and she knew that it wasn't worth explaining.

In the weighty silence that followed, Abe looked from one sister to the other and then examined with fake interest a ceramic frog on the mantel. He looked grateful when Penelope breezed into the room. He looked more than grateful. He looked as though he'd forgotten everything else and was melting with infatuation for his girlfriend.

"Cute frog, huh?" Penelope gave him a kiss on the cheek. She was wearing a sack of a blue linen halter dress that reached to her ankles, and she paused to retie the straps as she stood facing him.

"Shall we go?" She hooked her arm through his and said to her mother and aunt, "See you later."

"When's later?" Sally asked.

"The movie ends at eleven," Abe said.

"Midnight, then."

Penelope hadn't had a curfew for years, but Sally wanted to give her sister the impression that she had instilled in her daughter a sense of limits. Fortunately, Penelope didn't bother to protest.

In the lull that followed their departure, Sally gathered the cups and carried them into the kitchen. She hoped that her sister was convinced that she'd made a good life for herself here in Rondo. She had a pleasant, welcoming home and a lovely daughter who came home by midnight.

At the sink, she found herself watching with odd fascination as bubbles from the dish soap swelled and popped beneath the pressure of the running water. Tru, standing nearby, leaning against the counter to rest her weak leg, said something in a murmur.

"What's that?" Sally asked, setting a saucer to dry in the dish rack.

"Wouldn't you say he looks like a younger version of Loden?"

"Who?" Sally didn't look up from the sink.

"Your brother. He's the spitting image."

Of course Loden was her brother. But who was his spitting image? Why, Abe was. You could say that Abe resembled Clem Werner, too, and Willy when they were young, but most of all he looked like Loden.

Tru didn't say, *It's obvious.*

Sally didn't say, *Dear Lord in heaven.*

Instead, she coughed lightly into her fist before she said in the flattest voice possible, "Oh, that's because they're redheads. All redheads look alike."

Penelope had chosen Abe by chance, yet with the intuitive confidence that she was right. It was as easy as deciding on a favorite color. She just recognized him as the right man when she saw him, even before she knew him. They belonged together. They were destined to move along the paving stones to the driveway, both of them practically skipping, so happy to be with each other that it was hard to summon the desire for anything else. They certainly didn't want to waste their time in a movie theater, and so Abe drove directly to the house where he was renting a room on the third floor. They tried to climb up the rickety back staircase side by side, but the space was too narrow, so Penelope slipped in front and catapulted up the stairs two at a time while Abe scrambled to keep up and at one point used his hands, leapfrogging to the landing. He couldn't wait. She couldn't wait. They started kissing even before Abe had unlocked the door, and they kept kissing while he fumbled in his pocket for his keys.

Penelope had been around enough to know that the era's promotion of free love was not as much of a bargain as it first appeared. In her experiences so far, the boys she'd been intimate with were unreliable. While they didn't try to buy her off with the promise of commitment, neither did they want to limit themselves to just one girl. It was taken for granted that they would *play around,* as they put it, and they didn't want to be held accountable. Penelope thought she'd learned to expect nothing more than frivolity from love — until Abe Boyle came along, and then she realized that she could let herself expect more.

There was more *good* to be felt with him than she'd ever allowed herself to hope for. And with more good came the wish for more *time* to spend together. When she was with him, she'd let herself believe that the hours would last forever, but it was always over before she was ready to go home. When they were apart she would lose herself in an elaborate mix of fantasies and memories of him, reliving and imagining intimacy in daydreams that would absorb her so completely that she failed to notice when someone was trying to gain her attention. The phone would ring repeatedly before she heard it. Her mother would have to ask her a question at least twice before receiving an answer. And once when she was in the lifeguard chair at the pool, she didn't see the boy in the deep end splashing and flailing and calling for help, so his mother had to jump in to save him. It turned out that the boy had only been pretending to drown to impress his friends, but it was enough for the club manager to put Penelope on probation for a week.

Together in the rented room on the third floor of the house on Jay Street, the lovers began with their fingers to trace the curving lines of their ears, their chins, their shoulders, and soon they were pressed against each other, belly to belly, their mouths locked together, their hands exploring, working each other up until it became impossible not to go further than they'd meant to, and though neither was a virgin and both knew they should be using contraception, they weren't going to stop everything just because they didn't have a rubber handy. They'd use one the next time, or the time after that.

Buster Boy.

Baby Doll.

Because now was now, the present wouldn't last until the future and so must be lived in all its fullness, pleasures tangling in perfect proof of the rightness of their love. There was no question: it was breathtakingly clear that they were meant for each other. And how easy it had been to see the potential back when they first picked each other out from the group of their friends — as easy as recognizing a familiar face in a crowd.

Tru Werner stayed with her sister for three weeks, passing the time while Sally was at work watching the black-and-white TV, a treat for her, since she didn't have a TV of her own back in Lafayette. Sally didn't mention Arnie Caddeau to Tru and during this period saw him only in the office. They didn't return to the subject of Sally's son. Instead, they talked at length about their parents, about their habits and foibles and the faith that made them unforgiving.

In the evening, she would take her sister out on the town. They'd eat dinner at a strip-mall Chinese restaurant, and afterward they'd go to a movie or a nightclub. On Thursdays the department stores downtown were open late, so they went shopping. With Sally's help, Tru found bargains hidden on the racks and came away with a clutch made of lambskin, a linen pantsuit, a straw hat, and a red silk party dress, which she bought only reluctantly, at Sally's urging.

On a Sunday afternoon toward the end of her stay, Sally took Tru to see the new pedestrian bridge spanning the downtown gorge. It was a warm, humid day, but the gorge was cooled by the wind blowing across the crest of the falls, and a crowd of people lolled about, enjoying the breeze and listening to a man puffing on a harmonica. Tru couldn't walk far because of her bad leg, so they sat on a bench and tossed pieces of a roll to the pigeons that had followed them from the parking lot. Voices seemed to float around them, lingering, as if spoken by the shadows of passersby. At one point a gust of wind curled up from the chasm of the gorge, caught Tru's new straw hat by the brim, lifted it from her head, and blew it right off. It landed first on the pavement, but before Sally could retrieve it the wind blew it skittering across the bridge and over the edge.

One and two and three and —

That's about how long it took the straw hat to fall from the bridge to the river. In truth, though, Sally wasn't measuring the time. She was too mesmerized by the hat, which seemed to soar of its own volition, as if it had sprouted wings, and then slid at an angle through the air, descending along a steep invisible slope before disappearing into the river.

Sally sputtered an apology, and though Tru assured her that she wasn't to blame, Sally apologized again. She was sorry for bringing her sister to this windy site only to lose her nice hat, her nice *new* hat from McCurdy's, which Tru had gotten to wear just once. Sally should have thought about the wind before she dragged her sister onto the bridge. Tru reminded her that she hadn't been dragged; she'd come along happily, and she was glad of it, the breeze felt rejuvenating, and what did she need with a new hat anyway? She hardly ever wore hats anymore.

Though it was, as Tru indicated, a minor incident, the loss of the hat reminded Sally of the river's presence and power. She was compelled to notice it again, to remember that it was still there and still flowing from its source to its mouth. The ruddy, sludgy river, thick with sewage and chemicals. In

the depths lived strange, elusive little creatures, part worm, part human — river
angels, as Sally liked to think of them. She
had long since given up hope of ever catching sight of one again. She knew the Tuskee
well enough to expect that it would guard
its secrets. She knew more about the Tuskee
than most people knew, since she'd followed
it all the way from the spring on Thistle
Mountain. She knew that the headwaters
were gray with cement dust in Fishkill
Notch. She'd seen how the river widened
and surged along a shallow course on its
way through Helena, it deepened and flowed
calmly through the city that shared its
name, it tumbled down shelves of slate
through the ravine in the state park, and in
its last ten miles it plunged over three sets
of falls on its way to the lake.

The Tuskee River flowed north from the
Endless Mountains, and Sally Werner had
traveled north with it. Even when she'd
inadvertently wandered from it, she'd never
been so lost in her life that she couldn't find
her way back to the river. She'd come to
where the river had led her and was confident that she'd arrived in the place where
she was meant to be. But something about
that hat, that straw hat sliding along the
slope of wind and disappearing into the

river — that hat hadn't been bought in order to be lost. It had been lost by accident, and it made Sally wonder about other accidents that she might have mistaken for destiny.

She drove Tru back to the house after leaving the bridge. Following a simple dinner of deviled eggs and salad, Tru went to pack and then to bed, since she had an early bus to catch. Penelope was out for the evening, and Sally stayed up late reading magazines. Really, she didn't do much reading. She glanced at the photographs and their captions while she pondered how her life would have been altered if she hadn't followed the river all the way north.

She would have found a different job in a different office. She wouldn't have met Arnie and been swept up into an affair with him. Her daughter would have grown up with different influences and wouldn't be thinking about law school now. And Penelope certainly wouldn't have had the chance to meet the young man named Abe, who just happened, wouldn't you know, to be the spitting image of Loden Werner.

She spoke to Daniel Werner in her dreams, in her thoughts, in letters that she wrote and tore up. *Tell me where you sent him, tell me what's become of him!* She rehearsed what she would say to him so she'd be prepared when she finally tracked him down. *Did you give our son away, Daniel Werner? Tell me the truth! Did you give him away?* She pictured Daniel Werner's worn face in middle age. She imagined his response of a dull, mulish silence. She knew just how she'd fill in the blanks for him: *Yes, you did, you don't have to speak, I already know the answer. You couldn't handle the child, so you gave him away. You gave him away, I know you did.* Her sister had planted the idea, and now it was all too easy to guess what Daniel Werner wouldn't want to admit. *I gave the boy to my parents. They gave him to you. You gave him to strangers. Good for you. It's the one right thing you ever did in your life.* She imagined filling in the words for him. *You gave him to a family who could provide for him. And then you went away to start over. We both had to start over, from scratch, and we did, and that's good, that's the way it should be, that's what we were meant to do.* She even went so far as to plan what she knew she could never bring herself to say. *Good for you and good for me. Our son had a better life without us. I left him behind, and you gave him away. He's a happy, handsome young man by now, all grown up. Yes, sure, he's better off without us.*

She was inclined to let her thoughts circle around imagined conversations in order to avoid the implications of her uncertainty. She told herself what she wanted to hear: her child had not been harmed by her neglect. She wasn't to blame. If Daniel Werner couldn't handle him, then he'd done what Tru had suggested and given him away. It was the scenario that made the most sense. Of course Daniel Werner couldn't have raised a child on his own, so he'd given the baby up for adoption. And wasn't it likelier than not that the boy had grown up into a healthy, good-looking young man, a redhead just like her brothers?

In the first few weeks following her sister's departure, Sally caught up on some of the chores she'd been putting off. She cleaned the carpets, washed the windows, and hosed down the siding. At work she stayed late to sift through papers and reorganize files. Because it was summer, she saw less of Arnie than she did during the rest of the year. He took Fridays off and spent the long weekends with his family. But he came to Sally's for dinner on Mondays, and he'd stay with her through the evening. Penelope was usually out with Abe, and after dinner Sally and Arnie would close themselves in the bedroom and fall into each other's arms.

Arnie's most vocal expression to Sally was gratitude. He couldn't thank her enough for putting up with him, for being steadfast in her love despite the difficult circumstances. His wife was more dependent upon him than ever. If she suspected his infidelity, she gave no sign. Over the years she'd withdrawn from interactions and spent most of her time in bed, where she'd sleep for long stretches at irregular hours, eat her meals from a tray, and when awake knit a plain white scarf that just got longer and longer. She repeatedly reassured Arnie with a dreamy smile, insisting that she was contented with her life. Still, there were times when he became so overwhelmed by shame that he would arrive at Sally's unannounced, with the intention of breaking off the affair. In response, Sally would agree and even go so far as to say that nothing good could come of their cheating ways. All it took, though, was the prospect of saying goodbye to each other for their resolve to weaken. Their love, they'd decide, was not something they could just turn off with a switch. They were doomed to love each other. They'd become convinced of this all over again, and the affair would continue.

Despite her love for Arnie, or rather, because of it, she couldn't bring herself to confide in him about the mistakes of her youth. She kept her thoughts to herself. And as she pondered the news her sister had brought, her responses evolved. Her parents were gone, and she would never persuade them to forgive her, nor would they ever tell her about the fate of her child. They'd taken their secrets to the grave. For a while Sally just filled in the blanks and imagined a rich life for her son: he was movie-star hand-some; he worked in a fancy office in a distant city; he lived with his lovely young wife in a big house with a three-car garage.

It was Abraham Boyle who kept remind-ing her that she couldn't keep entertaining herself with fantasies. All he had to do was push the front door open and call, "Any-body home?" for Sally to be reminded of other possibilities. That he looked more like a Werner the more she stared at him . . . why, what an absurd idea, to think . . . she couldn't even allow herself to articulate it, not at first. But the absurdity presented itself for her perusal every time Abe arrived at the house. Just by being present and available for observation, he made it neces-sary for Sally to wonder if there was more than a coincidental resemblance.

She invited him to sit. She offered him a beer and took the opportunity to examine his features with more than just a glance. She noticed the dimple above the scruff of his beard, the line of his eyebrows, the curve of his nostrils, and his eyes, those green eyes speckled with flecks of brown. He was different from the other boys her daughter had brought home. It was a difference hard to define but apparent in his obvious devotion to Penelope. Sally saw why her daughter might come to love him, if given the chance. And she understood something about love, didn't she? Sure she did. She understood that the experience of love could be as vexing as it was rewarding. Love could be dangerous and beautiful at the same time, hurtful and healing, impossible and necessary. That's what Sally would have warned the couple if she'd had the courage to be frank.

To pass the time, she asked Abe about his parents. His father, he said, had died when he was a boy. She expressed her condolences. His mother lived on Long Island. She'd come down with some sort of flu, he said, a summer flu. Well, that was too bad. Sally hoped his mother recovered quickly. Mrs. Boyle lived on Long Island? She needed to hear him confirm it: yes, Long Island, though she was originally from Pittsburgh, that's where she'd grown up, as did Abe's father. Really? And they met there in Pittsburgh? Yes. And then moved to Long Island? Yes. And Abe was born on Long Island? Well, no, in fact, he'd been adopted. Sure, Sally murmured, he'd mentioned that before. So he'd been born . . . in Pittsburgh? He been adopted through the Roman Catholic Diocese in Pittsburgh. That's all he knew for certain.

She could see he was getting jittery. He was nervous, like a witness under cross-examination. She guessed that he wanted to hide the fact that there were missing pieces in the puzzle of his life. But he couldn't help it. She wanted to reassure him, to point out that he wasn't to blame for not knowing things he'd never been told. There were blanks in her own life story, as well, though she didn't come right out and admit this. She didn't mention that she had a son. He'd be about Abe's age, yes, just about, give or take a few months. Of course she didn't say this. Her daughter didn't know that she had an older half brother, and it was too late to tell her the truth. Sally had secrets; maybe Abe could find them just by searching her face, as she searched his.

"There's Penny. Ah, if you'll excuse me . . ."

"Sure, go along."

There he went, looking more like a Werner than ever.

That's because all redheads look alike.

Who are you?

Every question has an answer.

An answer is true until proven false. Or is it false until proven true? And what role does intuition play in the construction of the stories we tell ourselves? Guess.

Could you be . . . ?

Try out *no.* It felt thick and heavy, unproductive, pointless. Then try out *yes.* It was so much brighter, like the underside of a leaf turned up by a summer breeze. *Yes* was more appealing than *no.* But she had to be honest with herself and admit that it wasn't convincing. *Yes* was the sound of a whim.

Then how about *maybe,* with its respect for mystery and its promise of resolution? Try it out. Test the word for its resilience. *Maybe.* It was a hopeful word and for that reason alone was the best answer to the question Sally couldn't ask. *Maybe.* And out of *maybe,* she could begin to solve the riddle of her life and identify the consequence of that first decisive action she'd taken, when she'd given herself the chance to start over again.

Running, running, running.

Out of *maybe,* Sally Werner might learn who she'd been all along. *Maybe* seemed the most honest option and at the same time the most encouraging, giving her direction. She didn't bother to consider that it was the same direction she'd already allowed herself to follow in her imagination. It was the direction she'd come from, a return to the past. She told herself she'd go back and find out the truth about the child she'd abandoned, and *maybe, just maybe,* she'd learn that Abe Boyle was her son. She had figured out the right questions to ask, at last. She didn't stop to consider that she was framing the questions to produce the only answers she was prepared to accept. There wasn't time to reject the promise of her hunch. *Maybe* hid the truth, the ridiculous, exhilarating truth, which had to be disclosed if her daughter and Abe Boyle were going to be spared from making a terrible mistake.

Thinking back to that summer, Sally would remember that there was a sense of change in the air. The jobless rate was up across the country, car sales were falling, and in

Washington senators were talking about impeachment. Sally sat transfixed in front of the television, smoking her Lucky Strikes. And then she'd spend the nights tossing and turning, her thoughts racing.

She planned to drive to Tauntonville in mid-July, but that was the weekend Abe Boyle's mother took a turn for the worse. Abe's car was in the repair shop, so Penelope borrowed Sally's car to drive him to Long Island. That same week Arnie Caddeau took his family down to the Jersey Shore. Sally waited restlessly, counting the days. Once, just once, she met some of her girlfriends at Typhoon Sam's, and after too many gin daiquiris she showed off her talent with a song. She sang "Dream a Little Dream of Me."

In your dreams, whatever they be . . .

She could still belt it out. The noise in the bar subsided as everyone stopped talking to listen to Sally sing. They listened politely, and at the end there was scattered applause, but Sally could tell that she'd made a bad choice with that song. It was Mama Cass's hit, and anyone trying to outdo Mama Cass or even match her was bound to sound foolish.

Back home, with the song running through her head, she remembered the good times singing with Penny Campbell in Tuskee. She'd lost touch with Penny; she told herself that when she did go to Tauntonville she'd stop in Tuskee and look up her old friend. She'd be sure to bring along a photo of Penelope to show her that her namesake had grown up into a real beauty.

Penelope Bliss had plenty of talent to go with her looks, along with the good habit of persistence and irresistible charisma. For years, Sally had been convinced that her girl was a natural performer and would have grand success if she just set her mind to it. But being a star wasn't in Penelope's plan. Instead she'd been talking about law — a man's career, in Sally's opinion. In all her years as a secretary in the office of *Kendycandyc'doo,* she'd never met a single woman lawyer. It was true that she hadn't met any celebrities either, but she'd spent a lot of time looking at their pictures. They had a good life, an easy life. Sally wanted to remind her daughter to watch for opportunity.

Penelope thought she'd found an opportunity in Abe. No doubt about it — they were spending the week falling more deeply in love. They would come home from Long Island more attached to each other than ever, and it would be up to Sally to disclose to them the fact of their family connection, if there was indeed a fact.

She awoke to a soft summer rain the next morning. She made herself a cup of Nescafé and turned on the radio. The dj was saying something about Mama Cass of the Mamas and Papas. She didn't catch the details of his announcement. "Dream a Little Dream" came on, and as she blew out a stream of cigarette smoke she remembered with deprecating amusement how she'd tried to do justice to that song at Typhoon Sam's the night before.

She learned the sad news only at the end of the day, when she saw the headlines in the evening paper announcing that Mama Cass Elliot had been found dead in her bed in a London hotel room, clutching a half-eaten ham sandwich. What a lonely and humiliating way to go. How could a woman with a voice as delicate as Mama Cass's come to such a sorry end? Sally was reminded of her beloved Dara Bliss and of fleeting time stealing the sweetest voices from the world. As she crossed over the Court Street Bridge, she started humming, and then she started singing softly.

In your dreams, whatever they be . . .

She sang the whole song through and at the end felt oppressed by the weight of loneliness. She stopped and leaned against the embankment wall to watch the rust-streaked Tuskee moving lazily, spilling slowly toward the lip of the falls. She was forty-three years old, almost forty-four, old enough to realize how much she'd squandered in her life. And yet she told herself that she'd made the choices she thought would be best. She'd had to grow up too quickly, that was the problem. She'd become a mother at sixteen, and she'd never had a chance to finish being a child.

Shortly after she returned home, the phone rang. It was Penelope calling from Long Island to say that Abe's mother had died. Poor Abe, then, was an orphan again. Or maybe not. Maybe another mother would take over for the one he'd lost.

They'd be staying in Huntington through the funeral, which was scheduled for Wednesday, and would drive home the next day. By Friday, Sally would be able to track down the Werners and get some answers.

She stood in the parlor of Loden Werner's farmhouse. He'd purchased it more than twenty years earlier from his uncle, and from what Sally could tell, he'd let the fields lie fallow. He was telling her about the lumber company where he worked as a supervisor. Willy was a supervisor, as well, and Clem was a driver. Loden was cordial enough as he brought Sally up to date. He'd grown thick around the waist, and his hair had thinned, but she saw that his cheek still creased around the one big dimple, and his eyes were still the same green.

He introduced Sally to his wife — Betty Werner, daughter of Patrick Shaunessy of Peterkin. Shaunessy. Sally didn't recognize the name. She accepted Betty's offer of tea. While Betty was out of the room, Loden called loudly for Bonnie. From the way he was calling the name, Sally thought Bonnie was his dog. When Bonnie didn't appear, Sally asked about her and learned that she was Loden's twelve-year-old daughter. She was probably out doing chores at the neighbor's, Loden said. He explained that she was working hard to save up money to buy a pony. They couldn't have a pony, he said, they couldn't afford the upkeep. But he thought it was good to see his daughter working hard and saving money.

Betty brought a striped mug with the Lipton bag floating in tepid lemon-colored water. Sally took a sip and set it on the mantel. She announced that she wasn't going to beat around the bush. She reminded Loden that twenty-two years ago she'd come in search of news of her child. She asked him if he remembered that visit. He said no, he didn't recall it. Then he didn't recall telling Sally that she wasn't welcome at home. He spoke sharply in denial — he never said that. Then he did remember that visit twenty-two years ago? "I suppose," he admitted. Perhaps he might recall that when Sally had asked him about the whereabouts of her baby, he'd said, *What baby?* No, he didn't remember saying that.

Back and forth they continued, Sally offering Loden prompts, Loden denying, then hedging, then denying again. She quit pressing him and tried a different tack. She asked him if he knew where their cousin Daniel was. He said he hadn't heard hide nor hair of Daniel for years. Even his parents hadn't heard from him. He disappeared. He didn't even come home for his mother's funeral, Loden said. Sally remembered that Tru had remarked upon the same thing, with the same words. She'd thought this meant his absence signified a turning point in their understanding of him. Daniel Werner hadn't come home for his own mother's funeral. But standing with Loden, she realized that he was conveying his disgust for Daniel Werner as a way of conveying his disgust for her, since Sally had failed equally. Her father had died, and then her mother had died, and their eldest daughter hadn't come home for their funerals. The older generation had passed one by one, and Sally hadn't come home. Well, here she was, too late to ameliorate her brother's contempt for her.

There would be no reviving whatever familial ease they'd shared as children. Sally was Daniel's equal. Both were disgraceful in Loden's eyes. Fine. She didn't need his forgiveness. She just needed him to tell her what had happened to her baby.

He didn't know. Daniel disappeared, and he took the baby with him.

Really? Was Loden absolutely certain? Sally tried a small lie to nudge him: "I heard that Daniel gave the baby away."

"Where'd you hear that?" Loden asked sharply.

"It doesn't matter. I just want to know if it's true."

"What's true?"

"That he gave the baby away."

"I don't know."

"It's possible, isn't it? It's likely, eh?"

Loden didn't know. He couldn't say for certain one way or the other. He advised her to go talk to Clem. Clem was living in a house on Mosshill Lane. "Go talk to Clem,"

Loden advised.

Sally bid good-bye to Loden and his wife, Betty, with such abruptness that they didn't even have a chance to show her out. As she approached the front door, she felt that peculiar awareness that comes from being stared at, and she glanced up the well of the staircase and saw a girl with her face pressed between the rails of the banister. Sally expected the girl to draw back in shyness, but instead she kept staring down at her, as if Sally were an exotic animal in a zoo.

Sally offered a greeting in her friendliest voice. "I'm your aunt Sally," she said.

"Bonnie, come here!" At the sound of Loden's angry voice calling from the parlor, Sally and the girl engaged in a silent, powerful exchange, with the girl expressing fear and Sally trying to convey with a slight nod that she sympathized, for she knew herself how difficult it was to be a Werner. Loden called again, the girl fled from the stairs into a bedroom, and Sally let herself out.

From Loden's house to Clem's. What would her younger brother tell her that she didn't already know? The hedging, the obdurate denials, the feigned confusion — the Werner men could make it difficult to track down the truth. But Clem had always been nicer to Sally than Loden had, or at least he hadn't gone out of his way to humiliate her. And he was polite when he came home from work and found Sally talking to his wife, his gentle wife, who had gone ahead and invited her sister-in-law to stay for dinner. She'd made a meat loaf, enough to feed a crowd, she said. And those three boys of hers, Sally's nephews, why, they made as much noise as a crowd with their shouting and brawling as they came up the back steps. They yelled at their mother. They yelled at their beagle, who stood thumping his tail, blocking the doorway. Though they were still young, ranging in age from ten to fourteen, they were big and forceful in their actions and already they had that Werner way of looking askance, with obvious suspicion, at their guest.

Clem told Sally stories about the part of his growing up that she'd missed. He told her about the time he'd broken his arm falling off a tractor. He described how a tornado touched down in 1954 on the Jensons' farm, cut a swath across the edge of the field, and blew a cow right over the electric lines. He told her how he'd met his wife, Eveline, waiting outside the movie theater in Lafayette. And he told her about her parents' funerals, from the Gospel passages read right down to the meals that were served after the ceremony.

His words gave Sally a mixed feeling of guilt and relief. Clem Werner had always followed the rules and lived his life in a predictable fashion. Sally, on the other hand, had followed a river, and she'd run into new problems at every bend.

She couldn't ask outright about her child, not with Clem filling the air with small talk and their beagle braying on the porch and those three boys too restless to sit for long. Dinner was over in no time, and before Sally could have a proper conversation with her brother, Clem announced that he had to drive the boys to their Little League game. In a blink he already had his own cap on, his wife and the boys had said good-bye to Sally and were waiting in the pickup truck, and Clem was telling his sister how good it was to see her. Wasn't it a shame she'd stayed away, but she was always welcome in his house, he assured her with honest conviction. Sally thanked him for that. And out of the swell of gratitude she blurted, "Clem, I need to find our cousin Daniel."

"What could you possibly want with Daniel after all these years?" Clem asked. Only then, standing close to him by the screen door off the kitchen, did Sally realize how tall he'd grown, more than six feet, she guessed. And his hair was blonder than she'd remembered it, more strawberry blond than red.

"I want to find out what happened to my baby."

It was the final word that caused Clem to respond with a noisy inhalation, which he held inside puffed cheeks.

"Can you tell me about my baby, Clem?"

"I don't really know."

"I heard . . ." She paused, trying to sort out the difference between what she'd been told and what she'd imagined. "I heard he gave the baby away." There, she'd put her wish into words. She said it aloud to give Clem the chance to say it back to her. "Is it true, Clem? Did the baby go to strangers? It's all right, if that's what happened. I just want to know. Tell me, please, what you know. Was the baby put up for adoption?"

"Listen, Sally, I can't prove anything. But I think —"

"Yes?"

"I think you'd better go talk to Myra. You remember Myra, Daniel's sister. She'll be able to tell you more. You go talk to her and find out what Daniel did with that boy you left behind." The last words were pronounced slowly, with obvious accusation, and for the first time since she'd arrived at his house, she saw something cruel in his eyes, a look of unyielding blame that reminded her of her father.

"I'll do that," she said softly. "I'll find Myra and ask her. Thank you, Clem. You've been very helpful."

Only then did Sally hear the sound of Clem's sons arguing in the bed of the pickup truck, each one trying to yell louder than the next. Clem whistled with his fingers to quiet them. He apologized to Sally, but he had to run.

"Go on, sure," Sally said. "I'll follow you out."

She stayed with Tru in Lafayette, in her tidy little house lined floor-to-ceiling with green-and-brown-striped wallpaper, the rooms lit up with bulbs that were so bright Sally had to blink hard to adjust after stepping in from the dusk. Tru couldn't take off from work and accompany her on her visit to their cousin's the next day, but she called ahead to Myra to tell her that Sally would be coming. Myra said she was expecting her, since she'd already heard from Clem. Clem had called her that morning. Yes, Myra was expecting Sally, and if she could come to the Edelweiss Coffee Shop in Tauntonville, she'd be glad to treat her to lunch.

Sally remembered Myra, Daniel's older sister, as a strong, athletic girl. Waiting for her in a booth at the coffee shop was a stout woman with a broad, ruddy face and iron gray hair pulled into a bun. Myra Werner? Yes, of course, and here was Sally Werner. "Little Sally," she said, "who had been loved by all the boys." With a sweeping look around the coffee shop, she conveyed her disdain. She didn't need to speak her thoughts aloud to communicate them.

Word had it that Sally Werner was a loose girl — and the right words aren't easily forgotten, even after twenty-seven years.

Myra murmured, "You're all grown up."

"I guess I am."

As if she'd uttered plain nonsense, Sally's reply provoked a burst of laughter from Myra. Contemptuous laughter was what Sally heard. The bitter, ugly laughter of blame.

"What's so funny?" Sally asked in direct confrontation.

"Nothing," Myra said with a shrug. She stirred sugar into her watery coffee, clattering her spoon against the side of the cup. "Mmmhmmm. Are you hungry? I've already eaten."

"I'm fine."

"Yes, of course. Now Tru said you wanted to ask me something."

"Tru said that over the phone? I was standing right next to her. I didn't hear her say that."

"No? Well, then that's what Clem said. It's understandable. After all these years, it has occurred to you that pleasure isn't the only purpose of life. Yes, you've grown up."

Her iron-haired cousin with her clattering spoon was like a guard at the gate, playing with Sally, taunting her, denying her entrance for just a little while longer so she could mock her some more.

"You broke my brother's heart," she said. Her teeth remained clenched, and the spoon kept circling the cup.

"I would have broken more than that if I could have."

"Ah, you wicked girl. It's good you ran away."

"Tell me what happened to my baby. What did Daniel do with him?"

"Your baby?"

"Don't pretend you don't know, Myra. Daniel gave the baby away, didn't he? I've come to find out what happened to my son. Tell me —"

Sally Werner had already guessed that

there were no surprises awaiting her in the coffee shop in Tauntonville. She was wise to the game. Though her brothers and her cousins were in cahoots, they couldn't hide the truth from her, nor should they want to try, for Sally had never intended her son to be raised by Daniel. She'd left the baby in place of herself. He was supposed to fill the space of Sally's absence, to be raised by her parents, to endure in the household she had fled from and even to thrive, for she'd been providing for him, or she'd attempted to provide for him, she'd sent money, hundreds of dollars, which was intended to buy him special privaledges . . . no, privileges.

Myra couldn't tell Sally what had happened to all that money. It never made its way to Daniel, of that she was certain. And the boy, Daniel Junior, never received it, for he disappeared —

"What do you mean, he disappeared?"

If Sally would be patient, her cousin Myra would explain that the boy disappeared into the world after Daniel relinquished guardianship. He was given a different name and raised in a different family.

"What was his new name?" Sally asked.

"Why does it matter to you?"

"Because . . ." What could she say? She could make up a reason. After twenty-seven years, she wanted to know the name of her son because . . . because "I think I've found him."

The spoon stopped circling; the clenched teeth separated. When a strand of Myra's hair fell free of the pins, Sally was reminded of the ash breaking off a lit cigarette. She could have used a cigarette right then, but she'd smoked the last in the pack that morning. She sensed a tingling that began in her toes and spread up her ankles, as though she were being lowered into ice water. She would have welcomed help right then. If only she'd asked Arnie to come along for the ride. No, she couldn't have asked Arnie because he didn't know the truth about her past, nor did her daughter, which made Sally feel more alone than ever and more desperate to escape that loneliness through the boldest of admissions: *I think I've found him.* Now she'd not only thought it, she had said it aloud, and in doing so made it possible for Daniel Werner's sister to encourage Sally's fantasy, thus diverting her from any other line of inquiry that might have led her to the truth.

"Well." Myra shifted her weight and seemed to tilt her head to listen to the creaking of the bench's vinyl. "Well, well. Who is he, then?"

625

"That's what I'm trying to find out."

"But you said you've found him."

"I *think* I've found him. I'm not sure, Myra." By saying her cousin's name, she was attempting to signal a new potential for honesty. She'd revealed so much already, and now she needed Myra's help, dear Myra, please, if you can't help Sally, direct her to someone who can.

Myra mentioned Sylvia. Yes, she might be able to help. She didn't reveal that Sylvia was the sister of Myra's dead husband. She just said that her friend Sylvia worked in the county clerk's office, she had access to the records, and she could help Sally find out for sure, one way or the other, whether the fellow Sally thought was her son —

"What did you say his name was?" Myra asked.

"I didn't say." For some reason, Sally hesitated. But at this point she had nothing to hide; already she'd discovered that the more she revealed about her suspicions, the more she learned. "Abe Boyle."

"Abe . . . ?"

"Abraham. Abraham Boyle."

"Boyle . . . ah, yes, I do think that name . . . after all this time . . . that name does sound familiar. But I'm not much use, am I? Listen, go talk to Sylvia. Go to the county clerk's office in Peterkin and ask for Sylvia. She'll be able to help. I'll call her," Myra added, "to tell her that you're on your way."

See how easily one piece of evidence led to the next. Having followed through on a hunch, Sally was on the verge of finding her son. If her claim to him meant that he would have to redraw the boundaries in his relationship with her daughter, that was a small price, she thought. They were young and in the early stages of their courtship. Surely they each could be persuaded to fall in love with someone else and to share with Sally an appreciation of what had been recovered. *It's like he has risen from the grave* — a thought she was about to speak aloud but decided to keep to herself at the last moment, fearing that the iron-haired sister of Daniel would find her blasphemous.

Sally never guessed that the information she was gathering with her determined inquiry was invented to satisfy her leading questions. That there was a difference between the truth and the Werners' version of the truth didn't occur to her, for they gave the impression that they were offering the facts only with great reluctance. They were embarrassed, as well they should have been, by their hypocrisy: as Sally understood it, they blamed her for leaving her baby behind, yet there was no one among them who had been willing to care for the child, and they'd let Daniel Werner give him away. On top of that, all the money Sally had sent over the years in support of the child had disappeared into someone's pocket — whose, she would never know. It was inevitable, wasn't it, that her brothers and cousin would claim ignorance and reveal the truth only haltingly, in dribs and drabs?

There was evidence to be found at the county clerk's office in Peterkin, but it wasn't available to Sally just yet. When she spoke with Sylvia, Myra's sister-in-law, the following day, she was informed that a fire in 1957 had destroyed many of the county's files, and those remaining had been boxed haphazardly and stored in a basement vault in a different building. It would take weeks for the woman named Sylvia to sort through the files and find the relevant documents involving Sally's child. That's if the documents had survived at all.

Sally spoke with Sylvia across a scratched mahogany counter. This woman named Sylvia, masked with a thick coating of makeup that gave off a swampy smell, didn't have time to help Sally with her search right then. She had a line of impatient taxpayers to deal with, and all she would offer was that she'd look for any documents related to the adoption and get back to Sally as soon as possible. How soon would that be? Sally dared to ask, and Sylvia snapped back that it might be weeks.

There was no use staying in the area any longer. Tru, who with her forgiving disposition was set apart from the others, didn't hold Sally's past against her, but the other members of the family would only ever consider her an intruder. She spent one more day at Tru's house and over dinner described to her the nature of her search. She explained that she hoped to locate her son. She didn't admit that she might have already found him, and luckily Tru didn't think to remark upon Abe Boyle's resemblance to the Werners. Really, the prospect of hearing Abe's name spoken aloud was enough to remind Sally of how absolutely ridiculous the notion was, far beyond anything a reasonable person would be willing to believe. If someone had described it to her, she would have thought it sheer insanity to have pressed the issue this far, and she would have been willing to dismiss the evidence she'd begun to gather. Yet she'd settled into a new confidence after her meetings with her brothers and Myra and had come to understand her suspicion about Abe as more than a vague effort to sort out the facts. She wasn't just pursuing a possibility. She was actively trying to rule out the only other possibility she had allowed herself to entertain — the infinitely more likely possibility that while her son had been given up for adoption, he was not Abe Boyle. This was the falsehood she needed to disprove now that she was nearly convinced she was right. What she felt, or thought she felt, was instinct rather than suspicion — a mother's instinct, which she could allow herself to idealize, if only privately at this point, as an awareness surpassing plain knowledge.

It was August of 1974. The highway, completed in the mid-sixties, was the fastest route home, but Sally took a detour on the back roads to the city of Tuskee. She was dismayed to see so many storefronts boarded up along Main Street and the gutters full of trash and broken glass. The drawbridge she'd loved to watch yawning open was in such a state of disrepair that it had been permanently closed to traffic. She turned down State Street in search of Potter's Hardware and found in its place a convenience store. She stopped in the store to ask about Buddy Potter. The young teenage girl at the register had never heard of him. Sally borrowed a phone book and paged through the listings. Though there was no Buddy Potter listed, she found the address for Arthur Steerforth, husband to her old friend Penny Campbell, and she drove to their house. It was a large, well-kept Victorian on one of the thoroughfares leading out of town, belted around the front by a thick garden of black-eyed Susans. While there was a quaint homemade Welcome sign on the front door, the rooms were dark behind the sheer curtains, and Sally wasn't surprised when no one answered her knock.

She drove back to the city of R, arriving at home shortly after dark. Penelope was out, sparing Sally the effort of having to lie about the nature of her trip. Penelope knew where she'd been, but not why she'd gone. Sally wasn't ready to reveal anything until she had indisputable evidence. No matter what she felt instinctively, she had to be cautious, for she still could be wrong about Abe. Yet what if she was right? Then his relationship with her daughter was a perversion — unless, as she became increasingly convinced, there was nothing serious to it, nothing more than a few shared kisses at the movies, just another passing flirtation, forgettable in the long run. But really, she couldn't deny that her daughter was happy these days, happier than ever, and she went out with Abe at every opportunity. If she'd already begun thinking of him with the future in mind, well, this would complicate things. It was foolish for Sally to assume that she could take her time with this matter. She hadn't been home for an hour and she already regretted abandoning her search without having received the documents from the county clerk. Sylvia had said it might take weeks to sort through the files. Sally should have offered to search those boxes herself. Now she was obliged to wait for Sylvia to contact her, and for the time being she had to pretend to be absorbed by her normal routines.

As it turned out, the world didn't cooperate, and neither did her daughter, who late the next morning came out from her bedroom, poured herself a bowl of cereal, and as she ate her breakfast casually asked her mother why she'd gone back to Tauntonville after she'd said repeatedly that she would never go back.

Sally pretended that she'd been invited to visit her sister, which seemed to satisfy the girl. But then she decided to change the subject and say that she was concerned about all the time Penelope spent with Abe. "That Abe," she called him, infuriating her daughter and provoking her to remind her mother that she was twenty-one years old, she wasn't a baby, and she could make her own decisions when it came to love.

There, she'd used that word — *love.* She didn't mean it, she wasn't worldly enough to mean it, Sally thought. No, she mustn't love Abe, not that way, but Sally couldn't say so.

The best she could do was to make up distractions to keep the two apart. In the weeks left in the summer, she paid for her daughter to spend a few days in Niagara Falls with her girlfriends from high school. She took her on a trip to the Thousand Islands. She took her shopping and spent money extravagantly. When Abe called, she didn't relay his messages.

If only that woman named Sylvia would provide her with the information she sought. A whole week passed, and Sally didn't hear from her. Another week passed, and another. It was plenty of time for Penelope to get used to the feeling of *love,* and still Sally had no hard evidence in hand. She had to put a stop to the romance, but that was impossible. She had no justification for interfering, unless she made up some damning lie about Abe, and she didn't want to do that, for then when she actually said something that was factual, she wouldn't be believed.

As it happened, she didn't see Abe Boyle again for a long while. Her daughter went back to school, and Abe was mostly out of town, driving long hauls around the country. Sally waited to hear from Sylvia. And then came a turn of events that she had long since given up expecting.

That September, Arnie Caddeau's wife passed away in her sleep. The office of Kennedy, Kennedy and Caddeau closed for the day so the lawyers and staff could go to the funeral.

Even with the group from the office, the family and friends gathered for the funeral were dwarfed by the expansive sanctuary of the church; Sally sat in a rear pew, adding her own private prayers to the eulogies, pleading with the spirit of Arnie Caddeau's wife to forgive her. The closed coffin glistened in the mottled light shining through stained glass. Arnie sat in the front pew. Watching his shoulders shaking, Sally felt her own impurity so overwhelmingly and understood the inerasable effect of time so completely that for a moment the idea of ending her own life seemed attractive. Yet the lure only served to remind her of eternal damnation, for if she died at this point, whether by her own hand or by natural causes, she wouldn't have the chance to make reparations. Without reparations, there would be no salvation, not for a woman of such foul spirit. She would be rendered as she herself had rendered, she would be repaid double for her deeds . . .

Pestilence and mourning and famine —
She shall be burned with fire —
Blood will flow as high as a horse's bridle —
Folly is the garland of fools —
Help!
Who said that?
Help me!

She didn't want to go to hell. She wanted to disperse like the spirit of Arnie Caddeau's wife into heaven's rainbow light, up through the saints crowding the windowpanes, to be freed from the consequence of her mistakes once and for all. But if she was going to be spared, she had to repair the damage she'd caused and help those who needed her help.

As the organ wheezed into a hymn, Sally watched Arnie's shuddering shoulders. He was sobbing because he had never stopped loving his wife; he was sobbing from the agony of secret shame. It was terrible to have to sit in the back of the sanctuary and watch him endure his torment alone. Sally wished she could comfort him. He needed her, and so did her daughter and her son, even if they didn't yet know it. They needed her strength to get through their different losses.

It was all so confusing. She had always intended to live a righteous life. In the midst of any decision, she'd always thought she was doing what was justified and necessary. But how could she know, how did anyone know what the repercussions would be? Without the ability to see into the future, everyone was like Arnie's wife, working blindly on a scarf, which for the lucky ones grew longer and longer and for the unlucky ones became tangled in knots.

Sally was of the unlucky order, having inadvertently tied together strands that should have remained separate. Now it was her duty to untie those strands and rejoin them properly so they were connected in a complementary way, fortified by their place in the pattern rather than lost in a mess.

She went home instead of following the hearse to the cemetery. She doubted that Arnie would have wanted her at the burial. She made herself a cup of tea and stretched out across the bed. For the next hour she paged through *Daytime TV,* scanning the recaps of the soaps while tears soaked her cheeks. She thought about how sorry she felt for Arnie's wife. She felt sorry for Arnie, and she felt sorry for herself. She felt sorry even for those characters on the soaps who were slated to suffer terrible fates.

She was back at her desk the next day, but Arnie didn't appear or call in to say when he planned to return. He didn't show up at the office through the rest of the week, not until the end of the day on Friday, when he came in to collect his mail and begin to catch up on his work. He barely acknowledged Sally at first. Later, though, when she brought him some reports, he caught her from behind and wrapped his arms around her. "My dearest love," he whispered, burying his face in her hair. There was the familiar stinging guilt in his voice but also a sound that Sally heard as relief. "We'll be all right?" she whispered back. She regretted inflecting the words with uncertainty and so repeated them firmly, as a statement: "We'll be all right."

"Yes," he said.

A promise was contained in that brief exchange. It would take time, but they would learn to give up the furtiveness. They would allow their love for each other to be acknowledged by others, without fear of condemnation. They were too worn out by guilt to worry whether a love that had thrived for years in secret could survive out in the open. It was comforting just to look forward to the future and feel confident of the resolution.

Still, she was absorbed by the portion of her life that remained unresolved and hidden from others. She continued to tear through the mail each day looking for a letter from the woman named Sylvia. She grew annoyed by her desire to hear the phone ring.

She called the county clerk's office and then declined to leave a message with the stranger who answered. Another week passed without any news. One afternoon in late October, she decided she needed some fresh air. She would have gone to Sam's for a drink, but it was Sunday and Sam's was closed, so instead she got in her car, and on a whim she drove out to the pier at Canton Point, where the river empties into the lake.

It was late in the day and the sun hung low in the sky, burning red through a gauzy mist rising from the lake. There was no one on the pier, though up toward the end someone had left a chair unfolded, with a fishing rod leaning against it, along with an open tackle box and a bucket full of lake water so black with silt that it was hard for Sally to count the wriggling trout. She bent over to look more closely, counted three fish tails, or four, she wasn't sure, and then saw a filmy eye just beneath the surface staring helplessly. The eye of a small trout, it must have been, though Sally was immediately reminded of the creature she'd seen years earlier in the state park, that water fairy with its expressive face and two tiny hands that had gripped the rock, its humanlike features just an illusion, according to her sophisticated daughter, who blamed her mother's penchant for irrational belief on her lack of education. Penelope didn't fully remember what they'd seen in the park, but she was sure her mother was wrong to rely on a fantasy to explain a mystery. Now the dusk was tricking Sally again, coaxing her to believe in something that was impossible and to ignore the usual measures of reality.

She could have examined the fish in the bucket more carefully if she'd wanted to confirm what she was seeing. She could have reached in her hand and caught the trout and lifted it out of the murky water. Then there would have been no question about its features. But she didn't look more closely for a reason she'd later explain was perfectly simple: *there wasn't time,* she'd say, an easy excuse for the vagueness of her vision and a defense against the inevitable skepticism.

A minute later she was heading back along the pier when she saw the fisherman come out of the public restroom by the parking lot. She increased her pace and was stepping onto the pavement when she passed the man, a heavy middle-aged man in baggy overalls, with the lower half of his face wrapped in a brown beard. He offered an affable hello, and Sally returned his greeting with a nod. She hurried on so quickly that as he reached his chair and discovered that the entire contents of his bucket had been dumped into the lake, she was already in her car, turning the key in the ignition.

It took Myra's sister-in-law Sylvia more than two months to produce a letter verifying that the son of Daniel Werner indeed had been adopted through the Catholic Diocese of Pittsburgh. It was an official-looking letter, on stationery with the watermark of the county seal, and stated that the letter would serve in lieu of the original document, which had been destroyed in the fire of 1957, to affirm that a binding Relinquishment had been voluntarily signed by the birth father, Daniel Werner, in the presence of witnesses from the Werner family and a Notary Public, at the Peterkin county clerk's office in August of 1949. The original Relinquishment passed the parental rights of Daniel Werner to the Diocese of Pittsburgh, the letter stated. And since the letter did not specifically mention the name of the new parents, Sylvia had gone to the trouble of including a copy of the Decree of Adoption for the same child, who was identified as the boy legally relinquished to the Diocese in August of the same year. The Decree of Adoption was dated September 9, 1949, and signed by the adoptive parents, Redding and June Boyle.

Sally couldn't have guessed that by concocting a story to coincide with her hunch, the entire Werner family was spared from having to acknowledge their complicity in guarding the secret of the murder. And she would never have to learn that her real son was beaten to death by Daniel Werner and then buried by him in an unmarked grave on Thistle Mountain.

In defense of the Werner brothers, it should be said that they didn't know the truth about the child's fate until years after their cousin killed him. Their uncle, who had helped Daniel bury the baby and then given him the money to leave the region for good, had confessed only to their father, Dietrich Werner. Dietrich had immediately confided in his wife. And though she waited until after her husband's death, she had eventually confided in her sons. So it was an old secret by the time Sally's brothers learned it, and they received the news as more evidence of the wages of sin rather than as information about a crime that deserved an official investigation.

When their sister had arrived in Tauntonville, the Werner men feared that they would be unfairly accused of abetting the crime, and they demanded that Myra Werner deal with the problem Daniel had made for them. When Myra heard that Sally thought she'd located her son, she must have decided that this would be a convenient solution. With her sister-in-law's help, she assembled the proof that Sally sought. Between the false account of a Relinquishment and a copy of Abraham Boyle's real Decree of Adoption, she made sure that her brother wouldn't be held accountable for a murder that had happened by accident, when he was helplessly drunk. And Sally would never go looking for her son's grave.

Because Sally understood the necessity for sturdy proof in this important matter, she compared the papers to similar legal documents on file at Kennedy, Kennedy and Caddeau. And then she drove to Pittsburgh and made an appointment with the adoption agency of the diocese. After an initial meeting with the assistant director, she spoke with the woman who had sent the copy of the Decree of Adoption to the Peterkin clerk's office. Sally wasn't allowed to see the file, but the woman assured her that there could be no mistake with the document. The date was correct? Yes, the date was correct. And the names? It was an official document signed by a judge, the woman reminded her. Of course it was accurate. But were there, by chance, any other two-year-old boys in the care of the agency at the time? The woman perused the record of adoptions: there was only one adoption involving a two-year-old boy for the period from January of 1947 to December of 1950, and that boy was Abraham Boyle.

By the time she was in her car leaving Pittsburgh, Sally believed that she'd found what she was looking for. Just as the letter from Sylvia had said, the child relinquished by Daniel Werner of Tauntonville, Peterkin

County, in August of 1949 was the same child adopted by the Boyles of Pittsburgh that September. And he was the same young man whom fate had brought to the city of R. He was the same young man who had taken to opening the unlocked front door of Sally's house and calling, *Anybody home?*

Actually, he hadn't come around for several months, not since her daughter had returned to college. Sally inquired about him in her phone conversations with Penelope. Her daughter, who thought her mother had taken a dislike to Abe, responded vaguely, and Sally wondered if this indicated that her daughter's interest in him had waned. When Sally came right out and asked, Penelope explained what should have been obvious: she was busy with her studies, and he was busy with his work. When Sally asked if she was dating someone else, her daughter snapped back, telling her mother not to pry.

Since her daughter didn't want to be subjected to questions, Sally was left to search Penelope's bedroom at home for any information that might lead her to Abe Boyle.

It was the first week of November on a gray Tuesday, the clouds were thickening ahead of a storm, and with the shade drawn the room was dark, reminding her of entering the room early on winter mornings to wake Penelope for school. She switched on the light and immediately was struck by the stillness of the room. In her daughter's absence she dusted and vacuumed the bedroom every week, but now its neatness seemed to give the room an artificial quality, as though it had been arranged as a model of an earlier time rather than as a place Penelope still returned to between semesters. The smoothness of the quilt, the waxy white edges of the windowsill, the posters of rock singers Sally didn't recognize, the pens standing in a cup on the desk, the paperbacks on the shelves — everything remained too firmly in place, glued and bolted down so that years later visitors could come and see the typical bedroom, circa 1974, of a typical American girl.

The arrangement of the room was misleading. When occupied, it was messy, with tank tops and bell-bottoms piled on the floor, unmatched sandals cluttering the closet, papers and books stacked in a teetering tower on the little table beside the bed. Sally missed the dishevelment of her daughter's life. She missed the windswept, breathless presence of the girl as she spun from the kitchen down the hall, the radio blaring one of those screechy tunes that Penelope loved. She missed the noise of her daughter's life, the laughter and rush of it.

And yet there she was uselessly straightening a spiral notebook on the desk. Sally couldn't resist — it was in her nature to try to put the clutter of the world into some sort of respectable order. After all the mistakes she'd made in her life, she preferred to keep the floor clean, the blankets tucked tightly around the mattress. To Sally, the freedom young people claimed as a right was perilously close to chaos. She wanted to know what to believe. When she was sure of something, she wanted to remain sure.

In contrast to Sally, her daughter seemed drawn to things that were uncertain and unresolved. Here and there in the room, in corners that hadn't been touched by Sally, there was evidence of the girl's tolerance for confusion. The titles of the books she read, for instance — *Ends and Odds* and *Words in Commotion.* What did any of it mean? Sally could predict that these books held no answers. And what use did she have for riddles that couldn't be solved?

Her daughter was intent on learning about things that seemed to bear no direct relation to her life. It didn't matter to her that she was radiant and talented and could have become one of those glamorous celebrities whose photos Sally admired in the glossies. Penelope wanted to get herself educated and then put her education to practical use. She was too brainy for her own good.

Sally had to acknowledge that a life of glamour was not in the cards for her daughter. While she wasn't ready to admit that it was a naïve and empty ambition, she did see that Penelope wasn't interested in such things. And really, Sally was proud of her girl, proud of her smarts, proud of her determination to go out and find her own way. She was building a life for herself that Sally couldn't have imagined. Penelope wasn't afraid, like her mother was, of finding herself in the midst of a situation that she couldn't control. She trusted her own ability to handle any unpredictable challenges life delivered.

Sally had lost track of how much time had passed since she'd been in the room. She'd forgotten that she was looking for Abe's address. Instead, she was enjoying the feeling that her apprehension of her daughter was being expanded just by pondering the things she'd left behind. Her strong and capable daughter. Why, look, here was an essay she'd written for school, twelve typed pages about the poetry of Samuel Taylor Coleridge. Sally couldn't remember ever reading a poem by Samuel Taylor Coleridge, but her daughter had written a long essay, for which she received a big red A, along with a nice compliment from her teacher. Now, that was something. And here was a set of index cards upon which she'd jotted quotations from the Constitution. How could her daughter know so much! Her desk drawer was stuffed with notes she'd taken during lectures. Her old calculator had functions that Sally couldn't begin to figure out. She could see how much Penelope knew just by sifting through the mess in her desk drawer. And it was amusing to find things like a take-out menu from a Chinese restaurant, with circles around steamed dumplings and kung pao chicken. There was a plastic key-chain with the name of a moving van company on it. There was a box of thumbtacks and a chain of paper clips. And there was a small folded sheet with printed information.

At first glance, she thought the sheet explained how to work some sort of machine. But as she was stuffing the paper back in the crowded drawer, she happened to notice that the instructions included medical terminology. She unfolded the paper, smoothing out the creases, and looked more carefully at what she realized was a sheet of information from a medical lab. She had to read the sheet twice to understand that it included results of a mail-in pregnancy test.

She stared at the word *positive.* Why were there so many letters in the word? It was the wrong word, it didn't belong in her daughter's drawer. She wanted to rip up the sheet from the medical lab and throw it away. She also wanted to pick up the phone and call her daughter and demand an explanation. But she mustn't be harsh with her. She knew what it felt like to be caught by surprise in this way. And really, when Sally considered it, the notion that her daughter had left this piece of paper for her to find wasn't implausible, for how could Penelope not want to be comforted by her mother, to be soothed and told that everything would be all right? But maybe she had gotten things mixed up. How many girls were tricked into panic by a false-positive result? There was no reason to worry, and she'd know to be more careful in the future. Everything would be all right. But what if the result was a true positive, and the man involved was Abe? Then everything would not be all right. Nothing would ever be right again. If Abe was involved. If there was an accidental pregnancy. If it was too late. A brother with a sister. A terrible tangle of mistakes, and it was Sally's fault.

Sally Werner.

That whore.

Birthed a monster and ran away.

Left him for her family to raise.

Didn't even come back for her own parents' funerals.

That slut.

Look at the trouble she caused.

It would be all right. Or else it wouldn't be all right. The offense against nature had already been committed. It was too late. Or else it wasn't too late. Remember that God forgives the penitent. You just have to confess your wickedness and be sorry for your sin.

She had to find Abe and tell him he was her son. The monster she'd birthed. *Sally Werner . . . with her own cousin.* Why, cousins were one thing, but a brother and a sister were something else entirely! He'd agree that he had no choice but to leave town, he must go away forever, and then they would all start their lives over again, one by one. Abraham Boyle, Penelope Bliss, Sally Werner. As long as the offense produced no issue, they would be spared, and eventually, with God's grace, they would find peace within themselves. It would be as if none of this had ever happened.

Sally found Abe by calling the number on the moving company keychain in Penelope's drawer. Identifying herself as a relative, she asked for his address. She waited until the evening to visit him, though when she arrived he still wasn't home from work.

A storm system had stalled over the region, and a steady rain had been falling for two days. There were reports of localized flooding. The weather bureau in Buffalo warned that the rain could continue for another twenty-four hours.

Sally stood on the porch below Abe's rented room, watching the curtain of water spilling from a blocked gutter. While she waited she rehearsed in her mind what she would say. She was prepared for his doubt; of course he would doubt her, so she'd brought along the documents from Sylvia as proof.

She also had a separate envelope containing the money she'd kept with her since she was nineteen years old. Mason Jackson's money. Old Mason Jackson, of Fishkill Notch. After all these years she still hadn't spent any of his money. Yet that wasn't entirely true. Long ago, when she'd lost her purse and had no money of her own to spend, she'd had to use some of Mason Jackson's cash. She'd never thought of that money as hers. In a way, she'd only borrowed it . . . and she'd never managed to return it. She'd kept it because he'd given it to her. He'd wanted her to take it and to spend it wisely.

Now it seemed to her that Uncle Mason had told her to take the money for just this purpose — to give to her son so he could begin his new life. It made so much sense, like the design of a wheel. The things that made simple sense in the world were especially pleasing to think about right then. Wheels and roofs and rain. Why couldn't everything in the world make simple sense?

It was the fifth of November 1974. To Sally Bliss, standing on the porch of a rambling Victorian house in the Maplewood District, the political turmoil consuming the nation that week felt very far away, a dream being dreamed by a stranger while she was absorbed by her own strange dream. Her dream of the predicament she'd created. It made so little sense. Or else it made elaborate sense. Dreams could give a contradictory impression. Either way, the logic binding the elements of the situation couldn't have been more different from the logic of something as simple as a wheel.

She was there to meet her son. She was there to say, *Hello, I'm your mother, now go away.* She was there to give him the money she'd kept for nearly a quarter of a century, having touched none of it — except for the small portion she'd spent after she'd lost her purse in the alley behind Potter's Hardware.

She took out two tens from her wallet and added these to Mason Jackson's musty bills. Good, now it was all there, the full amount of what she'd stolen — rather, borrowed, or accepted as a gift back in 1950. In honor of Mason Jackson, she was giving the gift to her son. That's what Uncle Mason would have wanted. He was a prescient man, and he'd probably intended for Sally to use the money in just this fashion.

At quarter past eight, Sally lit another cigarette. She'd smoked half of it when she saw a car slow on the road. She watched the car back up until it was snug against the curb, and then Abe got out holding a brown bag full of groceries. He pushed the car door closed with his knee and approached the porch.

Though she'd planned a speech that was meant to combine disclosure with reassurance, her first reaction when she saw

653

him was to rush at him and start beating him for what he'd done to her daughter. He'd taken pleasure in unspeakable perversity, and now the damage was done. For the sake of his pleasure, he had violated God's law, and Sally wanted to punish him for this, to beat him with a stick until he understood that he must suffer for his sin.

But she didn't have a stick. She had a cigarette. The only thing she could think to do was to drop what remained of her cigarette and grind out the spark with her heel.

As he stepped onto the porch, he seemed to push apart the curtain of rain. "Mrs. . . . !" he said in surprise. Either he didn't immediately recognize her, or he'd forgotten her name. "Mrs. . . . Mrs. . . . Bliss, um, hello. Is everything all right?" How plaintive and meek his voice sounded. It was enough to remind Sally that of course he hadn't meant to do any harm. His mistake was her fault. Everything was her fault.

"May I come in?"

"Ah . . . yes, I live upstairs."

With one arm wrapped around the grocery bag, it was difficult for him to insert the key in the lock, but somehow he managed and swung open the door. He fumbled for the light in the foyer while behind him Sally took a step forward and stumbled. She reached out for his arm, instead grabbing the coatrack to keep herself from falling.

She followed him up the rickety stairs to the third-floor apartment. He set the groceries on the counter and offered her coffee. While he was filling up the kettle at the sink, she began, as she'd planned, by speaking his name aloud: "Abraham Boyle." When he turned to face her she saw his expression mixed utter bewilderment with fear, and she was reminded again that he was a good man and hadn't meant any harm. "I have news for you," she said. "Let's sit down."

She told him what she knew and, in detail, how she'd come to know it. She told him about riding on Daniel Werner's motorcycle. She told him about her parents' rage. She told him about leaving her baby like a loaf of bread on the kitchen table and running away. She told him that the river flowed north, so she'd gone north with it. She told him about the hamlet of Fishkill Notch, where she'd worked as a housekeeper for three years. She told him about Helena, where she'd fallen in love with a boy named Mole and then lost him. She told him about Benny Patterson, the father of Penelope. She told him about the haven that was the city of Tuskee. She told him why she'd fled

655

Tuskee and ended up here, in the city of R, this mixed-up city where things that didn't make sense were allowed to happen.

She said, "You're not going to believe me, Abe, when I tell you that I'm your mother."

She was right. He didn't believe her. He refused to believe her. Disbelief left him too appalled to argue with Sally's insane claims. All he could say was *That's impossible, that's impossible.* But he had to believe her, since she had incontrovertible proof both from the county clerk's office in Peterkin and the Catholic Diocese of Pittsburgh.

She would convince him that he had no choice but to accept her version of the truth as the one that would determine his course of action in the days and months ahead. But at the same time, the resolute conviction that she was wrong would plant itself just beyond articulable thought, where belief is experienced as a murky but potentially influential feeling. He didn't believe her, and with a similar vague awareness, she recognized this. Yet he couldn't deny that there were many reasons to believe her. She gave him more reasons than he could ever counter, and by the end of her visit he was forced to acknowledge with words that sounded artificial to both of them, when spoken aloud, that she must be right.

She was his mother, and she'd come to tell him what to do. Here was a hefty sum of money, more than two thousand dollars. Take it, Abe, and run. Run away. Leave Sally to explain to Penelope why she'd been abandoned by the man she loved. Or not to explain to her, *for such things,* she would think helplessly, *are inexplicable.* That's what she would offer instead of telling her the truth about Abe. Faced with the reality that her daughter would be raising a child who never should have been conceived, Sally would decide that the best comfort she could offer Penelope was to keep her ignorant.

Buster Boy,

Where are you?

You said you'd be here by four o'clock last Saturday. That was a week ago.

You said you loved me.

You said you would never leave me.

You stopped answering your phone.

You no longer live at the address I have for you.

You quit your job.

You broke your promise.

Why have you gone away? Answer me. But you can't answer me because you're not reading this letter. You're not reading this letter

657

because I don't know where to send it. I don't know where to send it because you went away without telling me where you were going. I'd hate you if I didn't love you so much. Nothing can make me stop loving you, even the fact that you've destroyed me. Abe, why have you done this?

There was a song my mother used to sing: it's simple to wish, and simple to dream.

I was singing that song in the shower on Saturday afternoon when I was getting ready to see you. You know a lot about me, but you haven't heard me sing, since I sing only in the shower. It made me laugh to think that some-day you'd hear the terrible noise I produce called singing. My mother is the singer in my family. She could have made a career of it. She might have tried if I hadn't come along. She had to find a job to support me. It's hard for single mothers. Did you ever consider that?

But I was telling you what I did on Saturday. I took a shower, dried my hair, put on the jeans you like, the skinny Levi's with the button-up fly. I watched the TV in the common room. There was an interview with an English-woman who was fired from a cannon. She wanted to break the human cannonball record and fly clear over a river, but she missed her mark and fell into the safety net. She said she thought they'd ironed out the troubles with the cannon, and she was going to try again. I was planning to tell you about her when you arrived. By then it was four o'clock, and I waited for your knock on the door. I kept waiting. At six o'clock I called your house, but there was no answer. At eight o'clock I called Stacey and got your friend Sam's number. But no one answered at Sam's all evening. I skipped dinner. I couldn't sleep. I kept picturing your car wrapped around a tree on some back road. My Buster Boy. What has happened to you? I finally got Sam on the phone the next morning, but he didn't know where you were. I called your work number, and they said you'd quit. I called Stacey and asked her to go to the address I had for you. She called me late in the afternoon. She'd talked to the landlord and learned that you'd packed your bags, paid up your rent for the month, and moved away.

That's impossible. You wouldn't have moved away without telling me.

Where are you?

Don't you love me anymore?

This is how I've been spending my days: I wake up in the dark, about five a.m. I look at the phone to see if it's ringing, and even though it's not ringing I pick up the receiver and wait for your voice to speak to me. But you don't speak. I hang up the phone and go down the hall to the bathroom, where I throw up. I throw up once every morning. Our child is a small hard bulge low in my belly. I sing to it in the shower, I sing, It's simple to guess that you and I will never stop being in love.

Where are you?

Why won't you answer me?

After I take a shower I get back into bed and read. I'm reading Dreiser's *American Tragedy*. I read chapter 41 this morning and thought of you. Here's a quote: "All that he would see or feel was that this meant the loss of everything to him." Here's another quote: "The loss of all his splendid dreams." Did this bulge in my belly threaten all your splendid dreams, Abe? Is that why you've gone away? We didn't need to have this child. These are modern times, and we have won the invaluable freedom to choose how to live our lives. I thought we'd made the choice together, Abe. You and me. We were committed to each other by the power of love. We were going to spend the rest of our lives together. Forever. You said that word to me. You whispered it to me, remember, when you were inside me.

I thought you meant that FOREVER went with the word LOVE. But now I wonder if I'd been deceived and you were only pretending to love me so you could fuck me on a regular basis. If that's true, Buster Boy, you deserve an Oscar, for you really had me fooled. When

I had my legs wrapped around you and we were both sloppy with sweat, you had me fooled. When you traced the center of me with kisses, you had me fooled. When we were pressed hip to hip, you had me fooled. When I spent the rest of the day smelling your after-shave on me and daydreaming about us together, I never guessed that I'd fallen for the oldest trick in the book.

I am baffled and disgusted and desperate. But I can't be angry with you, not until you admit that you were using me. I need you to put it into words. Say it, say that I am nothing to you. Nothing. I want you to whisper it in my ear. Repeat after me: You are nothing. I don't care about you. I don't love you and I never loved you. I want to hear you say it. You'd better say it over the phone and not in person, or otherwise I might tear your eyes out. Just kidding. But it would be a relief to be furious. I can't be furious at an absence. I am nothing, and you are nothing. We are the space left behind by broken promises.

I skipped classes on Wednesday and took the bus into New York. I walked from the Port Authority up to Columbus Circle and then across 59th and up Fifth Avenue. I stopped to browse at a book vendor, and I picked up a copy of a book. It was the Dreiser novel, *An American Tragedy.* Have you ever read it? It seems strange to have to ask, but I'm only just starting to realize how much I don't know about you. I was reading the description on the back of the book, when all of a sudden I heard your voice. You said, "And then we'll take the night train to Vienna." But it wasn't you, of course. It was another guy, he was about your age, a few inches shorter, and he was walking with his arm around a girl. They were planning a trip, I guess. They were talking about traveling around Europe together, and it made me so jealous and sad to think that we would never take a trip like that, and now it's too late, you've moved on to a better life and left me behind. I was thinking about this as I started to walk away. I kicked at the rotting leaves and thought about how alone I was. I was still holding the book, Dreiser's novel, and the vendor shouted at me, he called, "Hey, lady, are you going to pay for that or what?" And guess what I did in response. That's right, I started to cry. I stood there bawling on the sidewalk while appropriately clutching *An American Tragedy.* I am an American tragedy. I was duped into playing the role of the naïve girl. How did that happen? I would never have thought I could be so easily trapped. I'd always been so tough and independent, you said so yourself, you said I was the toughest girl you'd ever known.

But you wore me down, Abe. My love for you has made me pathetic. I was a pathetic mess, standing there bawling on Fifth Avenue. An American tragedy. It's an old story, a familiar story. Can tragedy be pathetic? That vendor, he must have felt sorry for me. He gave me the book for free. It was just a used paperback with a creased cover, priced at fifty cents. But the man wanted me to have it for free. So I said thank you, and I took the book and managed to stop crying. As I walked uptown carrying that thick book, I considered how stupid I'd been. I'd always thought I could recognize a trap when I saw it. But I was starting to realize that the world was like the unread book in my hand. Until I took the time to read it, I wouldn't be able to tell up from down. There was so much to learn. I needed to learn more about other lives in order to understand my own.

I felt a little better after spending a few hours in New York. I called my mother from a pay phone in the Port Authority and told her I was coming home. I got there at midnight. She was waiting for me at the station. On the car ride back to the house, I told her about us. I was surprised at how easily our story could be summed up, how small and predictable it seemed to my own ears. But mostly I was grateful because my mother didn't react to the news of my pregnancy with disappointment. She became suddenly practical and reminded me that abortion is safe and legal. She doesn't want me to repeat her mistake and become saddled with a child before I'm ready. But it's too late, I'm already committed, and I'm not going to let your cruelty change my mind. Once my mother understood that she couldn't talk me out of it, she was so quick to come up with a plan that it almost seemed like she'd rehearsed it. She reminded me that I must see a doctor for regular checkups. And she told me to get back to school so I could finish the semester. I'd take the spring off, she said, and then she would look after the baby when I returned to complete my degree in the fall. She said she wants me to prepare for whatever career I choose. This isn't the end of my life, she insisted. It is a beginning, she said, and she promised me that as long as I kept looking to the future, I'd get over you.

She's wrong about that. I won't get over you, Abe. I will think about you every day for the rest of my life. I will imagine you in different places around the world, caught up in different jobs, in bed with different women, enjoying new adventures to replace the old ones. I will come up with a thousand explanations for why you left me. Thirty years from now, I will smell your aftershave in a crowd, and it will be as if no time at all has passed since we last made love. I will love other men, but they will never replace you. I won't forgive you, but neither will I stop loving you. And even if I've discovered that I don't really know you as well as I thought I did, I know you well enough to continue believing that you would have chosen to stay with me forever if the situation had allowed you to choose. Something beyond your control drove you away. I want to blame you, but I can't. All of which is to say that despite the fact that you broke my heart, Buster Boy, you'll always be welcome if you ever want to come back. I am writing to tell you that.

The problem is, you'll never read this letter because without an address for you, I can't send it. I can't even say good-bye.

Penelope

He didn't intend to throw himself off the pedestrian bridge and drown in the river. He didn't leave his room early that morning to fulfill a specific plan. As he wove through the streets in the direction of the gorge, splashing through rivulets streaming toward sewer drains, stepping over branches that had been downed by the wind, he was thinking to himself that the whole situation was too absurd to take seriously, and he was everybody's favorite clown. Ha-ha, look at him go, staggering on tiptoes to the right, oops, then to the left. What a funny man.

Could he help it if the ground went one way and he went another? Having stayed up the night before washing down warm Smirnoff with warm Smirnoff, he wasn't completely balanced. He wanted to laugh at himself and was about to let out a big guffaw, but a car's horn preempted him, warning him to get out of the middle of the street. Geesh, he could have been killed!

There — he thought of it first as an accident narrowly averted, then as a prospect to consider, then as a direction to follow. Somewhere ahead of him was an end to the torture. Beyond that point, he would no longer have to think about what he'd done and what he'd have to live without.

He followed the street under the highway, across the intersection, and toward the river. By the time he reached the ruins of Boxman's Mill by the falls, the sky was a pale blue and most of the streetlights had blinked off. He stood for a few minutes by the stone steps leading to the old mill wheel. He pictured the wheel in motion, turned by the force of water surging through the race.

Standing by the ruined mill, he began to feel for a second time that morning that he was being watched. It seemed that he was being observed and judged by his willingness to follow through with his purpose, now that he had a purpose, which was . . . he had to think for a moment, yes, he was on his way to the pedestrian bridge that spanned the gorge. The bridge provided a convenient destination — the point from which he would not return. There, he could see the first lamppost behind the corner of the old button factory, and, as he approached, the second lamppost, and then the whole bridge and the smokestacks of the brewery on the opposite bank.

Good God, what was he doing?

He was walking onto the bridge, see, step by step with such balance he could have tricked a cop into thinking he was sober. He was leaning against the rail.

But he couldn't really be planning to jump, not Abe, who had always thought of himself as unusually sensitive to pain and would go out of his way to avoid the risk of physical danger. He wasn't about to let his body suffer bruising blows. No way. He preferred to be alive, even if it did mean living with the torment of his memory forever after. He would rather live with that torment than willfully throw himself off the bridge and fall seventy feet into a freezing river.

Still, in his current state of mind it helped to flirt with death by slinging one leg over the rail and balancing there while he pictured himself falling. It made him feel newly estimable to think of himself as a man with that much courage. He could hover there, straddling the rail, and rage at the heavens like a legitimate hero. He could tell himself that he was taking destiny into his own hands. The whole operation of consciousness was his own to start or stop at will, and he could pretend to make the final decision to jump without actually making it, leaving him free, when he was done pretending, to pull himself back to the inside of the rail and consider his next move.

Or else he could linger there a little longer, contemplating his nobility. And if he stayed long enough, lost in the drunken fantasy of suicide, then sooner or later he would be startled by a noise in the distance, perhaps the whistle of a train, or the chimes of St. Stephen's, causing him to loosen his grip, and before he could remind himself that the decision to jump was only hypothetical, it was too late.

One and two and three and . . .

Uh-oh, here comes another.

In the real world, he wouldn't be saved. In a world governed by the laws of physics, he would lose consciousness upon impact with the water and plunge to the bottom, bouncing up, to be seized by the surging river and carried through the gorge, his limp body remaining submerged, revolving head over heels with the swirling current. Silty water would fill his lungs, inhibiting the exchange of essential gases. His heart would race in an effort to compensate for the oxygen deficit even as the sensitive tissue of the brain would begin to die. Soon whatever glimmer of physical self-awareness the nervous system had retained within a state of unconsciousness would fade and go out altogether, leaving an eternal blackness, the soul fleeing, the mind emptied, the skin a bag stuffed with contents that had been abruptly stripped of their value. Without a reason to keep beating, the heart would stop. Eventually the body would float near the surface, facedown, only a patch on the back of the jacket visible, bloated by an air bubble.

But the way Sally explained it, when Abe disappeared into the Tuskee he left the real world behind.

■ ■ ■ ■

The river had been surging over the falls at twenty thousand cubic feet of water per second. Add the November storm, upstream rains, scum from overflowing sewers, a stopped-up cofferdam built by a corrupt construction company owner . . . and, in Sally's opinion, it still wasn't enough to make the current flow backward and propel Abe out of its depths.

She heard about it afterward. Abe wrote to her and described the event in an attempt to display the extent of his despair, which she, his mother, had provoked. Thanks to Sally Bliss, Abe had been compelled to try to drown himself. But the river wouldn't have him. The river hadn't liked the taste of him and spit him out.

It would have been natural for Sally to dismiss Abe's account as exaggeration. But Sally not only believed every word, she took it upon herself to enhance her son's version with her own fanciful additions. She made up a fairy tale to explain what happened that day in the gorge. It was the unreal counterpart to a real situation, the fanciful tag to experience, the portion that couldn't be verified with testimony and documents.

And in her understanding it was more than a necessary part of the story that began the day she climbed onto the back of her cousin's motorcycle; it was the salvation she'd been seeking for the last twenty-seven years.

Everything she'd learned during her early years in her parents' church had led her to believe that she would never be relieved of her responsibility. She was guilty and would always be guilty. But at the point when it really counted, the effort she'd made to see to her son's well-being and protect him in her absence had been rewarded. She had tried to do what was expected of her, to follow the path that was her destiny. And here, in the eleventh hour, was her reward: God summoned His little river angels, who made the river run backward in order to save a drowning man from death. Abe's survival was a gift to Sally, proof that she had been forgiven.

As much as she wanted to celebrate the miracle, she couldn't go around announcing that there were tiny angels living in the river. She didn't want the world to think she was crazy, even if she *was* crazy. But she couldn't deny what she'd seen with her own eyes, the glimpses she'd caught of the creatures over the years. There were strange and wonderful secrets hidden in the Tuskee, and they became Sally's handy explanation for an inexplicable event.

After she learned about the flood in the gorge and her son's improbable survival, she filled in the content to fit the event. And because it stretched even her own flexible credulity to the breaking point, she kept the details to herself for a long while. It was the part of the story that threatened to invalidate the rest. She had to remind herself that regarding the identity of Abraham Boyle, she had gone to great lengths to gather substantial proof. But there was nothing substantial about her version of the miracle that dumped Abe into the parking lot of the Beebee Electric plant.

She had to wait until a summer day in 1998, when she was at the county fair and happened to overhear an elderly native wood-carver reciting the legend of the Tuskawali. Only then would Sally realize that she wasn't the only one who knew the river's secrets. And if the rest of the crowd believed that they were hearing nothing more than superstition, so much the better, in Sally's opinion. Then no one would bring nets and poles and start hunting for them in the river — a good thing, since as the wood-carver warned, the Tuskawali don't like to be caught.

■ ■ ■ ■

In her letters to Abe, she pleaded with him to find happiness. She would do anything for him. She had failed him once but would not do so again. She sent him money. She shared all the good advice she could think of. As she wrote, she was reminded of the letters she used to type for the old woman in Helena, Mrs. Mellow. She remembered that Mrs. Mellow smelled of potpourri and that she seemed to know everything. Sally went to the public library and with the help of the reference librarian found some useful information to add to the letters she sent Abe.

He must live a full and happy life. Her daughter must live a full and happy life. Sally's own happiness depended upon theirs. She could accept that their definition of *happiness* differed from hers, as long as they were content. And neither of them should assume that trouble experienced at any point in their lives would cancel out future happiness. The ingredients for the feeling would change through the years, as they had for Sally. She'd learned to be open to unfamiliar prompts and find satisfying purpose where she would have least expected it. And she'd found a way to salvage a faith that had terrified her as a child and to experience it as a private set of beliefs, some borrowed, some eccentric, with fanciful and sentimental aspects, but all of them useful, as it turned out, during a crisis.

She would always regret that she was so poorly educated. But she made an effort to stay attentive to the dangers of ignorance. She'd done her best to be cautious. In her own estimate, she'd proven that she had a reliable instinct when it came to trusting people — or at least she'd worked to refine her perceptive skills and wasn't as easily misled as she'd been when she was younger. She liked to think that as she'd grown older, she'd become more adept at understanding bewildering experience. She didn't choose the beliefs that were most convenient, nor was she without skepticism. She simply remained open to persuasion and preferred to trust those who claimed to be telling the truth.

Without evidence to the contrary, she wouldn't guess that she'd been misled about Abe by the Werners of Tauntonville. She'd have no reason to suspect that the document Sylvia sent relating to his relinquishment was a forgery. It would never occur to her to doubt that the original document had been destroyed by fire. She wouldn't have a chance to learn that there hadn't been any fire. It was right and inevitable that her son had been returned to her, and she was always grateful to hear about his successes, which she interpreted as proof that he'd recovered from his unfortunate romance with her daughter. Abe and Penelope would both recover. And there'd be the addition of their child, Sally's granddaughter, her namesake, who, to her relief, wasn't born a monster. She thanked the grace of the good Lord that the girl wasn't marked by the sin that had produced her.

I was born on April 30, 1975. For the first five years of my life, my grandmother was my primary caregiver, while my mother finished her undergraduate degree and then attended law school in Buffalo. I don't remember the ranch house on Vernon Street, though I've seen photographs of it. After Arnie Caddeau and my grandmother were married in the spring of 1976, they bought a fancy Tudor backing up to the park behind the reservoir, and that's where I lived until 1980. I had a large bedroom shaded by a huge magnolia tree. I remember that in May when the blossoms were out, the sunlight would splash their tint on the walls of my room. And I remember hearing my grandmother singing while we wandered in opposite directions along the rim of the yard. By her late middle age, she'd stopped trying to stifle her urge to sing and had taken to singing easily, naturally, for the sheer pleasure of it. I'd listen to her while I greedily searched for weeds to add to my bouquet, hoping to make it bigger and more various than my grandmother's.

She wasn't willing to give up her job after she married. She continued to work part-time, three days a week. When she and Arnie were at the office and my mother was at school, I had a babysitter, an old woman who won my heart because she spread the peanut butter thickly on both slices of bread when she made me a sandwich.

My days were calm, structured by the reliable routines of meals and play. My grandmother was keen on convincing me that the world is fundamentally a peaceful place. I can recall only one unusual incident, and that was when a man came to the door and demanded to talk with Sally Mole. As it happened, my grandmother was out on an errand, so it was Arnie who answered the door. I was watching cartoons in the den when I heard voices coming from the front hall. The man had a loud voice to start with, and he grew louder as he grew angrier. Soon he was shouting. When I came to see what was going on, Arnie growled an order at me to go upstairs. It was the first time Arnie Caddeau had ever spoken harshly to me, and I was so offended that instead of obeying him I came farther into the hall and stood between the two men in defiance, my arms folded.

I remember the strange man quieted then as he asked me my name, and when he bent down to get a better look at me he blew out an unpleasant puff of sour breath. He moved to take me in his arms, but I jumped out of his reach, and as if there were a thread connecting me to the man's lips, my movement seemed to cause his smile to twist into a snarl.

I decided that I didn't like him and would rather be watching cartoons. I went back to the den, leaving Arnie to deal with the stranger.

That was the last I ever saw of the man. I learned later that he was my mother's father — my grandfather Benny Patterson. He hadn't sought out my grandmother because he wanted anything to do with us. He made it clear to Arnie that he didn't want to stick around for long. He'd gotten divorced and was moving out west, but he was strapped for cash. He said that if Arnie could loan him some money, he wouldn't bother us again. Arnie wrote him a check on the spot, a check for five hundred dollars, which was more than enough to satisfy Benny Patterson and send him to California.

Arnie never told my grandmother about the check. All she knew was that Benny had stopped by and grown belligerent but that Arnie had managed to calm him down.

Benny continued to write to Arnie every couple of years and ask for money. And later he'd do the same with my mother, after he got wind that she had, as he put it, a fancy-shmancy lawyer job. Though he never returned from the West Coast, he would depend upon Penelope to support him through the last decade of his life.

I learned about this only recently from my mother. I also learned that Benny's ex-wife, Harriet, came to visit her once, in 2004, a few months after my grandmother had died. Harriet was a bitter woman, full of resentment at having wasted the best years of her life as Mrs. Patterson. In the course of their conversation she told Penelope about Benny's role in an accident that had occurred downstate fifty years earlier, when Benny had run another car off the road on a rainy November night and then driven on without stopping. He found out later that a young couple was in that other car. The boy had been killed; the girl — my grandmother — survived without significant injury. People said they'd been drinking and had missed a curve. Benny wasn't ready to reveal his involvement in the accident, but he felt guilty enough to seek out Sally in Helena and start courting her, as though by winning her affection he could secure her forgiveness. She couldn't forgive him, though, for something he wouldn't admit. And when she ditched him, he went wild with anger. It took him a few years to find Sally, and then he beat her up, Harriet said. *He beat her up good.* And he never stopped being angry. He was so angry that sometimes when he got drunk, he'd boast about it all. He talked so freely that eventually most everyone within a hundred miles of his home knew what he'd done, and he had to move away to escape his own infamy.

Hearing about the accident from Harriet, my mother wondered if she'd underestimated my grandmother. She had always thought of Sally as a simple woman, easily categorized, raised in provincial circumstances, poorly educated, with naïve beliefs and limited experience of the world. Sally loved soap operas, Cracker Jacks and canned salmon, gaudy wallpaper, bargain-basement clothes. She had traveled the length of the Tuskee River and no farther. If she ever read a book, it was the *Reader's Digest* abridged version. She didn't drink often, but when she did, she didn't know when to stop. She smoked a pack of Lucky Strikes a day. My mother had always harbored a little bit of secret embarrassment about her mother, a feeling that through her childhood had become focused on Sally's singing. She loved to hear her mother sing, but she hadn't loved it when her loud singing kept the neighbors awake. It seemed to my mother that my grandmother had no idea when she was acting foolish.

Thanks to Harriet, my mother realized that there was more to my grandmother's life than she'd assumed. There was an old boyfriend who'd been killed in an accident. There was Benny and his anger. *He beat her up good.* If there was this much my mother hadn't known about my grandmother, there must have been more.

My grandmother had given her daughter the impression that she'd lived a relatively quiet life. For her own sake, she chose to cast her experiences as too ordinary to retell. And through most of her last two decades, she did live quietly, if you don't count her easy habit of singing as she moved around the house. She worked three days a week as a secretary in her husband's law firm. She kept a small vegetable garden out back. One spring, pumpkin seeds from the compost pile rooted, and she let the vines spread out across the yard. She harvested ten pumpkins that first year and thirty the next.

When my mother returned from law school, she was hired as an associate in Arnie's firm. She bought a house of her own in the suburbs, and I moved in with her. But I continued to stay over at my grandmother's house at least one night out of the week. Despite having only a seventh-grade education, she took out stacks of books from the library and taught me to read. When I was nine, Arnie lugged home an old IBM Selectric typewriter that had been replaced by an office computer, and my grandmother taught me to type. She said to me when I complained about the difficulty of matching the letters to the keys: *a girl can never know too much.*

Though she didn't use those same words, I imagine she was thinking them when she finally decided to confide in me. I could never know too much. Therefore, my grandmother was obliged to tell me everything she knew.

She'd been through surgery and two bouts of chemotherapy by then. Although her prognosis was encouraging, she probably realized that her thoughts were becoming increasingly scattered, with her memories getting mixed up with her dreams and even with some of the songs she sang. If she was going to communicate a long story coherently and include everything relating to the mistake of my conception, she'd better do it soon.

Her story was as long as the Tuskee and as full of surprises, she said to me. I was twenty-seven that year. I'd come home to the city of R and was living with Sebastian in an apartment on Westminster Street, working for an ad agency while I tried to figure out how to put my typing skills to better use. My grandmother would invite me over for a glass of sherry in the afternoon while Arnie was off playing golf. She told me about her various stops along the river, her different names, the adventures of her new beginnings. She told me who my parents were. She assured me that my father had gone on to find another woman to love, though she didn't offer to tell me where he was living, and I didn't ask. She made it clear that she didn't want me to repeat her story to anyone. But she did suggest that I go ahead and write a history of the Tuskawali — that would be a worthy subject for a book, she said, just as long as I pretended that I'd made it all up.

Spring officially arrived yesterday. Today is Good Friday. I'm just off the phone with my father, who called to say that he and Tracy and Marcia have arrived and checked in to the hotel. Now all our guests are in town, and we're ready for tomorrow. There's a full moon tonight, strangely veiled by a thin mist of snow. Earlier today I saw a flock of robins on the edge of the field by the reservoir. It's late. I'm alone. My fiancé is with his brothers, who have traveled from Oregon and New Mexico to be here. I'm staying over at my mother's house. She's gone to bed. I'm in the bedroom that used to be mine. My mother has talked about selling the house and downsizing, but she hasn't gotten around to it. She's been run ragged ever since the scandal hit Albany and the governor resigned. His tawdry fall will probably cause my mother to lose her job as the director of the urban renewal fund.

At the very least, there will be no money to distribute. The state is going broke. The country is going broke. We are spending ten billion dollars a month to press on with the war in Iraq. There have been between 80,000 and one million casualties since the war began in 2003 (the number varies among studies). The cost of a barrel of crude oil has reached an all-time high. Exxon-Mobil and Chevron are the most recent oil companies to post record profits. Truckers can't afford to fill their tanks. Railways can't afford to make repairs, and the trains are derailing. Our lakes are spiked with antibiotics and sex hormones. The earth is heating up. The frogs are dying. The bees are dying. The bats are dying. Floods follow droughts. Droughts follow floods. Tibetans are storming embassies on horseback. Darfur continues to burn. The crisis of hunger in Africa is matched by the crisis of obesity in North America. Gangs are using AK-47s to settle their scores. Average life expectancy is declining. Investors are worried that the subprime mortgage crisis will spread into other sectors of the economy. There's talk of a recession. The earth, astronomers inform us, is going to be sucked into the sun one day. We're all complaining. I can't find a decent-paying job since I left the ad agency. Sebastian, who teaches music in the city schools, is worried that he'll be a casualty of the impending cutbacks.

But tomorrow we will gather at the Lantern Restaurant by the falls, and we will celebrate. We're going to raise our glasses in defiance. We'll stab cheese cubes with toothpicks and scoop crackers in dip. Though snow is in the forecast, our guests will stroll along the pedestrian bridge. Feelings will be revealed and new commitments made. Lovers will toss coins into the river and make a wish. They will follow the new path leading through the ruins of Boxman's Mill. They will look at the huge mill wheel nestled between stone walls. They will walk along the metal grate that runs across the old race and hear the water surging below their feet. They will look deep into a pit lined with icicles and see the river below, boiling and foaming through the diversion. And when the harsh wind comes sweeping over the falls, they'll run back inside and grab drinks from the bar.

Some of our friends have formed a band for the occasion, and they've promised to play music that will make everyone get up and dance. We will spin across the room. We will grow giddy. We will ignore all the predictions. We will forget that we were ever worried.

Tomorrow we're getting married, and we're going to celebrate at a reception by the river with our family and friends. We'll toast to love and kiss whenever a spoon is clinked against a glass. We'll put on a show to demonstrate once again that joy is possible. We'll guzzle champagne. We'll remember the dead. We'll tell stories and laugh at every joke. No one will be blamed for mistakes or accused of being sentimental. When the band begins to play, Sebastian and I will lead the way onto the floor. My mother will be there. My father and sisters will be there. Music will fill the room, and we will dance.

ABOUT THE AUTHOR

Joanna Scott is the author of nine books, including *The Manikin,* which was a finalist for the Pulitzer Prize; *Various Antidotes* and *Arrogance,* which were both finalists for the PEN/Faulkner Award; and the critically acclaimed *Make Believe, Tourmaline,* and *Liberation.* A recipient of a MacArthur Fellowship, a Guggenheim Fellowship, and a Lannan Award, she lives with her family in upstate New York.

The employees of Thorndike Press hope you have enjoyed this Large Print book. All our Thorndike, Wheeler, and Kennebec Large Print titles are designed for easy reading, and all our books are made to last. Other Thorndike Press Large Print books are available at your library, through selected bookstores, or directly from us.

For information about titles, please call:
(800) 223-1244

or visit our Web site at:
http://gale.cengage.com/thorndike

To share your comments, please write:
Publisher
Thorndike Press
295 Kennedy Memorial Drive
Waterville, ME 04901